John Gilchrist

Scottish Songs, Ancient and Modern

John Gilchrist

Scottish Songs, Ancient and Modern

ISBN/EAN: 9783337180973

Printed in Europe, USA, Canada, Australia, Japan

Cover: Foto ©Andreas Hilbeck / pixelio.de

More available books at **www.hansebooks.com**

SCOTTISH SONGS,

Ancient and Modern.

CAREFULLY COLLATED AND CORRECTED FROM
THE MOST AUTHENTIC SOURCES.

WITH BRIEF NOTICES

BY

JOHN GILCHRIST.

EDINBURGH :
JAMES STILLIE, 79 PRINCES STREET.
1865.

This celebrated Collection was printed many years ago, but never published. Mr. Gilchrist is highly commended by Professor Aytoun for his selections, and Editorial care in his collection of Scottish Ballads and Songs.

The names of the Songs are printed on a larger type, the letters affixed, H. C., are from Herd's Collection, 1776, T. T. M., from Ramsay's Tea Table Miscellany, 1724-29.
The first lines of the Songs are on the smaller type.

Page

A cogie of ale, . . *Andrew Sheriff*, 412

A' bodie's like to be married, { *J. Hamilton of Edinr.*, } 408

Alloa House, *Rev. Dr. Alex. Webster of Edin.*, 149
Andro and his cutty gun, . *T. T. M.*, 73
Anna, ... *Burns*, 145
A red red rose, . . *Burns*, 194
Auld gudeman, . *Sir Alex. Boswell*, 328
Auld King Coul, . . 410
Auld lang syne, . . *Burns*, 322
Auld Rob Morris, . . *T. T. M.*, 357
Do. . . *Burns*, 358
Auld Robin Gray, *Lady Anne Lindsay*, 200
Awa, Whigs, awa, ✓ . *Jacobite Song*, 270
A waukrife minnie, { *Picked up by Burns from a country girl in Nithsdale*, . } 352

A boat danc'd on Clyde's bonny stream, . . 393
A friend of mine came here yestreen, ✓ . . 53
Again rejoicing nature sees, ✓ . . . 206
A Highland lad my love was born, ` . . 362

	Page
A laddie and a lassie, ✓	38
A lass that was laden with care, ✓	194
Altho' I be but a country lass,	350
Altho' my back be at the wa'	406
And are ye sure the news is true? ✓	238
And ye sall walk in silk attire, ✓	191
An O, for ane and twenty, Tam! ✓	187
As I came by Loch Eroch side, ✓	164
As I came in by Auchindown,	364
As I cam in by Calder fair,	335
As I was walking ae May morning, ✓	217
As I went forth to take the air, ✓	16
As Jenny sat down wi' her wheel,	408
As Patie came up frae the glen, ✓	34
As walking forth to view the plain,	93
At Polwart on the green, ✓	146
Auld Rob the laird o' muckle land,	400
Awa wi' your witchcraft o' beauty's alarms,	126
A wee bird cam to our ha' door,	380
Bagrie o't,	H. C. 323
Bannockburn,	Burns, 272
Bannocks o' barley,	Jacobite, 288
Bannocks o' barley meal,	318
Bauldy Fraser,	J. Hogg, 376
Bess the gawkee, Rev. Mr. Muirhead of Urr,	226
Bessy Bell and Mary Gray, partly by Ramsay,	104
Bide ye yet,	H. C., 235
Billet by Jeany Gradden,	258
Bonny Christy,	Ramsay, 160
Bonny laddie,	Jacobite, 371
Broom of the Cowdenknows,	T. T. M., 179
Busk ye, busk ye,	Ramsay, 358
Behind yon hills where Lugar flows,	118
Beneath a green shade I fand a fair maid,	156
Beyond thee, dearie, beyond thee, dearie,	180
Blyth, blyth, blyth was she,	78
Blythe, blythe, aroun' the nappy,	411
Blythe Jocky young and gay,	356
Blythe was the time when he fee'd wi' my father, O,	210
Blyth young Bess to Jean did say, ✓	226
Braw, braw lads of Galla water,	129

Page

Braw, braw lads on Yarrow braes,   .   130
By Logan's streams that ran sae deep,   .   197
By smooth-winding Tay a swain was reclining,   174
By yon castle wa', ...   283

Ca' the ewes to the knowes,   .   *Burns,* 135
Caledonia,   .   .   *Do.* 270
    Do.   .   *W. Lockhart of Edin.,* 387
Captain O'Kane,   .   .   *R. Gall,* 389
Carl an' the king come,   .   *Ramsay,* 367
Cauld kail in Aberdeen,   .   *Old words,* 85
    Do.   *Duke of Gordon,* 1785,   86
Charlie he's my darling,   .   *Jacobite,* 369
Clout the cauldron,   .   .   *T. T. M.* 41
Come under my plaidie,   *H. Macneill,* 223
Contented wi' little,   .   .   *Burns,* 331
Corn rigs are bonny,   .   .   *Ramsay,* 101
Country lassie,   .   .   *Burns,* 126
Craigieburn Wood,   .   .   *Do.,* 180
Crookie Den,   .   .   .   *Jacobite,* 299
Culloden,   .   .   *W. Nicholson,* 374
Cumberland and Murray's descent, *Jacobite,* 300

Published in Cromek's Remains of Nithsdale Song,
   probably written by Allan Cunningham, who con-
   tributed to the collection.

Cauld blaws the wind frae east to west,   .   265
Clavers and his Highland men,   .   .   302
Come boat me o'er, come row me o'er,   .   367
Come gie's a sang, Montgomery cry'd,   .   82
Come let's hae mair wine in,   .   .   325
Comin thro' the craigs o' Kyle,   .   .   97
Coming through the broom at e'en,   .   150
Coup sent a challenge frae Dunbar,   .   311

Donald Macdonald,   .   .   *J Hogg,* 315
Doun the burn, Davie,   *Col. Crawford,* 136
Drap o' cappie o',   .   .   55
Druken wife o' Galloway,   .   *H. C.* 58
Dumbarton drums,   .   .   *T. T. M.* 120
Duncan Davison,   .   .   *Burns,* 63

Page

Duncan Gray,   ·   *old words,* 233

Do.   ·   ·   ·   *Burns,* 234

Dear batchelour, I've read your billet,   .   .   258

Down in yon meadow a couple did tarie,   .   58

Ettrick banks,   .   .   . *T. T. M.,* 180

Ewe-bughts, Marion,   .   .   *Do.* 133

Fee him, faither, fee him,   *old song,* 10

For a' that,   .   .   . *Burns,* 314

For lack of gold,   .   *Dr. Austin,* 216

For the love of Jean,   .   . *T. T. M.* 166

For the sake o' somebody,   *old words,* 170

Do.   ·   ·   *Burns,* 172

Fareweel to auld Scotia,   .   *A. Bain,* 385

Farewell to Ayrshire,   .   .   *Burns,* 266

Farewell to Lochaber,   .   .   *Ramsay,* 193

Fareweel to a' our Scottish fame,   .   .   284

First when Maggy was my care,   .   :   :   72

Fy let us a' to the bridal,   .   :   .   29

Gala water,   .   .   *old words,* 129

Do.   .   .   *Burns,* 130

Garb of Old Gaul,   . *Sir Harry Erskine,* 270

Get up an' bar the door, { *another version of an old song in Johnson's Museum, titled,* " *Johnie Blunt,*" } 48

Gin e'er I'm in love,   .   .   248

Gloomy winter,   .   . *Tannahill,* 152

Go to Berwick, Johnny,   .   405

Green grow the rashes o',   .   *Burns,* 247

Gude nicht and joy,   .   :   382

Gudewife, count the lawin,   .   *Burns,* 332

Gane is the day and mirk the night,   .   .   332

Gi'e me a lass wi' a lump of land,   .   .   125

Gin I had a wee house, and a canty wee fire,   .   235

Gin living worth cou'd win my heart,   .   .   203

Go fetch to me a pint o' wine,   \   .   .   185

Haud awa' frae me, Donald,   \   154

Page

Hay's bonnie lassie, . . *Ramsay,* 174
Here awa', there awa', — *old words,* 195
Do. . . *Burns,* 196
Here's a health to them that's awa', *Jacobite,* 382
Here's his health in water, . *Do.,* 406
Here's to the king, sir, . *about* 1710, 313
Hey for a lass wi' a tocher, . *Burns,* 126
Hey, how, Johnny, lad, . *H. C.,* 338
Hey, Jenny, come doun to Jock, *Do.,* 37
Hey tutti taiti, . *altered by Burns,* 333
Highland laddie, . . *Ramsay,* 107
Highland lassie, . . *Do.,* 109
Highland laddie, . . 370
Highland Mary, . . *Burns,* 204
How lang and dreary, . . *Do.* 388

Harken, and I will tell you how, . . . 22
Have you any pots or pans, . . . 41
Hear me, ye nymphs, and ev'ry swain, . . 215
Here's a health to ane I lo'e dear, . . 208
Hersell pe Highland shentleman, . . 80
Honest man, John Ochiltree, . . . 338
How blythe, ilk morn, was I to see, . . 179
How sweet is the scene at the dawning o' morning, 213
How sweetly smells the simmer green! . . 160

I'm o'er young to marry yet, . *Burns,* 165
I carena for your e'en sae blue, . 403
I had a horse, . . . *H. C.,* 42
I hae a wife o' my ain, . . *Burns,* 262
I love my Jean, . . *Do.* 172
I loe na' a laddie but ane, { *Mr. J. Clunie of Borthwick,* } 164
It was a' for our rightfu' king, *Jacobite,* 383
I'll aye ca' in by yon toun, . *Burns,* 404
I'll cheer up my heart, . 217
I wonder when I'll be married, . 409

I am a batchelor winsome, . . . 256
I am an auld sodger, just come from the camp, . 318
I am my mammy's ae bairn, . . . 165
I gaed a waefu' gate, yestreen, . . . 113

	Page
I hae been courting at a lass, . . .	398
I ha'e laid a herring in sa't, . . .	9
I met four chaps yon birks amang, . .	249
I'm inspir'd, inspir'd, and fir'd, . . .	368
I'm wearin' awa, Jean, ...	245
In April when primroses paint the sweet plain, .	132
In coming by the brig o' Dye, . . .	263
In Scotland there liv'd a humble beggar, .	6
In summer when the hay was mawn, . .	126
In the garb of old Gaul, ...	270
In winter when the rain rain'd cauld, . .	46
Is there, for honest poverty, . .	314
It fell about the Martinmas time, . .	48
It was upon a Lammas night, . . .	144
I've heard them lilting, at the ewe milking, .	273
I've seen the smiling of fortune beguiling, .	274
I was anes a well-tocher'd lass, . . .	348
I will awa wi' my love, ...	121
I winna marry ony man but Sandy o'er the Lee,	124

Jamie o' the glen, . .	400
Jeanie's black e'e, .	*H. M'Neill,* 268
Jeanie, where hast thou been?	*Ramsay,* 337
Jenny's bawbee,	*Sir Alex. Boswell,* 249
Jenny Nettles, . . .	353
Jessie, . . .	*Burns,* 208
Jessie, the flower o' Dunblane,	*Tannahill,* 117
Jockie blythe and gay, .	356
Jockie fou and Jenny fair, .	*T. T. M.,* 359
Jockie said to Jenny, .	*old song,* 166
Jockie was the blythest lad, . . { an old song with additions by Burns. }	112
John Anderson my jo, .	*old song,* 240
John Barleycorn, . .	*Burns,* 326
John Highlandman, . .	*Do.* 362
John o' Badenyon,	*Rev. J. Skinner,* 90
John Ochiltree, . .	*T. T. M.,* 338
Johnie Coup, . . .	311
Johnny's grey breeks, . .	264

Jenny's heart was frank and free, . .	159
Jocky he came here to woo, . . .	37

Page

Katherine Ogie,   .   .   *T. T. M.*,   93
Kenmure's on and awa',   .   *Jacobite*, 281
Killicrankie,   .   .   .   *Do.*   275
    Do.   .   .   .   302
Kind Robin lo'es me,   .   .   *H. C.*, 123

Keen blaws the wind o'er the braes o' Gleniffer,   198
Ken ye whare cleekie Murray's gane,   .   .   300

Lass gin ye lo'e me, { *J. Tytler, from a frag-ment of an old song,* }   9
Lass wi' a lump o' land,   .   *Ramsay*, 125
Lassie lie near me,   .   *Dr. Blacklock*, 384
Lassie wi' the lint-white locks,   *Burns*, 139
Let me in this ae nicht,   .   *Do.* 142
Lewis Gordon, *ascribed to Rev. Dr. Geddes*, 282
Liza Baillie,   .   .   .   153
Lizzie Liberty,   .   .   *Rev. J. Skinner*, 319
Loch Eroch side, { *said to be by Duke of Gordon, 1750,* } 164
Logan braes,   .   .   *John Mayne*, 197
Logie o' Buchan, { *said to be by Mr. G. Halkett, 1750,* } 185
Lord Gregory,   .   .   *Burns*, 230
Louden's woods and braes,   *Tannahill*, 386
Low down in the broom, { *ascribed to Mr. J. Carnegie, 1765,* } 186

Landlady count the lawin,   .   .   .   333
Lang ha'e we parted been,   .   .   .   384
Lassie, lend me your braw hemp heckle,   .   76
Last May a braw wooer cam down the lang glen,   168
Late in an evening forth I went, .   .   .   50
Lovely lass of Inverness, ...   293
Love never more shall give me pain,   .   .   182

Maggie Lauder, { *supposed to have been written by Semple, a piper,* } 61
Maggie's Tocher,   .   .   25
Mary's dream,   .   .   *A. Lowe*, 202

		Page
Maun I still on Menie doat, .	*Burns,*	206
Medley, . . .		335
Do. . . .		413
Muirland Willie, { *old song, marked by Ramsay as such in T. T. M.,* }		22
My ain kind dearie O, .	*R. Fergusson,*	151
My Anna, . . .	*R. Gall,*	213
My bonny Mary, .	*Burns,*	185
My dear Highland laddie O, .	*Tannahill,*	210
My dearie, if thou die, .	*R. Crawford,*	182
My goddess, woman, .	*John Learmont,*	246
My Harry was gallant gay,	*Burns,*	209
My heart's in the Highlands,	*partly by Burns,*	267
My heart's my ain, .	*published* 1776,	218
My jo, Janet, . .	*T. T. M.,*	44
My Jockie blyth, .	*partly by Burns,*	351
My Johnnie, . .	*John Mayne,*	159
My love has forsaken me, .		407
My love she's but a lassie yet, . . { *old song, partly by Burns,* }		324
My Mary, dear departed shade,	*Burns,*	205
My Nannie O, . .	*Do.*	118
My only jo and dearie O, .	*R. Gall,*	212
My Peggie is a young thing, .	*Ramsay,*	99
My sheep I neglected,	*Sir G. Elliot,* 1743,	399
My tocher's the jewel, .	*Burns,*	221
My wife's a wanton wee thing, .	*H. C.,*	54
My wife's taen the gee, .	*Do.*	53
My bonny Liza Baillie, . . .		153
My daddy is a canker'd carle, . .		186
My father has forty good shillings, . .		409
My heart is a-breaking, dear Tittie, .		128
My heart is sair I dare na tell, . .		172
My love has built a bonny ship, and set her on the sea,		199
My love was born in Aberdeen, . .		209
My mither's ay glowran o'er me, .		107
My name is Bauldy Fraser, man, .		376
My name it is Donald MacDonald, .		315
My Patie is a lover gay, . . .		101

Page

Nac dominies for me, . . 16

Nae gentle the dames, tho' e'er sae fair, . . 183
Nansy's to the green-wood gane, . . . 14
Now wat ye wha I met yestreen, . . . 105

O an ye were dead, gudeman, . *H. C.* 362
O are ye sleepin', Maggie? *Tannahill,* 405
O for ane and twenty, Tam! . *Burns,* 187
O gin my love were yon red rose, *old words,* 403
    Do.   do. *Burns,* 403
O let me in this ae nicht, *old words,* 141
O Mary, turn awa', . . 392
O wat ye wha's in yon toun, . *Burns,* 116
O were I on Parnassus' Hill, . *Do.* 163
O' a, the ills on man that fa', . 253
Open the door to me O! . *Burns,* 231
Our gudeman cam' hame at e'en, *H. C..* 340
Our gudewife's aye in the richt, 330
O'er Bogie, . . . *Ramsay,* 121
O'er the moor amang the heather, *Jane Glover,* 97
O'er the water to Charlie, . *Jacobite,* 367

O Bessy Bell and Mary Gray, . . . 104
O cam ye here the fight to shun, . . . 304
O come awa, come awa, ... 154
O had awa, had awa, ... 154
O how can I be blythe and glad, . . . 188
O! I am come to the low countrie, . . 295
O Jeany, Jeany, where hast thou been, . . 337
O lassie are ye sleepin' yet, . . 141-142
O Logie o' Buchan, O Logie the laird, . . 185
O luve will venture in where it daur na weel be seen, 173
O meikle thinks my luve o' my beauty, . . 221
O merry may the maid be, . . . 167
On Ettrick banks, in a summer's night, . . 130
O' mighty Nature's handywarks, . . . 246
O mirk, mirk is this midnight hour, . . 230
O my luve's like a red red rose, . . . 194
One midsummer morning, . . . 396
O saw ye Jenny Nettles, ... 353
O saw ye my father, or saw ye my mither, . 140
O tell na me o' wind and rain, . . . 143

	Page
O Tibbie, I hae seen the day,	220
O this is no mine ain house,	237
O this is no my ain lassie,	115
O waly, waly up the bank,	229
O weel may the boatie row,	345
O wha my babie-clouts will buy?	76
O wha's at my chamber door,	344
O when she came ben she bobbed fu' law,	355
O whistle and I'll come to you, my lad,	170
O Willie brew'd a peck o' maut,	330
O wilt thou go wi' me, sweet Tibbie Dunbar,	247
Of a' the airts the wind can blaw,	172
Oh! how shall I venture, or dare to reveal,	289
Oh! I hae lost my silken snood,	232
Oh open the door some pity to shew,	231
Oh! send Lewis Gordon hame,	282
Our auld King Coul was a jolly auld soul,	410
Our gudeman cam hame at e'en,	340
Our guidwife's ay in the right,	330

Patie's wedding,	*prior to* 1776,	34
Polwart on the green,	*Ramsay*,	146
Princely is my luver's weed,		279

Red, red rose,	*Burns*,	194
Rigs o' barley,	*Do.*	144
Rise and follow Charlie,	*Jacobite*,	368
Roslin Castle,	*Mr. R. Hewit*,	111
Roy's wife of Aldivaloch,	*Mrs Grant of Carron*,	222
Robcyn's Jok came to woo our Jenny,		19
Robin is my only jo,		123
Row saftly thou stream, thro' the wild spangl'd valley,		389

Sae merry as we hae been,	*H. C.*,	194
Sandy o'er the lee,		124
Saw ye nae my Peggy,	*Ramsay*,	175
Scornfu' Nansy,	*prior to Gay, who adapted the air to one of his songs,*	14
Scotia's sons,	*Macphail*,	411
She's fair and fause,	*Burns*,	222
She raise and loot me in,	*Ramsay*,	347
She says she lo'es me best of a',	*Burns*,	114

Page

Sic a wife as Willie had, . *Burns*, 42
Slighted Nansy, . . *T. T. M.* 225
Some say kissing's a sin, . . 262
Strathallan's lament, . *Burns*, 1788, 287
Such a parcel of rogues, *Do.* 284
Sweet Annie, . . . 191
Sweet Kitty o' the Clyde, . 393
Sweet Susan, { *ascribed to R. Crawford,* } 176
           { *author of "Tweedside,"* }

Sae flaxen were her ringlets, . . . 114
Sair, sair was my heart, when I parted frae my Jean, 387
Saw ye Johnnie cumin' quo' she, . . . 10
Saw ye my wee thing? saw ye mine ain thing? . 214
Scenes of woe and scenes of pleasure, . . 266
Scots wha hae wi' Wallace bled, . . . 272
Sheriff-Muir, ... 304
Should auld acquaintance be forgot, . . 322
Sweet sir, for your courtesie, . . . 44

Tak your auld cloak about ye, { *early in the* } 46
                              { 17*th cent.*, }
Tam Glen, . . . *Burns*, 128
Tarry woo, . . . *Ramsay*, 360
The absent lover, . *Miss Blamyre*, 391
The auld goodman, . . *T. T. M.*, 50
The auld man's best argument, *Ramsay*, 344
The auld wife ayont the fire, . *T. T. M.*, 64
The banks o' Doon, . . *Burns*, 228
The banks of the Dee, { *J. Home, author of* } 197
                      { *"Douglas,"* }
The bard strikes his harp, . *R. Gall*, 395
The battle of Sheriff-muir, . *Burns*, 304
The birks of Invermay, . *D. Mallet*, 397
The blue-eyed lassie, . . *Burns*, 113
The blythsome bridal, *published in* 1706, 29
The boatie rows, *John Ewen of Aberdeen*, 345
The bob of Dumblane, *partly by Ramsay*, 76
The bonnie brucket lassie, . *J. Tytler*, 147
The bonnie lad that's far awa,' . *Burns*, 188

Page

The braes o' Ballochmyle, . *Burns,* 266
The braes o' Gleniffer, . . *Tannahill,* 198
The braw wooer, . . *Burns,* 168
The bridal o't, . *Alex. Ross,* 27
The bush aboon Traquair, *Wm. Crawford,* 215
The cauldrife wooer, . *prior to* 1756, 7
The chevalier's lament, . *Burns.* 286
The collier's bonnie lassie, . *Ramsay,* 161
The country lass, . . *T. T. M.* 350
The day returns, . . *Burns,* 243
The deil's awa' wi' the exciseman, *Do.* 61
The deuks dang o'er my daddie, O ! *Do.* 51
The ewie wi' the crookit horn, *Rev. J. Skinner,* 87
The flowers of the forest, *Miss J. Elliot,* 1755, 273
    Do. *Mrs. Cockburn,* 274
The gaberlunzie man, . . *James V.,* 1
The gray cock, . . *H. C.* 140
The haws o' Cromdale, . `. 364
The hawthorn, . ' . *J. Hamilton,* 396
The Highland laddie, . *Jacobite,* 279
The Highland lassie O ! . *Burns,* 183
The Highland widow's lament, *partly by Burns,* 295
The humble beggar, . . *H. C.* 6
The jolly beggars, . . *James V.* 4
The lammie, . . *H. M'Neill,* 98
The land o' the leal, . . 245
The lass o' Ballochmyle, . *Burns,* 390
The lass o' Gowrie, . . 137
The lass o' Patie's mill, . *Ramsay,* 95
The lass that winna sit down, . 401
The lovely lass of Inverness, *A. Cunningham,* 293
The lowlands of Holland, . *H. C.* 199
The maid that tends the goats, *W. Dudgeon,* 110
The mariner's wife, . *about* 1771, 238
The mill, mill O, . . *Ramsay,* 156
The miller, *Sir J. Clerk of Penicuick,* 1751, 167
The Miller's daughter, . . 398

Page

The pawky loon, the miller, . 334
The ploughman, . . . *II. C.* 236
The posie, . . . *Burns,* 173
The rantin' dog the daddie o't, . *Do.* 76
The rock and the wee pickle tow, *Alex. Ross,* 66
The runawa' bride, . *previous to* 1751, 38
The shepherd's son, . . 11
The silken snooded lassie, . 150
The siller crown, . *Miss Blamyre,* 191
The soger laddie, . . *Ramsay,* 121
The soger's return, . . *Burns,* 157
The step-daughter's relief, . *Ramsay,* 348
The Stuart's great line, . . 289
The tailor, . . *partly by Burns,* 354
The toast, . . . 325
The waefu' heart, . *Miss Blamyre,* 203
The weary pund o' tow, . *T. T. M.,* 71
The wee thing, . *II. M'Neill,* 214
The wee, wee German lairdie, *old words,* 290
    Do. another version, *ibid.*
The wee wifeikie, . *Rev. Dr. Geddes,* 77
The white cockade, *published in* 1776, 209
The widow, . . . *Ramsay,* 254
The wowing of Jok and Jynny, *published* 1568, 19
The yellow-hair'd laddie, . *old words,* 132
    Do. . . *Ramsay, ibid*
The young laird and Edinburgh Katy, *Do.* 105
The young lass contra auld man, *T T. M.* 255
The young Maxwell, . . *Jacobite,* 297
Then guidwife count the lawin, *Burns,* 332
Theniel Menzies' Bonny Mary, . *Do.* 263
There'll never be peace, . *Do.* 283
This is no my ain lassie, . *Do.* 115
Thou art gane awa', . . 394
Tibbie Dunbar, . . *Burns,* 247
Tibby Fowler, *attributed to Rev. Dr. Strachan,* 251
Tibbie, I hae seen the day, . *Burns,* 220

Page

Todlen hame, . . . *Ramsay,* 60
To daunton me, . . *Jacobite,* 278
Tranent Muir, . . *Adam Skirving,* 306
Tullochgorum, . . *Rev. J. Skinner,* 82
Turnimspike, . . . *H. C.* 80
Tweedside, . *old words by Lord Yester,* 102
  Do. *Patrick Crawford of Auchinames,* 1731, *ibid*
Twine weel the plaiden, . *H. C.* 232

The bairns gat out wi' an unco shout, . . 51
The bonniest lad that e'er I saw, . . 370
The carl he cam o'er the craft, . . . 255
The Catrine woods were yellow seen, . . 266
The Chevalier being void of fear, . . 306
The collier has a daughter, . . . 161
The deil cam fiddling thro' the town, . . 61
The heath-cock craw'd o'er muir and dale, . 374
The Lawland lads think they are fine, . . 107
The Lawland maids gang trig and fine, . . 109
The meal was dear short syne, . . . 25
The moon had climb'd the highest hill, . . 202
The morn was fair, saft was the air, . . 176
The night her silent sable wore, . . . 347
The night is my departing night, . . . 382
The pawky auld carl cam o'er the lee, . . 1
The small birds rejoice in the green leaves returning, 286
The smiling morn, the breathing spring, . . 397
The spring-time returns, and clothes the green plains, 149
The sun has gane down o'er the lofty Ben Lomond, 117
The sun in the west fa's to rest in the e'enin', . 211
The sun raise sae rosy, the grey hills adorning, . 268
The tailor fell thro' the bed, thimble an' a', . 354
The widow can bake, and the widow can brew, . 254
Their groves o' sweet myrtle let foreign lands reckon, 270
There came a young man to my daddie's door, . 7
There's auld Rob Morris, that wins in yon glen, . 358
There's cauld kail in Aberdeen, (old words) . 85
There's cauld kail in Aberdeen, (by the Duke of
  Gordon) 86
There liv'd a lass in Inverness, . . . 293
The liv'd a wife in our gate-end, . . . 55
There lives a lassie i' the braes, . . . 319
There was a jolly beggar, and a begging he was bound, 4
There was a lass, they ca'd her Meg, . . 63
There was a shepherd's son, . . . 11

Page

There was a wee bit wifeikie, was comin' frae the fair, 77
There was a wife won'd in a glen,   .   . 64
There was an auld wife an' a wee pickle tow,   . 66
There was anes a May, and she loo'd na men,   . 189
There were three kings into the East,   .   . 326
They say that Jockey'll speed weel o't,   .   . 27
Thickest night o'erhang my dwelling,   .   . 287
Thou ling'ring star, with less'ning ray,   .   . 205
Thy cheek is o' the rose's hue,   .   .   . 212
'Tis I have seven braw new gowns,   .   . 225
'Tis nae very lang sinsyne,   .   .   . 218
'Twas even—the dewy fields were green,   . 390
'Twas in that season of the year,   .   . 111
'Twas on a Monday morning,   .   .   . 369
'Twas summer, and softly the breezes were blowing, 197

Up in the morning early,   *partly by Burns,* 265

Up amang yon cliffy rocks,   .   .   . 110
Upon a simmer afternoon,   .   .   : 136

Wae's me for Prince Charlie,   { *W. Glen of Glasgow,* } 380
Waly, waly up the bank, *published in* 1666, 229
Welcome, Charley Stuart,   . 291
Were na my heart light I wad die, }   *Lady Grissel Baillie,* 189
Were thou but mine ain thing, 178
What ails the lasses at me,   *Alexander Ross,* 256
When she cam ben she bobbed, *partly by Burns,* 355
When I upon thy bosom lean,   *J. Lapraik,* 244
Whistle and I'll come to you, my lad, *Burns,* 170
Whistle o'er the lave o't,   .   *Do.* 72
Willie brew'd a peck o' maut,   .   *Do.* 330
Willie's rare,   .   .   . 393
Willy was a wanton wag, *Wm. Walkinshaw,* 74
Woo'd and married and a',   . *old song,* 32
    Do.   .   *Alex. Ross,* 259

Was ne'er in Scotland heard or seen,   .   . 413
Weary fa' you, Duncan Gray,   .   .   . 233
Were I but able to rehearse,   .   .   . 87

	Page
Were ye e'er at Crookie Den, . . .	299
Wha the deil hae we got for a king, . .	290
Wha wad na be in love, ...	61
Whare are you gaun, my bonny lass? . .	352
Whare gang ye, thou silly auld carle, . .	297
Whar' ha'e ye been a' day, . . .	371
Whar hae ye been a' day, my boy Tammy, .	98
Whare hae ye been sae braw, lad, . .	275
What ails this heart of mine, . . .	391
What beauties does Flora disclose, . .	102
What can a young lassie, what shall a young lassie,	45
What think ye o' the scornfu' quine, . .	401
When first I cam to be a man, . . .	90
When I have a saxpence under my thumb, .	60
When I think on this warld's pelf, . .	323
When I was in my se'enteenth year, . .	264
When Maggy and I were acquaint, . .	102
When the sheep are in the fauld and the kye at hame,	200
When trees did bud, and fields were green, .	136
When wild war's deadly blast was blawn, .	157
Will ye gang o'er the lee-rig, . . .	151
Will ye go to the ewe-bughts, Marion, . ' .	133
Willie Wastle dwalt on Tweed, . . .	52
Ye Jacobites by name, . *ascribed to Burns,*	285
Young Allan, . . *R. Gall,*	211
Ye banks, and braes, and streams around, .	204
Ye banks and braes o' bonnie Doon, . .	228
Yestreen I had a pint o' wine, . . .	145
Young Jocky was the blythest lad, . .	112
Young Peggy's to the mill gane, . . .	334
You're welcome, Charley Stuart, . . .	291

A

COLLECTION

OF

ANCIENT AND MODERN

SCOTTISH SONGS.

THE GABERLUNZIE MAN.

[Supposed to have been written by James V. on one of his intrigues.]

THE pawky auld carl came o'er the lee,
Wi' mony gude e'ens and days to me,
Saying, Gudewife, for your courtesie,
    Will ye lodge a silly poor man?
The night was cauld, the carl was wat,
And down ayont the ingle he sat,
My dochter's shouthers he 'gan to clap,
    And cadgily ranted and sang.

O wow! quo' he, were I as free,
As first when I saw this country,
How blyth and merry wad I be!
    And I wad never think lang.

A

He grew canty, and she grew fain;
But little did her auld minny ken
What thir slee twa together were say'ng,
  When wooing they were sae thrang.

And O! quo' he, an ye were as black
As e'er the crown o' your dady's hat,
'Tis I wad lay thee by my back,
  And awa wi' thee I wou'd gang.
And O! quo' she, an I were as white
As e'er the snaw lay on the dike,
I'd clead me braw and lady-like,
  And awa wi' thee I wou'd gang.

Between the twa was made a plot;
They raise a wee before the cock,
And wilily they shot the lock,
  And fast to the bent are they gane.
Upon the morn the auld wife raise,
And at her leisure pat on her claise;
Syne to the servant's bed she gaes,
  To speir for the silly poor man.

She gaed to the bed whar the beggar lay,
The strae was cauld, he was away;
She clapt her hands, cry'd, Waladay!
  For some o' our gear will be gane.
Some ran to coffers, and some to kists,
But nought was stown that cou'd be mist;
She danc'd her lane, cry'd, Praise be blest!
  I have lodg'd a leil poor man.

Since naething's awa, as we can learn,
The kirn's to kirn, and milk to earn,
Gae butt the house, lass, and wauken my bairn,
  And bid her come quickly ben.

The servant gade where the daughter lay,
The sheets were cauld, she was away,
And fast to her goodwife can say,
  She's aff wi' the gaberlunzie-man. *

O fy gar ride, and fy gar rin,
And haste ye find these traitors again;
For she's be burnt, and he's be slain,
  The wearifu' gaberlunzie-man.
Some rade upo' horse, some ran a-fit,
The wife was wood, and out o' her wit;
She cou'd na gang, nor yet cou'd she sit,
  But aye she curs'd and she bann'd.

Mean time, far hind out o'er the lee,
Fu' snug in a glen where nane could see,
The twa, with kindly sport and glee,
  Cut frae a new cheese a whang:
The priving was good, it pleas'd them baith,
To lo'e her for aye, he gae her his aith.
Quo' she, To leave thee I will be laith,
  My winsome gaberlunzie-man.

O kend my minny I were wi' you,
Ill-fardly wad she crook her mou,
Sic a poor man she'd never trow,
  After the gaberlunzie-man.
My dear, quo' he, ye're yet o'er young,
And ha' na learn'd the beggars' tongue,
To follow me frae town to town,
  And carry the gaberlunzie on.

Wi' cauk and keel I'll win your bread,
And spindles and whorles for them wha need,
Whilk is a gentle trade indeed,
  To carry the gaberlunzie on.

* A wallet-man or tinker, who appears to have been formerly a
jack-of-all-trades.

I'll bow my leg, and crook my knee,
And draw a black clout o'er my eye,
A cripple or blind they will ca' me,
While we shall be merry, and sing.

~~~~~~~~~~~

THE JOLLY BEGGAR.

[This song is also attributed to James V.]

THERE was a jolly beggar, and a begging he was bound,
And he took up his quarters into a land'art town.
*And we'll gang nae mair a roving sae late into the night,
And we'll gang nae mair a roving, let the moon shine
ne'er sae bright.
And we'll gang nae mair a roving.*

He wad neither ly in barn, nor yet wad he in byre,
But in ahint the ha' door, or else afore the fire.
And we'll gang nae mair, &c.

The beggar's bed was made at e'en, wi' good clean
straw and hay,
And in ahint the ha' door, and there the beggar lay.
And we'll gang nae mair, &c.

Up raise the goodman's dochter, and for to bar the door,
And there she saw the beggar standin' i' the floor.
And we'll gang nae mair, &c.

He took the lassie in his arms, and to the bed he ran,
O hooly, hooly wi' me, sir, ye'll waken our goodman.
And we'll gang nae mair, &c.

The beggar was a cunnin' loon, and ne'er a word he
    spak,
Until he got his turn done, syne he began to crack..
    And we'll gang nae mair, &c.

Is there ony dogs into this town? maiden, tell me true.
And what wad ye do wi' them, my hinny and my dow?
    And we'll gang nae mair, &c.

They'll rive a' my mealpocks, and do me meikle wrang.
O dool for the doing o't! are ye the poor man?
    And we'll gang nae mair, &c.

Then she took up the mealpocks, and flang them o'er
    the wa',
The de'il gae wi' the mealpocks, my maidenhead and a'.
    And we'll gang nae mair, &c.

I took ye for some gentleman, at least the laird of
    Brodie:
O dool for the doing o't! are ye the poor bodie?
    And we'll gang nae mair, &c.

He took the lassie in his arms, and gae her kisses three,
And four-and-twenty hunder merk to pay the nourice-
    fee.
    And we'll gang nae mair, &c.

He took a horn frae his side, and blew baith loud and
    shrill,
And four-and-twenty-belted knights came skipping
    o'er the hill.
    And we'll gang nae mair, &c.

And he took out his little knife, loot a' his duddies fa',
And he was the brawest gentleman that was amang
    them a'.
    And we'll gang nae mair, &c.

The beggar was a cliver loon, and he lap shoulder
    height,
O aye for sicken quarters as I gat yesternight.
    And we'll gang nae mair, &c.

~~~~~~~~~~~

THE HUMBLE BEGGAR.

In Scotland there liv'd a humble beggar,
    He had neither house, nor hald, nor hame,
But he was weel liked by ilka bodie,
    And they gae him sunkets to rax his wame.

A nivefow of meal, a handfow of groats,
    A dadd of bannock, or herring brie,
Cauld parradge, or the lickings of plates,
    Wad make him as blyth as a beggar could be.

This beggar he was a humble beggar,
    The feint a bit of pride had he,
He wad a ta'en his a'ms in a bikker,
    Frae gentleman, or poor bodie.

His wallets ahint and afore did hang,
    In as good order as wallets could be:
A lang kail-gooly hang down by his side,
    And a meikle nowt-horn to rout on had he.

It happen'd ill, it happen'd warse,
    It happen'd sae that he did die;
And wha do ye think was at his late-wake,
    But lads and lasses of a high degree.

Some were blyth, and some were sad,
  And some they play'd at Blind Harrie:
But suddenly up-started the auld carle,
  I redd ye, good folks, tak tent o' me.

Up gat Kate that sat i' the nook,
  Vow kimmer, and how do ye?
Up he gat, and ca'd her limmer,
  And ruggit and tuggit her cockernonie.

They houkit his grave in Duket's kirk-yard,
  E'en far frae the companie :
But when they were gaun to lay him i' the yird,
  The feint a dead nor dead was he.

And when they brought him to Duket's kirk-yard,
  He dunted on the kist, the boards did flee:
And when they were gaun to put him i' the yird,
  In fell the kist, and out lap he.

He cry'd, I'm cauld, I'm unco cauld;
  Fu' fast ran the fock, and fu' fast ran he:
But he was first hame at his ain ingle side,
  And he helped to drink his ain dirgie.

~~~~~~~~~

THE CAULDRIFE WOOER.

There came a young man to my daddie's door,
My daddie's door, my daddie's door,
There came a young man to my daddie's door,
  Came seeking me to woo.

And wow but he was a braw young lad,
A brisk young lad, and a braw young lad,
And wow but he was a braw young lad,
  Came seeking me to woo.

But I was baking when he came,
When he came, when he came;
I took him in; and gae him a scone,
  To thow his frozen mou'.
    And wow but, &c.

I set him in aside the bink,
I gae him bread and ale to drink,
But ne'er a blyth styme wad he blink,
  Until his wame was fou.
    And wow but, &c.

Gae, get ye gone, ye cauldrife wooer,
Ye sour-looking, cauldrife wooer:
I straightway show'd him to the door,
  Saying, Come nae mair to woo.
    And wow but, &c.

There lay a duck-dub before the door,
Before the door, before the door,
There lay a duck-dub before the door,
  And there fell he I trow.
    And wow but, &c.

Out came the goodman, and high he shouted,
Out came the goodwife, and low she louted,
And a' the town neighbours were gather'd about it,
  But there lay he, I trow.
    And wow but, &c.

Then out came I, and sneer'd, and smil'd,
Ye came to woo, but ye're a' beguil'd;
Ye've fa'en i' the dirt, and ye're a' befyl'd,
 We'll hae nae mair o' you.
  And now but, &c.

~~~~~~~~~~

LASS GIN YE LO'E ME.

I HA'E laid a herring in sa't,
 Lass gin ye lo'e me tell me now?
I ha'e brew'd a forpet o' ma't,
 And I canna come ilka day to woo.
I ha'e a calf will soon be a cow,
 Lass gin ye lo'e me tell me now?
I ha'e a pig will soon be a sow,
 And I canna come ilka day to woo.

I've a house on yonder moor,
 Lass gin ye lo'e me tell me now?
Three sparrows may dance upon the floor,
 And I canna come ilka day to woo.
I ha'e a butt and I ha'e a benn,
 Lass gin ye lo'e me tell me now?
I ha'e three chickens and a fat hen,
 And I canna come ony mair to woo.

I've a hen wi' a happity leg,
 Lass gin ye lo'e me tell me now?
Which ilka day lays me an egg,
 And I canna come ilka day to woo.
I ha'e a kebbock upon my shelf,
 Lass gin ye lo'e me tak me now!
I downa eat it a' myself,
 And I winna come ony mair to woo.

FEE HIM, FATHER, FEE HIM.

[" This song, for genuine humour in the verses, and lively origi-
nality in the air, is unparalleled. I take it to be very old."—
BURNS.]

Saw ye Johnnie cummin, quo' she,
  Saw ye Johnnie cummin;
O saw ye Johnnie cummin, quo' she,
  Saw ye Johnnie cummin;
Saw ye Johnnie cummin, quo' she,
  Saw ye Johnnie cummin,
Wi' his blue bonnet on his head,
  And his doggie rinnin, quo' she,
  And his doggie rinnin?

Fee him, father, fee him, quo' she,
  Fee him, father, fee him;
O fee him, father, fee him, quo' she;
  Fee him, father, fee him;
For he is a gallant lad,
  And a weel doin, quo' she;
And a' the wark about the house
  Gaes wi' me when I see him, quo' she,
  Gaes wi' me when I see him.

What will I do wi' him? quo' he,
  What will I do wi' him?
He's ne'er a sark upon his back,
  And I hae nane to gi'e him.
I hae twa sarks into my kist,
  And ane o' them I'll gie him;
And for a merk of mair fee,
  Dinna stand wi' him, quo' she,
  Dinna stand wi' him.

For well do I lo'e him, quo' she,
  Well do I lo'e him ;
For weel do I lo'e him, quo' she,
  Weel do I lo'e him.
O fee him, father, fee him, quo' she,
  Fee him, father, fee him ;
He'll had the pleugh,. thrash in the barn,
  And crack wi' me at e'en, quo' she,
  And crack wi' me at e'en.

THE SHEPHERD'S SON.

There was a shepherd's son,
  Kept sheep upon a hill,
He laid his pipe and crook aside,
  And there he slept his fill.
    Sing, fal deral, &c.

He looked east, he looked west,
  Then gave an under look,
And there he spy'd a lady fair,
  Swimming in a brook.
    Sing, fal deral, &c.

He rais'd his head frae his green bed,
  And then approach'd the maid,
Put on your claise, my dear, he says,
  And be ye not afraid.
    Sing, fal deral, &c.

'Tis fitter for a lady fair
  To sew her silken seam,
Than to get up in a May morning,
  And strive against the stream.
    Sing, fal deral, &c.

If you'll not touch my mantle,
  And let my claise alane,
Then I'll gi'e you as much money
  As you can carry hame.
    Sing, fal deral, &c.

O! I'll not touch your mantle,
  And I'll let your claise alane;
But I'll tak you out of the clear water,
  My dear to be my ain.
    Sing, fal deral, &c.

And when she out of the water came,
  He took her in his arms;
Put on your claise, my dear, he says,
  And hide those lovely charms.
    Sing, fal deral, &c.

He mounted her on a milk-white steed,
  Himself upon anither,
And all along the way they rode,
  Like sister and like brither.
    Sing, fal deral, &c.

When she came to her father's yett,
  She tirled at the pin;
And ready stood the porter there,
  To let this fair maid in.
    Sing, fal deral, &c.

And when the gate was opened,
  So nimbly she whipt in;
Pough! You're a fool without, she says,
  And I'm a maid within.
    Sing, fal deral, &c.

Then fare ye weel, my modest boy,
  I thank you for your care;
But had you done what you should done,
  I ne'er had left you there.
    Sing, fal deral, &c.

Oh! I'll cast aff my hose and shoon,
  And let my feet gae bare,
And gin I meet a bonny lass,
  Hang me, if her I spare.
    Sing, fal deral, &c.

In that do as you please, she says,
  But you shall never more
Have the same opportunity:
  With that she shut the door.
    Sing, fal deral, &c.

There is a gude auld proverb,
  I've often heard it told,
" He that would not, when he might,
  He should not when he would."
    Sing, fal deral, &c.

B

SCORNFU' NANSY.

Nansy's to the green-wood gane,
  To hear the gowdspink chatt'ring,
And Willie he has followed her,
  To gain her love by flatt'ring:
But a' that he cou'd say or do,
  She geck'd and scorned at him;
And ay when he began to woo,
  She bid him mind wha gat him.

What ails ye at my dad, quoth he,
  My minny or my aunty?
With crowdy-mowdy they fed me,
  Lang-kail and ranty-tanty:
With bannocks of good barley-meal,
  Of thae there was right plenty,
With chapped stocks fu' butter'd well;
  And was na that right dainty?

Although my father was nae laird,
  'Tis daffin to be vaunty,
He keepit ay a good kail-yard,
  A ha' house and a pantry:
A good blue bonnet on his head,
  An ourlay 'bout his craggy;
And ay until the day he dy'd,
  He rade on good shanks naggy.

Now wae and wonder on your snout,
  Wad ye hae bonny Nansy?
Wad ye compare ye'rsell to me,
  A docken till a tansy?

I have a wooer of my ain,
  They ca' him souple Sandy;
And well I wat his bonny mou'
  Is sweet like sugar-candy.

Wow, Nansy! what needs a' this din,
  Do I not ken this Sandy?
I'm sure the chief of a' his kin,
  Was Rab the beggar randy:
His minny, Meg, upo' her back,
  Bare baith him and his billy;
Will ye compare a nasty pack
  To me, your winsome Willy?

My gutcher left a gude braid sword,
  Tho' it be auld and rusty,
Yet ye may tak it on my word,
  It is baith stout and trusty:
And if I can but get it drawn,
  Which will be right uneasy,
I shall lay baith my lugs in pawn,
  That he shall get a heezy.

Then Nansy turn'd her round about,
  And said, Did Sandy hear ye,
Ye wadna miss to get a clout;
  I ken he disna fear ye:
Sae had ye'r tongue and say nae mair,
  Set somewhere else your fancy;
For as lang's Sandy's to the fore,
  Ye never shall get Nansy.

NAE DOMINIES FOR ME.

As I went forth to take the air,
　Into an evening clear, laddie,
I met a brisk young handsome spark,
　A new-made pulpitier, laddie:
An airy blade so brisk and bra',
　Mine eyes did never see, laddie;
A long cravat at him did wag,
　His hose girt 'boon the knee, laddie.

By-and-out o'er this young man had,
　A gallant douse black gown, laddie,
With cock'd up hat, and powder'd wig,
　Black coat, and muffs fu' clean, laddie.
At length he did approach me nigh,
　And bowing down full low, laddie;
He grasp'd me, as I did pass by,
　And would not let me go, laddie.

Said I, Pray, friend, what do you mean?
　Canst thou not let me be, laddie?
Says he, My heart, by Cupid's dart,
　Is captive unto thee, lassie.
I'll rather chuse to thole grim death;
　So cease and let me be, laddie.
For what? said he.—Good troth, said she,
　Nae dominies for me, laddie.

Ministers' stipends are uncertain rents
　For ladies' conjunct fee, laddie;
When books and gowns are all cry'd down,
　Nae dominies for me, laddie.

But for your sake I'll fleece the flock,
  Grow rich as I grow auld, lassie;
If I be spar'd, I'll be a laird,
  And thou be Madam call'd, lassie. ·

But what if ye should chance to die,
  Leave bairns ane or twa, laddie?
Naething would be reserv'd for them,
  But hair-mould books to gnaw, laddie.
At this he angry was, I wat,
  He gloom'd and look'd fu' hie, laddie;
When I perceived this, in haste
  I left my dominie, laddie.

Then I went hame to my step-dame, ·
  By this time it was late, laddie;
But she before had barr'd the door,
  I blush'd and look'd fu' blate, laddie.
Thinks I, I must ly in the street,
  Is there no room for me, laddie;
And is there neither plaid nor sheet
  With my young dominie, laddie?

Then with a humble voice, I cry'd,
  Pray open the door to me, laddie:
But he reply'd, I'm gone to bed,
  So cease, and let me be, lassie.
The sooner that you let me in,
  You'll be the more at ease, laddie;
And on the morrow I'll be gone,
  Then marry whom you please, laddie.

And what if I should chance to die,
  Leave bairns ane or twa, lassie,
Naething would be reserv'd for them,
  But hair-mould books to gna', lassie.

Ministers' stipends are uncertain rents
  For ladies' conjunct-fee, lassie;
When books and gowns are a' cry'd down, .
  Nae dominies for thee, lassie.

So fare you well, my charming maid,
  This lesson learn of me, lassie,
At the next offer hold him fast
  That first makes love to thee, lassie.
Then did I curse my doleful fate,
  Gin this had been my lot, laddie,
For to have match'd with such as you, -
  A good-for-nothing sot, laddie.

Then I returned hame again,
  And coming down the town, laddie,
By my good luck I chanc'd to meet
  A gentleman dragoon, laddie:
And he took me by baith the hands,
  'Twas help in time of need, laddie;
Fools on ceremonies stand,
  At twa words we agreed, laddie.

He led me to his quarter-house,
  Where we exchang'd a word, laddie;
We had nae use for black-gowns there,
  We marry'd o'er the sword, laddie.
Martial drums is music fine,
  Compar'd wi' tinkling bells, laddie;
Gold, red, and blue, is more divine
  Than black, the hue of hell, laddie.

Kings, queens, and princes, crave the aid
  Of the brave stout dragoons, laddie;
While dominies are much employ'd
  'Bout whores and sackcloth gowns, laddie.

Awa' then wi' these whining lowns,
   They look like let me be, laddie;
I've mair delight in roaring guns:
   Nae dominies for me, laddie.

THE WOWING OF JOK AND JYNNY.

[This song is preserved in the Bannatyne MS. and consequently
was written previous to 1568.]

Robeyn's Jok came to wow our Jynny,
   On our feist-evin quhen we were fow;
Scho brankit fast and maid hir bony,
   And said, Jok, come ye for to wow?
   Scho burneist hir baith breist and brow,
And maid her cleir as ony clok;
   Then spak hir dame, and said, I trow,
Ye come to wow our Jynny, Jok.

Jok said, Forsuth I zern full fane,
   To luk my heid, and sit doun by zow.
Than spak hir modir, and said agane,
   My bairne hes tocher gud annwch to ge zow:
   Te he! quoth Jynny, keik, keik, I se zow;
Muder, yone man maks zow a mok.
   I schro the lyar, full leis me zow,
I come to wow zour Jynny, quoth Jok.

My berne, scho sayis, hes of hir awin,
  Ane guss, ane gryce, ane cok, ane hen,
Ane calf, ane hog, ane futbraid sawin,
  Ane kirn, ane pin, that ze weill ken,
  Ane pig, ane pot, ane raip thair-ben,
Ane fork, ane flaik, ane reill, ane rok,
  Dischis and dublaris nyne or ten;
Come ze to wow our Jynny, Jok?

Ane blanket, and ane wecht also,
  Ane schule, ane scheit, and ane lang flail,
Ane ark, ane almry, and laidills two,
  Ane milk-syth, with ane swyne-taill,
  Ane rowsty quhittill to scheir the kaill,
Ane quheill, ane mell the beir to knok,
  Ane coig, ane caird wantand ane naill:
Come ze to wow our Jynny, Jok?

Ane furme, ane furlet, ane pott, ane pek,
  Ane tub, ane barrow, with ane quheilband,
Ane turs, ane troch, and ane meil-sek,
  Ane spurtil braid, and ane elwand.
  Jok tuk Jynny be the hand, ·
And cry'd, Ane feast! and slew ane cok,
  And maid a brydell up alland:
Now haif I gottin your Jynny, quoth Jok.

Now, deme, I haif zour bairne mareit;
  Suppois ye mak it nevir sa twche,
I latt zou wit schois nocht miskarrit,
  It is weill kend gud haif I annwch:
  Ane crukit gleyd fell our ane huch,
Ane spaid, ane speit, ane spur, ane sok,
  Withouttin oxin I haif a pluche,
To gang togiddir Jynny and Jok.

I haif ane helter, and eik ane hek,
　Ane cord, ane creill, and als an cradill,
Fyve fidder of raggis to stuff ane jak,
　Ane auld pannell of ane laid sadill,
　Ane pepper polk maid of a paddell,
Ane spounge, ane spindill wantand ane nok,
　Twa lusty lippis to lik ane laiddill,
To gang togidder Jynny and Jok.

Ane brechame, and twa brochis fyne,
　Weill buklit with a brydill renze,
Ane sark maid of the Linkome twyne,
　Ane gay grene cloke that will nocht stenze,
　And zit for mister I will nocht fenze,
Fyve hundrith fleis now in a flok;
　Call ze nocht that ane joly menze,
To gang togidder Jynny and Jok?

Ane trene truncheour, ane ramehorne spone,
　Twa buttis of barkit blasnit ledder,
All graith that gains to kobbill schone,
　Ane thrawcruk to twyne ane tedder,
　Ane brydill, ane girth, and ane swyne bledder,
Ane maskene fatt, ane fetterit lok,
　Ane scheip weill kepit fra ill wedder,
To gang togiddir Jynny and Jok.

Tak thair for my parte of the feist;
　It is weill knawin I am weill bodin;
Ze may nocht say my parte is leist.
　The wyfe said, Speid, the kaill ar soddin,
　And als the laverok is fust and loddin;
Quhen ze haif done tak hame the brok.
　The rost was twche, sa wer thay bodin;
Syn gaid togiddir Jynny and Jok.

MUIRLAND WILLIE.

Harken, and I will tell ye how
Young Muirland Willie came to woo,
Though he could neither say nor do,
 The truth I tell to you.
But aye he cries, Whate'er betide,
Maggy I'se hae to be my bride.
 With a fal dal, &c.

On his gray yade as he did ride,
With durk and pistol by his side,
He prick'd her on wi' meikle pride,
 Wi' meikle mirth and glee,
Out o'er yon moss, out o'er yon muir,
Till he came to her daddy's door.
 With a fal dal, &c.

Goodman, quoth he, be ye within,
I'm come your doghter's love to win,
I care na for making meikle din;
 What answer gi'e ye me?
Now, wooer, quoth he, would ye light down,
I'll gi'e ye my doghter's love to win:
 With a fal dal, &c.

Now, wooer, sin ye are lighted down,
Where do you win, or in what town?
I think my doghter winna gloom,
 On sic a lad as ye.
The wooer he stept up the house,
And wow but he was wond'rous crouse.
 With a fal dal, &c.

I have three owsen in a pleugh;
Twa gude ga'en yads, and gear enough;
The place they ca' it Cadeneugh;
    I scorn to tell a lie:
Besides, I hae frae the great laird,
A peat-pat, and a lang-kail-yard.
    With a fal dal, &c.

The maid pat on her kirtle brown,
She was the brawest in a' the town;
I wat on him she did na gloom,
    But blinkit bonnilie.
The lover he stendit up in haste,
And gript her hard about the waist;
    With a fal dal, &c.

To win your love, maid, I'm come here;
I'm young, and hae enough o' gear;
And for mysell you need na fear,
    Troth try me whan ye like.
He took aff his bannet, and spat in his chew,
He dighted his gab, and he prie'd her mou'.
    With a fal dal, &c.

The maiden blush'd and bing'd fu' law,
She had na will to say him na,
But to her daddy she left it a',
    As they twa could agree.
The lover ga'e her the tither kiss;
Syne ran to her daddy, and tell'd him this,
    With a fal dal, &c.

Your doghter wad na say me na,
As to yoursell she has left it a',
As we could 'gree between us twa;
    Say, what'll ye gi'e me wi' her?

Now, wooer, quo' he, I ha'e na meikle,
But sic's I ha'e ye's get a pickle,
    With a fal dal, &c.

A kilnfu o' corn I'll gi'e to thee,
Three soums of sheep, twa good milk kye,
Ye's ha'e the wedding-dinner free:
    Troth I dow do na mair.
Content, quo' he, a bargain be't;
I'm far frae hame, make haste let's do't.
    With a fal dal, &c.

The bridal day it came to pass,
Wi' mony a blithsome lad and lass;
But sicken a day there neyer was,
    Sic mirth was never seen.
This winsome couple straked hands,
Mess John ty'd up the marriage-bands.
    With a fal dal, &c.

And our bride's maidens were na few,
Wi' tap-knots, lug-knots, a' in blew,
Frae tap to tae they were braw new,
    And blinkit bonnilie:
Their toys and mutches were sae clean,
They glanced in our ladses' een.
    With a fal dal, &c.

Sic hirdum dirdum, and sic din,
Wi' he o'er her, and she o'er him;
The minstrels they did never blin,
    Wi' meikle mirth and glee.
And ay they bobit, and ay they beckt,
And ay their wames together met.
    With a fal dal, &c.

MAGIE'S TOCHER.

THE meal was dear short syne,
  We buckled us a' the gither;
And Maggie was in her prime,
  When Willie made courtship till her.
Twa pistols charg'd beguess,
  To gi'e the courting-shot,
And syne came ben the lass
  Wi' swats drawn frae the butt.
He first speer'd at the guidman,
  And syne at Giles the mither,
An ye wad gie's a bit land,
  We'd buckle us e'en the gither.

My doughter ye shall hae,
  I'll gi'e ye her by the hand;
But I'll part wi' my wife, by my fay,
  Or I part wi' my land.
Your tocher it sall be good,
  There's nane sall hae its maik,
The lass bound in her snood,
  And Crummie wha kens her stake;
With an auld bedding o' claiths,
  Was left me by my mither,
They're jet black o'er wi' fleas,
  Ye may cuddle in them the gither.

Ye speak right weel, guidman,
  But ye maun mend your hand,
And think o' modesty,
  Gin ye'll not quat your land.
                    c

We are but young, ye ken,
  And now we're gaun the gither,
A house is butt and ben,
  And Crummie will want her fother:
The bairns are coming on,
  And they'll cry, O their mither!
We have nonther pat nor pan,
  But four bare legs the gither.

Your tocher's be good enough,
  For that ye need nae fear,
Twa good stilts to the pleugh,
  And ye yoursell maun steer:
Ye sall hae twa good pocks
  That ance were of the tweel,
The tane to had the grots,
  The tither to had the meal:
With an auld kist made of wande,
  And that sall be your coffer,
Wi' aiken woody bands,
  And that may had your tocher.

Consider well, guidman,
  We hae but borrow'd gear,
The horse that I ride on
  Is Sandy Wilson's mare:
The saddle's nane of my ain,
  And thae's but borrow'd boots,
And when that I gae hame,
  I maun tak to my koots;
The cloak is Geordy Watt's,
  That gars me look sae crouse;
Come, fill us a cogue of swats,
  We'll mak nae mair toom roose.

I like you weel, young lad,
  For telling me sae plain,
I married when little I had
  O' gear that was my ain:
But sin that things are sae,
  The bride she maun come forth,
Tho' a' the gear she'll hae
  It'll be but little worth.
A bargain it maun be,
  Fy, cry on Giles the mither:
Content am I, quo' she,
  E'en gar the hissie come hither.
The bride she gade till her bed.
  The bridegroom he cam till her;
The fiddler crap in at the fit,
  And they cuddl'd it a' the gither.

THE BRIDAL O'T.

[By Mr Alex. Ross, late schoolmaster at Lochlee, and author of
The Fortunate Shepherdess.]

Tune—*Lucy Campbell.*

They say that Jockey'll speed weel o't,
  They say that Jockey'll speed weel o't,
For he grows brawer ilka day,
  I hope we'll hae a bridal o't.
For yesternight nae farder gane,
  The back house at the side wa' o't,
He there wi' Meg was mirden seen,
  I hope we'll hae a bridal o't.

An we had but a bridal o't,
  An we had but a bridal o't,
We'd leave the rest unto gude luck
  Altho' there should betide ill o't:
For bridal days are merry times,
  And young folks like the coming o't,
And scribblers they bang up their rhymes,
  And pipers they the bumming o't.

The lasses like a bridal o't,
  The lasses like a bridal o't,
Their braws maun be in rank and file
  Altho' that they should guide ill o't:
The boddom o' the kist is then
  Turn'd up unto the immost o't,
The end that held the keeks sae clean
  Is now become the teemest o't.

The bangster at the threshing o't,
  The bangster at the threshing o't,
Afore it comes is fidgin fain
  And ilka day's a clashing o't;
He'll sall his jerkin for a groat,
  His linder for anither o't,
And e'er he want to clear his shot,
  His sark'll pay the tither o't.

The pipers and the fiddlers o't,
  The pipers and tho fiddlers o't,
Can smell a bridal unco far,
  And like to be the middlers o't:
Fan thick and threefald they convene
  Ilk ane envies the tither o't,
And wishes naie but him alane
  May ever see anither o't.

Fan they hae done wi' eating o't,
  Fan they hae done wi' eating ô't,
For dancing they gae to the green,
  And aiblins to the beating o't:
He dances best that dances fast,
  And loups at ilka reesing o't,
And claps his hands frae hough to hough,
  And furls about the feezings o't.

〰〰〰〰〰〰

THE BLYTHSOME BRIDAL.

[This song is in Watson's collection of Scotch poems, printed at
Edinburgh in 1706.]

Fy let us a' to the bridal,
  For there will be lilting there;
For Jocky's to be married to Maggy,
  The lass wi' the gowden hair.
And there will be lang-kail and pottage,
  And bannocks of barley-meal;
And there will be good sawt herring,
  To relish a cog of good ale..
    Fy let us a' to the bridal,
    For there will be lilting there;
    For Jocky's to be married to Maggy,
    The lass wi' the gowden hair.

And there will be Sawney the sutor,
  And Will wi' the meikle mou';
And there will be Tam the blutter,
  With Andrew the tinkler, I trow;

And there will be bow'd-legged Robie,
  With thumbless Katie's goodman;
And there will blue-cheeked Dobie,
  And Lawrie the laird of the land.
    Fy let us, &c.

And there will be sow-libber Patie,
  And plucky-fac'd Wat i' the mill,
Capper-nos'd Francie and Gibbie,
  That wins i' the how of the hill;
And there will be Alaster Sibby,
  Wha in wi' black Bessy did mool,
With snivelling Lilly and Tibby,
  The lass that stands aft on the stool.
    Fy let us, &c.

And Madge that was buckl'd to Steenie,
  And coft him grey breeks to his a—e,
Wha after was hangit for stealing,
  Great mercy it happen'd nae warse:
And there will be gleed Geordy Janners,
  And Kirsh with the lily-white leg,
Wha gade to the south for manners,
  And bang'd up her wame in Mons-Meg.
    Fy let us, &c.

And there will be Judan Maclawrie,
  And blinkin daft Barbara Macleg,
Wi' flea-lugged sharney-fac'd Lawrie,
  And shangy-mou'd halucket Meg:
And there will be happer a—'d Nansy,
  And fairy-fac'd Florie by name,
Muck Madie, and fat-hippit Girsy,
  The lass wi' the gowden wame.
    Fy let us, &c.

And there will be girn-again Gibbie,
　With his glaikit wife Jeany Bell,
And misle-shinn'd Mungo Macapie,
　The lad that was skipper himsel.
The lads and lasses in pearlings,
　Will feast in the heart of the ha',
On sybows, and rifarts, and carlings,
　That are baith sodden and raw.
　　Fy let us, &c.

And there will be fadges and brachan,
　With fouth of good gabbocks of skate,
Powsowdy, and drammock, and crowdy,
　And caller nowt-feet in a plate.
And there will be partans and buckies,
　And whytens and speldings enew,
With singit sheep-heads, and a haggies,
　And scadlips to sup till ye spew.
　　Fy let us, &c.

And there will be lapper'd-milk kebbucks,
　And sowens, and farles, and baps,
With swats, and well-scraped paunches,
　And brandy in stoups and in caps:
And there will be meal-kail and castocks,
　With skink to sup till ye rive,
And roasts to roast on a brander,
　Of flowks that were taken alive.
　　Fy let us, &c.

Scrapt haddocks, wilks, dulse and tangle,
　And a mill of good snishing to prie;
When weary with eating and drinking,
　We'll rise up and dance till we die:
Then fy let us a' to the bridal,
　For there will be lilting there,
For Jocky's to be married to Maggy,
　The lass wi' the gowden hair.

WOO'D AND MARRIED AND A'.

Woo'd and married and a',
Woo'd and married and a',
Was she nae very weel aff
Was woo'd and married and a'.

The bride came out o' the byre,
  And O as she dighted her cheeks,
Sirs, I'm to be married the night,
  And has neither blankets nor sheets,
Has neither blankets nor sheets,
  Nor scarce a coverlet too;
The bride that has a' to borrow,
  Has e'en right meikle ado.
    Woo'd and married, &c.

Out spake the bride's father,
  As he came in frae the plough,
O had your tongue, my doughter,
  And ye's get gear enough;
The stirk that stands i' the tether,
  And our bra' basin'd yade,
Will carry ye hame your corn,
  What wad ye be at, ye jade?
    Woo'd and married, &c.

Out spake the bride's mither,
  What deil needs a' this pride!
I had nae a plack in my pouch
  That night I was a bride;
My gown was linsy-woolsy,
  And ne'er a sark ava;
And ye hae ribbons and buskins,
  Mae than ane or twa.
    Woo'd and married, &c.

What's the matter? quo' Willie,
  Tho' we be scant o' claise,
We'll creep the nearer thegither,
  And we'll smore a' the fleas:
Simmer is coming on,
  And we'll get teats of woo;
And we'll get a lass o' our ain,
  And she'll spin claise enew.
    Woo'd and married, &c.

Out spake the bride's brither,
  As he came in wi' the kie;
Poor Willie had ne'er a ta'en ye,
  Had he kent ye as weel as I;
For you're baith proud and saucy,
  And no for a poor man's wife;
Gin I canna get a better,
  Ise never tak ane i' my life.
    Woo'd and married, &c.

Out spake the bride's sister,
  As she came in frae the byre,
O gin I were but married,
  It's a' that I desire:
But we poor fo'k maun live single,
  And do the best we can;
I dinna care what I should want,
  If I could get but a man.
    Woo'd and married, &c.

PATIE'S WEDDING.

As Patie came up frae the glen,
  Driving his wethers before him,
He met bonnie Meg ganging hame,
  Her beauty was like for to smore him.
O dinna ye ken, bonnie Meg,
  That you and I's gaen to be married;
I rather had broken my leg
  Before sic a bargain miscarried.

Na, Patie,—O wha's tell'd you that?
  I think that of news they've been scanty,
That I should be married so soon,
  Or yet should hae been sae flanty:
I winna be married the year,
  Suppose I were courted by twenty;
Sae, Patie, ye need nae mair speer,
  For weel a wat I dinna want ye.

Now, Meggie, what maks ye sae swear,
  Is't cause that I hae na a maillin,
The lad that has plenty o' gear,
  Need ne'er want a half or a haill ane:
My dad has a gude gray mare,
  And yours has twa cows and a filly;
And that will be plenty o' gear,
  Sae, Maggie, be no sae ill-willy.

Indeed, Patie, I dinna ken,
  But first ye maun speer at my daddy;
You're as well born as Ben,
  And I canna say but I'm ready:

There's plenty o' yarn in clues,
  To make me a coat and a jimpy,
And plaiden enough to be trews,
  Gif ye get it, I shanna scrimp ye.

Now fair fa' ye, my bonny Meg,
  I'se let a wee smacky fa' on you;
May my neck be as lang as my leg,
  If I be an ill husband unto you;
Sae gang your way hame e'now,
  Make ready gin this day fifteen days,
And tell your father the news,
  That I'll be his son in great kindness.

It was nae lang after that,
  Wha came to our bigging but Patie,
Weel drest in a braw new coat,
  And wow but he thought himself pretty;
His bannet was little frae new,
  In it was a loop and a slitty
To tie in a ribbon sae blue,
  To bab at the neck o' his coaty.

Then Patie came in wi' a stend,
  Said, Peace be here to the bigging!
You're welcome, quo' William, come ben,
  Or I wish it may rive frae the rigging:
Now draw in your chair and sit down,
  And tell's a' your news in a hurry;
And haste ye, Meg, and be done,
  And hing on the pan wi' the berry.

Quoth Patie, My news is nae thrang,
  Yestreen I was wi' his Honour;
I've ta'en three riggs of bra' land,
  And hae bound mysel under a bonour;

And now my errand to you
  Is for Meggy to help me to labour;
I think you maun gie's the best cow,
  Because that our haddin's but sober.

Well, now for to help you through,
  I'll be at the cost of the bridal;
I'se cut the craig of the ewe
  That had amaist died of the side-ill,
And that'll be plenty of bree,
  Sae lang as our well is nae reisted,
To all the good neighbours and we,
  And I think we'll no be that ill feasted.

Quoth Patie, O that'll do well,
  And I'll gie you your brose in the morning,
O' kail that was made yestreen,
  For I like them best in the forenoon.
Sae Tam the piper did play,
  And ilka ane danc'd that was willing,
And a' the lave they ranked through,
  And they held the stoupy ay filling.

The auld wives sat and they chew'd,
  And when that the carles grew nappy,
They danc'd as weel as they dow'd,
  Wi' a crack o' their thumbs and a kappie.
The lad that wore the white band,
  I think they cau'd him Jamie Mather;
And he took the bride by the hand,
  And cry'd to play up Maggie Lauder.

HEY, JENNY, COME DOWN TO JOCK.

Jocky he came here to woo,
  On ae feast-day when we were fu';
And Jenny pat on her best array,
  When she heard Jocky was come that way.

Jenny she gaed up the stair,
  Sae privily to change her smock ;
And ay sae loud as her mother did rair,
  Hey, Jenny, come down to Jock.

Jenny she came down the stair,
  And she came bobbin and bakin ben ;
Her stays they were lac'd, and her waist it was jimp,
  And a bra' new-made manco gown.

Jocky took her by the hand,
  O Jenny, can ye fancy me ?
My father is dead, and he'as left me some land,
  And bra' houses twa or three ;

And I will gi'e them a' to thee.
  A haith, quo' Jenny, I fear you mock !
Then foul fa' me gin I scorn thee ;
  If ye'll be my Jenny, I'll be your Jock.

Jenny lookit, and syne she leugh,
  Ye first maun get my mither's consent.
A weel, goodwife, and what say ye ?
  Quo' she, Jocky, I'm weel content.

D

Jenny to her mither did say,
  O mither, fetch us some good meat;
A piece o' the butter was kirn'd the day,
  That Jocky and I thegither may eat.

Jocky unto Jenny did say,
  Jenny, my dear, I want nae meat;
It was nae for meat that I came here,
  But a' for the love of you, Jenny, my dear.

Then Jocky and Jenny were led to their bed,
  And Jocky he lay neist the stock,
And five or six times ere break of day,
  He ask'd at Jenny how she lik'd Jock.

Quo' Jenny, dear Jock, you gi'e me content,
  I bless my mither for gi'eing consent:
And on the next morning, before the first cock,
  Our Jenny did cry, I dearly love Jock.

Jenny she gaed up the gait,
  Wi' a green gown as side as her smock;
And ay sae loud as her mither did rair,
  Yow, sirs, has nae Jenny got Jock!

THE RINAWA' BRIDE.

A LADDIE and a lassie
  Dwelt in the south countrie,
And they hae cassen their claise thegither,
  And married they wad be.
The bridal day was set,
  On Tiseday for to be;
Then hey play up the rinawa' bride,
  For she has ta'en the gee.

The bridegroom hugg'd and kiss'd her,
   And press'd her to Mess John;
But she's run awa', and left him
   To face the priest alone.
From town to town they sought her,
   But found she cou'd na be:
Then hey play up, &c.

Her father and her mither
   Ran after her wi' speed,
And ay they ran until they came
   Unto the water of Tweed;
And when they came to Kelso town,
   They gart the clap gae thro',
Saw ye a lass wi' a hood and a mantle,
   The face o't lin'd up wi' blue;

The face o't lin'd up wi' blue,
   And the tail lin'd up wi' green,
Saw ye a lass wi' a hood and a mantle,
   Shou'd been married on Tiseday te'en?
With red stockings on her legs,
   'Twa coal-black blinkin' een;
Saw ye a lass wi' a hood and a mantle,
   Shou'd been married on Tiseday te'en?

When that she was a-wanting,
   And could not be found at all,
The bridegroom screech'd and tore himsel';
   Crying, his joy and only all;
Since she has gone and left me,
   Alas! for her I must die!
Then hey play up, &c.

Now wally fu' fa' the silly bridegroom,
   He was as saft as butter;

For had she play'd the like to me,
   I had nae sae easily quit her;
I'd gi'en her a tune o' my hoboy,
   And set my fancy free;
And syne play'd up our rinawa' bride,
   And lutten her tak the gee.

If he had but allow'd her
   To've come to hersel' again,
He needed not to have ru'd her,
   To ease him of his pain:
For if that he had been easy,
   She'd been more keener than he:
Then hey play up, &c.

She had nae run a mile or twa,
   When she began to consider,
The ang'ring of her father dear,
   The displeasing o' her mither,
The slighting of the silly bridegroom,
   The best o' a' the three;
Then hey play up, &c.

The bride's best maid was grieved
   To hear the bridegroom cry;
And so merrily as she cheer'd him,
   What think ye of you and I?
Let's join our hands right frankly,
   And wedded we will be;
And let Meg Dorts go belt hersel',
   Since she has ta'en the gee.

So, soon Mess John was sent for
   To tie up the marriage-bands;
When the saucy bride she heard it,
   She screech'd and clapp'd her hands:

But the bridegroom mock'd and jeer'd her,
  Saying, You've come too late for me;
Go tell your father and mother
  How I can cure the gee.

~~~~~~~~~~

CLOUT THE CALDRON.

[This song is supposed to have been composed on an amour of
one of the Kenmure family in the Cavalier times. The air was
such a favourite with the second Bishop Chisholm of Dumblane, that he used to say, that if he were going to be hanged,
nothing would sooth his mind so much by the way as to hear
it played.]

Have you any pots or pans,
  Or any broken chandlers?
I am a tinker to my trade,
  And newly come from Flanders,
As scant of siller as of grace,
  Disbanded we've a bad run;
Gar tell the lady of the place,
  I'm come to clout her caldron.
    Fa adrie, didle, didle, &c.

Madam, if you have wark for me,
  I'll do't to your contentment,
And dinna care a single flie
  For any man's resentment;
For, lady fair, though I appear
  To ev'ry ane a tinker,
Yet, to yoursel, I'm bauld to tell,
  I am a gentle jinker.
    Fa adrie, didle, didle, &c.

Love Jupiter into a swan
   Turn'd for his lovely **Leda** ;
He like a bull o'er meadows run,
   To carry aff Europa.
Then may not I, as well as he,
   To cheat your Argos blinker,
And win your love, like mighty Jove,
   Thus hide me in a tinker.
     Fa adrie, didle, didle, &c.

Sir, ye appear a cunning man,
   But this fine plot you'll fail in,
For there is neither pot nor pan
   Of mine you'll drive a nail in.
Then bind your budget on your back,
   And nails up in your apron,
For I've a tinker under tack
   That's us'd to clout my caldron.
     Fa adrie, didle, didle, &c.

I HAD A HORSE.

["This story was founded on fact. A John Hunter, ancestor to a very respectable farming family who live in a place in the parish, I think, of Galston, called Barr-mill, was the luckless hero that ' had a horse and had nae mair.'—For some little youthful follies he found it necessary to make a retreat to the West Highlands, where ' he foe'd himself to a *Highland* laird,' for that is the expression of all the oral editions of the song I ever heard.—The present Mr Hunter, who told me the anecdote, is the great-grandchild to our hero."—BURNS.]

I HAD a horse, and I had nae mair,
   I gat him frae my daddy;
My purse was light, and my heart was sair,
   But my wit it was fu' ready.

And sae I thought upon a wile,
  Outwittens o' my daddy,
To fee mysell to a Lawland laird,
  Who had a bonny lady.

I wrote a letter, and thus began,
  Madam, be not offended,
I'm o'er the lugs in love wi' you,
  And care nae tho' ye kend it:
For I get little frae the laird,
  And far less frae my daddy,
And I would blythly be the man
  Would strive to please my lady.

She read my letter, and she leuch,
  Ye need na been sae blate, man;
You might hae come to me yoursell,
  And tald me o' your state, man:
You might hae come to me yoursell,
  Outwittens o' your daddy,
And made John Goukston o' the laird,
  And kiss'd his bonny lady.

Then she pat siller in my purse,
  We drank wine in a cogie;
She fee'd a man to rub my horse,
  And wow but I was vogie:
But I gat ne'er sae sair a fleg
  Since I came frae my daddy,
The laird came tap, rap, to the yett,
  When I was wi' his lady.

Then she pat me below a chair,
  And happ'd me wi' a plaidie;
But I was like to swarf wi' fear,
  And wish'd me wi' my daddy.

The laird went out, he saw nae me,
  I went when I was ready:
I promis'd, but I ne'er gaed back,
  To see his bonny lady.

~~~~~~~~~~

MY JO JANET.

Sᴡᴇᴇᴛ sir, for your courtesie,
  When ye come by the Bass then,
For the love ye bear to me,
  Buy me a keeking-glass then.
Keek into the draw-well,
      Janet, Janet;
And there ye'll see your bonny sell,
      My jo Janet.

Keeking in the draw-well clear,
  What if I should fa' in, sir,
Syne a' my kin will say and swear,
  I drown'd mysell for sin, sir.
Had the better by the brae,
      Janet, Janet;
Had the better by the brae,
      My jo Janet.

Good sir, for your courtesie,
  Coming through Aberdeen then,
For the love ye bear to me,
  Buy me a pair of sheen then.
Clout the auld, the new are dear,
      Janet, Janet;
Ae pair may gain you ha'f a year,
      My jo Janet.

But what if dancing on the green,
   And skipping like a mawking,
If they should see my clouted sheen,
   Of me they will be tauking.
Dance ay laigh, and late at e'en,
       Janet, Janet;
Syne a' their fauts will no be seen,
       My jo Janet.

Kind sir, for your courtesie,
   When ye gae to the cross then,
For the love ye bear to me,
   Buy me a pacing-horse then.
Pace upo' your spinning-wheel,
       Janet, Janet;
Pace upo' your spinning-wheel,
       My jo Janet.

My spinning-wheel is auld and stiff,
   The rock o't winna stand, sir,
To keep the temper-pin in tiff,
   Employs aft my hand, sir.
Make the best o't that ye can,
       Janet, Janet;
But like it never wale a man,
       My jo Janet.

WHAT CAN A YOUNG LASSIE DO WI' AN AULD MAN?

[By Burns.]

What can a young lassie, what shall a young lassie,
What can a young lassie do wi' an auld man?

Bad luck on the pennie that tempted my minnie
  To sell her poor Jenny for siller an' lan'!
    Bad luck on the pennie, &c.

He's always compleenin frae mornin to e'enin,
  He hosts and he hirples the weary day lang;
He's deyl't and he's dozin, his bluid it is frozen,
  O, dreary's the night wi' a crazy auld man!

He hums and he hankers, he frets and he cankers,
  I never can please him do a' that I can;
He's peevish, and jealous of a' the young fellows,
  O, dool on the day I met wi' an auld man!

My auld auntie Katie upon me takes pity,
  I'll do my endeavour to follow her plan;
I'll cross him, and wrack him, until I heart break him,
  And then his auld brass will buy me a new pan.

TAK YOUR AULD CLOAK ABOUT YE.

[This must have been a popular song in the beginning of the
seventeenth century, one stanza of it being quoted in *Othello*,
in the scene where Iago entices Cassio to drink with him.]

In winter when the rain rain'd cauld,
  And frost and snaw on ilka hill,
And Boreas, with his blasts sae bauld,
  Was threat'ning a' our ky to kill:
Then Bell, my wife, wha loves nae strife,
  She said to me right hastily,
Get up, goodman, save Cromie's life,
  And tak your auld cloak about ye.

My Cromie is a usefu' cow,
　And she is come of a good kyne;
Aft has she wet the bairns' mou,
　And I am laith that she should tyne;
Get up, goodman, it is fu' time,
　The sun shines in the lift sae hie;
Sloth never made a gracious end,
　Go tak your auld cloak about ye.

My cloak was ance a good gray cloak,
　When it was fitting for my wear;
But now its scantly worth a groat,
　For I have worn't this thirty year;
Let's spend the gear that we have won,
　We little ken the day we'll die:
Then I'll be proud, since I have sworn
　To have a new cloak about me.

In days when our King Robert rang,
　His trews they cost but half a crown;
He said they were a groat o'er dear,
　And ca'd the taylor thief and loun.
He was the king that wore a crown,
　And thou'rt a man of laigh degree,
'Tis pride puts a' the country down,
　Sae tak thy auld cloak about thee.

Every land has its ain laugh,
　Ilk kind of corn it has its hool,
I think the warld is a' run wrang,
　When ilka wife her man wad rule;
Do ye not see Rob, Jock, and Hab,
　As they are girded gallantly,
While I sit hurklen in the ase?
　I'll have a new cloak about me.

Goodman, I wat 'tis thirty years
 Since we did ane anither ken;
And we have had between us twa
 Of lads and bonny lasses ten;
Now they are women grown and men,
 I wish and pray well may they be;
And if you'd prove a good husband,
 E'en tak your auld cloak about ye.

Bell, my wife, she lo'es nae strife,
 But she wad guide me, if she can;
And to maintain an easy life,
 I aft maun yield, tho' I'm gudeman:
Nought's to be won at woman's hand,
 Unless ye gi'e her a' the plea;
Then I'll leave aff where I began,
 And tak my auld cloak about me.

~~~~~~~~~~

GET UP AND BAR THE DOOR.

It fell about the Martinmas time,
 And a gay time it was then,
When our goodwife got puddings to make,
 And she's boil'd them in the pan.

The wind sae cauld blew south and north,
 And blew into the floor;
Quoth our goodman to our goodwife,
 Gae out and bar the door.

My hand is in my hussy'f-skap,
 Goodman, as ye may see,
An it should nae be barr'd this hundred year,
 It's no be barr'd for me.

They made a paction 'tween them twa,
   They made it firm and sure,
That the first word whae'er shou'd speak,
   Shou'd rise and bar the door.

Then by there came two gentlemen,
   At twelve o'clock at night,
And they could neither see house nor hall,
   Nor coal, nor candle light.

Now, whether is this a rich man's house?
   Or whether is't a poor?
But never a word wad ane o' them speak,
   For barring of the door.

And first they ate the white puddings,
   And then they ate the black;
Tho' muckle thought the goodwife to hersel,
   Yet ne'er a word she spake.

Then said the one unto the other,
   Here, man, tak ye my knife,
Do ye tak aff the auld man's beard,
   And I'll kiss the goodwife.

But there's nae water in the house,
   And what shall we do than?
What ails ye at the pudding-bree
   That boils into the pan?

O up then started our goodman,
   An angry man was he,
Will ye kiss my wife before my een,
   And scad me wi' pudding-bree?

E

Then up and started our goodwife,
  Gied three skips on the floor,
Goodman, you've spoken the foremost word,
  Get up and bar the door.

~~~~~~~~~~

THE AULD GOODMAN.

Late in an evening forth I went,
  A little before the sun gade down,
And there I chanc'd, by accident,
  To light on a battle new begun.
A man and his wife was fa'en in a strife,
  I canna weel tell you how it began;
But ay she wail'd her wretched life,
  And cry'd ever, Alake my auld goodman!

He.—Thy auld goodman that thou tells of,
  The country kens where he was born,
Was but a silly poor vagabond,
  And ilka ane leugh him to scorn;
For he did spend and make an end
  Of gear that his forefathers wan,
He gart the poor stand frae the door;
  Sae tell nae me of thy auld goodman.

She.—My heart, alake, is like to break,
  When I think on my winsome John;
His blinken ee, and gait sae free,
  Was naething like thee, thou dozen'd drone.
His rosy face, and flaxen hair,
  And a skin as white as ony swan,
Was large and tall, and comely withal,
  And thou'lt ne'er be like my auld goodman.

He.—Why dost thou 'pleen? I thee maintain,
　For meal and maut thou disna want;
But thy wild bees I canna please,
　Now when our gear 'gins to grow scant:
Of household-stuff thou hast enough,
　Thou wants for neither pot nor pan;
Of siclike ware he left thee bare,
　Sae tell nae mair of thy auld goodman.

She.—Yes, I may tell, and fret mysell,
　To think on those biyth days I had,
When he and I together lay
　In arms into a well-made bed:
But now I sigh, and may be sad,
　Thy courage is cauld, thy colour wan,
Thou falds thy feet, and fa's asleep,
　And thou'lt ne'er be like my auld goodman.

Then coming was the night sae dark,
　And gane was a' the light of day:
The carl was fear'd to miss his mark,
　And therefore wad nae langer stay;
Then up he gat, and ran away,
　I trow the wife the day she wan,
And ay the o'erword o' the fray
　Was ever, Alake my auld goodman!

~~~~~~~~~~

THE DEUKS DANG O'ER MY DADDIE, O!

[By Burns.]

The bairns gat out wi' an unco shout;
　The deuks dang o'er my daddie, O!
The fien-ma-care, quo' the feirrie auld wife,
　He was but a paidlin body, O!

He paidles out, and he paidles in,
　And he paidles late and early, O!
This seven lang years I hae lain by his side,
　And he is but a fusionless carlie, O!

O had your tongue my feirrie auld wife,
　O had your tongue now Nansie, O:
I've seen the day, and sae hae ye,
　Ye wad na been sae donsie, O.
I've seen the day ye butter'd my brose,
　And cuddled me late and early, O;
But downa do's come o'er me now,
　And, Oh, I find it sairly, O!

~~~~~~~~~

SIC A WIFE AS WILLIE HAD.

[By Burns.]

Willie Wastle dwalt on Tweed,
　The spot they ca'd it Linkumdoddiè,
Willie was a wabster gude,
　Cou'd stown a clue wi' ony boddie;
He had a wife was dour an' din,
　O Tinkler Madgie was her mither:
　　Sic a wife as Willie had,
　　I wad na gie a button for her.

She has an e'e, she has but ane,
　The cat has twa the very colour;
Five rusty teeth forbye a stump,
　A clapper tongue wad deave a miller;
A whiskin beard about her mou',
　Her nose and chin they threaten ither:
　　Sic a wife, &c.

She's bow-hough'd, she's hein-shinn'd,
    Ae limpin leg a hand-breed shorter;
She's twisted right, she's twisted left,
    To balance fair in ilka quarter:
She has a hump upon her breast,
    The twin o' that upon her shouther:
      Sic a wife, &c.

Auld baudrans by the ingle sits,
    An' wi' her loof her face a washin';
But Willie's wife is nae sae trig,
    She dights her grunzie wi' a hushion:
Her walie nieves' like midden-creels,
    Her face wad fyle the Logan water:
      Sic a wife, &c.

MY WIFE'S TA'EN THE GEE.

A FRIEND of mine came here yestreen,
    And he wou'd hae me down,
To drink a bottle of ale wi' him
    In the niest burrows-town:
But, O! indeed it was, sir,
    Sae far the war for me,
For lang or e'er that I came hame,
    My wife had ta'en the gee.

We sat sae late, and drank sae stout,
    The truth I tell to you,
That lang or e'er midnight came,
    We were a' roaring fou.
        E 3

My wife sits at the fire-side,
  And the tear blinds ay her e'ee,
The ne'er a bed will she gae to,
  But sit and tak the gee.

In the morning soon, when I came down,
  The ne'er a word she spake ;
But mony a sad and sour look,
  And ay her head she'd shake.
My dear, quoth I, what aileth thee,
  To-look sae sour on me ?
I'll never do the like again,
  If you'll ne'er tak the gee.

When that she heard, she ran, she flang
  Her arms about my neck ;
And twenty kisses in a crack,
  And, poor wee thing, she grat.
If you'll ne'er do the like again,
  But bide at hame wi' me,
I'll lay my life I'se be the wife
  That's never tak the gee.

MY WIFE'S A WANTON WEE THING.

My wife's a wanton wee thing,
My wife's a wanton wee thing,
My wife's a wanton wee thing,
  She winna be guided by me.
She play'd the loon or she was married,
She play'd the loon or she was married,
She play'd the loon or she was married,
  She'll do it again or she die.

She sell'd her coat and she drank it,
She sell'd her coat and she drank it,
She row'd hersell in a blanket,
   She winna be guided for me.
She mind't na when I forbade her,
She mind't na when I forbade her,
I took a rung and I claw'd her,
   And a braw gude bairn was she.

DRAP OF CAPPIE, O.

There lived a wife in our gate-end,
   She lo'ed a drap of cappie, O,
And all the gear that e'er she gat,
   She slipt it in her gabbie, O.

Upon a frosty winter's night,
   The wife had got a drappie, O,
And she had p——'d her coats sae well,
   She could not find the pattie, O.

But she's awa to her goodman,
   They ca'd him Tammie Lammie, O;
Gae ben and fetch the cave to me,
   That I may get a drammie, O.

Tammie was an honest man,
   Himsel he took a drappie, O,
It was nae weel out-o'er his craig,
   Till she was on his tappie, O.

She paid him weel, baith back and side,
　And sair she creish'd his backie, O,
And made his skin baith blue and black,
　And gar'd his shoulders crackie, O.

Then he's awa' to the malt-barn,
　And he has ta'en a pockie, O,
He put her in, baith head and tail,
　And cast her o'er his backie, O.

The carling spurn'd wi' head and feet,
　The carle he was sae aukie, O,
To ilka wa' that he came by
　He gar'd her head play knackie, O.

Goodman, I think you'll murder me,
　My brains you out will knockie, O:
He gi'd her ay the other hitch,
　Lie still, you devil's buckie, O.

Goodman, I'm like to make my burn,
　O let me out, good Tammie, O;
Then he set her upon a stane,
　And bade her p—h a dammie, O.

Then Tammie took her aff the stane,
　And put her in the pockie, O,
And when she did begin to spurn,
　He lent her ay a knockie, O.

Away he went to the mill-dam,
　And there ga'e her a duckie, O,
And ilka chiel that had a stick,
　Play'd thump upon her backie, O.

And when he took her hame again,
  He did hing up the pockie, O,
At her bed-side, as I heard say,
  Upon a little knagie, O.

And ilka day that she up-rose,
  In naething but her smockie, O.
Sae soon as she look'd o'er the bed,
  She might behold the pockie, O.

Now all ye men, baith far and near,
  That have a drunken tutie, O,
Duck ye your wives in time of year,
  And I'll lend you the pockie, O.

The wife did live for nineteen years,
  And was fu' frank and cuthie, O,
And ever since she got the duck,
  She never had the drouthie, O.

At last the carling chanc'd to die,
  And Tammie did her bury, O,
And, for the public benefit,
  He has gar'd print the curie, O.

And this he did her motto make:—
  " Here lies an honest luckie, O,
Who never left the drinking trade,
  Until she got a duckie, O."

DRUKEN WIFE O' GALLOWAY.

Down in yon meadow a couple did tarie,
The goodwife she drank naething but sack and canary;
The goodman complain'd to her friends right airly,
 O! gin my wife wad drink hooly and fairly.
Hooly and fairly, hooly and fairly,
O! gin my wife wad drink hooly and fairly.

First she drank Crommy, and syne she drank Garie,
And syne she drank my bonny grey marie,
That carried me thro' a' the dubs and the lairie.
 O! gin, &c.

She drank her hose, she drank her shoon,
And syne she drank her bonny new gown;
She drank her sark that cover'd her rarely.
 O! gin, &c.

Wad she drink her ain things, I wad na care,
But she drinks my claiths I canna weel spare;
When I'm wi' my gossips, it angers me sairly.
 O! gin, &c.

My Sunday's coat she's laid it a wad,
The best blue bonnet e'er was on my head;
At kirk and at market I'm cover'd but barely.
 O! gin, &c.

My bonny white mittens I wore on my hands,
Wi' her neighbour's wife she has laid them in pawn;
My bane-headed staff that I loo'd so dearly.
 O! gin, &c.

I never was for wrangling nor strife,
Nor did I deny her the comforts of life,
For when there's a war, I'm ay for a parley.
   O! gin, &c.

When there's ony money, she maun keep the purse;
If I seek but a bawbie, she'll scold and she'll curse;
She lives like a queen, I scrimped and sparely.
   O! gin, &c.

A pint wi' her cummers I wad her allow,
But when she sits down, she gets hersel fu',
And when she is fu' she is unco camstairie.
   O! gin, &c.

When she comes to the street, she roars and she rants,
Has no fear of her neighbours, nor minds the house
    wants;
She rants up some fool sang, like, " Up your heart,
    Charlie."
   O! gin, &c.

When she comes hame she lays on the lads,
The lasses she ca's them baith b——s and jades,
And ca's mysell ay an auld cuckold carlie.
   O! gin, &c.

TODLEN HAME.

[This is an old song; it was considered by Burns as " perhaps
the first bottle song that ever was composed."]

WHEN I have a saxpence under my thumb,
Then I'll get credit in ilka town:
But ay when I'm poor they bid me gang by;
O! poverty parts good company.
Todlen hame, todlen hame,
Cou'd na my love come todlen hame?

Fair fa' the goodwife, and send her good sale,
She gi'es us white bannocks to drink her ale,
Syne if that her tippenny chance to be sma',
We'll tak a good scour o't, and ca't awa'.
Todlen hame, todlen hame,
As round as a neep come todlen hame.

My kimmer and I lay down to sleep,
And twa pint-stoups at our bed's feet;
And ay when we waken'd, we drank them dry:
What think ye of my wee kimmer and I?
Todlen butt and todlen ben,
Sae round as my love comes todlen hame.

Leeze me on liquor, my todlen dow,
Ye're ay sae good-humour'd when weeting your
mou';
When sober, sae sour, ye'll fight with a flee,
That 'tis a blyth sight to the bairns and me,
When todlen hame, todlen hame,
When round as a neep ye come todlen hame.

THE DEIL'S AWA WI' THE EXCISEMAN.

[At a meeting of his brother excisemen in Dumfries, Burns being called upon for a song, handed these verses extempore to the president, written on the back of a letter.]

The Deil cam fiddling thro' the town,
 And danc'd awa wi' the exciseman;
And ilka wife cry'd, Auld Mahoun,
 We wish you luck o' the prize, man.
  The Deil's awa, the Deil's awa,
   The Deil's awa wi' the exciseman,
  He's danc'd awa, he's danc'd awa,
   He's danc'd awa wi' the exciseman.

We'll mak our maut, and brew our drink,
 We'll dance, and sing, and rejoice, man;
And mony thanks to the muckle black Deil
 That danc'd awa wi' the exciseman.
  The Deil's awa, &c.

There's threesome reels, and foursome reels,
 There's hornpipes and strathspeys, man,
But the ae best dance e'er cam to our lan',
 Was—the Deil's awa wi' the exciseman.
  The Deil's awa, &c.

MAGGY LAUDER.

Wha wad na be in love
 Wi' bonny Maggy Lauder?
A piper met her gaun to Fife,
 And speer'd what was't they ca'd her;

F

Right scornfully she answer'd him,
  Begone, ye hallanshaker,
Jog on your gate, you bladderskate,
  My name is Maggy Lauder.

Maggy, quoth he, and by my bags,
  I'm fidging fain to see you:
Sit down by me, my bonny bird,
  In troth I winna steer thee:
For I'm a piper to my trade,
  My name is Rob the Ranter;
The lasses loup as they were daft,
  When I blaw up my chanter.

Piper, quoth Meg, hae ye your bags,
  Or is your drone in order?
If you be Rob, I've heard of you,
  Live you upo' the border?
The lasses a', baith far and near,
  Have heard of Rob the Ranter;
I'll shake my foot wi' right good will,
  Gif you'll blaw up your chanter.

Then to his bags he flew wi' speed,
  About the drone he twisted:
Meg up and wallop'd o'er the green,
  For brawly cou'd she frisk it:
Weel done, quoth he: Play up, quoth she:
  Weel bob'd, quoth Rob the Ranter;
'Tis worth my while to play indeed,
  When I hae sic a dancer.

Weel hae you play'd your part, quoth Meg,
  Your cheeks are like the crimson;
There's nane in Scotland plays sae weel,
  Since we lost Habby Simpson.

I've liv'd in Fife, baith maid and wife,
　These ten years and a quarter;
Gin you should come to Enster fair,
　Speer ye for Maggy Lauder.

~~~~~~~~~~

DUNCAN DAVISON.

THERE was a lass, they ca'd her Meg,
　And she gaed o'er the muir to spin;
There was a lad that follow'd her,
　They ca'd him Duncan Davison;
The muir was dreigh, and Meg was skeigh,
　Her favour Duncan cou'd na win;
For wi' the rock she wad him knock,
　And ay she shook the temper pin.

As o'er the muir they lightly scoor,
　A burn was clear, a glen was green,
Upon the banks they eas'd their shanks,
　And ay she set the wheel between;
But Duncan swore a haly aith,
　That Meg should be a bride the morn,
Then Meg took up her spinnin graith,
　And flang them a' out o'er the burn.

O! we will big a wee, wee house,
　And we will live like king and queen,
Sae blythe and merry's we will be,
　When ye set by the wheel at e'en.
A man may drink and no be drunk,
　A man may fight, and no be slain;
A man may kiss a bonny lass,
　And ay be welcome back again.

THE AULD WIFE AYONT THE FIRE.

[In Ramsay's *Tea-Table Miscellany* this song is marked with the letter Q. as an old song with additions.]

THERE was a wife won'd in a glen,
And she had dochters nine or ten,
That sought the house baith butt and ben
    To find their mam a snishing. *
      The auld wife ayont the fire,
      The auld wife aniest the fire,
      The auld wife aboon the fire,
        She died for lack of snishing.

Her mill into some hole had fawn,
What recks, quoth she, let it be gawn,
For I maun hae a young goodman,
    Shall furnish me with snishing.
      The auld wife, &c.

Her eldest dochter said right bauld,
Fy, mother, mind that now ye're auld,
And if you with a yonker wald,
    He'll waste away your snishing.
      The auld wife, &c.

The youngest dochter ga'e a shout,
O mother dear! your teeth's a' out,
Besides ha'f blind, ye hae the gout,
    Your mill can had nae snishing.
      The auld wife, &c.

---

* Snishing, in its literal meaning, is snuff made of tobacco; but in this song it means sometimes contentment, a husband, love, money, &c.

Ye lie, ye limmers, cries auld mump,
For I hae baith a tooth and stump,
And will nae langer live in dump,
   By wanting of my snishing.
    The auld wife, &c.

Thole ye, says Peg, that pauky slut,
Mother, if you can crack a nut,
Then we will a' consent to it,
   That you shall have a snishing.
    The auld wife, &c.

The auld ane did agree to that,
And they a pistol-bullet gat;
She powerfully began to crack,
   To won hersell a snishing.
    The auld wife, &c.

Braw sport it was to see her chow't,
And 'tween her gums sae squeeze and row't,
While frae her jaws the slaver flow'd,
   And ay she curst poor stumpy.
    The auld wife, &c.

At last she ga'e a desperate squeeze,
Which brak the lang tooth by the neeze,
And syne poor stumpy was at ease,
   But she tint hopes of snishing.
    The auld wife, &c.

She of the task began to tire,
And frae her dochters did retire,
Syne lean'd her down ayont the fire,
   And died for lack of snishing.
    The auld wife, &c.

Ye auld wives, notice well this truth,
As soon as ye're past mark of mouth,
Ne'er do what's only fit for youth,
 And leave aff thoughts of snishing:
  Else, like this wife ayont the fire,
  Your bairns against you will conspire ;
  Nor will you get, unless ye hire,
   A young man with your snishing.

THE ROCK AND THE WEE PICKLE TOW.

[By Mr Alex. Ross, late schoolmaster at Lochlee.]

There was an auld wife an' a wee pickle tow,
 An' she wad gae try the spinning o't,
She louted her down, an' her rock took a low,
 And that was a bad beginning o't:
She sat an' she grat, an' she flet an' she flang,
An' she threw an' she blew, an' she wrigl'd an' wrang,
An' she choked, an' boaked, an' cry'd like to mang,
 Alas! for the dreary spinning o't.

I've wanted a sark for these eight years an' ten,
 An' this was to be the beginning o't,
But I vow I shall want it for as lang again,
 Or ever I try the spinning o't;
For never since ever they ca'd me as they ca' me,
Did sic a mishap an' misanter befa' me,
But ye shall hae leave baith to hang me an' draw me,
 The niest time I try the spinning o't.

I hae keeped my house for these threescore o' years,
    An' ay I kept free o' the spinning o't,
But how I was sarked foul fa' them that speers,
    For it minds me upo' the beginning o't.
But our women are now a-days a' grown sae bra', –
That ilk ane maun hae a sark an' some maun hae **twa,**
The warlds were better when ne'er ane ava
    Had a rag but ane at the beginning o't.

Foul fa' her that ever advis'd me to spin,
    That had been sae lang a beginning o't,
I might well have ended as I did begin,
    Nor have got sic a skair with the spinning o't.
But they'll say, she's a wyse wife that kens her ain
    weerd,
I thought on a day it should never be speer'd,
How loot ye the low tak your rock be the beard,
    When ye yeed to try the spinning o't?

The spinning, the spinning it gars my heart sab,
    When I think upo' the beginning o't,
I thought ere I died to have anes made a wab,
    But still I had weers o' the spinning o't.
But had I nine dathers, as I hae but three,
The safest and soundest advice I cou'd gie,
Is that they frae spinning wad keep their hands free,
    For fear of a bad beginning o't.

Yet in spite of my counsel if they will needs run
    The drearysome risk o' the spinning o't,
Let them seek out a lythe in the heat of the sun,
    And there venture on the beginning o't:
But to do as I did, alas, and awow!
To busk up a rock at the cheek of the low,
Says, that I had but little wit in my pow,
    And as little ado with the spinning o't.

But yet after a', there is ae thing that grieves
   My heart to think o' the beginning o't,
Had I won the length but of ae pair o' sleeves,
   Then there had been word o' the spinning o't;
This I wad ha' washen an' bleech'd like the snaw,
And o' my twa gardies like moggans wad draw,
An' then fouk wad say, that auld Girzy was bra',
   An' a' was upon her ain spinning o't.

But gin I wad shog about till a new spring,
   I should yet hae a bout of the spinning o't,
A mutchkin of linseed I'd i' the yerd fling,
   For a' the wan-chansie beginning o't.
I'll gar my ain Tammie gae down to the how,
An' cut me a rock of a widdershines grow,
Of good rantry-tree for to carry my tow,
   An' a spindle of the same for the twining o't.

For now when I mind me, I met Maggy Grim,
   This morning just at the beginning o't,
She was never ca'd chancy, but canny an' slim,
   An' sae it has far'd of my spinning o't:
But an my new rock were anes cutted an' dry,
I'll a' Maggie's can an' her cantraps defy,
An' but onie sussie the spinning I'll try,
   An' ye's a' hear o' the beginning o't.

Quo' Tibby, her dather, tak tent fat ye say,
   The never a rag we'll be seeking o't,
Gin ye anes begin, ye'll tarveal's night an' day,
   Sae it's vain ony mair to be speaking o't.
Since Lambas I'm now gaen thirty an' twa,
An' never a dud sark had I yet gryt or sma',
An' what war am I? I'm as warm an' as bra',
   As thrummy-tail'd Meg that's a spinner o't.

To labor the lint-land, an' then buy the seed,.
   An' then to yoke me to the harrowing o't,
An' syn loll amon't an' pike out ilka weed,
   Like swine in a sty at the farrowing o't;
Syn powing and ripling an' steeping, an' then
To gar's gae an' spread it upo' the cauld plain,
An' then after a' may be labor in vain,
   When the wind and the weet gets the fusion o't.

But tho' it should anter the weather to byde,
   Wi' beetles we're set to the drubbing o't,
An' then frae our fingers to gnidge aff the hide,
   With the wearisome wark o' the rubbing o't.
An' syn ilka tait maun be heckl'd out throw,
The lint putten ae gate, anither the tow,
Syn on on a rock wi't, an' it taks a low ;—
   The back o' my hand to the spinning o't.

Quo' Jenny, I think 'oman ye're i' the right,
   Set your feet ay a-spar to the spinning o't,.
We may tak our advice frae our ain mither's fright,.
   That she gat when she try'd the beginning o't.
But they'll say that auld fouk are twice bairns indeed,
An' sae she has kythed it, but there's nae need
To sickan an amshack that we drive our head,
   As lang's we're sae skair'd frae the spinning o't.

Quo' Nanny the youngest, I've now heard you a',
   An' dowie's your doom o' the spinning o't,
Gin ye, fan the cow flings, the cog cast awa',
   Ye may see where ye'll lick up your winning o't.
But I see that but spinning I'll never be bra',
But gae by the name of a dilp or a da,
Sae lack where ye like I shall anes shak a fa',.
   Afore I be dung with the spinning o't.

For well I can mind me when black Willie Bell
   Had Tibbie there just at the winning o't,
What blew up the bargain, she kens well hersell,
   Was the want of the knack of the spinning o't.
An' now, poor 'oman, for ought that I ken,
She may never get sic an offer again,
But pine away bit and bit, like Jenkin's hen,
   An' naething to wyte but the spinning o't.

But were it for naething, but just this alane,
   I shall yet hae a bout o' the spinning o't,
They may cast me for ca'ing me black at the bane,
   But nae cause I shun'd the beginning o't.
But, be that as it happens, I care not a strae,
But nane of the lads shall hae it to say,
When they come till woo, she kens naething avae,
   Nor has onie can o' the spinning o't.

In the days they ca'd yore, gin auld fouks had but won,
   To a surkoat hough-side for the winning o't,
Of cot raips well cut by the cast o' their bum,
   They never sought mair o' the spinning o't.
A pair of grey hoggers well clinked benew,
Of nae other lit but the hue of the ew,
With a pair of rough rullions to scuff thro' the dew,
   Was the fee they sought at the beginning o't.

But we maun hae linen, an' that maun hae we,
   An' how get we that, but the spinning o't?
How can we hae face for to seek a gryt fee,
   Except we can help at the winning o't?
An' we maun hae pearlins, and mabbies, an' cocks,
An' some other thing that the ladies ca' smokes,
An' how get we that, gin we tak na our rocks,
   And pow what we can at the spinning o't?

'Tis needless for us for to tak our remarks
    Frae our mither's miscooking the spinning o't,
She never kend ought o' the guid of the sarks,
    Frae this aback to the beginning o't.
Twa-three ell of plaiden was a' that was sought
By our auld warld bodies, an' that boot be bought,
For in ilka town sickan things was na wrought,
    So little they kend o' the spinning o't.

THE WEARY PUND O' TOW.

The weary pund, the weary pund,
    The weary pund o' tow ;
I think my wife will end her life,
    Before she spin her tow.

I bought my wife a stane o' lint
    As gude as e'er did grow;
And a' that she has made o' that,
    Is ae poor pund o' tow.
      The weary pund, &c.

There sat a bottle in a bole,
    Beyont the ingle low ;
And ay she took the tither souk,
    To drouk the stourie tow.
      The weary pund, &c.

Quoth I, for shame; ye dirty dame,
    Gae spin your tap o' tow !
She took the rock, and wi' a knock,
    She brak it o'er my pow.
      The weary pund, &c.

At last her feet, I sang to see't,
  Gaed foremost o'er the knowe;
And or I wed anither jad,
  I'll wallop in a tow.
  The weary pund, &c.

WHISTLE O'ER THE LAVE O'T.

[By BURNS.]

FIRST when Maggy was my care,
Heaven, I thought, was in her air;
Now we're married—spier nae mair—
  Whistle o'er the lave o't.

Meg was meek, and Meg was mild,
Bonnie Meg was nature's child—
Wiser men than me's beguil'd—
  Whistle o'er the lave o't.

How we live, my Meg and me,
How we love and how we 'gree,
I care na by how few may see;
  Whistle o'er the lave o't.

Wha I wish were maggots meat,
Dish'd up in her winding-sheet;
I could write—but Meg maun see't—
  Whistle o'er the lave o't.

ANDRO AND HIS CUTTY GUN.

Blyth, blyth, blyth was she,
  Blyth was she butt and ben;
And well she loo'd a Hawick gill,
  And leugh to see a tappit hen.
She took me in, and set me down,
  And heght to keep me lawing free;
But, cunning carling that she was,
  She gart me birl my bawbee.

We loo'd the liquor well enough;
  But waes my heart my cash was done,
Before that I had quench'd my drouth,
  And laith I was to pawn my shoon.
When we had three times toom'd our stoup,
  And the niest chappin new begun,
In started, to heeze up our hope,
  Young Andro with his cutty gun.

The carling brought her kebbuck ben,
  With girdle-cakes well toasted brown,
Well does the canny kimmer ken,
  They gar the scuds gae glibber down.
We ca'd the bicker aft about;
  Till dawning we ne'er jee'd our bum;
And ay the cleanest drinker out,
  Was Andro with his cutty gun.

He did like ony mavis sing,
  And as I in his oxter sat,
He ca'd me ay his bonny thing,
  And mony a sappy kiss I gat.
G

I hae been east, I hae been west,
   I hae been far ayont the sun ;
But the blythest lad that e'er I saw,
   Was Andro with his cutty gun.

        ~~~~~~~~~~

WILLY WAS A WANTON WAG.

[By Mr WALKINSHAW of Walkinshaw.]

WILLY was a wanton wag,
   The blythest lad that e'er I saw,
At bridals still he bore the brag,
   And carried ay the gree awa;
His doublet was of Zetland shag,
   And wow ! but Willy he was braw,
And at his shoulder hang a tag,
   That pleas'd the lasses best of a'.

He was a man without a clag,
   His heart was frank without a flaw ;
And ay whatever Willy said,
   It was still hadden as a law.
His boots they were made of the jag ;
   When he went to the weaponshaw,
Upon the green nane durst him brag,
   The feind a ane amang them a'.

And was not Willy well worth gowd?
   He wan the love of great and sma' ;
For after he the bride had kiss'd,
   He kiss'd the lasses hale-sale a' :

Sae merrily round the ring they row'd,
  When by the hand he led them a',
And smack on smack on them bestow'd,
  By virtue of a standing law.

And was nae Willy a great lown,
  As shyre a lick as e'er was seen?
When he danc'd with the lasses round,
  The bridegroom speer'd where he had been.
Quoth Willy, I've been at the ring,
  With bobbing, faith, my shanks are sair;
Gae ca' your bride and maidens in,
  For Willy he dow do nae mair.

Then rest ye, Willy; I'll gae out,
  And for a wee fill up the ring:
But, shame light on his souple snout,
  He wanted Willy's wanton fling.
Then straight he to the bride did fare,
  Says, Well's me on your bonny face,
With bobbing Willy's shanks are sair,
  And I am come to fill his place.

Bridegroom, she says, you'll spoil the dance;
  And at the ring you'll ay be lag,
Unless like Willy ye advance;
  O! Willy has a wanton leg:
For we't he learns us a' to steer,
  And foremast ay bears up the ring;
We will find nae sic dancing here,
  If we want Willy's wanton fling.

THE BOB OF DUMBLANE.

[The two first lines are old, the rest of the song is by RAMSAY.]

LASSIE, lend me your braw hemp heckle,
  And I'll lend you my thripling kame;
For fainness, deary, I'll gar ye keckle,
  If ye'll go dance the Bob of Dumblane.
Haste ye, gang to the ground of your trunkies,
  Busk ye braw, and dinna think shame;
Consider in time, if leading of monkies
  Be better than dancing the Bob of Dumblane.

Be frank, my lassie, lest I grow fickle,
  And tak my word and offer again,
Syne ye may chance to repent it mickle,
  Ye did nae accept of the Bob of Dumblane.
The dinner, the piper, and priest shall be ready,
  For I'm grown dowy wi' lying my lane;
Away then, leave baith minny and daddy,
  And try with me the Bob of Dumblane.

THE RANTIN DOG THE DADDIE O'T.

[Composed by BURNS when a very young man, and sent by him
  to a young girl, a particular acquaintance of his, at that time
  under a cloud.]

O WHA my babie-clouts will buy?
Wha will tent me when I cry?
Wha will kiss me whare I lie?
  The rantin dog the daddie o't.—

Wha will own he did the faut?
Wha will buy my groanin maut?
Wha will tell me how to ca't?
    The rantin dog the daddie o't.—

When I mount the creepie-chair,
Wha will sit beside me there?
Gie me Rob, I seek nae mair,
    The rantin dog the daddie o't.—

Wha will crack to me my lane?
Wha will mak me fidgin fain?
Wha will kiss me o'er again?
    The rantin dog the daddie o't.—

THE WEE WIFEIKIE.

[This very excellent song is said to be the composition of the
learned Dr Alexander Geddes, well known in the literary world
for his translation of the Bible into English, and other works.]

There was a wee bit wifeikie, was comin frae the fair,
Had got a little drappikie, that bred her meikle care;
It gaed about the wifie's heart, and she began to spew,
Oh! quo' the wee wifeikie, I wish I binna fou.
   I wish I binna fou, quo' she, I wish I binna fou,
   Oh! quo' the wee wifeikie, I wish I binna fou.

If Johnnie find me barley-sick, I'm sure he'll claw my
    skin;
But I'll lye down and tak a nap before that I gae in,
Sitting at the dyke-side, and taking o' her nap,
By came a packman wi' a little pack,
   Wi' a little pack, quo' she, wi' a little pack,
   By came a packman wi' a little pack.

G 3

He's clippit a' her gowden locks sae bonnie and sae
    lang;
He's ta'en her purse and a' her placks, and fast awa
    he ran. .
And when the wifie waken'd her head was like a bee,
Oh! quo' the wee wifeikie, this is nae me,
    This is nae me, quo' she, this is nae me,
    Somebody has been felling me, and this is nae me.

I met with kindly company, and birl'd my babee!
And still, if this be Bessikie, three placks remain wi'
    me;
But I will look the pursie nooks, see gin the cunzie
    be;—
There's neither purse nor plack about me!—this is
    nae me.
    This is nae me, &c.

But I have a little housekie, but and a kindly man;
A dog, they ca' him Doussekie, if this be me he'll
    faun,
And Johnnie, he'll come to the door, and kindly wel-
    come gie,
And a' the bairns on the floor will dance if this be me.
    This is nae me, &c.

The night was late, and dang out weet, and oh but it
    was dark,
The doggie heard a body's foot, and he began to bark.
Oh when she heard the doggie bark, and kenning it
    was he,
Oh well ken ye, Doussie, quo' she, this is nae me.
    This is nae me, &c.

When Johnnie heard his Bessie's word, fast to the
    door he ran;
Is that you, Bessikie?—Wow na, man!
Be kind to the bairns, and weel mat ye be;
And farewell, Johnnie, quo' she, this is nae me!
   This is nae me, &c.

John ran to the minister, his hair stood a' on end,
I've gotten sic a fright, sir, I fear I'll never mend;
My wife's come hame without a head, crying out most
    piteously,
Oh farewell, Johnnie, quo' she, this is nae me!
   This is nae me, &c.

The tale you tell, the parson said, is wonderful to me,
How that a wife without a head could speak, or hear,
    or see!
But things that happen hereabout, so strangely alter'd
    be,
That I could almost wi' Bessie say, 'tis neither you
    nor she.
   Neither you nor she, quo' he, neither you nor she,
   Wow na, Johnnie man, 'tis neither you nor she.

Now Johnnie he came hame again, and oh! but he
    was fain,
To see his little Bessikie come to hersell again.
He got her sitting on a stool with Tibbek on her knee,
Oh! come awa, Johnnie, quo' she, come awa to me,
For I've got a nap wi' Tibbekie, and this is now me.
   This is now me, quo' she, this is now me,
   I've got a nap wi' Tibbekie, and this is now me.

THE TURNIMSPIKE.

Tune—*Clout the Caldron.*

Hᴇʀsᴇʟʟ pe Highland shentleman,
　Pe auld as Pothwel-prig,* man;
An' mony alterations seen
　Amang te Lawland Whig, man.
　　Fal, lal, &c.

First when her to the Lawlands came,
　Nainsell was driving cows, man:
There was nae laws about him's nerse,
　About the preeks or trews, man.
　　Fal, lal, &c.

Nainsell did wear the philabeg,
　The plaid prick't on her shou'der;
The guid claymore hung pe her pelt,
　The pistol sharg'd wi' pouder.
　　Fal, lal, &c.

But for whereas these cursed precks,
　Wherewith her nerse be lockit,
O hon! that e'er she saw the day!
　For a' her houghs be prokit.
　　Fal, lal, &c.

---

* The battle of Bothwell-bridge was fought on the 22d July 1679, in which the Covenanters, under General Hamilton, were totally defeated by the royal army commanded by the Duke of Monmouth.

Every t'ing in te Highlands now
  Pe turn't to alteration:
The sodger dwall at our toor-sheek,
  And tat's te great vexation.
    Fal, lal, &c.

Scotland be turn't a Ningland now
  An' laws pring on te cadger:
Nainsell wad durk him for her deeds,
  But oh! she fears te sodger.
    Fal, lal, &c.

Anither law cam after that,
  Me never saw te like, man,
They mak a lang road on te crund,
  And ca' him Turnimspike, man.
    Fal, lal, &c.

An' wow! she pe a ponny road,
  Like Louden corn-rigs, man,
Where twa carts may gang on her,
  An' no preak ithers legs, man.
    Fal, lal, &c.

They sharge a penny for ilka horse
  In troth she'll no pe sheaper,
For nought put gaen upo' the crund,
  And they gi'e me a paper.
    Fal, lal, &c.

They tak te horse t'en py te head,
  And t'ere they mak' him stand, man:
Me tell tem me hae seen te day
  Tey had nae sic command, man.
    Fal, lal, &c.

Nae doubts, Nainsell maun tra her purse,
  And pay them what hims like, man:
I'll see a shugement on his toor,
  T'at filthy Turnimspike, man!
    Fal, lal, &c.

But I'll awa to te Highland hills,
  Where te'il a ane dare turn her,
And no come near her Turnimspike,
  Unless it pe to purn her.
    Fal, lal, &c.

TULLOCHGORUM.

[Written by the late Rev. John Skinner, sixty-four years Episcopal clergyman at Longside, Aberdeenshire. "He was passing
the day," says Burns, "at the town of [Ellon] in a friend's
house, whose name was Montgomery. Mrs Montgomery ob-
serving, *en passant*, that the beautiful reel of Tullochgorum
wanted words, she begged them of Mr Skinner, who gratified
her wishes, and the wishes of every lover of Scottish song, in
this most excellent ballad."]

COME gie's a sang, Montgomery cry'd,
And lay your disputes all aside,
What singifies't for folks to chide
    For what was done before them:.
Let Whig and Tory all agree,
  Whig and Tory, Whig and Tory,
  Whig and Tory all agree,
    To drop their Whig-mig-morum;
Let Whig and Tory all agree
To spend the night wi' mirth and glee,
And cheerful sing alang wi' me
    The reel o' Tullochgorum.

O Tullochgorum's my delight,
It gars us a' in ane unite,
And ony sumph that keeps a spite,
    In conscience I abhor him:
For blythe and cheerie we'll be a',
    Blythe and cheerie, blythe and cheerie,
    Blythe and cheerie we'll be a',
    And make a happy quorum,
For blythe and cheerie we'll be a'
As lang as we hae breath to draw,
And dance till we be like to fa'
    The reel o' Tullochgorum.

What needs there be sae great a fraise
Wi' dringing dull Italian lays,
I wad na gie our ain Strathspeys
    For half a hunder score o' them;
They're dowf and dowie at the best,
    Dowf and dowie, dowf and dowie,
    Dowf and dowie at the best,
    Wi' a' their variorum;
They're dowf and dowie at the best,
Their *allegros* and a' the rest,
They canna' please a Scottish taste
    Compar'd wi' Tullochgorum.

Let warldly worms their minds oppress
Wi' fears o' want and double cess,
And sullen sots themsells distress
    Wi' keeping up decorum:
Shall we sae sour and sulky sit,
    Sour and sulky, sour and sulky,
    Sour and sulky shall we sit
    Like old philosophorum!

Shall we sae sour and sulky sit,
Wi' neither sense, nor mirth, nor wit,
Nor ever try to shake a fit
        To th' reel o' Tullochgorum?

May choicest blessings ay attend
Each honest, open-hearted friend,
And calm and quiet be his end,
        And a' that's good watch o'er him;
May peace and plenty be his lot,
        Peace and plenty, peace and plenty,
        Peace and plenty be his lot,
        And dainties a great store o' them;
May peace and plenty be his lot,
Unstain'd by any vicious spot,
And may he never want a groat,
        That's fond o' Tullochgorum!

But for the sullen frumpish fool,
That loves to be oppression's tool,
May envy gnaw his rotten soul,
        And discontent devour him;
May dool and sorrow be his chance,
        Dool and sorrow, dool and sorrow,
        Dool and sorrow be his chance,
        And nane say, wae's me for him!
May dool and sorrow be his chance,
Wi' a' the ills that come frae France,
Whae'er he be that winna dance
        The reel o' Tullochgorum.

CAULD KAIL IN ABERDEEN.

[The old words.]

THERE's cauld kail in Aberdeen,
  And castocks in Stra'bogie,
Where ilka lad maun hae his lass,
  But I maun hae my cogie.
    For I maun hae my cogie, troth,
      I canna want my cogie;
    I wadna gie my three-gird cog
      For a the wives in Bogie.

Johnnie Smith has got a wife
  Wha scrimps him o' his cogie;
But were she mine, upon my life,
  I'd duck her in a bogie.
    For I maun hae, &c.

Twa or three toddlin weans they hae,
  The pride o' a' Stra'bogie;
Whene'er the totums cry for meat,
  She curses ay his cogie;
    Crying, Wae betide the three-gird cog!
      Oh, wae betide the cogie!
    It does mair skaith than a' the ills
      That happen in Stra'bogie.

She fand him ance at Willie Sharp's,
  · And, what they maist did laugh at,
She brake the bicker, spilt the drink,
  And tightly gowff'd his haffet,
    · *Crying, Wae betide, &c.*
                II

Yet here's to ilka honest soul
Wha'll drink wi' me a cogie;
And for ilk silly whingin fool,
We'll duck him in the bogie.
For I maun hae my cogie, sirs,
I canna want my cogie;
I wadna gie my three-gird cog
For a' the queans in Bogie.

~~~~~~~~~~

[By the Duke of Gordon.]

There's cauld kail in Aberdeen,
And castocks in Stra'bogie;
Gin I hae but a bonny lass,
- Ye're welcome to your cogie.
And ye may sit up a' the night,
And drink till it be braid day-light;
Gie me a lass baith clean and tight,
To dance the reel of Bogie.

In cotillons the French excel;
John Bull in country-dances;
The Spaniards dance fandangos well;
Mynheer an all'mande prances:
In foursome reels the Scots delight,
The threesome maist dance wondrous light,
But twasome ding a' out o' sight,
Danc'd to the reel of Bogie.

Come, lads, and view your partners well,
Wale each a blythsome rogie;
I'll tak this lassie to mysell,
She seems sae keen and vogie:

Now, piper lad, bang up the spring ;
The country fashion is the thing,
To prie their mou's ere we begin
   To dance the reel o' Bogie.

Now ilka lad has got a lass,
   Save yon auld doited fogie,
And ta'en a fling upo' the grass,
   As they do in Stra'bogie.
But a' the lasses look sae fain,
We canna think oursels to hain,
For they maun hae their come-again,
   To dance the reel of Bogie.

Now a' the lads hae done their best,
   Like true men of Stra'bogie ;
We'll stop a while and tak a rest,
   And tipple out a cogie :
Come now, my lads, and tak your glass,
And try ilk other to surpass,
In wishing health to every lass
   To dance the reel of Bogie.

THE EWIE WI' THE CROOKIT HORN.

[By the Rev. JOHN SKINNER].

WERE I but able to rehearse;
My ewie's praise in proper verse,
I'd sound it forth as loud and fierce
   As ever piper's drone could blaw ;

The ewie wi' the crookit horn,
Wha had kent her might hae sworn
Sic a ewe was never born,
    Hereabout nor far awa',
Sic a ewe was never born,
    Hereabout nor far awa'.

I never needed tar nor keil
To mark her upo' hip or heel,
Her crookit horn did as weel
    To ken her by amo' them a';
She never threaten'd scab nor rot,
But keepit ay her ain jog-trot,
Baith to the fauld and to the cot,
    Was never sweir to lead nor ca',
Baith to the fauld and to the cot, &c.

Cauld nor hunger never dang her,
Wind nor wet could never wrang her,
Anes she lay an ouk and langer
    Furth aneath a wreath o' snaw:
Whan ither ewie's lap the dyke,
And eat the kail for a' the tyke,
My ewie never play'd the like,
    But tyc'd about the barn wa';
My ewie never play'd the like, &c.

A better or a thriftier beast,
Nae honest man could weel hae wist,
For, silly thing, she never mist
    To hae ilk' year a lamb or twa';
The first she had I gae to Jock,
To be to him a kind o' stock,
And now the laddie has a flock
    O' mair nor thirty head ava';
And now the laddie has a flock, &c.

I lookit aye at even' for her,
Lest mishanter shou'd come o'er her,
Or the fowmart might devour her,
 'Gin the beastie bade awa';
My ewie wi' the crookit horn,
Well deserv'd baith girse and corn,.
Sic a ewe was never born,
 Hereabout nor far awa'.
Sic a ewe was never born, &c.

Yet last onk, for a' my keeping,
(Wha can speak it without greeting?)
A villain cam when I was sleeping,
 Sta' my ewie, horn and a':
I sought her sair upo' the morn;
And down aneath a buss o' thorn
I got my ewie's crookit horn,
 But my ewie was awa'.
I got my ewie's crookit horn, &c.

O! gin I had the loun that did it,
Sworn I have as well as said it,
Tho' a' the warld should forbid it,
 I wad gie his neck a thra':
I never met wi' sic a turn
As this sin ever I was born,
My ewie wi' the crookit horn,
 Silly ewie stown awa',
My ewie wi' the crookit horn, &c.

O! had she died o' crook or cauld,
As ewies do when they grow auld,
It wad na been, by mony fauld,
 Sae sair a heart to nane o's a':

For a' the claith that we hae worn,
Frae her and her's sae aften shorn,
The loss o' her we cou'd hae born,
 Had fair strae-death ta'en her awa'.
The loss o' her we cou'd hae born, &c.

But thus, poor thing, to lose her life,
Aneath a bleedy villain's knife,
I'm really fley't that our guidwife
 Will never win aboon't ava':
O! a' ye bards benorth Kinghorn,
Call your muses up and mourn,
Our ewie wi' the crookit horn,
 Stown frae's, and fellt and a'!
Our ewie wi' the crookit horn, &c.

JOHN O' BADENYON.

[Written by the Rev. JOHN SKINNER, about 1763, when Mess.
Wilkes, Horne, &c. were making a noise about liberty.]

WHEN first I cam to be a man
 Of twenty years or so,
I thought myself a handsome youth,
 And fain the world would know;
In best attire I stept abroad,
 With spirits brisk and gay,
And here and there and every where
 Was like a morn in May;
No care I had nor fear of want,
 But rambled up and down,
And for a beau I might have past
 In country or in town;

I still was pleas'd where'er I went,
  And when I was alone,
I tun'd my pipe and pleas'd myself
  Wi' John o' Badenyon.

Now in the days of youthful prime
  A mistress I must find,
For love, I heard, gave one an air
  And ev'n improv'd the mind:
On Phillis fair above the rest
  Kind fortune fixt my eyes,
Her piercing beauty struck my heart,
  And she became my choice;
To Cupid now with hearty prayer
  I offer'd many a vow;
And danc'd and sung, and sigh'd and swore,
  As other lovers do;
But, when at last I breath'd my flame,
  I found her cold as stone;
I left the girl, and tun'd my pipe
  To John o' Badenyon.

When love had thus my heart beguil'd
  With foolish hopes and vain;
To friendship's port I steer'd my course,
  And laugh'd at lovers' pain;
A friend I got by lucky chance,
  'Twas something like divine,
An honest friend's a precious gift,
  And such a gift was mine;
And now whatever might betide
  A happy man was I,
In any strait I knew to whom
  I freely might apply;

A strait soon came: my friend I try'd;
  He heard, and spurn'd my moan;
I hy'd me home, and tun'd my pipe
  To John o' Badenyon.

Methought I should be wiser next
  And would a patriot turn,
Began to doat on Johnny Wilkes
  And cry up Parson Horne.
Their manly spirit I admir'd,
  And prais'd their noble zeal,
Who had with flaming tongue and pen
  Maintain'd the public weal;
But ere a month or two had past,
  I found myself betray'd,
'Twas self and party after all,
  For a' the stir they made;
At last I saw the factious knaves
  Insult the very throne,
I curs'd them a', and tun'd my pipe
  To John o' Badenyon.

What next to do I mus'd a while,
  Still hoping to succeed,
I pitch'd on books for company,
  And gravely try'd to read:
I bought and borrowed every where,
  And study'd night and day,
Nor mist what dean or doctor wrote
  That happen'd in my way:
Philosophy I now esteem'd
  The ornament of youth,
And carefully through many a page
  I hunted after truth.

A thousand various schemes I try'd,
    And yet was pleas'd with none,
I threw them by, and tun'd my pipe
    To John o' Badenyon.

And now ye youngsters every where,
    That wish to make a show,
Take heed in time, nor fondly hope
    For happiness below;
What you may fancy pleasure here,
    Is but an empty name,
And girls, and friends, and books, and so,
    You'll find them all the same:
Then be advised and warning take
    From such a man as me;
I'm neither Pope nor Cardinal,
    Nor one of high degree;
You'll meet displeasure every where;
    Then do as I have done,
Ev'n tune your pipe and please yourselves
    With John o' Badenyon.

KATHARINE OGIE.

[About 1680, this song was sung by Mr Abell at his concert in
Stationers Hall, London.—RITSON.]

As walking forth to view the plain,
    Upon a morning early,
While May's sweet scent did cheer my brain,
    From flowers which grew so rarely:

I chanc'd to meet a pretty maid,
  She shin'd though it was fogie:
I ask'd her name: Sweet sir, she said,
  My name is Katharine Ogie.

I stood a while, and did admire
  To see a nymph so stately;
So brisk an air there did appear,
  In a country maid so neatly:
Such natural sweetness she display'd,
  Like a lillie in a bogie;
Diana's self was ne'er array'd
  Like this same Katharine Ogie.

Thou flow'r of females, Beauty's queen,
  Who sees thee sure must prize thee;
Though thou art drest in robes but mean,
  Yet these cannot disguise thee:
Thy handsome air, and graceful look,
  Far excels any clownish rogie;
Thou'rt match for laird, or lord, or duke,
  My charming Katharine Ogie.

O were I but a shepherd swain!
  To feed my flock beside thee,
At boughting time to leave the plain,
  In milking to abide thee;
I'd think myself a happier man,
  With Kate, my club, and dogie,
Than he that hugs his thousands ten,
  Had I but Katharine Ogie.

Than I'd despise th' imperial throne,
  And statesmen's dangerous stations;
I'd be no king, I'd wear no crown,
  I'd smile at conqu'ring nations;

Might I caress and still possess
  This lass, of whom I'm vogie;
For these are toys, and still look less
  Compar'd with Katharine Ogie.

But I fear the gods have not decreed
  For me so fine a creature,
Whose beauty rare makes her exceed
  All other works of nature:
Clouds of despair surround my love,
  That are both dark and fogie;
Pity my case, ye powers above!
  Else I die for Katharine Ogie.

THE LASS OF PATIE'S MILL.

[Written by RAMSAY while residing at Loudon Castle with the
then Earl. One forenoon, riding, or walking out together,
his Lordship and Allan passed a sweet romantic spot on Irvine
water, still called " Patie's Mill," where a bonnie lass was
" tedding hay," bareheaded on the green. My Lord observed
to Allan, that it would be a fine theme for a song. Ramsay
took the hint, and, lingering behind, he composed the first
sketch of it, which he produced at dinner.—BURNS.]

THE lass of Patie's mill,
  So bonny, blyth and gay,
In spite of all my skill,
  She stole my heart away.
When tedding of the hay,
  Bare-headed on the green,
Love 'midst her locks did play,
  And wanton'd in her een.

Her arms, white, round, and smooth,
  Breasts rising in their dawn,
To age it would give youth,
  To press 'em with his hand.
Through all my spirits ran
  An extasy of bliss,
When I such sweetness fand
  Wrapt in a balmy kiss.

Without the help of art,
  Like flowers which grace the wild,
She did her sweets impart,
  Whene'er she spoke or smil'd.
Her looks they were so mild,
  Free from affected pride;
She me to love beguil'd,
  I wish'd her for my bride.

O! had I all that wealth
  Hopetoun's high mountains * fill,
Insur'd long life and health,
  And pleasure at my will;
I'd promise and fulfil,
  That none but bonny she,
The lass of Patie's mill,
  Should share the same with me.

* Thirty-three miles south-west of Edinburgh, where the Right
Honourable the Earl of Hopetoun's mines of gold and lead are.—
RAMSAY.

O'ER THE MOOR AMANG THE HEATHER.

["This is the composition of a Jean Glover, a girl who was not
only a whore, but also a thief; and in one or other character
has visited most of the correction houses in the west. She was
born I believe in Kilmarnock,—I took the song down from
her singing as she was strolling through the country with a
slight-of-hand blackguard."—BURNS.]

COMIN thro' the craigs o' Kyle,
Amang the bonnie·blooming heather,
There I met a bonnie lassie,
Keeping a' her yowes thegither,
   O'er the moor amang the heather,
   O'er the moor amang the heather,
   There I met a bonnie lassie,
   Keeping a' her yowes thegither.

Says I, My dearie where is thy hame,
In moor or dale pray tell me whether?
She said, I tent the fleecy flocks
That feed amang the blooming heather.
   O'er the moor, &c.

We laid us down upon a bank,
Sae warm and sunny was the weather,
She left her flocks at large to rove
Amang the bonnie blooming heather.
   O'er the moor, &c.

While thus we lay, she sang a sang,
Till echo rang a mile and farther,
And ay the burden o' the sang
Was o'er the moor amang the heather.
   O'er the moor, &c.

She charm'd my heart, and aye sinsyne,
I could na think on any ither:
By sea and sky she shall be mine!
The bonnie lass amang the heather.
O'er the moor, &c.

~~~~~~~~~~~~

THE LAMMIE.

[By H. MACNEILL, Esq.]

WHAR hae ye been a' day, my boy Tammy?
  Whar hae ye been a' day, my boy Tammy?
I've been by burn and flow'ry brae,
  Meadow green and mountain grey,
Courting o' this young thing
  Just come frae her mammy.

And whar gat ye that young thing,
  My boy Tammy?
I gat her down in yonder how,
  Smiling on a broomy know,
Herding ae wee lamb and ewe
  For her poor mammy.

What said ye to the bonnie bairn,
  My boy Tammy?
I prais'd her een, so lovely blue,
  Her dimpled cheek, and cherry mou ;—
I pree'd it aft as ye may trou !—
  She said, she'd tell her mammy.

I held her to my beating heart,
  My young, my smiling lammie!

I hae a house, it cost me dear,
  I've walth o' plenishen and gear;
Ye'se get it a' wer't ten times mair,
  Gin ye will leave your mammy.

The smile gaed aff her bonnie face—
  I maun nae leave my mammy;
She's gi'en me meat, she's gi'en me claise,
  She's been my comfort a' my days:—
My father's death brought mony waes—
  I canna leave my mammy.

We'll tak her hame and mak her fain,
  My ain kind-hearted lammie;
We'll gie her meat, we'll gie her claise,
  We'll be her comfort a' her days.
The wee thing gies her hand, and says,
  There! gang and ask my mammy.

Has she been to the kirk with thee,
  My boy Tammy?
She has been to the kirk wi' me,
  And the tear was in her ee,—
But O! she's but a young thing
  Just come frae her mammy.

MY PEGGY IS A YOUNG THING.

[By RAMSAY.]

Tune—*The wawking of the fauld.*

My Peggy is a young thing,
  Just enter'd in her teens,
Fair as the day, and sweet as May,
Fair as the day, and always gay;

My Peggy is a young thing,
   And I'm nae very auld,
Yet well I like to meet her at
   The wawking of the fauld.

My Peggy speaks sae sweetly,
   Whene'er we meet alane,
I wish nae mair to lay my care,
I wish nae mair of a' that's rare.
My Peggy speaks sae sweetly,
   To a' the lave I'm cauld;
But she gars a' my spirits glow,
   At wawking of the fauld.

My Peggy smiles sae kindly,
   Whene'er I whisper love,
That I look down on a' the town,
That I look down upon a crown.
My Peggy smiles sae kindly,
   It makes me blyth and bauld;
And naething gi'es me sic delight,
   As wawking of the fauld.

My Peggy sings sae saftly,
   When on my pipe I play;
By a' the rest it is confest,
By a' the rest, that she sings best.
My Peggy sings sae saftly,
   And in her sangs are tauld,
With innocence, the wale of sense,
   At wawking of the fauld.

CORN RIGS ARE BONNY.

[By RAMSAY.]

My Patie is a lover gay,
　His mind is never muddy,
His breath is sweeter than new hay,
　His face is fair and ruddy.
His shape is handsome, middle size,
　He's stately in his wa'king;
The shining of his een surprise;
　'Tis heaven to hear him ta'king.

Last night I met him on a bawk,
　Where yellow corn was growing,
There mony a kindly word he spake,
　That set my heart a-glowing.
He kiss'd, and vow'd he wad be mine,
　And loo'd me best of ony;
That gars me like to sing sinsyne,
　" O corn rigs are bonny."

Let maidens of a silly mind
　Refufe what maist they're wanting;
Since we for yielding are design'd,
　We chastely should be granting;
Then I'll comply, and marry Pate,
　And syne my cockernony
He's free to touzle air or late
　Where corn rigs are bonny.

TWEED-SIDE.

[These verses are the old words to this tune, and are said to have been composed by a Lord Yester.]

When Maggy and I were acquaint,
  I carried my noddle fu' hie;
Nae lint white on all the gay plain,
  Nor gowdspink sae bonny as she.
I whistled, I pip'd, and I sang,
  I woo'd, but I came nae great speed;
Therefore I maun wander abroad,
  And lay my banes over the Tweed.

To Maggy my love I did tell,
  Saut tears did my passion express;
Alas! for I lo'ed her o'er well,
  And the women lo'e sic a man less.
Her heart it was frozen and cauld,
  Her pride had my ruin decreed,
Therefore I will wander abroad,
  And lay my banes far frae the Tweed.

TWEED-SIDE.

[Written about 1731 by Robert Crawford of Auchinames, who was unfortunately drowned coming from France. The Mary to whom the lines are addressed, says the learned author of *Marmion*, was a Miss Mary Lilias Scott of the Harden family.]

What beauties does Flora disclose!
  How sweet are her smiles upon Tweed!
Yet Mary's still sweeter than those,
  Both nature and fancy exceed.

No daisy, nor sweet blushing rose,
  Not all the gay flowers of the field,
Nor Tweed gliding gently thro' those,
  Such beauty and pleasure does yield.

The warblers are heard in the grove,
  The linnet, the lark, and the thrush,
The blackbird, and sweet cooing dove,
  With music enchant ev'ry bush.
Come, let us go forth to the mead,
  Let us see how the primroses spring ;
We'll lodge in some village on Tweed,
  And love while the feather'd folks sing.

How does my love pass the long day ?
  Does Mary not 'tend a few sheep ?
Do they never carelessly stray,
  While happily she lies asleep ?
Tweed's murmurs should lull her to rest ;
  Kind nature indulging my bliss,
To relieve the soft pains of my breast,
  I'd steal an ambrosial kiss.

'Tis she does the virgins excel,
  No beauty with her may compare ;
Love's graces around her do dwell,
  She's fairest where thousands are fair.
Say, charmer, where do thy flocks stray ?
  Oh ! tell me at noon where they feed ;
Shall I seek them on sweet winding Tay,
  Or the pleasanter banks of the Tweed ?

BESSY BELL AND MARY GRAY.

[The first stanza is supposed to be part of the original song,
which, it is to be regretted, RAMSAY altered, substituting his
own verses in its stead, it being highly probable that the present song is much inferior to the old one which was founded on
the following story :—" The celebrated Bessie Bell and Mary
Gray are buried near Lyndoch. * The common tradition is, that
the father of the former was laird of Kinvaid, in the neighbourhood of Lyndoch, and the father of the latter laird of Lyndoch ;
that these two young ladies were both very handsome, and a
most intimate friendship subsisted between them ; that while
Miss Bell was on a visit to Miss Gray, the plague broke out in
the year 1666, in order to avoid which, they built themselves a
bower, about three quarters of a mile west from Lyndoch-
house, in a very retired and romantic place, called Burn-braes,
on the side of Brauchie-burn.   Here they lived for some time,
but the plague raging with great fury, they caught the infec-
tion, it is said; from a young gentleman, who was in love with
them both, and here they died.   The burial place lies about
half a mile west from the present house of Lyndoch." *Muses
Threnodie*, p. 19, Perth, 1774.]

O BESSY BELL and Mary Gray,
　They are twa bonny lasses,
They bigg'd a bower on yon burn brae,
　And theeked it o'er wi' rashes.
Fair Bessy Bell I loo'd yestreen,
　And thought I ne'er could alter ;
But Mary Gray's twa pawky een,
　They gar my fancy falter.

Now Bessy's hair's like a lint-tap ;
　She smiles like a May morning,
When Phœbus starts frae Thetis' lap,
　The hills with rays adorning :

* The seat of that gallant officer, Lord Lyndoch.

White is her neck, saft is her hand,
  Her waist and feet's fu' genty;
With ilka grace she can command;
  Her lips, O wow! they're dainty.

And Mary's locks are like a craw,
  Her een like diamonds glances;
She's ay sae clean, redd up, and braw,
  She kills whene'er she dances:
Blyth as a kid, with wit at will,
  She blooming, tight, and tall is;
And guides her airs sae gracefu' still,
  O Jove! she's like thy Pallas.

Dear Bessy Bell and Mary Gray,
  Ye unco sair oppress us;
Our fancies jee between you twae,
  Ye are sic bonny lasses:
Waes me! for baith I canna get,
  To ane by law we're stented;
Then I'll draw cuts, and tak my fate,
  And be with ane contented.

THE YOUNG LAIRD AND EDINBURGH KATY.

[By RAMSAY.]

Now wat ye wha I met yestreen,
  Coming down the street, my jo?
My mistress in her tartan screen,
  Fu' bonny, braw, and sweet, my jo.

My dear, quoth I, thanks to the night,
　　That never wish'd a lover ill,
Since ye're out of your mither's sight,
　　Let's tak a wauk up to the Hill.

O Katy, wiltu' gang wi' me,
　　And leave the dinsome town a while?
The blossom's sprouting frae the tree,
　　And a' the simmer's gaw'n to smile:
The mavis, nightingale, and lark,
　　The bleeting lambs, and whistling hind;
In ilka dale, green, shaw, and park,
　　Will nourish health, and glad your mind.

Soon as the clear goodman of day
　　Does bend his morning draught of dew,
We'll gae to some burn-side and play,
　　And gather flowers to busk your brow:
We'll pu' the daisies on the green,
　　The lucken gowans frae the bog;
Between hands now and then we'll lean,
　　And sport upo' the velvet fog.

There's up into a pleasant glen,
　　A wee piece frae my father's tow'r,
A canny, saft, and flow'ry den,
　　Where circling birks have form'd a bow'r:
Whene'er the sun grows high and warm,
　　We'll to the cauler shade remove,
There will I lock thee in my arms,
　　And love and kiss, and kiss and love.

KATY'S ANSWER.

My mither's ay glowran o'er me,
Though she did the same before me ;
   I canna get leave
   To look to my loove,
Or else she'll be like to devour me.

Right fain wad I take your offer,
Sweet sir, but I'll tine my tocher,
   Then, Sandy, ye'll fret,
   And wyte your poor Kate,
Whene'er ye keek in your toom coffer.

For, though my father has plenty
Of siller, and plenishing dainty,
   Yet he's unco sweer
   To twin wi' his gear,
And sae we had need to be tenty.

Tutor my parents wi' caution,
Be wylie in ilka motion ;
   Brag weel o' your land,
   And there's my leal hand,
Win them, I'll be at your devotion.

HIGHLAND LADDIE.

[By Ramsay.]

The Lawland lads think they are fine ;
   But O, they're vain and idly gaudy !
How much unlike that gracefu' mein,
   And manly looks of my Highland laddie

O my bonny Highland laddie,
   My handsome charming Highland laddie!
May Heaven still guard, and love reward
   Our Lawland lass and her Highland laddie!

If I were free at will to chuse,
   To be the wealthiest Lawland lady,
I'd tak young Donald without trews,
   With bonnet blue, and belted plaidy.
      O my bonny, &c.

The brawest beau in burrows-town,
   In a' his airs, with art made ready,
Compar'd to him he's but a clown;
   He's finer far in's tartan plaidy.
      O my bonny, &c.

O'er benty hill with him I'll run,
   And leave my Lawland kin and daddy,
Frae winter's cauld, and summer's sun,
   He'll screen me with his Highland plaidy.
      O my bonny, &c.

A painted room, and silken bed,
   May please a Lawland laird and lady;
But I can kiss, and be as glad,
   Behind a bush in's Highland plaidy.
      O my bonny, &c.

Few compliments between us pass,
   I ca' him my dear Highland laddie,
And he ca's me his Lawland lass,
   Syne rows me in beneath his plaidie.
      O my bonny, &c.

Nae greater joy I'll e'er pretend,
　Than that his luve prove true and steady,
Like mine to him, which ne'er shall end,
　While Heaven preserves my Highland laddie.
　　O my bonny, &c.

⁕⁕⁕⁕⁕⁕⁕⁕⁕⁕⁕

THE HIGHLAND LASSIE.

The Lawland maids gang trig and fine,
　But aft they're sour and unco saucy;
Sae proud, they never can be kind
　Like my good-humour'd Highland lassie,
　　O my bonny Highland lassie,
　　　My hearty smiling Highland lassie;
　　May never care make thee less fair,
　　　But bloom of youth still bless my lassie!

Than ony lass in burrows-town,
　Wha mak their cheeks with patches mottie,
I'd take my Katy but a gown,
　Bare-footed in her little coatie.
　　O my bonny, &c.

Beneath the brier, or brecken bush,
　Whene'er I kiss and court my dawtie;
Happy and blyth as ane wad wish,
　My flighteren heart gangs pittie pattie.
　　O my bonny, &c.

O'er highest hethery hills I'll sten,
　With cockit gun and ratches tenty,
To drive the deer out of their den,
　To feast my lass on dishes dainty.
　　O my bonny, &c.

K

There'e nane shall dare by deed or word,
  'Gainst her to wag a tongue or finger,
While I can wield my trusty sword,
  Or frae my side whisk out a whinger.
    O my bonny, &c.

The mountains clad with purple bloom,
  And berries ripe, invite my treasure.
To range with me; let great fowk gloom,
  While wealth and pride confound their pleasure.
    O my bonny, &c.

THE MAID THAT TENDS THE GOATS.

[Written by Mr DUDGEON, a respectable farmer's son in Berwick-
shire.—BURNS.]

Up amang yon cliffy rocks,
Sweetly rings the rising echo,
To the maid that tends the goats,
Lilting o'er her native notes.
Hark, she sings, Young Sandy's kind,
And he's promis'd ay to lo'e me;
Here's a brotch, I ne'er shall tin'd,
'Till he's fairly married to me;
Drive away, ye drone time,
And bring about our bridal day.

Sandy herds a' flock o' sheep,
Aften does he blaw the whistle,
In a strain sae saftly sweet,
Lammies list'ning dare nae bleat;

He's as fleet's the mountain roe,
Hardy as the Highland heather,
Wading thro' the winter snow,
Keeping ay his flock together;
But a plaid, wi' bare houghs,
He braves the bleakest norlin blast.

Brawly he can dance, and sing
Canty glee or Highland cronach;
Nane can ever match his fling
At a reel or round a ring;
Wightly can he wield a rung,
In a brawl he's ay the bangster:
A' his praise can ne'er be sung
By the langest winded sangster.
Sangs that sing o' Sandy,
Come short, tho' they were, e'er sae lang.

ROSLIN CASTLE.

[By Mr RICHARD HEWIT, whom the celebrated Dr Blacklock
kept for some years as an amanuensis. The air was composed
by Mr Oswald, a music-seller in London, who about the year
1750 published a large collection of Scotch tunes, under the title
of *The Caledonian Pocket Companion.*]

'Twas in that season of the year,
When all things gay and sweet appear,
That Colin with the morning ray,
Arose and sung his rural lay.
Of Nanny's charms the shepherd sung,
The hills and dales with Nanny rung;
While Roslin Castle heard the swain,
And echo'd back the chearful strain.

Awake, sweet muse! the breathing spring
With rapture warms; awake and sing!
Awake and join the vocal throng,
Who hail the morning with a song;
To Nanny raise the chearful lay,
O! bid her haste and come away;
In sweetest smiles herself adorn,
And add new graces to the morn!

O hark, my love! on ev'ry spray
Each feather'd warbler tunes his lay;
'Tis beauty fires the ravish'd throng;
And love inspires the melting song:
Then let my raptur'd notes arise;
For beauty darts from Nanny's eyes;
And love my rising bosom warms,
And fills my soul with sweet alarms.

O! come, my love! thy Colin's lay
With rapture calls, O come away!
Come, while the muse this wreath shall twine
Around that modest brow of thine;
O! hither haste, and with thee bring
That beauty blooming like the spring,
Those graces that divinely shine,
And charm this ravish'd breast of mine!

JOCKEY WAS THE BLYTHEST LAD.

[This song is marked with the letter Z. in Johnson's *Musical Museum*, as being an old song with corrections or additions.]

Young Jockey was the blythest lad
In a' our town, or here awa';
Fu' blythe he whistled at the gaud,
Fu' lightly danc'd he in the ha'.

He roos'd my een sae bonnie blue,
   He roos'd my waist sae genty sma' ;
And ay my heart came to my mou',
   When ne'er a body heard or saw.

My Jockey toils upon the plain,
   Thro' wind and weet, thro' frost and sna' ;
And o'er the lee I leuk fu' fain,
   When Jockey's owsen hameward ca'.
An' ay the night comes round again,
   When in his arms he taks me a' ;
An' ay he vows he'll be my ain
   As lang's he has a breath to draw.

~~~~~~~~~~

THE BLUE-EYED LASSIE.

[By Burns. " The heroine of this song," says Dr Currie, " was
Miss J———, of Lochmaban. This lady, now Mrs R———,
after residing some time in Liverpool, is settled with her husband in New-York, North America."—Burns's *Works*, vol.
iv. 299.]

I gaed a waefu' gate, yestreen,
   A gate, I fear, I'll dearly rue ;
I gat my death frae twa sweet een,
   Twa lovely een o' bonnie blue.
'Twas not her golden ringlets bright ;
   Her lips, like roses wat wi' dew,
Her heaving bosom, lily-white—
   It was her een sae bonnie blue.

She talk'd; she smil'd, my heart she wyl'd,
   She charm'd my soul I wist na how ;
And ay the stound, the deadly wound,
   Cam frae her een sae bonnie blue.

But spare to speak, and spare to speed;
  She'll aiblins listen to my vow:
Should she refuse, I'll lay my dead
  To her twa een sae bonnie blue.

~~~~~~~~~~

SHE SAYS SHE LO'ES ME BEST OF A'.

[By BURNS.]

Tune—*Onagh's water-fall.*

SAE flaxen were her ringlets,
  Her eye-brows of a darker hue,
Bewitchingly o'er-arching
  Twa laughing een o' bonnie blue.
Her smiling sae wyling,
  Wad make a wretch forget his woe;
What pleasure, what treasure,
  Unto these rosy lips to grow:
Such was my Chloris' bonnie face,
  When first her bonnie face I saw,
And ay my Chloris' dearest charm,
  She says she lo'es me best of a'.

Like harmony her motion;
  Her pretty ancle is a spy
Betraying fair proportion,
  Wad make a saint forget the sky.
Sae warming, sae charming,
  Her fau'tless form and gracefu' air;
Ilk feature—auld Nature
  Declar'd that she could do nae mair:
Her's are the willing chains o' love,
  By conquering beauty's sovereign law;
And ay my Chloris' dearest charm,
  She says she lo'es me best of a'.

Let others love the city,
  And gaudy shew at sunny noon ;
Gie me the lonely valley,
  The dewy eve, and rising moon
Fair beaming, and streaming,
  Her silver light the boughs amang ;
While falling, recalling,
  The amorous thrush concludes his sang :
There, dearest Chloris, wilt thou rove
  By wimpling burn and leafy shaw,
And hear my vows o' truth and love,
  And say thou lo'es me best of a'.

THIS IS NO MY AIN LASSIE.

[By Burns.]

Tune—*This is no my ain house.*

O THIS *is no my ain lassie,*
  Fair tho' the lassie be ;
O weel ken I my ain lassie,
  Kind love is in her e'e.

I see a form, I see a face,
Ye weel may wi' the fairest place :
It wants to me the witching grace,
  The kind love that's in her e'e.
    O this is no, &c.

She's bonnie, blooming, straight, and tall,
And lang has had my heart in thrall ;
And ay it charms my very saul,
  The kind love that's in her e'e.
    O this is no, &c.

A thief sae pawkie is my Jean,
To steal a blink, by a' unseen,
But gleg as light are lovers' een,
   When kind love is in the e'e.
     O this is no, &c.

It may escape the courtly sparks,
It may escape the learned clerks;
But weel the watching lover marks,
   The kind love that's in her e'e.
     O this is no, &c.

'O WAT YE WHA'S IN YON TOWN.

[By BURNS. " The heroine of this song," says Dr Currie,
" Mrs O. (formerly Miss L. J.) died lately (1799) at Lisbon.
This most accomplished and most lovely woman was worthy of
this beautiful strain of sensibility. The song is written in the
character of her husband."—BURNS's *Works*, vol. iv. 312.]

O WAT ye wha's in yon town,
   Ye see the e'enin sun upon,
The fairest dame's in yon town,
   That e'enin sun is shining on.

Now haply down yon gay green shaw,
   She wanders by yon spreading tree:
How blest ye flowers that round her blaw,
   Ye catch the glances o' her e'e.

How blest ye birds that round her sing,
   And welcome in the blooming year,
And doubly welcome be the spring,
   The season to my Lucy dear.

The sun blinks blythe on yon town,
    And on yon bonnie braes of Ayr;
But my delight in yon town,
    And dearest bliss, is Lucy fair.

Without my love, not a' the charms
    O' Paradise could yield me joy;
But gie me Lucy in my arms,
    And welcome Lapland's dreary sky.

My cave wad be a lover's bower,
    Tho' raging winter rent the air;
And she a lovely little flower,
    That I wad tent and shelter there.

O sweet is she in yon town,
    Yon sinkin sun's gane down upon;
A fairer than's in yon town,
    His setting beam ne'er shone upon.

If angry fate is sworn my foe,
    And suffering I am doom'd to bear;
I careless quit aught else below,
    But spare me, spare me Lucy dear.

For while life's dearest blood is warm,
    Ae thought frae her shall ne'er depart,
And she—as fairest is her form!
    She has the truest kindest heart.

JESSIE THE FLOWER O' DUMBLANE.

[BY TANNY HILL.]

THE sun has gane down o'er the lofty Ben Lomon,
    And left the red clouds to preside o'er the scene;

While lanely I stray on a calm simmer gloamin'.
  To muse on sweet Jessie, the flower o' Dumblane.
How sweet is the brier, wi' its saft faulding blossom!
  And sweet is the birk, wi' its mantle o' green;
Yet sweeter and fairer, and dear to this bosom,
  Is lovely young Jessie, the flower o' Dumblane,
    Is lovely young Jessie, &c.

She's modest as ony, and blythe as she's bonnie,
  For guileless simplicity marks her its ain;
Accurs'd be the villain, divested o' feeling,
  Wou'd blight in its bloom the sweet flower o' Dum-
    blane.
Sing on, thou sweet mavis, thy hymn to the e'ening,
  Thou'rt dear to the echoes of Calder-wood glen;
Sae dear to this bosom, sae artless an' winning,
  Is charming young Jessie, the flower o' Dumblane.
    Is charming young Jessie, &c.

How lost were my days, till I met wi' my Jessie,
  The sports o' the city seem'd foolish and vain;
I ne'er saw a nymph I could call my dear lassie,
  Till charm'd wi' young Jessie the flower o' Dumblane.
Though mine were the station o' loftiest grandeur,
  Amid'st it's profusion I'd languish in pain,
An' reckon as naething the height o' it's-splendour,
  If wanting sweet Jessie, the flower o' Dumblane.
    If wanting sweet Jessie, &c.

~~~~~~~~~~

MY NANNIE, O.

[By Burns.]

Tune—*My Nannie, O.*

Behind yon hills where Lugar flows,
  'Mang moors an' mosses many, O,

The wintry sun the day has clos'd,
  And I'll awa to Nannie, O.

The westlin wind blaws loud an' shill;
  The night's baith mirk and rainy, O;
But I'll get my plaid an' out I'll steal,
  An' owre the hill to Nannie, O.

My Nannie's charming, sweet, and young;
  Nae artfu' wiles to win ye, O:
May ill befa' the flattering tongue
  That wad beguile my Nannie, O.

Her face is fair, her heart is true,
  As spotless as she's bonnie, O;
The op'ning gowan, wet wi' dew,
  Nae purer is than Nannie, O.

A country lad is my degree,
  An' few there be that ken me, O;
But what care I how few they be,
  I'm welcome ay to Nannie, O.

My riches a's my penny-fee,
  An' I maun guide it cannie, O;
But warl's gear ne'er troubles me,
  My thoughts are a' my Nannie, O.

Our auld guidman delights to view
  His sheep an' kye thrive bonnie, O;
But I'm as blythe that hauds his pleugh,
  An' has nae care but Nannie, O.

Come weel, come woe, I care na by,
  I'll tak' what Heav'n will sen' me, O;
Nae ither care in life have I,
  But live an' love my Nannie, O.

DUMBARTON DRUMS.

Dumbarton's drums beat bonny, O,
When they mind me of my dear Johnny, O,
 How happy am I,
 When my soldier is by,
While he kisses and blesses his Annie, O!
'Tis a soldier alone can delight me, O,
For his graceful looks do invite me, O:
 While guarded in his arms,
 I'll fear no war's alarms,
Neither danger nor death shall e'er fright me, O.

My love is a handsome laddie, O,
Genteel, but ne'er foppish nor gaudy, O:
 Tho' commissions are dear,
 Yet I'll buy him one this year;
For he shall serve no longer a cadie, O.
A soldier has honour and bravery, O,
Unacquainted with rogues and their knavery, O:
 He minds no other thing
 But the ladies or the king;
For every other care is but slav'ry, O.

Then I'll be a captain's lady, O;
Farewell all my friends, and my daddy, O;
 I'll wait no more at home,
 But I'll follow with the drum,
And whene'er that beats I'll be ready, O.
Dumbarton's drums sound bonny, O,
They are sprightly like my dear Johnny, O:
 How happy shall I be,
 When on my soldier's knee,
And he kisses and blesses his Annie, O!

THE SOGER LADDIE.

[The first verse of this is old; the rest is by RAMSAY.—BURNS.]

My soger laddie is over the sea,
And he will bring gold and money to me;
And when he comes hame, he'll make me a lady,
My blessings gang wi' my soger laddie.

My doughty laddie is handsome and brave,
And can as a soger and lover behave;
True to his country; to love he is steady;
There's few to compare with my soger laddie.

Shield him, ye angels! frae death in alarms,
Return him with laurels to my longing arms,
Syne frae all my care ye'll presently free me,
When back to my wishes my soger ye gie me.

O! soon may his honours bloom fair on his brow,
As quickly they must, if he get his due:
For in noble actions his courage is ready,
Which makes me delight in my soger laddie.

~~~~~~~~~~

O'ER BOGIE.

[By RAMSAY.]

I WILL *awa wi' my love,*
I will awa wi' her,
Tho' a' my kin had sworn and said,
I'll o'er Bogie wi' her.

L

If I can get but her consent,
  I dinna care a strae
Though ilka ane be discontent,
  Awa wi' her I'll gae.
    I will awa, &c.

For now she's mistress of my heart,
  And wordy of my hand,
And well I wat we shanna part
  For siller or for land.
Let rakes delight to swear and drink,
  And beaus admire fine lace;
But my chief pleasure is to blink
  On Betty's bonnie face.
    I will awa, &c.

There a' the beauties do combine,
  Of colour, traits, and air;
The saul that sparkles in her een
  Maks her a jewel rare;
Her flowing wit gives shining life
  To a' her other charms;
How blest I'll be when she's my wife,
  And lock'd up in my arms!
    I will awa, &c.

There blythly will I rant and sing,
  While o'er her sweets I range,
I'll cry, Your humble servant, king,
  Shame fa' them that wad change.
A kiss of Betty and a smile,
  Albeit ye wad lay down
The right ye hae to Britain's isle,
  And offer me your crown.
    I will awa, &c.

KIND ROBIN LO'ES ME.

Robin is my only jo,
Robin has the art to lo'e,
So to his suit I mean to bow,
   Because I ken he lo'es me.
Happy, happy was the show'r,
That led me to his birken bow'r,
Whare first of love I fand the pow'r,
   And kend that Robin lo'ed me.

They speak of napkins, speak of rings,
Speak of gloves and kissing strings,
And name a thousand bonny things,
   And ca' them signs he lo'es me.
But I'd prefer a smack of Rob,
Sporting on the velvet fog,
To gifts as lang's a plaiden wob,
   Because I ken he lo'es me.

He's tall and sonsy, frank, and free,
Lo'ed by a', and dear to me,
Wi' him I'd live, wi' him I'd die,
   Because my Robin lo'es me.
My titty Mary said to me,
Our courtship but a joke wad be,
And I, or lang, be made to see,
   That Robin did na lo'e me.

But little kens she what has been
Me and my honest Rob between,
And in his wooing, O so keen
   Kind Robin is that lo'es me.

Then fly, ye lazy hours, away,
And hasten on the happy day,
When, Join your hands, Mess John shall say,
   And mak him mine that lo'es me.

Till then, let ev'ry chance unite,
To weigh our love, and fix delight,
And I'll look down on such wi' spite,
   Who doubt that Robin lo'es me.
O hey, Robin, quo' she,
O hey, Robin, quo' she,
O hey, Robin, quo' she,
   Kind Robin lo'es me.

SANDY O'ER THE LEE.

I winna marry ony man but Sandy o'er the lee,
I winna marry ony man but Sandy o'er the lee;
I winna hae the dominie, for gude he canna be,
But I will hae my Sandy lad, my Sandy o'er the lee,
   For he's aye a kissing, kissing, aye a kissing me,
   He's aye a kissing, kissing, aye a kissing me.

I winna hae the minister for a' his godly looks,
Nor yet will I the lawyer hae, for a' his wily crooks:
I winna hae the ploughman lad, nor yet will I the
   miller,
But I will hae my Sandy lad, without ae penny siller.
   For he's aye a kissing, kissing, &c.

I winna hae the soger lad, for he gangs to the war,
I winna hae the sailor lad, because he smells of tar;
I winna hae the lord nor laird, for a' their meikle gear,
But I will hae my Sandy lad, my Sandy o'er the moor.
   For he's aye a kissing, kissing, &c.

LASS WITH A LUMP OF LAND.

[By Ramsay.]

Gi'e me a lass with a lump of land,
   And we for life shall gang thegither,
Tho' daft or wise, I'll ne'er demand,
   Or black or fair, it maksna whether.
I'm aff with wit, and beauty will fade,
   And blood alane is no worth a shilling,
But she that's rich, her market's made,
   For ilka charm about her is killing.

Gi'e me a lass with a lump of land,
   And in my bosom I'll hug my treasure;
Gin I had ance her gear in my hand,
   Should love turn dowf, it will find pleasure.
Laugh on wha likes, but there's my hand,
   I hate with poortith, tho' bonny, to meddle;
Unless they bring cash, or a lump of land,
   They'se never get me to dance to their fiddle.

There's meikle good love in bands and bags,
   And siller and gowd's a sweet complexion;
But beauty, and wit, and virtue in rags,
   Have tint the art of gaining affection;
Love tips his arrows with woods and parks,
   And castles and rigs, and muirs and meadows,
And naething can catch our modern sparks,
   But well-tocher'd lasses, or jointur'd widows.

HEY FOR A LASS WI' A TOCHER.

[By Burns.]

Tune—*Balinamona ora.*

Awa wi' your witchcraft o' beauty's alarms,
The slender bit beauty you grasp in your arms:
O, gie me the lass that has acres o' charms,
O, gie me the lass wi' the weel-stockit farms.
  Then hey for a lass wi' a tocher, then hey for a lass
  wi' a tocher,
  Then hey for a lass wi' a tocher; the nice yellow
  guineas for me.

Your beauty's a flower, in the morning that blows,
And withers the faster, the faster it grows;
But the rapturous charm o' the bonnie green knowes,
Ilk spring they're new deckit wi' bonnie white yowes.
  Then hey, &c.

And e'en when this beauty your bosom has blest,
The brightest o' beauty may cloy when possest;
But the sweet yellow darlings wi' Geordie imprest,
The langer ye hae them—the mair they're carest.
  Then hey, &c.

COUNTRY LASSIE.

[By Burns.]

In simmer when the hay was mawn,
  And corn wav'd green in ilka field,
While claver blooms white o'er the lea,
  And roses blaw in ilka bield;

Blythe Bessie in the milking shiel,
 Says, I'll be wed, come o't what will:
Out spak a dame in wrinkled eild,
 O' gude advisement comes nae ill.

It's ye hae wooers mony ane,
 And lassie ye're but young ye ken:
Then wait a wee, and cannie wale
 A routhie butt, a routhie ben:
There's Johnie o' the Buskie-glen,
 Fu' is his barn, fu' is his byre;
Tak this frae me, my bonnie hen,
 It's plenty beets the luver's fire.

For Johnie o' the Buskie-glen,
 I dinna care a single flee;
He lo'es sae well his craps and kye,
 He has nae luve to spare for me:
But blythe's the blink o' Robie's e'e,
 And weel I wat he lo'es me dear:
Ae blink o' him I wad nae gie
 For Buskie-glen and a' his gear.

O thoughtless lassie, life's a faught;
 The canniest gate, the strife is sair:
But ay fu' han't is fechtin best,
 A hungry care's an unco care:
But some will spend, and some will spare,
 And wilfu' folk maun hae their will;
Syne as ye brew, my maiden fair,
 Keep mind that ye maun drink the yill.

O gear will buy me rigs o' land,
 And gear will buy me sheep and kye;
But the tender heart o' leesome luve,
 The gowd and siller canna buy:

We may be poor,—Robie and I,
 Light is the burden luve lays on;
Content and luve brings peace and joy,
 What mair hae queens upon a throne?

●●●●●●●●●●●

TAM GLEN.

[By Burns.]

Tune—The mucking o' Geordie's byre.

My heart is a-breaking, dear Tittie,
 Some counsel unto me come len',
To anger them a' is a pity,
 But what will I do wi' Tam Glen?

I'm thinking, wi' sic a braw fellow,
 In poortith I might mak a fen';
What care I in riches to wallow,
 If I mauna marry Tam Glen.

There's Lowrie the laird o' Drumeller,
 " Gude day to you," brute! he comes ben;
He brags and he blaws o' his siller,
 But when will he dance like Tam Glen?

My minnie does constantly deave me,
 And bids me beware o' young men;
They flatter, she says, to deceive me,
 But wha can think sae o' Tam Glen?

My daddie says, gin I'll forsake him,
 He'll gie me gude hunder marks ten:
But, if it's ordain'd I maun take him,
 O wha will I get but Tam Glen?

Yestreen at the Valentines' dealing,
  My heart to my mou' gied a sten;
For thrice I drew ane without failing,
  And thrice it was written, Tam Glen.

The last Halloween I was waukin
  My droukit sark sleeve, as ye ken;
His likeness cam up the house staukin,
  And the very grey breeks o' Tam Glen.

Come counsel, dear Tittie, don't tarry;
  I'll gie you my bonnie black hen,
Gif ye will advise me to marry
  The lad I lo'e dearly, Tam Glen.

~~~~~~~~~~

GALLA WATER.

[The old words.]

Braw, braw lads of Galla water,
  O! braw lads of Galla water;
I'll kilt my coats aboon my knee,
  And follow my love thro' the water.

Sae fair her hair, sae brent her brow,
  Sae bonnie blue her een, my dearie;
Sae white her teeth, sae sweet her mou',
  I aften kiss her till I'm wearie.

O'er yon bank, and o'er yon brae,
  O'er yon moss amang the heather,
I'll kilt my coats aboon my knee,
  And follow my love thro' the water.

Down amang the broom, the broom,
  Down amang the broom, my dearie;
The lassie lost her silken snood,
  That cost her mony a blirt and bleary.

~~~~~~~~~~

GALLA WATER.

[By Burns.]

Braw, braw lads on Yarrow braes,
  Ye wander thro' the blooming heather;
But Yarrow braes, nor Ettric shaws,
  Can match the lads o' Galla water.

But there is ane, a secret ane,
  Aboon them a' I loe him better;
And I'll be his, and he'll be mine,
  The bonny lad o' Galla water.

Altho' his daddie was nae laird,
  And tho' I hae nae meikle tocher;
Yet rich in kindest, truest love,
  We'll tent our flocks by Galla water.

It ne'er was wealth, it ne'er was wealth,
  That coft contentment, peace, or pleasure;
The bands and bliss o' mutual love,
  O that's the chiefest warld's treasure!

~~~~~~~~~~

ETTRICK BANKS.

On Ettrick banks, in a summer's night,
  At gloaming when the sheep drave hame;

I met my lassie braw and tight,
　Come wading, barefoot, a' her lane:
My heart grew light; I ran, I flang
　My arms about her lily neck,
And kiss'd and clap'd her there fou lang,
　My words they were na mony feck.

I said, My lassie, will ye go
　To the Highland hills, the Erse to learn?
I'll baith gie thee a cow and ewe,
　When ye come to the Brig of Earn.
At Leith auld meal comes in, ne'er fash,
　And herrings at the Broomy-Law,
Cheer up your heart, my bonny lass,
　There's gear to win we never saw.

All day when we have wrought enough,
　When winter-frosts, and snaw begin,
Soon as the sun gaes west the loch,
　At night when ye sit down to spin,
I'll screw my pipes, and play a spring;
　And thus the weary night we'll end,
Till the tender kid and lamb-time bring
　Our pleasant summer back again.

Syne when the trees are in their bloom,
　And gowans glent o'er ilka field,
I'll meet my lass amang the broom,
　And lead you to my summer shield.
Then far frae a' their scornfu' din,
　That mak the kindly hearts their sport,
We'll laugh, and kiss, and dance, and sing,
　And gar the langest day seem short.

THE YELLOW-HAIR'D LADDIE.

[The old words.]

THE yellow-hair'd laddie sat down on yon brae,
Cries, Milk the ewes, lassie, let nane of them gae:
And ay she milked, and ay she sang,
The yellow-hair'd laddie shall be my goodman.
    And ay she milked, &c.

The weather is cauld, and my claithing is thin,
The ewes are new clipped, they winna bught in;
They winna bught in tho' I shou'd die,
O yellow-hair'd laddie, be kind to me.
    They winna bught in, &c.

The goodwife cries butt the house, Jenny come ben,
The cheese is to mak, and the butter's to kirn;
Tho' butter, and cheese, and a' shou'd sour,
I'll crack and kiss wi' my love ae haff hour;
It's ae haff hour, and we's e'en mak it three,
For the yellow-hair'd laddie my husband shall be.

THE YELLOW-HAIR'D LADDIE.

[By RAMSAY.]

IN April when primroses paint the sweet plain,
And summer approaching rejoiceth the swain;
The yellow-hair'd laddie would oftentimes go
To wilds and deep glens where the hawthorn trees
    grow.

There, under the shade of an old sacred thorn,
With freedom he sung his loves ev'ning and morn;
He sang with so saft and enchanting a sound,
That sylvans and fairies unseen danc'd around.

The shepherd thus sung, Tho' young Maya be fair,
Her beauty is dash'd with a scornfu' proud air;
But Susie was handsome, and sweetly cou'd sing;
Her breath like the breezes perfum'd in the spring.

That Madie, in all the gay bloom of her youth,
Like the moon was inconstant, and never spoke truth;
But Susie was faithful, good-humour'd, and free,
And fair as the goddess who sprung from the sea.

That mamma's fine daughter, with all her great dow'r,
Was awkwardly airy, and frequently sour;
Then, sighing, he wish'd, would parents agree,
The witty sweet Susie his mistress might be.

~~~~~~~

EWE-BUGHTS MARION.

[In Ramsay's *Tea-Table Miscellany* this song is marked with the letter Q. as an old song with additions.]

WILL ye go to the ewe-bughts, Marion,
    And wear in the sheep wi' me?
The sun shines sweet, my Marion,
    But nae half sae sweet as thee.,

O Marion's a bonny lass,
  And the blyth blinks in her e'e;
And fain wad I marry Marion,
  Gin Marion wad marry me.

There's gowd in your garters, Marion,
  And silk on your white hauss-bane;
Fu' fain wad I kiss my Marion,
  At e'en when I come hame!

There's braw lads in Earnslaw, Marion,
  Wha gape, and glowr with their e'e,
At kirk when they see my Marion;
  But nane of them lo'es like me.

I've nine milk ewes, my Marion,
  A cow and a brawny quey,
I'll gi'e them a' to my Marion,
  Just on her bridal day;

And ye's get a green sey apron,
  And waistcoat of the London brown,
And wow but ye will be vap'ring,
  Whene'er ye gang to the town!

I'm young and stout, my Marion;
  Nane dances like me on the green;
And gin ye forsake me, Marion,
  I'll e'en gae draw up wi' Jean:

Sae put on your pearlins, Marion,
  And kyrtle of the cramasie;
And soon as my chin has nae hair on,
  I shall come west and see ye.

CA' THE EWES TO THE KNOWES.

[Was first published in Johnson's *Musical Museum*, to which it was sent by BURNS, who added some stanzas, and altered others. The poet got it taken down from the singing of a clergy-man, a Mr Clunie.]

Ca' the ewes to the knowes,
. Ca' them whare the heather grows,
Ca' them whare the burnie rows,
My bonnie dearie.

As I gaed down the water side
There I met my shepherd lad,
He row'd me sweetly in his plaid,
And he ca'd me his dearie.
Ca' the ewes, &c.

Will ye gang down the water side,
And see the waves sae sweetly glide
Beneath the hazels spreading wide,
The moon it shines fu' clearly.
Ca' the ewes, &c.

I was bred up at nae sic school,
My shepherd lad, to play the fool,
And a' the day to sit in dool,
And naebody to see me.
Ca' the ewes, &c.

Ye sall get gowns and ribbons meet,
Cauf-leather shoon upon your feet,
And in my arms ye's lie and sleep,
And ye sall be my dearie.
Ca' the ewes, &c.

If ye'll but stand to what ye've said,
  I'se gang wi' you, my shepherd lad,
And ye may row me in your plaid,
  And I sall be your dearie.
    Ca' the ewes, &c.

While waters wimple to the sea,
  While day blinks in the lift sae hie;
Till clay-cauld death sall blin' my e'e,
  Ye sall be my dearie.
    Ca' the ewes, &c.

DOWN THE BURN, DAVIE.

[This song is signed C. in the *Tea-Table Miscellany,* and is ascribed to Colonel GEORGE CRAWFORD, by the late Mr Ramsay of Ochtertyre.]

WHEN trees did bud, and fields were green,
  And broom bloom'd fair to see;
When Mary was complete fifteen,
  And love laugh'd in her e'e;
Blyth Davie's blinks her heart did move
  To speak her mind thus free,
Gang down the burn, Davie, love,
  And I shall follow thee.

Now Davie did each lad surpass,
  That dwelt on this burn side,
And Mary was the bonniest lass,
  Just meet to be a bride;
Her cheeks were rosie, red and white,
  Her een were bonnie blue;
Her looks were like Aurora bright,
  Her lips like dropping dew.

As down the burn they took their way,
　What tender tales they said!
His cheek to her's he aft did lay,
　And with her bosom play'd;
Till baith at length impatient grown,
　To be mair fully blest,
In yonder vale they lean'd them down;
　Love only saw the rest.

What pass'd, I guess was harmless play,
　And naething sure unmeet;
For ganging hame, I heard them say,
　They lik'd a wawk sae sweet;
And that they aften should return
　Sic pleasure to renew.
Quoth Mary, Love, I like the burn,
　And ay shall follow you.

THE LASS O' GOWRIE.

Upon a simmer afternoon,
A wee before the sun gade down,
My lassie, in a braw new gown,
　Cam o'er the hills to Gowrie.
The rose-bud, ting'd with morning show'r,
Blooms fresh within the sunny bow'r;
But Katie was the fairest flower
　That ever bloom'd in Gowrie.

Nae thought had I to do her wrang,
But round her waist my arms I flang,
And said, My dearie, will ye gang,
　To see the Carse o' Gowrie?

M 3

I'll tak ye to my father's ha',
In yon green fields beside the shaw ;
I'll mak you lady o' them a',
   The brawest wife in Gowrie.

A silken gown o' siller grey,
My mither coft last new-year's day,
And buskit me frae tap to tae,
   To keep me out o' Gowrie.
Daft Will, short syne, cam courting Nell,
And wan the lass, but what befel,
Or whare she's gane, she kens hersel,
   She staid na lang in Gowrie.

Sic thoughts, dear Katie, ill combine
Wi' beauty rare, and wit like thine ;
Except yoursel, my bonny quean,
   I care for nought in Gowrie.
Since first I saw you in the sheal,
To you my heart's been true and leal ;
The darkest night I fear nae de'il,
   Warlock, or witch, in Gowrie.

Saft kisses on her lips I laid,
The blush upon her cheeks soon spread ;
She whisper'd modestly, and said,
   O Pate, I'll stay in Gowrie !
The auld folks soon gae their consent,
Syne for Mess John they quickly sent,
Wha ty'd them to their heart's content,
   And now she's Lady Gowrie.

LASSIE WI' THE LINT-WHITE LOCKS.

[By Burns.]

Tune—*Rothemurche's rant.*

LASSIE *wi' the lint-white locks,*
Bonnie lassie, artless lassie,
Wilt thou wi' me tent the flocks,
Wilt thou be my dearie O!

Now Nature cleeds the flowery lea,
And a' is young and sweet like thee;
O wilt thou share its joys wi' me,
   And say thou'lt be my dearie O?
    Lassie wi', &c.

And when the welcome simmer-shower
Has cheer'd ilk drooping little flower,
We'll to the breathing woodbine bower
   At sultry noon, my dearie O.
    Lassie wi', &c.

When Cynthia lights, wi' silver ray,
The weary shearer's hameward way;
Thro' yellow waving fields we'll stray,
   And talk o' love, my dearie O.
    Lassie wi', &c.

And when the howling wintry blast,
Disturbs my lassie's midnight rest;
Enclasped to my faithfu' breast,
   I'll comfort thee, my dearie O.
    Lassie. wi', &c.

THE GRAY COCK.

O saw ye my father, or saw ye my mither,
  Or saw ye my true love John?
I saw not your father, I saw not your mither,
  But I saw your true love John.

It's now ten at night, and the stars gie nae light,
  And the bells they ring, ding dong;
He's met wi' some delay, that causeth him to stay,
  But he will be here ere long.

The surly auld carl did naething but snarl,
  And Johnny's face it grew red;
Yet, tho' he often sigh'd, he ne'er a word reply'd,
  Till all were asleep in bed.

Up Johnny rose, and to the door he goes,
  And gently tirled the pin;
The lassie taking tent, unto the door she went,
  And she open'd, and let him in.

And are ye come at last, and do I hold ye fast,
  And is my Johnny true!
I have nae to time tell, but sae lang's I like mysell,
  Sae lang shall I like you.

Flee up, flee up, my bonny gray cock,
  And craw when it is day;
Your neck shall be like the bonny beaten gold,
  And your wings of the silver gray.

The cock prov'd false, and untrue he was,
  For he crew an hour o'er soon;
The lassie thought it day, when she sent her love away,
  And it was but a blink of the moon.

LET ME IN THIS AE NIGHT.

[The old words.]

O LASSIE are ye sleepin yet,
Or are ye waukin, I wad wit,
For luve has bound me hand and fit,
  And I wad fain be in, jo.
    O let me in this ae night,
      This ae, ae, ae night,
    O let me in this ae night,
      And I'll no come back again, jo.

The morn it is the term-day,
I maun awa, I canna stay;
O pity me before I gae,
  And rise and let me in, jo.
    O let me in, &c.

The night it is baith cauld and weet,
The morn it will be snaw and sleet,
My shoon are frozen to my feet
  In standing here my lane, jo.
    O let me in, &c.

I am the laird o' Windy-wa's,
I cam na here without a cause,
And I hae gotten mony fa's
  In comin thro' the plain, jo.
    O let me in, &c.

My father's walking in the street,
My mither the chamber keys does keep,
My chamber door does chirp and cheep,
   I daur na let you in, jo.
     O gae your ways this ae night,
      This ae, ae, ae night,
     O gae your ways this ae night,
      For I daur na let you in, jo.

But I'll come stealing saftly in,
And cannily mak little din;
My fitstep-tread there's nane can ken
   For the sughin wind and rain, jo.
     O let me in, &c.

Cast up the door unto the weet,
Cast aff your shoon frae aff your feet,
Syne to my chamber ye may creep,
   But ye maun na do't again, jo.
     O leeze me on this ae night,
      This ae, ae, ae night,
     The joys we've had this ae night,
      Your chamber wa's within, jo!

LET ME IN THIS AE NIGHT.

[By BURNS.]

O LASSIE, art thou sleeping yet,
Or art thou wakin, I would wit,
For love has bound me hand and foot,
   And I would fain be in, jo.
     O let me in this ae night,
      This ae, ae, ae night;
     For pity's sake this ae night,
      O rise and let me in, jo.

Thou hear'st the winter wind and weet,
Nae star blinks thro' the driving sleet;
Tak pity on my weary feet,
   And shield me frae the rain, jo.
     O let me in, &c.

The bitter blast that round me blaws,
Unheeded howls, unheeded fa's;
The cauldness o' thy heart's the cause
   Of a' my grief and pain, jo.
     O let me in, &c.

HER ANSWER.

O tell na me o' wind and rain,
Upbraid na me wi' cauld disdain!
Gae back the gait ye cam again,
   I winna let you in, jo.
     I tell you now this ae night,
       This ae, ae, ae night,
     And ance for a' this ae night,
       I winna let you in, jo.

The snellest blast, at mirkest hours,
That round the pathless wand'rer pours,
Is nocht to what poor she endures
   That's trusted faithless man, jo.
     I tell you now, &c.

The sweetest flower that deck'd the mead,
Now trodden like the vilest weed:
Let simple maid the lesson read,
   The weird may be her ain, jo.
     I tell you now, &c.

The bird that charm'd his summer-day,
Is now the cruel fowler's prey;
Let witless, trusting, woman say
  How aft her fate's the same, jo.
  I tell you now, &c.

<hr>

RIGS O' BARLEY.

[By Burns.]

Tune—*Corn rigs are bonnie.*

It was upon a Lammas night,
  When corn rigs are bonnie,
Beneath the moon's unclouded light,
  I held awa to Annie;
The time flew by wi' tentless heed,
  Till 'tween the late and early,
Wi' sma' persuasion she agreed
  To see me thro' the barley.
    Corn rigs, an' barley rigs,
      An' corn rigs are bonnie:
    I'll ne'er forget that happy night,
      Amang the rigs wi' Annie.

The sky was blue, the wind was still,
  The moon was shining clearly;
I set her down wi' right good will,
  Amang the rigs o' barley:
I ken'd her heart was a' my ain;
  I lov'd her most sincerely;
I kiss'd her owre and owre again
  Amang the rigs o' barley.
    Corn rigs, &c.

I lock'd her in my fond embrace;
  Her heart was beating rarely:
My blessings on that happy place,
  Amang the rigs o' barley!
But by the moon and stars so bright,
  That shone that hour so clearly!
She ay shall bless that happy night,
  Amang the rigs o' barley.
    Corn rigs, &c.

I hae been blythe wi' comrades dear;
  I hae been merry drinkin;
I hae been joyfu' gath'ring gear;
  I hae been happy thinkin:
But a' the pleasures e'er I saw,
  Tho' three times doubl'd fairly,
That happy night was worth them a',
  Amang the rigs o' barley.
    Corn rigs, &c.

~~~~~~~~~~~

ANNA.

[By Burns.]

Tune—*Banks of Banna.*

Yestreen I had a pint o' wine,
  A place where body saw na';
Yestreen lay on this breast o' mine
  The gowden locks of Anna.
The hungry Jew in wilderness
  Rejoicing o'er his manna,
Was naething to my hinny bliss
  Upon the lips of Anna.

N

Ye monarchs tak the east and west,
   Frae Indus to Savannah!
Gie me within my straining grasp,
   The melting form of Anna.
There I'll despise imperial charms,
   An Empress or Sultana,
While dying raptures in her arms
   I give and take with Anna.

Awa thou flaunting god of day!
   Awa thou pale Diana!
Ilk star gae hide thy twinkling ray
   When I'm to meet my Anna.
Come, in thy raven plumage, night,
   Sun, moon, and stars, withdrawn a';
And bring an angel pen to write
   My transports wi' my Anna!

POLWART ON THE GREEN.

[By RAMSAY.]

At Polwart on the green,
   If you'll meet me the morn,
Where lasses do convene
   To dance about the thorn;
A kindly welcome you shall meet,
   Frae her wha likes to view
A lover and a lad complete,
   The lad and lover you.

Let dorty dames say Na,
   As lang as e'er they please,
Seem caulder than the sna',
   While inwardly they bleeze;

But I will frankly shaw my mind,,
  And yield my heart to thee;
Be ever to the captive kind,
  That langs nae to be free.

At Polwart on the green,
  Amang the new-mawn hay,
With sangs and dancing keen,
  We'll pass the heartsome day.
At night, if beds be o'er thrang laid,
  And thou be twin'd of thine,
Thou shalt be welcome, my dear lad,
  To tak a part of mine.

THE BONNY BRUCKET LASSIE.

[The two first lines of this song are all of it that is old. The rest of the song was written by JAMES TYTLER, editor of the second edition of the celebrated Encyclopedia Britannica, and well known in Edinburgh by the name of Balloon Tytler, from having ascended from Comely Garden in a fire balloon, constructed after the plan of Montgolfier. For an account of this very eccentric character, see CROMEK's *Reliques of Burns*, 8vo. p. 306.]

THE bonny brucket lassie,
  She's blue beneath the een;
She was the fairest lassie
  That danc'd on the green.
A lad he loo'd her dearly,
  She did his love return;
But he his vows has broken,
  And left her for to mourn.

My shape, she says, was handsome,
  My face was fair and clean,
But now I'm bonny brucket,
  And blue beneath the een:
My eyes were bright and sparkling,
  Before that they turn'd blue;
But now they're dull with weeping,
  And a', my love, for you.

My person it was comely,
  My shape they said was neat;
But now I am quite changed,
  My stays they winna meet.
A' night I sleeped soundly,
  My mind was never sad;
But now my rest is broken,
  Wi' thinking o' my lad.

O could I live in darkness,
  Or hide me in the sea,
Since my love is unfaithful,
  And has forsaken me!
No other love I suffer'd
  Within my breast to dwell;
In nought I have offended
  But loving him too well.

Her lover heard her mourning,
  As by he chanc'd to pass;
And press'd unto his bosom
  The lovely brucket lass.
My dear, he said, cease grieving,
  Since that your love's so true,
My bonny brucket lassie,
  I'll faithful prove to you.

ALLOA HOUSE.

[The air of this song was composed by Mr Oswald, a music-
seller in London.]

The spring-time returns, and clothes the green plains,
 And Alloa shines more cheerful and gay;
The lark tunes his throat, and the neighbouring swains,
 Sing merrily round me wherever I stray:
But Sandy nae mair returns to my view;
 Nae spring-time me cheers, nae music can charm;
He's gane! and, I fear me, for ever: adieu!
 Adieu every pleasure this bosom can warm!

O Alloa house! how much art thou chang'd!
 How silent, how dull to me is each grove!
Alane I here wander where ance we both rang'd,
 Alas! where to please me my Sandy ance strove!
Here, Sandy, I heard the tales that you tauld,
 Here list'ned too fond whenever you sung;
Am I grown less fair then, that you are turn'd cauld?
 Or, foolish, believ'd a false flattering tongue?

So spoke the fair maid, when sorrow's keen pain,
 And shame, her last fault'ring accents supprest;
For fate, at that moment, brought back her dear swain,
 Who heard, and with rapture his Nelly addrest:
My Nelly! my fair, I come; O my love!
 Nae power shall thee tear again from my arms,
And Nelly! nae mair thy fond shepherd reprove,
 Who knows thy fair worth, and adores a' thy charms.

She heard; and new joy shot thro' her saft frame;
 And will you, my love! be true? she replied:
And live I to meet my fond shepherd the same?
 Or dream I that Sandy will make me his bride?

N 3

O Nelly! I live to find thee still kind:
Still true to thy swain, and lovely as true:
Then adieu to a' sorrow; what soul is so blind,
As not to live happy for ever with you?

~~~~~~~~~~~~

THE SILKEN SNOODED LASSIE.

[The first and second verses of this song are the same with the
last and second verses of the old song of Galla Water, of which
it was probably intended by some good-natured poet to be the
continuation.]

Coming through the broom at e'en,
  And coming through the broom sae dreary,
The lassie lost her silken snood,
  Which cost her many a blurt and blear-eye.

Fair her hair, and brent her brow,
  And bonny blue her een when near ye;
The mair I priv'd her bonny mou',
  The mair I wish'd her for my deary.

The broom was lang, the lassie gay,
  And O but I was unco cheary;
The snood was tint, a well-a-day!
  For mirth was turn'd to blurt and blear-eye.

I prest her hand, she sigh'd, I woo'd,
  And spear'd, What gars ye sob, my deary?
Quoth she, I've lost my silken snood,
  And never mair can look sae cheary.

I said, Ne'er mind the silken snood,
    Nae langer mourn, nor look sae dreary ;
I'll buy you ane that's twice as good,
    If you'll consent to be my deary.

Quoth she, If you will aye be mine,
    Nae mair the snood shall make me dreary :
I vow'd, I seal'd, and bless the time
    That in the broom I met my deary.

MY AIN KIND DEARY O.

[Mostly composed by FERGUSSON, in one of his merry humours,
from an old song beginning, " I'll rowe thee o'er the lea-rig."
—BURNS.]

WILL ye gang o'er the lee-rig,
    My ain kind deary O,
And cuddle there sae kindly,
    Wi' me, my kind deary O.

At thorny dike, and birken tree,
    We'll daff, and ne'er be weary O ;
They'll scug ill een frae you and me,
    Mine ain kind deary O.

Nae herds wi' kent, or colly there,
    Shall ever come to fear ye O ;
But lavrocks whistling in the air,
    Shall woo, like me, their deary O.

While others herd their lambs and ewes,
    And toil for warld's gear, my jo,
Upon the lee my pleasure grows,
    Wi' you, my kind deary O !

GLOOMY WINTER.

[By Tanny Hill.]

Gloomy winter's now awa,
Saft the western breezes blaw;
'Mang the birks o' Stanley shaw
  The mavis sings fu' cheerie O.
Sweet the crow-flower's early bell
Decks Gleniffer's dewy dell,
Blooming like thy bonnie sell,
  My young, my artless dearie O.
Come, my lassie, let us stray
O'er Glenkilloch's sunny brae,
Blythely spend the gowden day,
  'Midst joys that never weary O.

Tow'ring o'er the Newton woods,
Lavrocks fan the snaw-white clouds,
Siller saughs wi' downy buds
  Adorn the bank sae briery O.
Round the silvan fairy nooks,
Feath'ry brackens fringe the rocks,
'Neath the brae the burnie jouks,
  And ilka thing is cheery O.
Trees may bud, and birds may sing,
Flowers may bloom, and verdure spring,
Joy to me they canna bring,
  Unless wi' thee, my dearie O.

LIZA BAILLIE.

My bonny Liza Baillie,
  I'll row you in my plaidie,
If you will gang alang wi' me
  And be a Highland lady.]

If I wad gang alang wi' you,
  They wadna ca' me wise, sir,
For I can neither card nor spin,
  Nor yet can I speak Erse, sir.

My bonny Liza Baillie,
  Your minny canna want you;
Sae let the trooper gang his lane,
  And carry his ain portmanteau.

But she's cast aff her bonny shoon,
  Made o' the Spanish leather,
And she's put on her Highland progues
  To skip amang the heather.

And she's cast aff her bonny gown,
  A' wrought wi' gowd and satin,
And she's put on a tartan plaid,
  To sport among the braken.

She wadna hae a Lawland laird,
  Nor be an English lady;
But she's awa wi' Duncan Grahame,
  He's row'd her in his plaidie.

HAD AWA FRAE ME, DONALD.

O COME awa, come awa,
    Come awa wi' me, Jenny;
Sic frowns I canna bear frae ane
    Whase smiles ance ravish'd me, Jenny:
If you'll be kind, you'll never find
    That aught sall alter me, Jenny;
For you're the mistress of my mind,
    Whate'er you think of me, Jenny.

First when your sweets enslav'd my heart,
    You seem'd to favour me, Jenny;
But now, alas! you act a part
    That speaks inconstancy, Jenny;
Inconstancy is sic a vice,
    'Tis not befitting thee, Jenny;
It suits not wi' your virtue nice
    To carry sae to me, Jenny,

HER ANSWER.

O had awa, had awa,
    Had awa frae me, Donald;
Your heart is made o'er big for ane,
    It is not meet for me, Donald.
Some fickle mistress you may find,
    Will change as aft as thee, Donald;
To ilka swain she will prove kind,
    And nae less kind to thee, Donald.

But I've a heart that's naething such,
    'Tis fill'd with honesty, Donald;
I'll ne'er love mony, I'll love much,
    I hate all levity, Donald.

Therefore nae mair with art pretend
  Your heart is chained to mine, Donald,
For words of falsehood ill defend
  A roving love like thine, Donald.

First when you courted, I must own
  I frankly favour'd you, Donald;
Apparent worth, and fair renown,
  Made me believe you true, Donald.
Ilk virtue then seem'd to adorn
  The man esteem'd by me, Donald;
But now, the mask fall'n aff, I scorn
  To ware a thought on thee, Donald.

And now, for ever, had awa,
  Had awa frae me, Donald;
Gae seek a heart that's like your ain,
  And come nae mair to me, Donald;
For I'll reserve mysell for ane,
  For ane that's liker me, Donald;
If sic a ane I canna find,
  I'll ne'er lo'e man, nor thee, Donald.

DONALD.

Then I'm thy man, and false report
  Has only tald a lie, Jenny;
To try thy truth, and make us sport,
  The tale was rais'd by me, Jenny.

JENNY.

When this ye prove, and still can love,
  Then come awa to me Donald;
I'm weel content ne'er to repent
  That I hae smil'd on thee, Donald.

THE MILL, MILL O.

[The original, or at least a song evidently prior to this one of
RAMSAY'S, is still extant. It begins,—
"The mill, mill O, and the kill, kill O,
And the coggin o' Peggy's wheel O," &c.
BURNS.]

BENEATH a green shade I fand a fair maid,
Was sleeping sound and still O;
A' lowan wi' love, my fancy did rove
Around her wi' good will O:
Her bosom I prest; but sunk in her rest,
She stirr'd na my joy to spill O:
While kindly she slept, close to her I crept,
And kiss'd, and kiss'd her my fill O.

Oblig'd by command in Flanders to land,
T' employ my courage and skill O,
Frae her quietly I staw, hoist sails and awa,
For the wind blew fair on the bill O.
Twa years brought me hame, where loud-fraising fame
Tald me with a voice right shrill O,
My lass, like a fool, had mounted the stool,
Nor kend wha had done her the ill O.

Mair fond of her charms, with my son in her arms,
I ferlying speir'd how she fell O.
Wi' the tear in her eye, quoth she, Let me die,
Sweet sir, gin I can tell O.
Love gave the command, I took her by the hand,
And bade a' her fears expel O,
And nae mair look wan, for I was the man
Wha had done her the deed mysel O.

My bonny sweet lass, on the gowany grass,
  Beneath the shellin-hill O,
If I did offence, I'se make ye amends
  Before I leave Peggy's mill O.
O the mill, mill O, and the kill, kill O,
  And the coggin of the wheel O:
The sack and the sieve, a' that ye maun leave,
  And round with a sodger reel O.

~~~~~~~~~~

THE SODGER'S RETURN.

[By BURNS.]

Air—*The Mill, Mill o.*

WHEN wild war's deadly blast was blawn,
  And gentle peace returning,
Wi' mony a sweet babe fatherless,
  And mony a widow mourning:
I left the lines and tented field,
  Where lang I'd been a lodger,
My humble knapsack a' my wealth,
  A poor and honest sodger.

A leal, light heart was in my breast,
  My hand unstain'd wi' plunder:
And for fair Scotia, hame again,
  I cheery on did wander.
I thought upon the banks o' Coil,
  I thought upon my Nancy,
I thought upon the witching smile
  That caught my youthful fancy.

o

At length I reach'd the bonny glen,
  Where early life I sported;
I pass'd the mill, and trysting thorn,
  Where Nancy aft I courted:
Wha spied I but my ain dear maid,
  Down by her mother's dwelling!
And turn'd me round to hide the flood
  That in my een was swelling.

Wi' alter'd voice, quoth I, sweet lass,
  Sweet as yon hawthorn's blossom,
O! happy, happy may he be,
  That's dearest to thy bosom!
My purse is light, I've far to gang,
  And fain would be thy lodger;
I've serv'd my king and country lang,
  Take pity on a sodger.

Sae wistfully she gaz'd on me,
  And lovelier was than ever;
Quo' she, a sodger ance I lo'ed,
  Forget him shall I never:
Our humble cot, and hamely fare,
  Ye freely shall partake it,
That gallant badge, the dear cockade,
  Ye're welcome for the sake o't.

She gaz'd—she redden'd like a rose—
  Syne pale like ony lily;
She sank within my arms and cried,
  Art thou my ain dear Willie?
By Him who made yon sun and sky—
  By whom true love's regarded,
I am the man; and thus may still
  True lovers be rewarded.

The wars are o'er, and I'm come hame,
  And find thee still true-hearted!
Tho' poor in gear, we're rich in love,
  And mair we'se ne'er be parted.
Quo' she, my grandsire left me gowd,
  A mailen plenish'd fairly;
And come, my faithfu' sodger lad,
  Thou'rt welcome to it dearly!

For gold the merchant ploughs the main,
  The farmer ploughs the manor;
But glory is the sodger's prize,
  The sodger's wealth is honour;
The brave poor sodger ne'er despise,
  Nor count him as a stranger,
Remember he's his country's stay
  In day and hour of danger.

* * * * *

MY JOHNIE.

Tune—*Johnny's gray brecks.*

Jenny's heart was frank and free,
  And wooers she had mony, yet
Her sang was aye, Of a' I see,
  Commend me to my Johnie yet.
For, air and late, he has sic gate
  To mak a body cheary, that
I wish to be, before I die,
  His ain kind deary yet.

Now Jenny's face was fu' o' grace,
  Her shape was sma' and genty-like,
And few or nane in a' the place
  Had gowd and gear mair plenty yet;

Tho' war's alarms, and Johnie's charms,
  Had gart her aft look eerie, yet
She sung wi' glee, I hope to be
  My Johnie's ain kind deary yet:

What tho' he's now gaen far awa,
  Where guns and cannons rattle, yet
Unless my Johnie chance to fa'   .
  In some uncanny battle, yet
Till he return, his breast will burn
  Wi' love that will confound me yet,
For I hope to see, before I die,
  His bairns a' dance around me yet.

~~~~~~~~~~~

BONNY CHRISTY,

[By RAMSAY.]

How sweetly smells the simmer green!
  Sweet taste the peach and cherry;
Painting and order please our een,
  And claret makes us merry:
But finest colours, fruits, and flowers,
  And wine, tho' I be thirsty,
Lose a' their charms, and weaker powers,
  Compar'd with those of Christy.

When wand'ring o'er the flow'ry park,
  No nat'ral beauty wanting,
How lightsome is't to hear the lark,
  And birds in concert chanting!
But if my Christy tunes her voice,
  I'm rapt in admiration;
My thoughts with ecstasies rejoice,
  And drap the haill creation.

Whene'er she smiles a kindly glance,
  I take the happy omen,
And aften mint to make advance,
  Hoping she'll prove a woman:
But, dubious of my ain desert,
  My sentiments I smother;
With secret sighs I vex my heart,
  For fear she love another.

Thus sang blate Edie by a burn,
  His Christy did o'erhear him;
She doughtna let her lover mourn,
  But e'er he wist drew near him;
She spake her favour with a look,
  Which left nae room to doubt her;
He wisely this white minute took,
  And flang his arms about her.

My Christy!—witness, bonny stream,
  Sic joys frae tears arising,
I wish this mayna be a dream;
  O love the maist surprising!
Time was too precious now for tauk;
  This point of a' his wishes
He wadna with set speeches bauk,
  But war'd it a' on kisses.

THE COLLIER'S BONNY LASSIE.

[The first half stanza is old; the rest of the song is Ramsay's.]

The collier has a daughter,
  And O she's wond'rous bonny;
A laird he was that sought her,
  Rich baith in lands and money:

The tutors watch'd the motion
  Of this young honest lover;
But love is like the ocean,
  Wha can its depth discover!

He had the art to please ye,
  And was by a' respected;
His airs sat round him easy,
  Genteel, but unaffected.
The collier's bonny lassie,
  Fair as the new-blown lilie,
Ay sweet, and never saucy,
  Secur'd the heart of Willie.

He lov'd beyond expression
  The charms that were about her,
And panted for possession;
  His life was dull without her.
After mature resolving,
  Close to his breast he held her,
In saftest flames dissolving,
  He tenderly thus tell'd her:

My bonny collier's daughter,
  Let naething discompose ye,
'Tis no your scanty tocher
  Shall ever gar me lose ye;
For I have gear in plenty,
  And love says, 'tis my duty
To ware what Heaven has lent me,
  Upon your wit and beauty.

O WERE I ON PARNASSUS' HILL.

[Composed by BURNS out of compliment to Mrs B.]

Tune—*My love is lost to me.*

O WERE I on Parnassus' hill!
Or had of Helicon my fill;
That I might catch poetic skill,
    To sing how dear I love thee.
But Nith maun be my muse's well,
My muse maun be thy bonnie sell;
On Corsincon I'll glowr and spell,
    And write how dear I love thee.

Then come, sweet muse, inspire my lay,
For a' the lee-lang simmer's day,
I coudna sing, I coudna say,
    How much, how dear I love thee.
I see thee dancing o'er the green,
Thy waist sae jimp, thy limbs sae clean,
Thy tempting lips, thy roguish e'en—
    By heaven and earth I love thee!

By night, by day, a-field, at hame,
The thoughts o' thee my breast inflame;
And ay I muse and sing thy name,
    I only live to love thee.
Tho' I were doom'd to wander on,
Beyond the sea, beyond the sun,
Till my last weary sand was run;
    Till then—and then I love thee.

LOCH EROCH SIDE.

As I came by Loch Eroch side,
   The lofty hills surveying,
The water clear, the heather blooms,
   Their fragrance sweet conveying,
I met, unsought, my lovely maid,
   I found her like May morning;
With graces sweet, and charms so rare,
   'Her' person all adorning.

How kind her looks, how blest was I,
   While in my arms I press'd her!
And she her wishes scarce conceal'd,
   As fondly I caress'd her.
She said, If that your heart be true,
   If constantly you'll love me,
I heed not cares, nor fortune's frowns;
   Nor ought but death shall move me.

But faithful, loving, true, and kind,
   For ever you shall find me;
And of our meeting here so sweet,
   Loch Eroch side will mind me.
Enraptur'd then, My lovely lass!
   I cry'd, no more we'll tarry;
We'll leave the fair Loch Eroch side,
   For lovers soon should marry.

~~~~~~~~~~~

I LOE NA A LADDIE BUT ANE.

Tune—*Happy Dick Dawson.*

I loe nae a laddie but ane,
   He loes na a lassie but me;

He's willing to make me his ain,
   An' his ain I am willing to be.
Ho coft me a rokley o' blue,
   ' A pair o' mittens o' green,
And his price was a kiss o' my mou;
   An' I paid him the debt yestreen.

My mither's ay makin' a phraze,
   That I'm lucky young to be wed;
But lang ere she countit my days,
   O' me she was brought to bed:
Sae mither, just settle your tongue,
   An' dinna be flytin' sae bauld,
For we can do the thing when we're young,
   That we canna do weel when we're auld.

~~~~~~~~~

I'M O'ER YOUNG TO MARRY YET.

[The chorus is old; the rest is BURNS's.]

I AM my mammy's ae bairn,
   Wi' unco folk I weary, sir,
And lying in a man's bed,
   I'm fley'd it make me irie, sir.
     I'm o'er young, I'm o'er young,
      I'm o'er young to marry yet,
     I'm o'er young, 'twad be a sin
      To tak me frae my mammy yet.

Hallowmass is come and gane,
   The nights are lang in winter, sir;
And you an' I in ae bed,
   In trowth, I dare na venture, sir.
     I'm o'er young, &c.

Fu' loud and shill the frosty wind
  Blaws thro' the leafless timmer, sir;
But if ye come this gate again,
  I'll aulder be gin simmer, sir.
    I'm o'er young, &c.

~~~~~~~~~~

FOR THE LOVE OF JEAN.

[In the *Tea-Table Miscellany* this song is marked with the letter Z. as being an old song.]

Jocky said to Jeany, Jeany, wilt thou do't?
Ne'er a fit, quo' Jeany, for my tocher good,
For my tocher good, I winna marry thee.
E'en's ye like, quo' Johny, ye may let it be.

I hae gowd and gear, I hae land enough,
I hae seven good owsen ganging in a pleugh,
Ganging in a pleugh, and linking o'er the lee,
And gin ye winna tak me, I can let ye be.

I hae a good ha' house, a barn, and a byre,
A stack afore the door, I'll make a rantin fire,
I'll make a rantin fire, and merry shall we be,
And gin ye winna tak me, I can let ye be.

Jeany said to Jocky, Gin ye winna tell,
Ye shall be the lad, I'll be the lass mysell;
Ye're a bonny lad, and I'm a lassie free,
Ye're welcomer to tak me than to let me be.

THE MILLER.

O MERRY may the maid be
   That marries the miller,
For foul day, and fair day,
   He's ay bringing till her;
He's ay a penny in his purse,
   For dinner and for supper;
And, gin she please, a good fat cheese,
   And lumps of yellow butter.

When Jamie first did woo me,
   I speir'd what was his calling;
Fair maid, says he, O come and see,
   Ye're welcome to my dwalling:
Though I was shy, yet I cou'd spy
   The truth of what he told me,
And that his house was warm and couth,
   And room in it to hold me.

Behind the door a bag of meal,
   And in the kist was plenty
Of good hard cakes, his mither bakes,
   And bannocks were na scanty;
A good fat sow, a sleeky cow
   Was standing in the byre;
Whilst lazy puss with mealy mouse
   Was playing at the fire.

Good signs are these, my mither says,
   And bids me tak the miller;
For foul day, and fair day,
   He's ay bringing till her:

For meal and malt she does na want,
  Nor ony thing that's dainty;
And now and then a keckling hen
  To lay her eggs in plenty.

In winter when the wind and rain
  Blaws o'er the house and byre,
He sits beside a clean hearth-stane
  Before a rousing fire;
With nut-brown ale he tells his tale,
  Which rows him o'er fu' nappy:
Who'd be a king?—a petty thing,
  When a miller lives so happy.

~~~~~~~~~~

THE BRAW WOOER.

[By Burns.]

Tune—*The Lothian lassie.*

Last May a braw wooer cam down the lang glen,
  And sair wi' his love he did deave me;
I said there was naething I hated like men,
  The deuce gae wi'm to believe me, believe me,
  The deuce gae wi'm to believe me.

He spak o' the darts in my bonnie black een,
  And vow'd for my love he was dying;
I said he might die when he liked for Jean,
  The Lord forgie me for lying, for lying,
  The Lord forgie me for lying!

A weel-stocked mailen, himsel for the laird,
  And marriage aff-hand, were his proffers:
I never loot on that I kenn'd it, or car'd,
  But thought I might hae waur offers, waur offers,
  But thought I might hae waur offers.

But what wad ye think? in a fortnight or less,
  The deil tak his taste to gae near her!
He up the lang loan to my black cousin Bess,
  Guess ye how, the jad! I could bear her, could
    bear her,
  Guess ye how, the jad! I could bear her.

But a' the niest week as I fretted wi' care,
  I gaed to the tryste o' Dalgarnock,
And wha but my fine fickle lover was there,
  I glowr'd as I'd seen a warlock, a warlock,
  I glowr'd as I'd seen a warlock.

But owre my left shouther I gae him a blink,
  Least neebors might say I was saucy;
My wooer he caper'd as he'd been in drink,
  And vow'd I was his dear lassie, dear lassie,
  And vow'd I was his dear lassie.

I spier'd for my cousin fu' couthy and sweet,
  Gin she had recover'd her hearin,
And how her new shoon fit her auld shachl't feet,
  But, heavens! how he fell a swearin, a swearin,
  But, heavens! how he fell a swearin.

He begged, for Gudesake! I wad be his wife,
  Or else I wad kill him wi' sorrow:
So e'en to preserve the poor body in life,
  I think I maun wed him to-morrow, to-morrow,
  I think I maun wed him to-morrow.

WHISTLE AND I'LL COME TO YOU, MY LAD.

[By Burns.]

O whistle and I'll come to you, my lad,
O whistle and I'll come to you, my lad :
Tho' father and mither and a' should gae mad,
Thy Jeany will venture wi' ye, my lad.

But warily tent, when you come to court me,
And come nae unless the back-yett be a-jee ;
Syne up the back-stile and let naebody see,
And come as ye were na comin to me.
And come, &c.
 O whistle, &c.

At kirk or at market, whene'er ye meet me,
Gang by me as tho' that ye car'd not a flie ;
But steal me a blink o' your bonnie black e'e,
Yet look as ye were na lookin at me.
Yet look, &c.
 O whistle, &c.

Ay vow and protest that ye care na for me,
And whyles ye may lightly my beauty a wee ;
But court nae anither, tho' jokin ye be,
For fear that she wyle your fancy frae me.
For fear, &c.
 O whistle, &c.

FOR THE SAKE OF SOMEBODY.

[The old words.]

For the sake of somebody,
 For the sake of somebody ;
I could wake a winter night,
 For the sake of somebody.

I am gawn to seek a wife,
   L am gawn to buy a plaidy;
I have three stane of woo,
   Carlin, is thy daughter ready?
     For the sake, &c.

Betty, lassy, say't thysell,
   Tho' thy dame be ill to shoo,
First we'll buckle, then we'll tell,
   Let her flyte and syne come too:
What signifies a mither's gloom,
   When love in kisses come in play?
Shou'd we wither in our bloom,
   And in simmer mak nae hay?
     For the sake, &c.

SHE.—Bonny lad, I carena by,
   Tho' I try my luck with thee,
Since ye are content to tye
   The ha'f-mark bridal band with me;
I'll slip hame and wash my feet,
   And steal on linens fair and clean,
Syne at the trysting-place we'll meet,
   To do but what my dame has done.
     For the sake, &c.

HE.—Now my lovely Betty gives
   Consent in sic a heartsome gate,
It me frae a' my care relieves,
   And doubts that gart me aft look blate:
Then let us gang and get the grace,
   For they that have an appetite
Should eat;—and lovers should embrace;
   If these be faults, 'tis nature's wyte.
     For the sake, &c.

FOR THE SAKE O' SOMEBODY.

[By Burns.]

My heart is sair I dare na tell,
　My heart is sair for somebody ;
I could wake a winter night
　For the sake o' somebody.
　　Oh-hon ! for somebody !
　　Oh-hey ! for somebody !
I could range the world around,
For the sake o' somebody.

Ye powers that smile on virtuous love,
　O sweetly smile on somebody !
Frae ilka danger keep him free,
　And send me safe my somebody.
　　Oh-hon ! for somebody !
　　Oh-hey ! for somebody !
I wad do—what wad I not,
For the sake o' somebody ?

~~~~~~~~

I LOVE MY JEAN.

[By Burns.]

Tune—*Miss Admiral Gordon's strathspey.*

Of a' the airts the wind can blaw,
　I dearly like the west,
For there the bonnie lassie lives,
　The lassie I lo'e best :

There wild woods grow, and rivers row,
    And mony a hill between;
But day and night my fancy's flight
    Is ever wi' my Jean.

I see her in the dewy flowers,
    I see her sweet and fair:
I hear her in the tunefu' birds,
    I hear her charm the air:
There's not a bonnie flower that springs
    By fountain, shaw, or green,
There's not a bonnie bird that sings,
    But minds me o' my Jean.

THE POSIE.

[By Burns.]

O luve will venture in where it daur na weel be seen,
O luve will venture in where wisdom ance has been;
But I will down yon river rove, amang the wood sae
    green,
    And a' to pu' a posie to my ain dear May.

The primrose I will pu', the firstling o' the year,
And I will pu' the pink, the emblem o' my dear,
For she's the pink o' womankind, and blooms without
    a peer;
    And a' to be a posie to my ain dear May.

I'll pu' the budding rose, when Phœbus peeps in view,
For it's like a baumy kiss o' her sweet bonnie mou;
The hyacinth's for constancy wi' its unchanging blue,
    And a' to be a posie to my ain dear May.

The lily it is pure, and the lily it is fair,
And in her lovely bosom I'll place the lily there;
The daisy's for simplicity and unaffected air,
    And a' to be a posie to my ain dear May.

The hawthorn I will pu', wi' its locks o' siller grey,
Where, like an aged man, it stands at break o' day,
But the songster's nest within the bush I winna tak
    away;
    And a' to be a posie to my ain dear May.

The woodbine I will pu' when the e'ening star is near,
And the diamond draps o' dew shall be her een sae
    clear;
The violet's for modesty which weel she fa's to wear,
    And a' to be a posie to my ain dear May.

I'll tie the posie round wi' the silken band o' luve,
And I'll place it in her breast, and I'll swear by a' above,
That to my latest draught o' life the band shall ne'er
    remove,
    And this will be a posie to my ain dear May.

HAY'S BONNY LASSIE.

[By RAMSAY. The heroine was daughter of John Hay, Earl
or Marquis of Tweeddale, and late Countess-dowager of Rox-
burgh. She died at Broomlands, near Kelso, some time between the years 1720 and 1740.—BURNS.]

By smooth-winding Tay a swain was reclining,
Aft cry'd he, Oh hey! maun I still live pining
Mysell thus awa, and dare na discover
To my bonny Hay, that I am her lover?

Nae mair it will hide, the flame waxes stronger;
If she's not my bride, my days are nae longer;
Then I'll tak a heart, and try at a venture,
May be, ere we part, my vows may content her.

She's fresh as the spring, and sweet as Aurora,
When birds mount and sing, bidding day a good-mor-
    row;
The swaird of the mead, enamell'd with daisies,
Looks wither'd and dead when twin'd of her graces.

But if she appear where verdure invites her,
The fountains run clear, and flowers smell the sweeter;
'Tis heaven to be by when her wit is a-flowing,
Her smiles and bright eye set my spirits a-glowing.

The mair that I gaze, the deeper I'm wounded;
Struck dumb with amaze, my mind is confounded;
I'm all in a fire, dear maid, to caress ye,
For a' my desire is Hay's bonny lassie.

SAW YE NAE MY PEGGY.

Saw ye nae my Peggy,
Saw ye nae my Peggy,
Saw ye nae my Peggy,
    Coming o'er the lee?
Sure a finer creature
Ne'er was form'd by nature,
So complete each feature,
    So divine is she.

O, how Peggy charms me!
Every look still warms me;
Every thought alarms me,
   Lest she love nae me.
Peggy doth discover
Nought but charms all over;
Nature bids me love her;
   That's a law to me.

Who would leave a lover,
To become a rover?
No, I'll ne'er give over,
   'Till I happy be.   .
For since love inspires me,.
As her beauty fires me,
And her absence tires me,
   Nought can please but she..

When I hope to gain her,
Fate seems to detain her;
Cou'd I but obtain her,
   Happy wou'd I be.
I'll ly down before her,.
Bless, sigh, and adore her,
With faint looks implore her,
   'Till she pity me.

~~~~~~~~~~~

SWEET SUSAN.

Tune—*Leader-haughs.*

THE morn was fair, saft was the air,
   All nature's sweets were springing;
The buds did bow with silver dew,
   Ten thousand birds were singing:

When on the bent, with blythe content,
　Young Jamie sang his marrow,
Nae bonnier lass e'er trod the grass
　On Leader-haughs and Yarrow.

How sweet her face, where ev'ry grace
　In heavenly beauty's planted:
Her smiling een, and comely mein,
　That nae perfection wanted.
I'll never fret, nor ban my fate,
　But bless my bonny marrow;
If her dear smile my doubts beguile,
　My mind shall ken nae sorrow.

Yet tho' she's fair, and has full share
　Of ev'ry charm enchanting,
Each good turns ill, and soon will kill
　Poor me, if love be wanting.
O bonny lass! have but the grace
　To think ere ye gae furder,
Your joys maun flit, if ye commit
　The crying sin of murder.

My wand'ring ghaist will ne'er get rest,
　And day and night affright ye;
But if ye're kind, with joyful mind,
　I'll study to delight ye.
Our years around with love thus crown'd,
　From all things joy shall borrow;
Thus none shall be more blest than we
　On Leader-haughs and Yarrow.

O sweetest Sue! 'tis only you
　Can make life worth my wishes,
If equal love your mind can move
　To grant this best of blisses.

Thou art my sun, and thy least frown
  Would blast me in the blossom:
But if thou shine, and make me thine,
  I'll flourish in thy bosom.

WERT THOU BUT MINE AIN THING.

WERT thou but mine ain thing,
  I would love thee, I would love thee;
Wert thou but mine ain thing,
  How dearly would I love thee.

As round the elm th' enamour'd vine
Delights with wanton arms to twine,
So I'd encircle thee in mine,
  And show how much I love thee.
    Wert thou but, &c.

This earth my paradise should be,
I'd grasp a heav'n of joys in thee,
For thou art all thy sex to me,
  So fondly do I love thee.
    Wert thou but, &c.

Should thunder roar its loud alarms,
Amidst the clash of hostile arms,
I'd softly sink among thy charms,
  And only live to love thee.
    Wert thou but, &c.

Let Fortune drive me far away,
Or make me fall to foes a prey,
My flame for thee shall ne'er decay,
  And dying I would love thee.
    Wert thou but, &c.

Tho' I were number'd with the dead,
My soul should hover round thy head:
I may be turn'd a silent shade,
  But cannot cease to love thee.
    Wert thou but, &c.

BROOM OF COWDENKNOWS.

How blythe, ilk morn, was I to see
  My swain come o'er the hill:
He skipt the burn, and flew to me;
  I met him wi' good will.
    O the broom, the bonny bonny broom,
      The broom of Cowdenknows;
    I wish I were with my dear swain,
      With his pipe and my ewes.

I neither wanted ewe nor lamb,
  While his flock near me lay;
He gather'd in my sheep at night,
  And cheer'd me a' the day.
    O the broom, &c.

He tun'd his pipe and reed sae sweet,
  The birds stood list'ning by;
Ev'n the dull cattle stood and gaz'd,
  Charm'd with his melody.
    O the broom, &c.

While thus we spent our time, by turns
  Betwixt our flocks and play,
I envy'd not the fairest dame,
  Tho' ne'er sae rich and gay.
    O the broom, &c.

Hard fate! that I should banish'd be,
  Gang heavily and mourn,
Because I lov'd the kindest swain
  That ever yet was born.
    O the broom, &c.

He did oblige me ev'ry hour;
  Cou'd I but faithfu' be?
He staw my heart; cou'd I refuse
  Whate'er he ask'd of me?
    O the broom, &c.

My doggie, and my little kit
  That held my wee soup whey,
My plaidy, broach, and crooked stick,
  May now ly useless by.
    O the broom, &c.

Adieu, ye Cowdenknows, adieu,
  Farewell a' pleasures there;
Ye gods restore me to my swain,
  Is a' I crave, or care.
    O the broom, &c.

~~~~~~~

CRAIGIE-BURN WOOD.

[By Burns, who composed the song on a passion which a Mr
Gillespie, a particular friend of his, had for a Miss Lorimer,
afterwards a Mrs Whelpdale.—The young lady was born at
Craigie-burn wood. The chorus is part of an old ballad.]

Beyond thee, dearie, beyond thee, dearie,
  And O to be lying beyond thee,
O sweetly, soundly, weel may he sleep,
  That's laid in the bed beyond thee.

Sweet closes the evening on Craigie-burn wood,
   And blythely awakens the morrow;
But the pride of the spring in the Cragie-burn wood,
   Can yield to me nothing but sorrow.
     Beyond thee, &c.

I see the spreading leaves and flowers,
   I hear the wild birds singing;
But pleasure they hae nane for me,
   While care my heart is wringing.
     Beyond thee, &c.

I canna tell, I maun na tell,
   I dare na for your anger;
But secret love will break my heart,
   If I conceal it langer.
     Beyond thee, &c.

I see thee gracefu', straight, and tall,
   I see thee sweet and bonnie,
But oh, what will my torments be,
   If thou refuse thy Johnie!
     Beyond thee, &c.

To see thee in anither's arms,
   In love to lie and languish,
'Twad be my dead, that will be seen,
   My heart wad burst wi' anguish.
     Beyond thee, &c.

But Jeanie, say thou wilt be mine,
   Say, thou lo'es nane before me;
And a' my days o' life to come
   I'll gratefully adore thee.
     Beyond thee, &c.

MY DEARY, IF THOU DIE.

[By Mr ROBERT CRAWFORD of Auchinames.]

Love never more shall give me pain,
    My fancy's fix'd on thee;
Nor ever maid my heart shall gain,
    My Peggy, if thou die.
Thy beauties did such pleasure give,
    Thy love's so true to me;
Without thee I shall never live,
    My deary, if thou die.

If fate shall tear thee from my breast,
    How shall I lonely stray.!
In dreary dreams the night I'll waste,
    In sighs the silent day.
I ne'er can so much virtue find,
    Nor such perfection see:
Then I'll renounce all womankind,
    My Peggy, after thee.

No new-blown beauty fires my heart
    With Cupid's raving rage,
But thine, which can such sweets impart,
    Must all the world engage.
'Twas this that, like the morning sun,
    Gave joy and life to me;
And when its destined day is done,
    With Peggy let me die.

Ye powers that smile on virtuous love,
    And in such pleasures share;
You who its faithful flames approve,
    With pity view the fair.

Restore my Peggy's wonted charms,
Those charms so dear to me ;
Oh ! never rob me from these arms »
I'm lost if Peggy die.

~~~~~~~~~~

THE HIGHLAND LASSIE, O.

[Written by BURNS when a very young man. It breathes his
unalterable attachment to a young woman, the first object of
his love, but whose premature death at once dissipated his
dreams of pleasure, and cast a gloom upon his mind, which
hung upon it for several years. Their last interview was cal-
culated to make a deep and lasting impression on youthful
sensitive minds. The lovers met on the banks of Ayr to bid
each other farewell, the young woman being to proceed to the
West Highlands to arrange matters with her friends for their
intended union. They stood on each side of a small purling
brook ; they laved their hands in its limpid stream, and hold-
ing a Bible between them, pronounced their vows to be faithful
to each other. They parted, but never met again. This interesting female, faithful to her promise, crossed the sea at
Greenock on her return, where she had scarcely landed when
she was seized with a malignant fever, of which she died in a
few days, and before her admirer even heard of her illness.—
It is in reference to this melancholy occurrence that Burns composed his *Highland Mary*, and the elegy *To Mary in Heaven.*]

NAE gentle the dames, tho' e'er sae fair,
Shall ever be my muse's care ;
Their titles a' are empty show ;
Gie me my Highland lassie, O.
   Within the glen sae bushy, O,
   Aboon the plain sae rushy, O,
   I set me down wi' right good will,
   To sing my Highland lassie, O.

O were yon hills and vallies mine,
Yon palace and yon gardens fine!
The world then the love should know
I bear my Highland·lassie, O.
Within the glen, &c.

But fickle fortune frowns on me,
And I maun cross the raging sea:
But while my crimson currents flow
I'll love my Highland lassie, O.
Within the glen, &c.

Altho' thro' foreign climes I range,
I know her heart will never change,
For her bosom burns with honour's glow,
My faithful Highland lassie, O.
Within the glen, &c.

For her I'll dare the billow's roar;
For her I'll trace a distant shore,
That Indian wealth may lustre throw,
Around my Highland lassie, O.
Within the glen, &c.

She has my heart, she has my·hand,
By sacred truth and honour's band!
Till the mortal stroke shall·lay me low,
I'm thine my Highland lassie, O.
Farewell the glen sae bushy, O!
Farewell the plain sae rushy, O!
To other lands I now must go
To sing my Highland lassie, O!

MY BONNIE MARY.

[The first half stanza is old; the rest is BURNS'S.]

Go fetch to me a pint o' wine,
    And fill it in a silver tassie;
That I may drink before I go,
    A service to my bonnie lassie;
The boat rocks at the pier o' Leith;
    Fu' loud the wind blaws frae the Ferry;
The ship rides by the Berwick-law,
    And I maun lea'e my bonnie Mary.

The trumpets sound, the banners fly,
    The glittering spears are ranked ready;
The shouts o' war are heard afar,
    The battle closes thick and bloody;
But 'tis not the roar o' sea or shore
    Wad make me langer wish to tarry;
Nor shouts o' war that's heard afar,
    'Tis leaving thee, my bonnie Mary.

LOGIE O' BUCHAN.

O LOGIE o' Buchan, O Logie the laird,
They ha'e ta'en awa Jamie that delv'd in the yard,
Wha play'd on the pipe an' the viol sae sma';
They ha'e ta'en awa Jamie the flower o' them a'.
    He said, Think na lang, lassie, tho' I gang awa',
    He said, Think na lang, lassie, tho' I gang awa';
    For the simmer is coming, cauld winter's awa',
    And I'll come and see thee in spite o' them a'.

Q 3

O Sandy has owsen, and siller, and kye,
A house and a haddin, and a' things forbye;
But I wad hae Jamie wi's bonnet in's hand,
Before I'd hae Sandy wi' houses and land.
 He said, &c.

My daddy looks sulky, my minny looks sour,
They frown upon Jamie because he is poor;
But daddy and minny, altho' that they be,
There's nane o' them a' like my Jamie to me.
 He said, &c.

I sit on my creepie, and spin at my wheel,
And think on the laddie that loo'd me sae weel;
He had but a sixpence, he brak it in twa,
And he gied me the ha'f o't when he gaed awa'.
 Then haste ye back, Jamie, and bide na awa',
 Then haste ye back, Jamie, and bide na awa';
 Simmer is coming, cauld winter's awa',
 And ye'll come and see me in spite o' them a'.

LOW DOWN IN THE BROOM.

My daddy is a canker'd carle,
 He'll nae twine wi' his gear;
My minny she's a scalding wife,
 Hads a' the house a-steer:
  But let them say, or let them do,
   It's a' ane to me;
  For he's low down, he's in the broom,
   That's waiting on me:
  Waiting on me, my love,
   He's waiting on me,
  For he's low down, he's in the broom,
   That's waiting on me.

My aunty Kate sits at her wheel,
    And sair she lightlies me;
But weel ken I it's a' envy,
    For ne'er a jo has she.
      But let them say, &c.

My cousin Kate was sair beguil'd
    Wi' Johnnie i' the glen;
And ay sinsyne she cries, Beware
    Of false deluding men.
      But let them say, &c.

Gleed Sandy he came wast ae night,
    And speer'd when I saw Pate;
And ay sinsyne the neighbours round
    They jeer me air and late.
      But let them say, &c.

O FOR ANE AND TWENTY, TAM!.

[By Burns.].

Tune—*The Moudiewort.*.

An O, for ane and twenty, Tam!
    An hey, sweet ane and twenty, Tam!
I'll learn my kin a rattlin sang,
    An I saw ane and twenty, Tam.

They snool me sair, and haud me down,
    And gar me look like bluntie, Tam!
But three short years will soon wheel roun',
    And then comes ane and twenty, Tam.
      An O, for ane, &c.

A gleib o' lan', a claut o' gear,
   Was left me by my auntie, Tam ;
At kith or kin I need na spier,
   An I saw ane and twenty, Tam.
    An O, for ane, &c.

They'll hae me, wed a wealthy coof,
   Tho' I mysel hae plenty, Tam ;
But hear'st thou, laddie, there's my loof,
   I'm thine at ane and twenty, Tam !
    An O, for ane, &c.

THE BONIE LAD THAT'S FAR AWA.

[By Burns.]

O now can I be blythe and glad,
   Or how can I gang brisk and braw,
When the bonie lad that I lo'e best
   Is o'er the hills and far awa ?

Its no the frosty winter wind,
   Its no the driving drift and snaw ;
But ay the tear comes in my e'e,
   To think on him that's far awa.

My father pat me frae his door,
   My friends they hae disown'd me a' ;
But I hae ane will tak my part,
   The bonie lad that's far awa.

A pair o' gloves he gave to me,
   And silken snoods he gave me twa ;
And I will wear them for his sake,
   The bonie lad that's far awa.

The weary winter soon will pass,
  And spring will cleed the birken-shaw;
And my sweet babie will be born,
  And he'll come hame that's far awa.

~~~~~~~~~~~~

WERE NA MY HEART LIGHT I WAD DIE.

[By Lady GRISSEL BAILLIE, eldest daughter of Patrick first
  Earl of Marchmont, and wife to George Baillie of Jerviswood,
  Esq. whose widow she died on the 6th December 1746.]

THERE was anes a may, and she loo'd na men,
She biggit her bonny bow'r down in yon glen;
But now she cries dool! and a well a-day!
Come down the green gate, and come here away.
  But now she cries, &c.

When bonny young Johny came o'er the sea,
He said he saw naething sae lovely as me;
He hecht me baith rings and mony braw things;
And were na my heart light I wad die.
  He hecht me, &c.

He had a wee titty that loo'd na me,
Because I was twice as bonny as she;
She rais'd such a pother 'twixt him and his mother,
That were na my heart light I wad die.
  She rais'd, &c.

The day it was set, and the bridal to be,
The wife took a dwam, and lay down to die;
She main'd and she grain'd out of dolour and pain,
Till he vow'd he never wad see me again.
  She main'd, &c.

His kin was for ane of a higher degree,
Said, What had he to do with the like of me?
Albeit I was bonny, I was na for Johny;
And were na my heart light I wad die.
 Albeit I was, &c.

They said, I had neither cow nor caff,
Nor dribbles of drink rins throw the draff,
Nor pickles of meal rins throw the mill-eye;
And were na my heart light I wad die.
 Nor pickles of, &c.

His titty she was baith wylie and slee,
She spy'd me as I came o'er the lee;
And then she ran in and made a loud din,
Believe your ain een, an ye trow na me.
 And then she, &c.

His bonnet stood ay fou round on his brow;
His auld ane look'd ay as well as some's new:
But now he lets't wear ony gate it will hing,
And casts himself dowie upon the corn-bing.
 But now he, &c.

And now he gaes dandering about the dykes,
And a' he dow do is to hund the tykes:
The live-lang night he ne'er steeks his eye,
And were na my heart light I wad die.
 The live-lang, &c.

Were I young for thee, as I hae been,
We shou'd hae been galloping down on yon green,
And linking it on the lily-white lee;
And wow gin I were but young for thee!
 And linking, &c.

THE SILLER CROWN.

AND ye sall walk in silk attire,
  And siller hae to spare,
Gin ye'll consent to be his bride,
  Nor think o' Donald mair.
Oh! wha wad buy a silken gown,
  Wi' a poor broken heart?
Or what's to me a siller crown,
  Gin frae my love I part?

The mind whase every wish is pure,
  Far dearer is to me;
And ere I'm forc'd to break my faith,
  I'll lay me down and die:
For I hae pledged my virgin troth
  Brave Donald's fate to share;
And he has gi'en to me his heart,
  Wi' a' its virtues rare.

His gentle manners wan my heart,
  He, gratefu', took the gift;
Cou'd I but think to seek it back,
  It wou'd be war than thift.
For langest life can ne'er repay
  The love he bears to me;
And ere I'm forced to break my troth,
  I'll lay me down and die.

SWEET ANNIE.

SWEET Annie frae the sea-beech came,
  Where Jocky speel'd the vessel's side;
Ah! wha can keep their heart at hame,
  When Jocky's tost aboon the tide?

Far aff to distant realms he gangs,
  Yet I'll be true as he has been;
And when ilk lass about him thrangs,
  He'll think on Annie, his faithful ain.

I met our wealthy laird yestreen,
  Wi' gowd in hand he tempted me;
He prais'd my brow, my rolling een,
  And made a brag of what he'd gi'e:
What tho' my Jocky's far awa,
  Tost up and down the awsome main,
I'll keep my heart anither day,
  Since Jocky may return again.

Nae mair, false Jamie, sing nae mair,
  And fairly cast your pipe away,
My Jocky wad be troubled sair,
  To see his friend his love betray:
For a' your songs and verse are vain,
  While Jocky's notes do faithful flow;
My heart to him shall true remain,
  I'll keep it for my constant jo.

Bla' saft, ye gales, round Jocky's head,
  And gar your waves be calm and still;
His hameward sail with breezes speed,
  And dinna a' my pleasure spill!
What tho' my Jocky's far away,
  Yet he will braw in siller shine:
I'll keep my heart anither day,
  Since Jocky may again be mine.

FAREWELL TO LOCHABER.

[By Ramsay.]

Tune—*Lochaber no more.*

Farewell to Lochaber, and farewell, my Jean,
Where heartsome with thee I have mony days been;
For Lochaber no more, Lochaber no more,
We'll may be return to Lochaber no more.
These tears that I shed, they are a' for my dear,
And no for the dangers attending on weir;
Tho' bore on rough seas to a far bloody shore,
May be to return to Lochaber no more.

Tho' hurricanes rise, and rise every wind,
They'll ne'er make a tempest like that in my mind;
Tho' loudest of thunder on louder waves roar,
That's naething like leaving my love on the shore.
To leave thee behind me, my heart is sair pain'd;
By ease that's inglorious no fame can be gain'd;
And beauty and love's the reward of the brave,
And I must deserve it before I can crave.

Then glory, my Jeany, maun plead my excuse;
Since honour commands me, how can I refuse?
Without it I ne'er can have merit for thee,
And without thy favour I'd better not be!
I gae then, my lass, to win honour and fame,
And if I should luck to come gloriously hame,
I'll bring a heart to thee with love running o'er,
And then I'll leave thee and Lochaber no more.

R

A RED RED ROSE.

[By Burns.]

O my luve's like a red red rose,
  That's newly sprung in June :
O my luve's like the melodie
  That's sweetly play'd in tune.

As fair art thou, my bonnie lass,
  So deep in luve am I :
And I will love thee still, my dear,
  Till a' the seas gang dry.

Till a' the seas gang dry, my dear,
  And the rocks melt wi' the sun :
I will love thee still, my dear,
  While the sands o' life shall run.

And fare thee weel, my only luve !
  And fare thee weel a-while !
And I will come again, my luve,
  Tho' it were ten thousand mile.

SAE MERRY AS WE HAE BEEN.

A lass that was laden with care
  Sat heavily under yon thorn ;
I listen'd a while for to hear,
  When thus she began for to mourn :

Whene'er my dear shepherd was there,
  The birds did melodiously sing,
And cold nipping winter did wear
  A face that resembled the spring.
    Sae merry as we twa hae been,
    Sae merry as we twa hae been ;
    My heart it is like for to break,
    When I think on the days we have seen.

Our flocks feeding close by his side,
  He gently pressing my hand,
I view'd the wide world in its pride,
  And laugh'd at the pomp of command !
My dear, he would oft to me say,
  What makes you hard-hearted to me ?
Oh ! why do you thus turn away
  From him who is dying for thee ?
    Sae merry, &c.

But now he is far from my sight,
  Perhaps a deceiver may prove ;
Which makes me lament day and night,
  . That ever I granted my love.
At eve when the rest of the folk
  Were merrily seated to spin,
I set myself under an oak,
  And heavily sighed for him.
    Sae merry, &c.

HERE AWA, THERE AWA.

[The old words.]

Here awa, there awa, here awa, Willie,
Here awa, there awa, here awa hame ;
Lang have I sought thee, dear have I bought thee,
Now I have gotten my Willie again.

Thro' the lang muir I have follow'd my Willie,
Thro' the lang muir I have follow'd him hame,
Whatever betide us, nought shall divide us,
Love now rewards all my sorrow and pain.

Here awa, there awa, here awa, Willie,
Here awa, there awa, here awa hame,
Come, love, believe me, nothing can grieve me,
Ilka thing pleases while Willie's at hame.

WANDERING WILLIE.

[By Burns.]

Here awa, there awa, wandering Willie,
Here awa, there awa, haud awa hame;
Come to my bosom, my ain only dearie,
Tell me thou bring'st me my Willie the same.

Winter winds blew loud and cauld at our parting,
Fears for my Willie brought tears in my e'e,
Welcome now simmer, and welcome my Willie;
The simmer to nature, my Willie to me.

Rest, ye wild storms, in the cave of your slumbers,
How your dread howling a lover alarms!
Wauken ye breezes, row gently ye billows,
And waft my dear laddie ance mair to my arms.

But oh, if he's faithless, and minds na his Nanie,
Flow still between us, thou wide-roaring main!
May I never see it, may I never trow it,
But, dying, believe that my Willie's my ain.

LOGAN BRAES.

By Logan's streams that run sae deep,
Fu' aft wi' glee I've herded sheep,—
Herded sheep, or gather'd slaes,
Wi' my dear lad on Logan braes.
But wae's my heart these days are gane,
And I wi' grief may herd alane,
While my dear lad maun face his faes,
Far, far frae me, and Logan braes.

Nae mair at Logan kirk will he,
Atween the preachings meet wi' me;
Meet wi' me, or when its mirk,
Convoy me hame frae Logan kirk.
Well may I sing these days are gane;
Frae kirk or fair I come alane;
While my dear lad maun face his faes,
Far, far frae me, and Logan braes.

****

THE BANKS OF THE DEE.

[By Mr John Home, author of the tragedy of *Douglas*.]

Tune—*Langolee.*

'Twas summer, and softly the breezes were blowing,
   And sweetly the nightingale sung from the tree,
At the foot of a rock, where the river was flowing,
   I sat myself down on the banks of the Dee.
Flow on, lovely Dee, flow on, thou sweet river;
Thy banks' purest streams shall be dear to me ever;
For there I first gain'd the affection and favour
   Of Sandy, the glory and pride of the Dee.

But now he's gone from me, and left me thus mourning,
  To quell the proud rebels, for valiant is he ;
And, ah ! there's no hope of his speedy returning,
  To wander again on the banks of the Dee.
He's gone, helpless youth! o'er the rude roaring billows;
The kindest and sweetest of all the gay fellows ;
And left me to stray 'mongst the once-loved willows,
  The loneliest maid on the banks of the Dee.

But time and my pray'rs may perhaps yet restore him;
  Blest peace may restore my dear shepherd to me ;
And when he returns, with such care I'll watch o'er
      him,
  He never shall leave the sweet banks of the Dee.
The Dee then shall flow, all its beauties displaying ;
The lambs on its banks shall again be seen playing ;
While I with my Sandy am carelessly straying,
  ‧ And tasting again all the sweets of the Dee.

THE BRAES O' GLENIFFER.

[By TANNY HILL.]

Tune—*Bonny Dundee.*

KEEN blaws the wind o'er the braes o' Gleniffer,
  The auld wa's and turrets are cover'd wi' snaw ;
How changed sin the days that I met wi' my lover
  Amang the green bushes by Stanley-green shaw !
The wild flow'r o' simmer was springing sae bonny ;
  The mavis sang sweet frae the green birken tree ;
But far to the camp they hae march'd aff my Johnie ;
  And now it is winter wi' nature and me.

Then ilk thing around us was blythsome and cheerie ;
  Then ilk thing around us was bonny and braw :
Now naething is heard but the wind whistling drearie ;
  Now naething is seen but the wide spreading snaw.
The trees are a' bare, and the birds mute and dowie,
    They shake the cauld drift frae their wings as they
      flee ;
They chirp out their plaints, seeming wae for my
    Johnie ;
  'Tis winter wi' them, and 'tis winter wi' me.

Yon cauld sleety cloud as it skiffs the bleak mountain,
  And shakes the dark furs on its stey rocky brae,
While down the deep glen bawls the sna'-flooded
    fountain,
  That murmur'd sae sweet to my laddie and me.
'Tis no the loud roar o' the wint'ry wind swelling ;
  'Tis no the cauld blast brings the tear i' my e'e ;
For O gin I saw but my bonnie Scots callan,
  The dark days o' winter were simmer to me.

THE LOWLANDS OF HOLLAND.

My love has built a bonny ship, and set her on the sea,
With sevenscore good mariners to bear her company ;
There's threescore is sunk, and threescore dead at sea,
And the Lowlands of Holland has twin'd my love and
  me.

My love he built another ship, and set her on the main,
And nane but twenty mariners for to bring her hame ;
But the weary wind began to rise, and the sea began
  to rout,
My love then and his bonny ship turn'd withershins
  about.

There shall neither coif come on my head, nor comb
 come in my hair,
There shall neither coal nor candle light shine in my
 bower mair;
Nor will I love another one, until the day I die:
For I never lov'd a love but one, and he's drown'd in
 the sea.

O had your tongue, my daughter dear, be still and be
 content;
There are mair lads in Galloway, ye need nae sair lament.
O! there is nane in Galloway, there's nane at a' for me:
For I never lov'd a love but ane, and he's drown'd in
 the sea.

AULD ROBIN GRAY.

[Written by Lady ANN LINDSAY, daughter to the late Earl of
 Balcarras.]

Tune—*The Bridegroom greets.*

WHEN the sheep are in the fauld and the kye at hame,
And a' the weary warld to rest are gane;
The waes of my heart fa' in show'rs frae my e'e,
While my gudeman lyes sound by me.

Young Jamie loo'd me weel, and he sought me for his
 bride,
But saving a crown, he had naething beside;
To mak' that crown a pound, my Jamie gade to sea,
And the crown and the pound were baith for me.

He had na been awa a week but only twa,
When my mither she fell sick, and the cow was stoun
   away ;
My father brak' his arm, and my Jamie at the sea,
And auld Robin Gray came a courting me.

My father coudna work, and my mother coudna spin,
I toil'd day and night, but their bread I coudna win ;
Auld Rob maintain'd them baith, and wi' tears in his ee,
Said, Jenny, for their sakes, O marry me.

My heart it said nay, I look'd for Jamie back ;
But the wind it blew high, and the ship it was a wreck :
The ship it was a wreck, why didna Jenny die ?
And why do I live to say, Wae's me ?

My father argued sair, tho' my mother didna speak,
She look'd in my face till my heart was like to break ;
So they gied him my hand, tho' my heart was in the sea,
And auld Robin Gray is gudeman to me.

I hadna been a wife a week but only four,
When sitting sae mournfully ae night at the door,
I saw my Jamie's wraith, for I coudna think it he,
Till he said, I'm come back for to marry thee.

O sair did we greet, and muckle did we say,
We took but ae kiss, and we tore ourselves away :
I wish I were dead ! but I'm no like to die ;
And why do I live to say, Wae's me ?

I gang like a ghaist, and carena to spin ;
I darena think on Jamie, for that would be a sin ;
But I'll do my best a gude wife to be,
For auld Robin Gray is kind unto be.

MARY'S DREAM.

[Written by Mr ALEX. LOWE, who lived for some time at Airds
in Galloway, from whence he went to North America. The
Mary alluded to is supposed to be Miss Mary Macghie, daughter of the proprietor of Airds.—BURNS.]

THE moon had climb'd the highest hill
    Which rises o'er the source of Dee,
And from the eastern summit shed
    Her silver light on tow'r and tree.
When Mary laid her down to sleep,
    Her thoughts on Sandy far at sea;
When soft and low a voice was heard,
    Say, Mary, weep no more for me!

She from her pillow gently rais'd
    Her head, to ask who there might be?
She saw young Sandy shiv'ring stand,
    With visage pale and hollow eye:
O Mary, dear! cold is my clay;
    It lies beneath a stormy sea;
Far, far from thee I sleep in death;
    So, Mary, weep no more for me!

Three stormy nights and stormy days,
    We toss'd upon the raging main;
And long we strove our bark to save,
    But all our striving was in vain.
Ev'n then, when horror chill'd my blood,
    My heart was fill'd with love for thee:
The storm is past, and I at rest,
    So, Mary, weep no more for me!

O maiden, dear! thyself prepare,
  We soon shall meet upon that shore,
Where love is free from doubt and care,
  And thou and I shall part no more.
Loud crow'd the cock, the shadow fled;
  No more of Sandy could she see;
But soft the passing spirit said,
  Sweet Mary, weep no more for me!

THE WAEFU' HEART.

Gin living worth cou'd win my heart,
  You wou'd na speak in vain,
But in the darksome grave it's laid,
  Never to rise again.
My waefu' heart lies low wi' his
  Whose heart was only mine;
And oh! what a heart was that to lose,
  But I maun no repine.

Yet oh! gin Heav'n in mercy soon
  Wou'd grant the boon I crave,
And tak this life, now naething worth
  Sin Jamie's in his grave.
And see! his gentle spirit come
  To show me on my way,
Surprised, nae doubt, I still am here,
  Sair wond'ring at my stay.

I come, I come, my Jamie dear;
  And oh! wi' what gude will
I follow, wharsoe'er ye lead,
  Ye canna lead to ill.

She said, and soon a deadly pale
  Her faded cheek possest;
Her waefu' heart forgot to beat;
  Her sorrows sunk to rest.

HIGHLAND MARY.

[By Burns, in remembrance of his last interview with Mary
Campbell. *Vide supra*, p. 183.]

Tune—*Katharine Ogie.*

Ye banks, and braes, and streams around
  The castle o' Montgomery,
Green be your woods, and fair your flowers,
  Your waters never drumlie!
There simmer first unfald her robes,
  And there the langest tarry:
For there I took the last fareweel
  O' my sweet Highland Mary.

How sweetly bloom'd the gay, green birk,
  How rich the hawthorn's blossom;
As underneath their fragrant shade,
  I clasp'd her to my bosom!
The golden hours, on angel wings,
  Flew o'er me and my dearie;
For dear to me, as light and life,
  Was my sweet Highland Mary.

Wi' mony a vow, and lock'd embrace,
  Our parting was fu' tender;
And, pledging aft to meet again,
  We tore oursels asunder;

But Oh! fell death's untimely frost,
  That nipt my flower sae early!
Now green's the sod, and cauld's the clay,
  That wraps my Highland Mary!

O pale, pale now, those rosy lips,
  I aft hae kiss'd sae fondly!
And clos'd for ay, the sparkling glance,
  That dwalt on me sae kindly!
And mouldering now in silent dust
  That heart that lo'ed me dearly!
But still within my bosom's core,
  Shall live my Highland Mary.

MY MARY, DEAR DEPARTED SHADE.

[This sublime elegy was composed by BURNS, under great agitation of mind, on the anniversary of the death of his beloved Mary Campbell. *Vide supra*, p. 251.]

Tune—*Captain Cook's death, &c.*

THOU ling'ring star, with less'ning ray,
  That lov'st to greet the early morn,
Again thou usher'st in the day
  My Mary from my soul was torn.
O Mary! dear departed shade!
  Where is thy place of blissful rest?
Seest thou thy lover lowly laid?
  Hear'st thou the groans that rend his breast?

That sacred hour can I forget,
  Can I forget the hallow'd grove,
Where, by the winding Ayr, we met
  To live one day of parting love!

s

Eternity cannot efface
  Those records dear of transports past;
Thy image at our last embrace,
  Ah, little thought we 'twas our last!

Ayr, gurgling, kiss'd his pebbled shore,
  O'erhung with wild-woods thick'ning green;
The fragrant birch and hawthorn hoar,
  Twin'd amorous round the raptur'd scene:
The flowers sprang wanton to be prest,
  The birds sang love on every spray,
Till too, too soon the glowing west
  Proclaim'd the speed of winged day.

Still o'er these scenes my mem'ry wakes,
  And fondly broods with miser care;
Time but th' impression stronger makes,
  As streams their channels deeper wear:
My Mary, dear departed shade!
  Where is thy place of blissful rest?
Seest thou thy lover lowly laid?
  Hear'st thou the groans that rend his breast?

MAUN I STILL ON MENIE DOAT.

[By BURNS. The chorus is part of a song composed by a gentleman of Edinburgh, a particular friend of the bard's.]

Tune—*Johnny's gray-breeks.*

AGAIN rejoicing nature sees
  Her robe assume its vernal hues,
Her leafy locks wave in the breeze,
  All freshly steep'd in morning dews.

And maun I still on Menie doat,
  And bear the scorn that's in her e'e!
For it's jet, jet black, ... like a hawk.
  An' it winna let a body be!

In vain to me the cowslips blaw,
  In vain to me the vi'lets spring;
In vain to me, in glen or shaw,
  The mavis and the lintwhite sing.
    And maun I still, &c.

The merry ploughboy cheers his team,
  Wi' joy the tentie seedsman stalks,
But life to me's a weary dream,
  A dream of ane that never wauks.
    And maun I still, &c.

The wanton coot the water skims,
  Amang the reeds the ducklings cry,
The stately swan majestic swims,
  And ev'ry thing is blest but I.
    And maun I still, &c.

The sheep-herd steeks his faulding slap,
  And owre the moorlands whistles shill,
Wi' wild, unequal, wand'ring step
  I meet him on the dewy hill.
    And maun I still, &c.

And when the lark, 'tween light and dark,
  Blythe waukens by the daisy's side,
And mounts and sings on flittering wings,
  A woe-worn ghaist I hameward glide.
    And maun I still, &c.

Come winter, with thine angry howl,
  And raging bend the naked tree ;
  ~~~~ ~~~~~ ~~~~ soothe my cheerless soul
When nature all is sad like me !
  And maun I still, &c.

JESSY.

[This song was written by BURNS in the summer of 1796, when
he was descending rapidly to the grave, and is the last finished
offspring of his muse.]

Tune—Here's a health to them that's awa, hiney.

HERE'S *a health to ane I lo'e dear,*
Here's a health to ane I lo'e dear ;
Thou art sweet as the smile when fond lovers meet,
And soft as their parting tear—Jessy !

Altho' thou maun never be mine,
  Altho' even hope is denied ;
'Tis sweeter for thee despairing,
  Than aught in the world beside—Jessy !
    Here's a health, &c.

I mourn thro' the gay, gaudy day,
  As, hopeless, I muse on thy charms ;
But welcome the dream o' sweet slumber,
  For then I am lockt in thy arms—Jessy !
    Here's a health, &c.

I guess by the dear angel smile,
  I guess by the love rolling e'e ;
But why urge the tender confession
  'Gainst fortune's fell cruel decree—Jessy !
    Here's a health, &c.

MY HARRY WAS A GALLANT GAY.

[This song is BURNS's, with the exception of the chorus, which he picked up from an old woman in Dumblane.]

Tune—*Highlander's Lament.*

My Harry was a gallant gay,
  Fu' stately strade he on the plain,
But now he's banish'd far away,
  I'll never see him back again.
    O for him back again!
    O for him back again!
    I wad gie a' Knockhaspie's land
    For Highland Harry back again.

When a' the lave gae to their bed,
  I wander dowie up the glen;
I set me down and greet my fill,
  And ay I wish him back again.
    O for him, &c.

O were some villains hangit high,
  And ilka body had their ain!
Then I might see the joyful sight,
  My Highland Harry back again.
    O for him, &c.

THE WHITE COCKADE.

My love was born in Aberdeen,
The boniest lad that e'er was seen,
But now he makes our hearts fu' sad,
He takes the field wi' his white cockade.

s 3

O he's a ranting, roving lad,
He is a brisk an' a bonny lad,
Betide what may, I will be wed,
And follow the boy wi' the white cockade.

I'll sell my rock, my reel, my tow,
My gude gray mare, and hawkit cow,
To buy mysel a tartan plaid,
To follow the boy wi' the white cockade.
   O he's a ranting, &c.

MY DEAR HIGHLAND LADDIE, O.

Air—*Morneen I Gaberland.*

Blythe was the time when he fee'd wi' my father, O,
Happy war the days when we herded thegither, O,
Sweet war the hours when he row't me in his plaidie, O,
An' vow't to be mine, my dear Highland laddie, O;
But ah, waes me! wi' their sodg'ring sae gaudy, O,
The laird's wys't away my braw Highland laddie, O;
Misty are the glens, and the dark hills sae cloudy, O,
That ay seem't sae blythe wi' my dear Highland
   laddie, O.

The blae-berry banks now are lonesome and dreary, O,
Muddy are the streams that gush'd down sae clearly, O,
Silent are the rocks that echoed sae gladly, O,
The wild-melting strains o' my dear Highland laddie, O.
Oh! love is like the morning, sae gladsome and
   bonny, O,
Till winds fa' a-storming, and clouds low'r sae rainy, O:
As nature in winter droops withering sae sadly, O,
Sae lang may I mourn for my dear Highland laddie, O.

He's pu'd me the crawberry ripe frae the scroggie
    glen,
He's pu'd me the strawberry ripe frae the foggy fen,
He's pu'd me the rowan frae the wild steep sae gaudy, O,
Sae loving and kind was my dear Highland laddie, O.
Farewell my ewes, and farewell my dogie, O,
Farewell Glenfiach, my mammy, and my daddy, O,
Farewell ye mountains, sae cheerless and cloudy, O,
Where aft I have been wi' my dear Highland laddie, O.

YOUNG ALLAN.

[By RICHARD GALL, a young man of promising genius. He
was bred to the printing profession, which consequently en-
grossed much of his time and attention; his leisure hours he
devoted to the cultivation of his mind, which he improved con-
siderably, but the bent of his inclination was directed to Scottish
poetry, in which, we are assured by those who have inspected
his unpublished poems, he would probably have attained to no
ordinary celebrity, had not an abscess broke out in his breast,
that cut him off in May 1801, in the twenty-fifth year of his
age. He was the friend and correspondent of Burns, and lived
in terms of the greatest intimacy with M'Neill, to whom he
addressed an epistle, prefixed to the works of that ingenious
poet.]

THE sun in the west fa's to rest in the e'enin';
    Ilk morn blinks cheerfu' upon the green lee;
But, ah! on the pillow o' sorrow ay leanin',
    Nae mornin' nae e'enin' brings pleasure to me.
O! waefu' the parting, when, smiling at danger,
    Young Allan left Scotia to meet wi' the fae;
Cauld, cauld now he lies in a land amang strangers,
    Frae friends, and frae Helen for ever away.

As the aik on the mountain resists the blast rairin',
    Sae did he the brunt o' the battle sustain,
Till treach'ry arrested his courage sae darin',
    And laid him pale, lifeless upon the drear plain.
Cauld winter the flower divests o' its cleidin',
    In simmer again it blooms bonny to see;
But naething, alas! can e'er hale my heart bleidin',
    Drear winter remaining for ever wi' me.

MY ONLY JO AND DEARIE, O.

[By RICHARD GALL.]

Thy cheek is o' the rose's hue,
    My only jo and dearie, O;
Thy neck is like the siller dew
    Upon the bank sae brierie, O:
Thy teeth are o' the ivory,
O sweet's the twinkle o' thine e'e!
Nae joy, nae pleasure blinks on me,
    My only jo and dearie, O.

The birdie sings upon the thorn
    Its sang o' joy, fu' cheerie, O,
Rejoicing in the simmer morn,
    Nae care to mak it eerie, O:
But little kens the sangster sweet
Aught o' the care I hae to meet,
That gars my restless bosom beat,
    My only jo and dearie, O.

When we were bairnies on yon brae,
    And youth was blinkin bonny, O,
Aft we wad daff the lee lang day,
    Our joys fu' sweet and mony, O.

Aft I wad chase thee o'er the lee·
And ~~~~~ ~~~~ ~~~ ~~~~~y tree,
Or pu' the wild flowers a' for thee,
   My only jo and dearie, O.

I hae a wish I canna tine,
   'Mang a' the cares that grieve me, O,
A wish that thou wert ever mine,
   And never mair to leave me, O!
Then I wad daut thee night and day,
Nae ither warl'ly care wad hae,
Till life's warm stream forgot to play, `
   My only jo and dearie, O.

MY ANNA.

[By Richard Gall.]

How sweet is the scene at the dawning o' morning!
   How fair ilka object that lives in the view!
Dame Nature the valley and hillock adorning;
   The primrose and blue-bells yet wet wi' the dew.
How sweet in the morning o' life is my Anna!
   Her smile like the sun-beam that glents o'er the lee!
To wander and leave her, dear lassie, I canna,
   Frae love and frae beauty I never can flee.

O! lang hae I lo'ed her, and lo'e her fu' dearly,
   And aft hae I preed o' her bonny sweet mou';
And aft hae I read, in her e'e blinkin' clearly,
   A language that bade me be constant and true!
Then others may doat on their fond warl'ly treasure,
   For pelf, silly pelf, they may brave the rude sea;
To love my sweet lassie be mine the dear pleasure,
   Wi' her let me live, and wi' her let me die!

THE WEE THING.

[By H. MACNEILL, Esq.]

SAW ye my wee thing? saw ye mine ain thing?
    Saw ye my true love down by yon lee;
Cross'd she the meadow yestreen at the gloaming?
    Sought she the burnie whar flow'rs the haw-tree?

Her hair it is lint-white; her skin it is milk-white;
    Dark is the blue o' her saft rolling ee;
Red, red her ripe lips! And sweeter than roses:—
    Whar could my wee thing wander frae me?

I saw nae your wee thing, I saw nae your ain thing,
    Nor saw I your true love down by yon lee;
But I met my bonny thing late in the gloaming,
    Down by the burnie whar flow'rs the haw-tree.

Her hair it was lint-white; her skin it was milk-white;
    Dark was the blue o' her saft rolling ee;
Red were her ripe lips, and sweeter than roses:
    Sweet were the kisses that she gae to me!

It was nae my wee thing; it was nae my ain thing,
    It was nae my true love ye met by the tree:
Proud is her leel heart! modest her nature!
    She never loo'd ony till ance she loo'd me.

Her name it is Mary; she's frae Castle-Cary:
    Aft has she sat, when a bairn, on my knee:—
Fair as your face is, war't fifty times fairer,
    Young bragger, she ne'er wad gie kisses to thee!

It was then your Mary; she's frae Castle-Cary;
    It was then your true love I met by the tree:
Proud as her heart is, and modest her nature,
    Sweet were the kisses that she gae to me.

Sair gloom'd his dark brow, blood-red his cheek grew,
  Wild flash'd the fire frae his red-rolling ee !—
Ye's rue sair, this morning, your boasts and your scorn-
    ing :
  Defend ye, fause traitor ! fu' loudly ye lie.

Awa wi' beguiling, cried the youth, smiling.—
  Aff went the bonnet; the lint-white locks flee :
The belted plaid fa'ing, her white bosom shawing,
  Fair stood the lov'd maid wi' the dark rolling ee !

Is it my wee thing ! is it mine ain thing !
  Is it my true love here that I see !
O Jamie, forgi'e me ; your heart's constant to me ;
  I'll never mair wander, dear laddie, frae thee !

~~~~~~~~

THE BUSH ABOON TRAQUAIR.

[By Mr ROBERT CRAWFORD of Auchinames.]

HEAR me, ye nymphs, and ev'ry swain,
  I'll tell how Peggy grieves me ;
Though thus I languish, thus complain,
  Alas ! she ne'er believes me :
My vows and sighs, like silent air,
  Unheeded never move her ;
At the bonny bush aboon Traquair,
  'Twas there I first did love her.

That day she smil'd, and made me glad,
  No maid seem'd ever kinder ;
I thought myself the luckiest lad,
  So sweetly there to find her :

I try'd to sooth my am'rous flame,
　In words that I thought tender;
If more there pass'd, I'm not to blame,
　I meant not to offend her.

Yet now she scornful flees the plain,
　The fields we then frequented;
If e'er we meet, she shews disdain,
　She looks as ne'er acquainted.
The bonny bush bloom'd fair in May,
　Its sweets I'll ay remember;
But now her frowns make it decay,
　It fades as in December.

Ye rural powers, who hear my strains,
　Why thus should Peggy grieve me?
Oh! make her partner in my pains,
　Then let her smiles relieve me:
If not, my love will turn despair,
　My passion nae mair tender;
I'll leave the bush aboon Traquair,
　To lonely wilds I'll wander.

FOR THE LACK OF GOLD.

[By the late Dr AUSTIN, physician in Edinburgh, on the marriage of Jean, daughter of John Drummond of Megginich, Esq. to James Duke of Atholl, on whose death she married General Lord Adam Gordon, whose widow she died at Edinburgh about 1800.]

For he lack of gold she's left me, O,
And of all that's dear bereft me, O;
She me forsook for a great duke,
　And to endless woes she's left me, O.

A star and garter have more art,
Than youth, a true and faithful heart;
For empty titles we must part,
   And for glitt'ring show she's left me, O.

No cruel fair shall e'er more move
My injured heart again to love;
Through distant climates I must rove,
   Since Jeany she has left me, O.
Ye pow'rs above! I to your care
Give up my charming lovely fair;
Your choicest blessings be her share,
   Tho' she's for ever left me, O.

I'LL CHEAR UP MY HEART.

As I was walking ae May morning,
   The fiddlers an' youngsters were making their game;
And there I saw my faithless lover,
   And a' my sorrows return'd again.
Well since he is gane, joy gang wi' him;
   It's ne'er be he shall gar me complain:
I'll chear up my heart, and I will get another;
   I'll never lay a' my love upon ane.

I could na get sleeping yestreen for weeping,
   The tears ran down like showers o' rain;
An' had na I got greiting my heart wad a broken;
   And O! but love's a tormenting pain.
But since he is gane, may joy gae wi' him;
   It's never be he that shall gar me complain:
I'll chear up my heart, and I will get another;
   I'll never lay a' my love upon ane.

T

When I gade into my mither's new house,
    I took my wheel and sat down to spin;
'Twas there I first began my thrift;
    And a' the wooers came linking in.
It was gear he was seeking, but gear he'll na get;
    And its never be he that shall gar me complain:
For I'll chear up my heart, and I'll soon get another;
    I'll never lay a' my love upon ane.

MY HEART'S MY AIN.

'Tis nae very lang sinsyne,
    That I had a lad o' my ain;
But now he's awa to anither,
    And left me a' my lain.
The lass he's courting has siller,
    And I hae nane at a';
And 'tis nought but the love of the tocher
    That's tane my lad awa.

But I'm blyth that my heart's ain,
    And I'll keep it a' my life,
Until that I meet wi' a lad
    Who has sense to wale a good wife.
For though I say't mysell,
    That shou'd nae say't, 'tis true,
The lad that gets me for a wife,
    He'll ne'er hae occasion to rue.

I gang ay fou clean and fou tosh,
    As a' the neighbours can tell;
Tho' I've seldom a gown on my back,
    But sic as I spin mysell:

And when I'm clad in my curtsey,
   I think mysell as braw
As Susie, wi' a' her pearling,
   That's tane my lad awa.

But I wish they were buckled together,
   And may they live happy for life ;
Tho' Willie does slight me, and's left me,
   The chield he deserves a good wife.
But, O ! I'm blyth that I've miss'd him,
   As blyth as I weel can be ;
For ane that's sae keen o' the siller
   Will ne'er agree wi' me.

But as the truth is, I'm hearty,
   I hate to be scrimpit and scant ;
The wee thing I hae I'll make use o't,
   And nae ane about me shall want :
For I'm a good guide o' the warld,
   I ken when to ha'd and to gi'e ;
For whinging and cringing for siller
   Will ne'er agree wi' me.

Contentment is better than riches,
   An' he wha has that has enough ;
The master is seldom sae happy
   As Robin that drives the plough.
But if a young lad wou'd cast up,
   To make me his partner for life,
If the chield has the sense to be happy,
   He'll fa' on his feet for a wife.

TIBBIE, I HAE SEEN THE DAY.

[By Burns.]

Tune—*Invercald's Reel.*

O TIBBIE, *I hae seen the day,*
Ye would nae been sae shy ;
For laik o' gear ye lightly me,
But, trowth, I care na by.

Yestreen I met you on the moor,
Ye spak na, but gaed by like stoure :
Ye geck at me because I'm poor,
But fient a hair care I.
O Tibbie, I hae, &c.

I doubt na, lass, but ye may think,
Because ye hae the name o' clink,
That ye can please me at a wink,
Whene'er ye like to try.
O Tibbie, I hae, &c.

But sorrow tak him that's sae mean,
Altho' his pouch o' coin were clean,
Wha follows ony saucy quean
That looks sae proud and high.
O Tibbie, I hae, &c.

Altho' a lad were e'er sae smart,
If that he want the yellow dirt,
Ye'll cast your head anither airt,
And answer him fu' dry.
O Tibbie, I hae, &c.

But if he hae the name o' gear,
Ye'll fasten to him like a brier,
Tho' hardly he for sense or lear,
  Be better than the kye.
    O Tibbie, I hae, &c.

But, Tibbie, lass, tak my advice,
Your daddie's gear maks you sae nice;
The deil a ane wad spier your price,
  Were ye as poor as I.
    O Tibbie, I hae, &c.

There lives a lass in yonder park,
I would nae gie her in her sark,
For thee wi' a' thy thousan' mark;
  Ye need na look sae high.
    O Tibbie, I hae, &c.

MY TOCHER'S THE JEWEL.

[By Burns.]

O MEIKLE thinks my luve o' my beauty,
  And meikle thinks my luve o' my kin;
But little thinks my luve I ken brawlie,
  My tocher's the jewel has charms for him.
It's a' for the apple he'll nourish the tree;
  It's a' for the hiney he'll cherish the bee,
My laddie's sae meikle in luve wi' the siller,
  He canna hae luve to spare for me.

Your proffer o' luve's an airl-penny,
  My tocher's the bargain ye wad buy;
But an ye be crafty, I am cunnin,
  Sae ye wi' anither your fortune maun try.
    T 3

Ye're like to the timmer o' yon rotten wood,
Ye're like to the bark o' yon rotten tree,
Ye'll slip frae me like a knotless thread,
And ye'll crack your credit wi' mae nor me.

SHE'S FAIR AND FAUSE.

[By Burns.]

She's fair and fause that causes my smart,
I lo'ed her meikle and lang;
She's broken her vow, she's broken my heart,
And I may e'en gae hang.
A coof cam in wi' rowth o' gear,
And I hae tint my dearest dear,
But woman is but warld's gear,
Sae let the bonnie lass gang.

Whae'er ye be that woman love,
To this be never blind,
Nae ferlie 'tis tho' fickle she prove,
A woman has't by kind:
O woman, lovely, woman fair!
An angel form's faun to thy share,
'Twad been o'er meikle to gi'en thee mair,
I mean an angel mind.

ROY'S WIFE OF ALDIVALOCH.

[By Mrs Grant of C****n.]

Roy's wife of Aldivaloch,
  Roy's wife of Aldivaloch,
Wat ye how she cheated me,
  As I came o'er the braes of Balloch?

She vow'd, she swore she wad be mine;
　　She said she lo'ed me best of ony;
But oh! the fickle, faithless quean,
　　She's ta'en the carl, and left her Johnie.
　　　　Roy's wife, &c.

O she was a canty quean,
　　And weel cou'd dance the Highland walloch;
How happy I, had she been mine,
　　Or I'd been Roy of Aldivaloch.
　　　　Roy's wife, &c.

Her hair's sae fair, her een's sae clear,
　　Her wee bit mou's sae sweet and bonny,
To me she ever will be dear,
　　Tho' she's for ever left her Johnie.
　　　　Roy's wife, &c.

COME UNDER MY PLAIDY.

[By H. M'NEILL, Esq.]

Tune—*Johnie M'Gill.*

COME under my plaidy, the night's gaun to fa';
Come in frae the cauld blast, the drift, and the snaw;
Come under my plaidy, and sit down beside me;
There's room in't, dear lassie! believe me, for twa.
Come under my plaidy, and sit down beside me,
I'll hap ye frae every cauld blast that will blaw:
O! come under my plaidy, and sit down beside me,
There's room in't, dear lassie! believe me, for twa.

Gae 'wa wi' your plaidy! auld Donald, gae 'wa,
I fear na the cauld blast, the drift, nor the snaw;
Gae 'wa wi' your plaidy! I'll no sit beside ye;
Ye may be my gutcher, auld Donald, gae 'wa:—
I'm gaun to meet Johnie, he's young and he's bonie,
He's been at Meg's bridal, sae trig and sae braw;
O nane dances sae lightly! sae gracefu'! sae tightly!
His cheek's like the new rose, his brow's like the snaw!

Dear Marion, let that flee stick fast to the wa',
Your Jock's but a gowk, and has naithing ava;
The hale o' his pack he has now on his back,
He's thretty, and I am but threescore and twa.
Be frank now and kindly; I'll busk you aye finely;
At kirk or at market they'll nane gang sae braw;
A bein house to bide in, a chaise for to ride in,
And flunkies to 'tend you as aft as ye ca'.

My father's ay tauld me, my mither and a',
Ye'd mak a gude husband, and keep me aye braw
It's true I loo Johnie, he's gude and he's bonie,
But, waes me! ye ken he has naething ava!
I hae little tocher; you've made a gude offer;
I'm now mair than twenty; my time is but sma'!
Sae gi'e me your plaidy, I'll creep in beside ye,
I thought ye'd been aulder than threescore and twa.

She crap in ayont him, aside the stane wa',
Whar Johnie was list'ning, and heard her tell a';
The day was appointed!—his proud heart it dunted,
And struck 'gainst his side as if bursting in twa.
He wander'd hame weary, the night it was dreary!
And thowless, he tint his gate deep 'mang the snaw;
The howlet was screaming, while Johnie cried, Women
Wad marry auld Nick if he'd keep them aye braw!—

O the deel's in the lasses! they gang now sae braw,
They'll lie down wi' auld men o' fourscore and twa;
The hale o' their marriage is gowd and a carriage;
Plain luve is the cauldest blast now that can blaw!

***

SLIGHTED NANSY.

Tune—The Kirk wad let me be.

'Tis I have seven braw new gowns,
  And ither seven better to mak,
And yet for a' my new gowns,
  My wooer has turn'd his back.
Besides I have seven milk ky,
  And Sandy he has but three;
And yet for a' my good ky,
  The laddie winna ha'e me.

My dadie's a delver of dikes,
  My mither can card and spin,
And I am a fine fodgel lass,
  And the siller comes linkin in:
The siller comes linkin in,
  And it is fou fair to see,
And fifty times wow! O wow!
  What ails the lads at me?

Whenever our Baty does bark,
  Then fast to the door I rin,
To see gin ony young spark
  Will light and venture but in:
But never a ane will come in,
  Tho' many a ane gaes by,
Syne far ben the house I rin,
  And a weary wight am I.

When I was at my first prayers,
  I pray'd but anes i' the year,
I wish'd for a handsome young lad,
  And a lad with muckle gear.
When I was at my neist prayers,
  I pray'd but now and than,
I fash'd na my head about gear,
  If I got a handsome young man.

Now when I'm at my last prayers,
  I pray on baith night and day,
And O! if a beggar wad come,
  With that same beggar I'd gae.
And O! and what'll come o' me?
  And O! and what'll I do?
That sic a braw lassie as I
  Shou'd die for a wooer I trow!

BESS THE GAWKIE.

Blyth young Bess to Jean did say,
Will ye gang to yon sunny brae,
Where flocks do feed, and herds do stray,
  And sport a while wi' Jamie?
Ah na, lass, I'll no gang there,
Nor about Jamie tak nae care,
Nor about Jamie tak nae care,
  For he's ta'en up wi' Maggy.

For hark, and I will tell you, lass,
Did I not see your Jamie pass,
Wi' meikle gladness in his face,
  Out o'er the muir to Maggy.

I wat he gae her mony a kiss,
And Maggy took them ne'er amiss;
'Tween ilka smack pleas'd her wi' this,
   That Bess was but a gawkie.

For when a civil kiss I seek,
She turns her head, and thraws her cheek,
And for an hour she'll scarcely speak;
   Who'd not ca' her a gawkie?
But sure my Maggy has mair sense,
She'll gi'e a score without offence:
Now gi'e me ane into the mense,
   And ye shall be my dawtie.

O Jamie, ye hae mony tane,
But I will never stand for ane
Or twa, when we do meet again;
   Sae ne'er think me a gawkie.
Ah na, lass, that ne'er can be,
Sic thoughts as these are far frae me,
Or ony thy sweet face that see,
   E'er to think thee a gawkie.

But whisht!—nae mair of this we'll speak,
For yonder Jamie does us meet;
Instead of Meg he kiss'd sae sweet,
   I trow he likes the gawkie.—
O dear Bess, I hardly knew,
When I came by, your gown's sae new,
I think you've got it wat wi' dew.
   Quoth she, That's like a gawkie.

It's wat wi' dew, and 'twill get rain,
And I'll get gowns when it is gane,
Sae you may gang the gate you came,
   And tell it to your dawtie.

The guilt appear'd in Jamie's cheek,
He cry'd, O cruel maid, but sweet,
If I should gang another gate,
    I ne'er could meet my dawtie!

The lasses fast frae him they flew,
And left poor Jamie sair to rue,
That ever Maggy's face he knew,
    Or yet ca'd Bess a gawkie.
As they gade o'er the muir they sang,
The hills and dales with echoes rang,
The hills and dales with echoes rang,
    Gang o'er the muir to Maggy.

THE BANKS O' DOON.

[By Burns.]

Ye banks and braes o' bonnie Doon,
    How can ye bloom sae fresh and fair;
How can ye chant, ye little birds,
    And I sae weary, fu' o' care!
Thou'll break my heart, thou warbling bird,
    That wantons thro' the flowering thorn:
Thou minds me o' departed joys,
    Departed never to return.

Oft hae I rov'd by bonnie Doon,
    To see the rose and woodbine twine;
And ilka bird sang o' its luve,
    And fondly sae did I o' mine.
Wi' lightsome heart I pu'd a rose,
    Fu' sweet upon its thorny tree;
And my fause luver stole my rose,
    But, ah! he left the thorn wi' me.

WALY, WALY UP THE BANK.

[A song with this title is quoted in a *Musical Medley*, published in 1666.]

O WALY, waly up the bank,
    And waly, waly down the brae,
And waly, waly yon burn-side,
    Where I and my love wont to gae!
I lean'd my back unto an aik,
    I thought it was a trusty tree,
But first it bow'd, and syne it brak,
    Sae my true love did lightly me.

O waly, waly but love be bonny,
    A little time whan it is new,
But when 'tis auld, it waxeth cauld,
    And fades away like the morning dew.
O wherefore shou'd I busk my head?
    Or wherefore shou'd I kame my hair?
For my true love has me forsook,
    And says he'll never lo'e me mair.

Now Arthur-Seat shall be my bed,
    The sheets shall ne'er be fyl'd by me,
Saint Anton's well shall be my drink,
    Since my true love has forsaken me.
Martinmas wind, when wilt thou blaw,
    And shake the green leaves aff the tree?
O gentle death, when wilt thou come?
    For of my life I am weary.

U

'Tis not the frost that freezes fell,
  Nor blawing snaw's inclemency ;
'Tis not sic cauld that makes me cry,
  But my love's heart's grown cauld to me.
When we came in by Glasgow town,
  We were a comely sight to see ;
My love was cled in the black velvet,
  And I mysell in cramasie.

But had I wist before I kiss'd,
  That love had been sae ill to win,
I'd lock'd my heart in a case of gold,
  And pinn'd with a silver pin.
Oh, oh ! if my young babe were born,
  And set upon the nurse's knee ;
And I mysell were dead and gane,
  For a maid again I'll never be.

~~~~~~~~

LORD GREGORY.

[By Burns, on the same subject as an ode of Dr Walcott's founded on a passage in the beautiful ballad of *Fair Annie of Lochroyan.*]

O MIRK, mirk is this midnight hour,
  And loud the tempest's roar ;
A waefu' wanderer seeks thy tow'r,
  Lord Gregory ope thy door.

An exile frae her father's ha',
  And a' for loving thee ;
At least some pity on me shaw,
  If love it may na be.

Lord Gregory, mind'st thou not the grove,
  By bonnie Irwine side,
Where first I own'd that virgin-love
  I lang, lang had denied?

How aften did'st thou pledge and vow
  Thou wad for ay be mine!
And my fond heart, itsel sae true,
  It ne'er mistrusted thine.

Hard is thy heart, Lord Gregory,
  And flinty is thy breast:
Thou dart of heav'n that flashest by,
  O wilt thou give me rest!

Ye mustering thunders from above
  Your willing victim see!
But spare, and pardon my fause love,
  His wrangs to heaven and me!

<hr />

OPEN THE DOOR TO ME, OH!

[By Burns]

Oh open the door, some pity to shew,
  Oh, open the door to me, Oh!
Tho' thou hast been false, I'll ever prove true,
  Oh, open the door to me, Oh!

Cauld is the blast upon my pale cheek,
  But caulder thy love for me, Oh!
The frost that freezes the life at my heart,
  Is nought to my pains frae thee, Oh!

The wan moon is setting behind the white wave,
  And time is setting with me, Oh!
False friends, false love, farewell! for mair
  I'll ne'er trouble them, nor thee, Oh!

She has open'd the door, she has open'd it wide;
  She sees his pale corse on the plain, Oh!
My true love, she cried, and sank down by his side,
  Never to rise again, Oh!

TWINE WEEL THE PLAIDEN.

Oh! I hae lost my silken snood,
  That tied my hair sae yellow;
I've gi'en my heart to the lad I loo'd,
  He was a gallant fellow.
    And twine it weel, my bonny dow,
      And twine it weel, the plaiden;
    The lassie lost her silken snood
      In pu'ing of the bracken.

He prais'd my een sae bonny blue,
  Sae lily white my skin, O;
And syne he prie'd my bonny mou',
  And swore it was nae sin, O.
    And twine it weel, &c.

But he has left the lass he loo'd,
  His ain true love forsaken,
Which gars me sair to greet the snood,
  I lost amang the bracken.
    And twine it weel, &c.

DUNCAN GRAY.

[In Johnson's *Musical Museum* this song is marked with the letter Z. as being an old song with corrections or additions. Tradition ascribes the air to a carman in Glasgow.]

Weary fa' you, Duncan Gray,
   Ha, ha the girdin o't,
Wae gae by you, Duncan Gray,
   Ha, ha the girdin o't;
When a' the lave gae to their play,
Then I maun sit the lee lang day,
And joeg the cradle wi' my tae,
   And a' for the girdin o't,

Bonnie was the Lammas moon,
   Ha, ha, &c.
Glowrin a' the hills aboon,
   Ha, ha, &c.
The girdin brak, the beast cam down,
I tint my curch and baith my shoon,
And Duncan, ye're an unco loun;
   Wae on the bad girdin o't.

But Duncan, gin ye'll keep your aith,
   Ha, ha, &c.
I'se bless you wi' my hindmost breath,
   Ha, ha, &c.
Duncan, gin ye'll keep your aith,
The beast again can bear us baith,
And auld Mess John will mend the skaith,
   And clout the bad girdin o't.

DUNCAN GRAY.

[By Burns.]

Duncan Gray cam here to woo,
  Ha, ha the wooing o't,
On blythe Yule night when we were fou,
  Ha, ha the wooing o't.
Maggie coost her head fu' high,
Look'd asklent and unco skeigh,
Gart poor Duncan stand abeigh;
  Ha, ha the wooing o't.

Duncan fleech'd, and Duncan pray'd:
  Ha, ha, &c.
Meg was deaf as Ailsa craig,
  Ha, ha, &c.
Duncan sigh'd baith out and in,
Grat his een baith bleert and blin',
Spak o' lowpin o'er a linn;
  Ha, ha, &c.

Time and chance are but a tide,
  Ha, ha, &c.
Slighted love is sair to bide,
  Ha, ha, &c.
Shall I, like a fool, quoth he,
For a haughty hizzie die;
She may gae to—France for me!
  Ha, ha, &c.

How it comes let Doctors tell,
  Ha, ha, &c.
Meg grew sick—as he grew heal,
  Ha, ha, &c.

Something in her bosom wrings,
For relief a sigh she brings ;
And O, her een, they spak sic things !.
    Ha, ha, &c.

Duncan was a lad o' grace,
    Ha, ha, &c.
Maggie's was a piteous case,
    Ha, ha, &c.
Duncan could na be her death,
Swelling pity smoor'd his wrath ;
Now they're crouse and canty baith.
    Ha, ha, &c.

BIDE YE YET.

G<small>IN</small> I had a wee house, and a canty wee fire,
A bonny wee wifie to praise and admire,
A bonny wee yardy aside a wee burn ;
Fareweel to the bodies that yammer and mourn !
    Sae bide ye yet, and bide ye yet,
    Ye little ken what may betide ye yet ;
    Some bonny wee body may be my lot,
    And I'll ay be canty wi' thinking o't.

When I gang a-field, and come hame at e'en,
I'll get my wee wifie fou neat and fou clean,
And a bonny wee bairnie upon her knee,
That will cry Papa, or Daddy, to me.
    Sae bide ye yet, &c.

And if there should happen ever to be
A diff'rence a'tween my wee wifie and me,
In hearty good humour, altho' she be teaz'd,
I'll kiss her, and clap her, until she be pleas'd.
    Sae bide ye yet, &c.

THE PLOUGHMAN.

THE ploughman he's a bonny lad,
  His mind is ever true, jo,
His garters knit below his knee,
  His bonnet it is blue, jo.
    Then up wi't a', my ploughman lad,
      And hey, my merry ploughman;
    Of a' the trades that I do ken,
      Commend me to the ploughman.

My ploughman he comes hame at e'en,
  He's aften wat and weary:
Cast aff the wat, put on the dry,
  And gae to bed, my dearie.
    Then up wi't a', &c.

I will wash my ploughman's hose,
  And I will dress his o'erlay:
I will mak my ploughman's bed,
  And cheer him late and early.
    Then up wi't a', &c.

I hae been east, I hae been west,
  I hae been at Saint Johnston,
The bonniest sight that e'er I saw
  Was the ploughman laddie dancin.
    Then up wi't a', &c.

Snaw-white stockings on his legs,
  And siller buckles glancin;
A gude blue bannet on his head,
  And Oh! but he was handsome.
    Then up wi't a', &c.

THIS IS NO MINE AIN HOUSE.

[The first half stanza is old; the rest is Ramsay's.]

O THIS is no mine ain house,
   I ken by the rigging o't,
Since with my love I've changed vows,
   I dinna like the bigging o't.
For now that I'm young Robie's bride,
And mistress of his fire-side,
Mine ain house I like to guide,
   And please me wi' the trigging o't.

Then farewell to my father's house,
   I gang where love invites me;
The strictest duty this allows,
   When love with honour meets me.
When Hymen moulds us into ane,
My Robie's nearer than my kin,
And to refuse him were a sin,
   Sae lang's he kindly treats me.

When I am in mine ain house,
   True love shall be at hand ay,
To make me still a prudent spouse,
   And let my man command ay;
Avoiding ilka cause of strife,
The common pest of married life,
That makes ane wearied of his wife,
   And breaks the kindly band ay.

THE MARINER'S WIFE.

[This fine song is long posterior to Ramsay's days. About the year 1771 or 1772 it came first on the streets as a ballad.—BURNS.]

AND are ye sure the news is true?
  And are ye sure he's well?
Is this a time to tawk o' wark?
  Mak haste, set by your wheel.
Is this a time to tawk o' wark,
  When Colin's at the door?
Gie me cloak, I'll to the quay,
  And see him come ashore.
      For there's nae luck about the house,
        There's nae luck ava;
      There's little pleasure in the house,
        When our goodman's awa.

Rise up and mak a clean fire-side,
  Put on the muckle pat;
Gie little Kate her cotton gown,
  And Jock his Sunday's coat:
And mak their shoon as black as slaes,
  Their hose as white as snaw;
It's a' to please my ain goodman,
  For he's been lang awa.
      For there's nae luck, &c.

There are twa hens upon the bauk,
  Have fed this month and mair,
Mak haste, and thraw their necks about,
  That Colin weel may fare:

And spread the table neat and clean,
  Gar ilka thing look bra';
It's a' for love of my goodman,
  For he's been lang awa.
    For there's nae luck, &c.

O gie down my bigonet,
  My bishóp-satin gown,
For I maun tell the bailie's wife,
  That Colin's come to town.
My Sunday's shoon they maun gae on,
  My hose o' pearl blue,
It's a' to please my ain goodman,
  For he's baith leel and true.
    For there's nae luck, &c.

Sae true's his words, sae smooth's his speech,
  . His breath's like caller air,
His very foot has music in't,
  When he comes up the stair.
And will I see his face again?
  And will I hear him speak?
I'm downright dizzy wi' the thought;
  In troth I'm like to greet.
    For there's nae luck, &c.

The cauld blasts of the winter wind,
  That thrilled thro' my heart,
They're a' blawn by, I hae him safe,
  Till death we'll never part:
But what puts parting in my head?
  It may be far awa:
The present moment is our ain;
  The neist we never saw.
    For there's nae luck, &c.

Since Colin's weel, I'm weel content,
  I hae nae mair to crave;
Could I but live to mak him blest,
  I'm blest aboon the lave.
And will I see his face again?
And will I hear him speak?
I'm downright dizzy wi' the thought;
  In troth I'm like to greet.
    For there's nae luck, &c.

JOHN ANDERSON, MY JO.

[This song, in its present shape, was first published by Brash and
Reid of Glasgow, about 1796, in a collection of poetry, in which
it was said to have been improved by Burns. This assertion
Dr Currie positively denies, and supposes the poet wrote no
more of the song than the two stanzas (which are here distinguished by inverted commas) that appeared originally in Johnson's *Musical Museum.*

" It is a received tradition in Scotland," says Dr Percy, " that
at the time of the Reformation, ridiculous and obscene songs
were composed, to be sung by the rabble, to the tunes of the
most favourite hymns in the Latin service. *Green sleeves and
pudding pies,* (designed to ridicule the Popish clergy) is said to
be one of those metamorphosed hymns: *Maggy Lauder* was
another: *John Anderson my jo* was a third. The original
music of all these burlesque sonnets," continues he, " was
very fine."—The last mentioned song is preserved by Dr
Percy.

WOMAN.

" John Anderson my jo, cum in as ze gae bye,
And ze sall get a sheips heid weel baken in a pye;
Weel baken in a pye, and the haggis in a pat;
John Anderson, my jo, cum in, and ze's get that.

MAN.

" And how do ze, Cummer? and how hae ze threven?
And how mony bairns hae ze ? Wom. Cummer, I hae seven.
MAN. Are they to zour awin gude man ? Wom. Na, Cum-
mer, na;
For five of them were gotten quhan he was awa."

" The ' seven bairns' are," Ritson observes, " with great proba-
bility, thought to allude to the *seven sacraments*; five of which,
it is observed, were the spurious offspring of Mother church: as
the first stanza is supposed to contain a satirical allusion to the
luxury of the Popish clergy; which, however, is not so evident.
In Dr Percy's first edition, the second stanza ran thus :—

" And how doe ze Cummer? and how *do ze thrive?*
And how mony bairns hae ze ? Wom. Cummer, I hae *five.*
MAN. Are they all to zour ain gude man? Wom. Na,
Cummer na,
For *three* of them were gotten quhan *Willie* was awa.

" This, therefore, seems to have been the original ballad; of
which the satire was transferred, by the easy change of two or
three words, from common life to holy church. It is, however,
either way, a great curiosity."—RITSON'S *Scottish Songs,*
vol. i. p. ci.
John Anderson is said by tradition to have been town-piper of
Kelso.—*Musical Museum,* vol. iii.]

JOHN ANDERSON, my jo, John, I wonder what you
mean,
To rise so soon in the morning, and sit up so late at e'en,
Ye'll blear out a' your een, John, and why should you
do so?
Gang sooner to your bed at e'en, John Anderson, my jo.

John Anderson, my jo, John, when nature first began
To try her canny hand, John, her master-work was
man ;
And you among them a' John, sae trig frae tap to toe ;
She prov'd to be nae journey-work, John Anderson,
my jo.

x

John Anderson, my jo, John, ye were my first conceit,
And ye need na think it strange, John, tho' I ca' ye
trim and neat;
Tho' some folks say ye're auld, John, I never think ye so,
But I think ye're ay the same to me, John Anderson,
my jo.

John Anderson, my jo, John, we've seen our bairns'
bairns,
And yet, my dear John Anderson, I'm happy in your
arms,
And sae are ye in mine, John,—I'm sure ye'll ne'er
say no,
Tho' the days are gane that we have seen, John Anderson, my jo.

John Anderson, my jo, John, what pleasure does it gie,
To see sae many sprouts, John, spring up 'tween you
and me.
And ilka lad and lass, John, in our footsteps to go,
Makes perfect heaven here on earth, John Anderson,
my jo.

" John Anderson, my jo, John, when we were first
acquaint,
" Your locks were like the raven, your bonnie brow
was brent;
" But now your head's turn'd bald, John, your locks
are like the snow,
" Yet blessings on your frosty pow, John Anderson,
my jo."

John Anderson, my jo, John, frae year to year we've past,
And soon that year maun come, John, will bring us
to our last;
But let na that affright us, John, our hearts were ne'er
our foe,
While in innocent delight we liv'd, John Anderson, my jo.

" John Anderson, my jo, John, we clamb the hill the-
        gither,
" And mony a canty day, John, we've had wi' ane an-
        ither ;
" Now we maun totter down, John, but hand in hand
        we'll go,
" And we'll sleep thegither at the foot, John Anderson,
        my jo."

~~~~~~~~~~

THE DAY RETURNS, MY BOSOM BURNS.

[By Burns, out of compliment to Robert Riddel, Esq. of Glen-
riddel, and his lady.]

Tune—*Seventh of November.*

The day returns, my bosom burns,
    The blissful day we twa did meet,
Tho' winter wild in tempest toil'd,
    Ne'er summer-sun was half sae sweet.
Than a' the pride that loads the tide,
    And crosses o'er the sultry line ;
Than kingly robes, than crowns and globes,
    Heaven gave me more, it made thee mine.

While day and night can bring delight,
    Or nature aught of pleasure give !
While joys above, my mind can move,
    For thee, and thee alone, I live !
When that grim foe of life below
    Comes in-between to make us part ;
The iron hand that breaks our band,
    It breaks my bliss—it breaks my heart.

WHEN I UPON THY BOSOM LEAN.

[This song was the work of a very worthy facetious old fellow,
JOHN LAPRAIK, late of Dalfram, near Muirkirk; which little
property he was obliged to sell in consequence of some con-
nexion as security for some persons concerned in that villanous
bubble, the Ayr Bank. He has often told me that he composed this song one day when his wife had been fretting o'er
their misfortunes.—BURNS.]

Tune—*Scots Recluse.*

W HEN I upon thy bosom lean,
    And fondly clasp thee a' my ain,
I glory in the sacred ties
    That made us ane, wha ance were twain:
A mutual flame inspires us baith,
    The tender look, the melting kiss:
Even years shall ne'er destroy our love,
    But only gie us change o' bliss.

Hae I a wish? 'tis a' for thee;
    I ken thy wish is me to please;
Our moments pass sae smooth away,
    That numbers on us look and gaze.
Weel pleas'd they see our happy days,
    Nor envy's sel finds aught to blame;
And ay when weary cares arise,
    Thy bosom still shall be my hame.

I'll lay me there, and take my rest,
    And if that aught disturb my dear,
I'll bid her laugh her cares away,
    And beg her not to drap a tear:

Hae I a joy ! 'tis a' her ain ;
　United still her heart and mine ;
They're like the woodbine round the tree,
　That's twin'd till death shall them disjoin.

THE LAND OF THE LEAL.

Tune—Tulie taitie.

I'm wearin' awa, Jean,
Like sna' when 'tis thaw, Jean,
I'm wearin' awa
　To the land o' the leal !
There's nae sorrow there, Jean,
There's nae cauld nor care, Jean,
The day is ay fair
　In the land o' the leal.

Ye were ay leal an' true, Jean,
Your task's ended now, Jean,
And I'll welcome you
　To the land o' the leal.
Our bonnie bairn's there, Jean,
She was baith gude and fair, Jean,
And we grudg'd her right sair
　To the land o' the leal.

Then dry that tearfu' ee, Jean,
My saul langs to be free, Jean,
For angels wait on me
　To the land o'. the leal.
Now, fare ye weel, my ain Jean,
This warld's care is vain, Jean,
We'll meet and ay be fain
　In the land o' the leal.

MY GODDESS, WOMAN.

[By Mr LEARMONT at Dalkeith.]

Tune—*The Butcher boy.*

O' MIGHTY Nature's handywarks,
  The common, or uncommon,
There's nocht thro' a' her limits wide
  Can be compar'd to woman.
The farmer toils, the merchant trokes,
  Fra dawin to the gloamin;
The farmer's pains, the merchant's cares,
  Are baith to please a woman.

The sailor spreads the daring sail,
  Thro' angry seas a foaming;
The jewels, gems o' foreign shores,
  He gies to please a woman.
The sodger fights o'er crimson fields,
  In distant climates roaming;
Yet lays, wi' pride, his laurels down,
  Before all-conquering woman.

A monarch lea'es his golden throne,
  Wi' other men in common,
He flings aside his crown, and kneels
  A subject to a woman.
Tho' I had a' e'er man possess'd,
  Barbarian, Greek, or Roman,
It wad nae a' be worth a strae,
  Without my goddess, woman.

TIBBIE DUNBAR.

Tune—*Johnny M'Gill.*

O WILT thou go wi' me, sweet Tibbie Dunbar?
O wilt thou go wi' me, sweet Tibbie Dunbar?
Wilt thou ride on a horse, or be drawn in a car,
Or walk by my side, O sweet Tibbie Dunbar?

I care na thy daddie, his lands and his money,
I care na thy kin, sae high and sae lordly:
But say thou wilt hae me for better for waur,
And come in thy coatie sweet Tibbie Dunbar.

~~~~~~~~~~

GREEN GROW THE RASHES.

[By BURNS.]

GREEN grow the rashes, O ;
   Green grow the rashes, O ;
The sweetest hours that e'er I spend,
   Are spent amang the lasses, O.

There's nought but care on ev'ry han',
   In ev'ry hour that passes, O :
What signifies the life o' man,
   An' 'twere na for the lasses, O.
     Green grow, &c.

The warldly race may riches chase,
   An' riches still may fly them, O ;
An' tho' at last they catch them fast,
   Their hearts can ne'er enjoy them, O.
     Green grow, &c.

But gie me a canny hour at e'en,
  My arms about my dearie, O;
An' warldly cares, and warldly men.
  May a' gae tapsalteerie, O!
    Green grow, &c.

For you sae douse, ye sneer at this,
  Ye're nought but senseless asses, O:
The wisest man the warld e'er saw,
  He dearly lov'd the lasses, O.
    Green grow, &c.

Auld Nature swears, the lovely dears
  Her noblest work she classes, O:
Her prentice hand she try'd on man,
  An' then she made the lasses, O.
    Green grow, &c.

GIN E'ER I'M IN LOVE.

Gin e'er I'm in love, it shall be with a lass
As sweet as the morn-dew that ligs on the grass;
Her cheeks maun be ruddy, her een maun be bright,
Like stars in the sky on a cauld frosty night.
    Oh! cou'd I but ken sic a lassie as this,
    Oh! cou'd I but ken sic a lassie as this,
      I'd freely gang to her,
      Caress her, and woo her,
  At once take up heart, and solicit a kiss.

My daddy wad ha'e me to marry wi' Bell,
But wha wad hae ane that he canna like well?
What tho' she has meikle, she's bleary and auld,
Camstarie, and saucy, and a terrible scauld.

Oh! gin I get sic a vixen as this,
Oh! gin I get sic a vixen as this,
   I'd whap her, and strap her,
   And bang her, and slap her,
The devil for me shou'd solicit a kiss.

There's Maggy wad fain lug me into the chain,
She spiers frisky at me, but blinks it in vain:
She trows that I'll ha'e her—but, faith, I think no,
For Willy did for her a long while ago.
   Oh! gin I get sic a wanton as this,
   Oh! gin I get sic a wanton as this,
      She'd horn me, and scorn me,
      And hugely adorn me,
And, ere she kiss'd me, gi'e another a kiss.

But find me a lassie, that's youthfu' and gay,
As blithe as a starling, as pleasant as May;
Wha's free from a' wrangling, and jangling, and strife,
And I'll tak her, and mak her my ain thing for life.
   Oh! gin I get sic a lassie as this,
   Oh! gin I get sic a lassie as this,
      I'll kiss her and press her,
      Preserve and caress her,
And think myself greater than Jove is in bliss.

JENNY'S BAWBEE.

I MET four chaps yon birks amang,
Wi' hanging lugs and faces lang,
I spier'd at neibour Bauldy Strang,
       Wha are they these we see?

Quoth he, Ilk cream-fac'd pauky chiel,
Thinks himsell cunning as the de'il,
And here they came awa to steal
          Jenny's bawbee.

The first, a capt:'n to his trade,
Wi' ill-lin'd scull, and back weel clad,
March'd roun' the barn and by the shade,
          And papped on his knee:
Quoth he, My goddess, nymph, and queen,
Your beauty's dazzl'd baith my een;
But de'il a beauty he had seen
          But Jenny's bawbee.

A norlan' laird neist trotted up,
Wi' bassen'd nag and siller whup,
Cry'd, Here's my beast, lad, had the grup,
          Or tie him to a tree:
What's goud to me? I've walth o' lan',
Bestow on ane o' worth your han';
He thought to pay what he was awn
          Wi' Jenny's bawbee.

A lawyer neist, wi' blatherin' gab,
Wi' speeches wove like ony wab,
In ilk ane's corn he took a dab,
          And a' for a fee:
Accounts he owed thro' a' the town,
And tradesmen's tongues nae mair cou'd drown,
But now he thought to clout his gown
          Wi' Jenny's bawbee.

Quite spruce, just frae the washing tubs,
A fool cam neist, but life has rubs,
Foul were the roads, and fu' the dubs,
          And sair besmear'd was he;

He danc'd up, squintin' thro' a glass,
And grinn'd, I' faith a bonny lass,
He thought to win, wi' front o' brass,
    Jenny's bawbee.

She bade the laird gae kaim his wig,
The soger not to strut sae big,
The lawyer not to be a prig;
    The fool he cried, Tee hee,
I ken'd that I could never fail;
But she prinn'd the dish-clout to his tail,
And cool'd him wi' a water pail,
    And kept her bawbee.

Then Johnny cam, a lad o' sense,
Altho' he had na mony pence,
He took young Jenny to the spence,
    Wi' her to crack a wee.
Now Johnny was a clever chiel,
And here his suit he press'd sae weel,
That Jenny's heart grew saft as jeel,
    And she birl'd her bawbee.

TIBBY FOWLER.

'Tibby Fowler o' the glen,
 There's o'er mony wooing at her;
Tibby Fowler o' the glen,
 There's o'er mony wooing at her.
  Courting at her, wooing at her,
  Seeking at her, canna get her;
  Filthy elf, it's for her pelf
  That a' the lads are wooing at her.

Ten came east, and ten came west,
  And ten came rowing o'er the water;
Twa gaid down the lang dyke side,
  There's twa-and-thirty wooing at her.
    Courting at her, &c.

Fye upon the filthy snort,
  There's o'er mony wooing at her;
Fifteen came frae Aberdeen;
  There's seven-and-forty wooing at her.
    Courting at her, &c.

In came Frank wi' his lang legs,
  Gar'd a' the stairs play clitter clatter;
Had awa, young men, he begs,
  For, by my sooth, I will be at her.
    Courting at her, &c.

She's got pendels to her lugs,
  Cockle-shells wad set her better;
High-heel'd shoon, and siller studs,
  And a' the lads are courting at her.
    Courting at her, &c.

Be a lassie ne'er sae fine,
  Gin she want the penny siller,
She may live till ninety-nine
  Ere she get a man till her.
    Courting at her, &c.

Be a lassie ne'er sae black,
  An' she hae the name o' siller,
Set her upo' Tintock tap,
  The wind will bla' a man till her.
    Courting at her, &c.

O' A' THE ILLS ON MAN THAT FA'.

O' a' the ills on man that fa'
   Maist poverty I drie;
For canny up life's hill we ca',
   Whan that our purse grows wee.

Whan siller's gane, an' credit lost,
   There's no ane cares for me,
'Tis then I feel life's cauldest frost,
   Whan that my purse grows wee.

Fu' mony a day blythe Maggy fair
   I loo'd, and she loo'd me;
To please her aye was a' my care,
   Whan my purse was na wee.

Yestreen I wander'd o'er to Maggy,
   An' love gleam'd in my ee;
But whan I kiss'd the fickle jaddie,
   Howt, haud awa, quoth she.

I look'd at her wi' fondest glance,
   An' spier'd her ails at me;
But she replied, wi' mou' askance,
   Wow but your purse is wee.

O' a' the ills on man that fa'
   Maist poverty I drie,
For wi' us ilk ane finds a flaw,
   Whan that our purse grows wee.

Y

THE WIDOW.

[By Ramsay.]

The widow can bake, and the widow can brew,
The widow can shape, and the widow can sew,
And mony braw things the widow can do;
   Then have at the widow, my laddie.
With courage attack her baith early and late,
To kiss her and clap her ye manna be blate;
Speak well, and do better; for that's the best gate
   To win a young widow, my laddie.

The widow she's youthfu', and never ae hair
The waur of the wearing, and has a good skair
Of every thing lovely; she's witty and fair,
   And has a rich jointure, my laddie.
What could you wish better your pleasure to crown,
Than a widow, the bonniest toast in the town,
Wi' naething but draw in your stool and sit down,
   And sport wi' the widow, my laddie.

Then till'er, and kill'er with courtesy dead,
Though stark love and kindness be a' ye can plead;
Be heartsome and airy, and hope to succeed
   Wi' a bonny gay widow, my laddie.
Strike iron while 'tis het, if ye'd have it to wauld,
For fortune ay favours the active and bauld,
But ruins the wooer that's thowless and cauld,
   Unfit for the widow, my laddie.

THE YOUNG LASS CONTRA AULD MAN.

THE carl he came o'er the craft,
  And his beard new shav'n,
He look'd at me as he'd been daft,
  The carl trows that I would hae him.
Howt awa, I winna hae him!
  Na, forsooth, I winna hae him!
For a' his beard new shav'n,
  Ne'er a bit I winna hae him.

A siller broach he gae me neist,
  To fasten on my curchea nooked;
I wor'd awee upon my breast,
  But soon, alake! the tongue o't crooked;
And sae may his; I winna hae him,
  Na, forsooth, I winna hae him;
Ane twice a bairn's a lass's jest;
  Sae ony fool for me may hae him.

The carl has nae faut but ane;
  For he has land and dollars plenty;
But wae's me for him! skin and bane
  Is no for a plump lass of twenty.
Howt awa, I winna hae him,
  Na, forsooth, I winna hae him!
What signifies his dirty riggs
  And cash, without a man wi' them?

But shou'd my canker'd daddy gar
  Me tak him 'gainst my inclination,
I warn the fumbler to beware,
  That antlers dinna claim their station.

Howt awa, I winna hae him!
  Na, forsooth, I winna hae him!
I'm flee'd to crack the haly band,
  Sae lawty says, I shou'd na hae him.

~~~~~~~~~~

WHAT AILS THE LASSES AT ME.

[By Mr ALEX. Ross, late schoolmaster at Lochlee.]

Tune—*Kirk wad let me be.*

I AM a batchelor winsome,
  A farmer by rank and degree,
An' few I see gang out mair handsome,
  To kirk or to market than me;
I have outsight and insight and credit,
  And from any eelist I'm free,
I'm well enough boarded and bedded;
  And what ails the lasses at me?

My boughts of good store are no scanty,
  My byres are well stocked wi' ky,
Of meal i' my girnels is plenty,
  An' twa or three easments forby.
A horse to ride out when they're weary,
  An' cock with the best they can see,
An' then be ca'd dawty and deary;
  I fairly what ails them at me.

Behind backs, afore fouk I've woo'd them,
  An' a' the gates o't that I ken,
An' when they leugh o' me, I trow'd them,
  An' thought I had won, but what then;

When I speak of matters they grumble,
  Nor are condescending and free,
But at my proposals ay stumble;
  I wonder what ails them at me.

I've tried them baith Highland and Lowland,
  Where I a good bargain cou'd see,
But nane o' them fand I wad fall in,
  Or say they wad buckle wi' me.
With jooks an' wi' scraps I've address'd them,
  Been with them baith modest and free,
But whatever way I caress'd them,
  There's something still ails them at me.

O, if I kend how but to gain them,
  How fond of the knack wad I be!
Or what an address could obtain them,
  It should be twice welcome to me.
If kissing an' clapping wad please them,
  That trade I should drive till I die;
But, however I study to ease them,
  They've still an exception at me.

There's wratacks, an' cripples, an' cranshaks,
  An' a' the wandoghts that I ken,
No sooner they speak to the wenches,
  But they are ta'en far onough ben;
But when I speak to them that's stately,
  I find them ay ta'en with the gee,
An' get the denial right flatly;
  What, think ye, can ail them at me?

I have yet but ae offer to make them,
  If they wad but hearken to me,
And that is, I'm willing to tak them,
  If they their consent wad but gie;

Let her that's content write a billet;
  And get it transmitted to me,
I hereby engage to fulfill it,
  Tho' cripple, tho' blind she sud be.

~~~~~~~~~

BILLET BY JEANY GRADDEN.

Dear batchelour, I've read your billet,
  Your strait an' your hardships I see,
An' tell you it shall be fulfilled,
  Tho' it were by none other but me.
These forty years I've been neglected,
  An' nane has had pity on me;
Such offers should not be rejected,
  Whoever the offerer be.

For beauty I lay no claim to it,
  Or, may be, I had been away;
Tho' tocher or kindred could do it,
  I have no pretensions to they:
The most I can say, I'm a woman,
  An' that I a wife want to be;
An' I'll tak exception at no man,
  That's willing to tak nane at me.

And now I think I may be cocky,
  Since fortune has smurtl'd on me,
I'm Jenny, an' ye shall be Jockie,
  'Tis right we together sud be;
For nane of us cou'd find a marrow,
  So sadly forfairn were we;
Fouk sud no at any thing tarrow,
  Whose chance looked naething to be.

On Tuesday speer for Jeany Gradden,
  When I i' my pens ween to be,
Just at the sign of the Old Maiden,
  Where ye shall be sure to meet me:
Bring with you the priest for the wedding,
  That a' things just ended may be,
An' we'll close the whole with the bedding;
  An' wha'll be sae merry as we?

A cripple I'm not, ye forsta me,
  Tho' lame of a hand that I be;
Nor blind is there reason to ca' me,
  Altho' I see but with ae eye:
But I'm just the chap that you wanted,
  So tightly our state doth agree;
For nane wad hae you, ye have granted,
  As few I confess wad hae me.

WOO'D AND MARRIED AND A'.

[By Mr Alex. Ross, late schoolmaster at Lochlee.]

Woo'd and married and a',
  Married and woo'd and a',
The dandilie lass of our parish
  Is now by hand and awa.

The grass had nae freedom of growing
  As lang as she was nae awa;
Nor in the town could there be stowing
  For wooers that wanted to ca'.

For dancing, and drinking, and bruilzies,
    And boxing, and shaking of fu's,
The town was ever in toulzies,
    But now the lassie's awa.
        Woo'd and married, &c.

He'll roose her but little that's gotten her,
    Wi' her tocher and ribbons and a';
I doubt he'll wish he had miscarried
    Or he had married her ava':
For a' her ken lay in her dressing;
    But if ance her braws were awa,
She'll soon turn out o' the fashion,
    And knit up her moggins wi' stra'.
        Woo'd and married, &c.

For yesterday I went to see her,
    And wow! she was wondrous bra',
She called to her husband to gie her
    An ell o' new ribbons or twa:
He up, and set down beside her
    A reel and a wheelie to ca',
She said, Was he this gate to guide her?
    And out at the door and awa.
        Woo'd and married, &c.

Her neist road was hame to her mither,
    Wha spier'd, Lassie, how goes a'?
She said, Was it for mae ither,
    That she was married and awa,
But for to sit down at a wheelie,
    And at it baith wallop and ca',
And hae the yarn reel'd by a cheelie,
    Wha was ever crying to dra'?
        Woo'd and married, &c.

Her mother says to her, Hech! lassie,
  He's wisest I fear o' the twa;
Ye'll hae little to put in the bassie,
  If ye be sae backward to draw:
For just now you should work like a tiger,
  And at it baith wallop and ca',
As lang as ye hae youth and vigour,
  And little anes and debt keep awa.
    Woo'd and married, &c.

Sae swith awa hame to your hadden,
  Mair fool than ye came awa;
Ye maunna be ilka day wedden,
  Nor gang sae white-finger'd and braw:
For ye ken wi' a neighbour your yoked,
  At the end o' the yoke ye maun dra',
Or else ye deserve to be docked;
  So that is an answer for a'.
    Woo'd and married, &c.

Young luckie she sees herself nidder'd,
  And wish'd nae weel what way to ca',
But yet wi' hersel she consider'd,
  That hamewards 'twas better to dra',
And even tak her chance o' her landing,
  However the matter might fa';—
Folks need no' on frets to be standing,
  That's woo'd and married and a'.
    Woo'd and married, &c.

I HAE A WIFE O' MY AIN.

[By Burns, in 1788, when engaged in rebuilding the dwelling-house on his farm; he then looked forward to scenes of domestic content and peace.]

I hae a wife o' my ain,
I'll partake wi' naebody;
I'll tak cuckold frae nane,
I'll gie cuckold to naebody.

I hae a penny to spend,
There—thanks to naebody;
I hae naething to lend,
I'll borrow frae naebody.

I am naebody's lord,
I'll be slave to naebody;
I hae a guid braid sword,
I'll tak dunts frae naebody.

I'll be merry and free,
I'll be sad for naebody;
If naebody care for me,
I'll care for naebody.

~~~~~~~~~~

SOME SAY KISSING'S A SIN.

Tune—*Auld Sir Simon the King.*

Some say kissing's a sin,
But I say that winna stand;
It is a most innocent thing,
And allow'd by the laws of the land.

If it were a transgression,
  The ministers it would reprove,
But they, their eldèrs, and session,
  Can do it as well as the lave.

It's lang since it came in fashion,
  I'm sure it will never be done,
As laing as there's in the nation
  A lad, lass, wife, or a lown.

What can I say more to commend it,
  Tho' I should speak all my life;
Yet this will I say in the end o't,
  Let every man kiss his ain wife.

Let him kiss her, clap her, and dawt her,
  And gie her benevolence due,
And that will a thrifty wife make her,
  And sae I'll bid farewell to you.

* * * * * * * * *

THENIEL MENZIES' BONIE MARY.

[In Johnson's *Musical Museum* this song is marked with the
  letter Z. as being an old song with corrections or additions.]

Tune—*Ruffian's Rant.*

In coming by the brig o' Dye,
  At Darlet we a blink did tarry;
As day was dawin in the sky,
  We drank a health to bonie Mary.
  Theniel Menzies' bonie Mary,
    Theniel Menzies' bonie Mary,
  Charlie Grigor tint his plaidie,
    Kissin' Theniel's bonie Mary.

Her een sae bright, her brow sae white,
　Her haffet locks as brown's a berry;
And ay they dimpl't wi' a smile,
　The rosy cheeks o' bonie Mary.
　　Theniel Menzies', &c.

We lap and danc'd the lee-lang day.
　Till piper lads were wae and weary;
But Charlie gat the spring to pay
　For kissing Theniel's bonie Mary.
　　Theniel Menzies', &c.

JOHNNY'S GRAY BREEKS.

W HEN I was in my se'enteenth year,
　I was baith blythe and bonny, O;
The lads loo'd me baith far and near,
　But I loo'd nane but Johnny, O.
He gain'd my heart in twa three weeks,
　He spak sae blythe and kindly, O;
And I made him new gray breeks
　That fitted him most finely, O.

He was a handsome fellow,
　His humour was baith frank and free;
His bonny locks sae yellow,
　Like goud they glitter'd in my ee;
His dimpl'd chin and rosy cheeks,
　And face so fair and ruddy, O;
And then, a' day, his gray breeks
　Were neither auld nor duddy, O.

But now they're thread-bare worn,
    They're wider than they wont to be:
They're tashed like and torn,
    And clouted sair on ilka knee.
But gin I had a summer's day,
    As I have had right mony, O,
I'll mak a web o' new gray,
    To be bréeks to my Johnny, O.

For he's well wordy o' them,
    And better gin I had to gie,
And I'll tak pains upon them,
    Frae faults I'll strive to keep them free.
To clead him weel shall be my care,
    And please him a' my study, O;
But he maun wear the auld pair
    Awee, tho' they be duddy, O.

UP IN THE MORNING EARLY.

[The chorus is old; the other two verses are by Burns.]

Cauld blaws the wind frae east to west,
    The drift is driving sairly;
Sae loud and shrill's I hear the blast,
    I'm sure it's winter fairly.
        Up in the morning's no for me,
            Up in the morning early;
        When a' the hills are cover'd wi' snaw,
            I'm sure it's winter fairly.

The birds sit chittering in the thorn,
    A' day they fare but sparely;
And lang's the night frae e'en to morn,
    I'm sure it's winter fairly.
        Up in the morning's, &c.

z

THE BRAES O' BALLOCHMYLE.

[Composed by BURNS on the amiable and excellent family of Whitefoord's leaving Ballochmyle, when Sir John's misfortunes had obliged him to sell the estate.]

THE Catrine woods were yellow seen
   The flowers decay'd on Catrine lee;
Nae lavrock sang on hillock green,
   But nature sicken'd on the e'e.
Thro' faded groves Maria sang,
   Hersel in beauty's bloom the whyle,
And ay the wild-wood echoes rang,
   Fareweel the braes o' Ballochmyle.

Low in your wintry beds, ye flowers,
   Again ye'll flourish fresh and fair;
Ye birdies dumb, in with'ring bowers,
   Again ye'll charm the vocal air.
But here, alas! for me nae mair,
   Shall birdie charm, or flow'ret smile;
Fareweel the bonnie banks of Ayr,
   Fareweel, fareweel! sweet Ballochmyle!

FAREWELL TO AYRSHIRE.

[By BURNS.]

SCENES of woe and scenes of pleasure,
   Scenes that former thoughts renew,
Scenes of woe and scenes of pleasure,
   Now a sad and last adieu!

Bonny Doon, sae sweet at gloaming,
  Fare thee weel before I gang!
Bonny Doon, whare, early roaming,
  First I weav'd the rustic sang!

Bowers adieu, whare love, decoying,
  First enthrall'd this heart o' mine,
There the saftest sweets enjoying—
  Sweets that mem'ry ne'er shall tine!

Friends, so near my bosom ever,
  Ye hae render'd moments dear;
But, alas! when forc'd to sever;
  Then the stroke, O how severe!

Friends! that parting tear reserve it,
  Tho' 'tis doubly dear to me!
Could I think I did deserve it,
  How much happier would I be!

Scenes of woe and scenes of pleasure,
  Scenes that former thoughts renew,
Scenes of woe and scenes of pleasure,
  Now a sad and last adieu!

MY HEART'S IN THE HIGHLANDS.

[The first half stanza is old; the rest is BURNS's.]

Tune—*Failte na miosg.*

My heart's in the Highlands, my heart is not here;
My heart's in the Highlands a chasing the deer;
Chasing the wild deer, and following the roe,
My heart's in the Highlands wherever I go.

Farewell to the Highlands, farewell to the north,
The birth-place of valour, the country of worth;
Wherever I wander, wherever I rove,
The hills of the Highlands for ever I love.

Farewell to the mountains high cover'd with snow;
Farewell to the straths and green vallies below:
Farewell to the forests and wild-hanging woods;
Farewell to the torrents and loud-pouring floods.
My heart's in the Highlands, my heart is not here;
My heart's in the Highland's a chasing the deer:
Chasing the wild deer, and following the roe;
My keart's in the Highlands wherever I go.

~~~~~~~~

JEANIE'S BLACK EE;

OR

THA MI 'N AM CHODAL, 'SNA DUISGIBH MI.

[By H. MACNEILL, Esq.]

Air—*Cauld frosty morning.*

THE sun raise sae rosy, the grey hills adorning!
Light sprang the levroc and mounted sae hie;
When true to the tryst o' blythe May's dewy morning,
    My Jeanie cam linking out owre the green lea.
To mark her impatience, I crap 'mang the brakens,
Aft, aft to the kent gate she turned her black ee;
Then lying down dowylie, sighed by the willow tree,
    Ha me mohátel na dousku me. *

----

* " I am asleep, do not waken me."—The Gaelic chorus is
pronounced according to the present orthography.

Saft through the green birks I sta' to my jewel,
Streik'd on spring's carpet aneath the saugh tree!
Think na, dear lassie, thy Willie's been cruel,—
   Ha me mohátel na dousku me.
Wi' luve's warm sensations I've marked your impatience,
Lang hid 'mang the brakens I watch'd your black ee.—
You're no sleeping, pawkie Jean! open thae lovely
      een!
   Ha me mohátel na dousku me.

Bright is the whin's bloom ilk green know adorning!
Sweet is the primrose bespangled wi' dew!
Yonder comes Peggy to welcome May morning!
   Dark waves her haffet locks owre her white brow!
O! light! light she's dancing keen on the smooth
      gowany green,
Barefit and kilted half up to the knee!
While Jeanie is sleeping still, I'll rin and sport my
      fill,—
   I was asleep, and ye've waken'd me!

I'll rin and whirl her round; Jeanie is sleeping sound;
Kiss her frae lug to lug; nae ane can see!
Sweet! sweet's her hinny mou!—Will, I'm no sleep-
     ing now,
   I was asleep, but ye waken'd me.
Laughing till like to drap, swith to my Jean I lap,
Kiss'd her ripe roses and blest her black ee!
And ay since whane'er we meet, sing, for the sound
     is sweet,
   Ha me mohátel na dousku me.

CALEDONIA.

[By BURNS.]

Tune—*Humours of Glen.*

THEIR groves o' sweet myrtle let foreign lands reckon,
 Where bright-beaming summers exalt the perfume,
Far dearer to me yon lone glen o' green breckan,
 Wi' the burn stealing under the lang yellow broom.
Far dearer to me are yon humble broom bowers,
 Where the blue-bell and gowan lurk lowly unseen:
For there, lightly tripping amang the wild flowers,
 A listening the linnet, aft wanders my Jean.

Tho' rich is the breeze in their gay sunny vallies,
 And cauld, Caledonia's blast on the wave;
Their sweet-scented woodlands that skirt the proud
  palace,
 What are they? The haunt o' the tyrant and slave!
The slave's spicy forests, and gold-bubbling fountains,
 The brave Caledonian views wi' disdain;
He wanders as free as the winds of his mountains,
 Save love's willing fetters, the chains o' his Jean.

GARB OF OLD GAUL.

[Written by Sir HARRY ERSKINE. The tune was composed by
 General Reid, and called by him, " The Highland, or 42d
 Regiment's March."—BURNS.]

IN the garb of old Gaul, wi' the fire of old Rome,
From the heath-cover'd mountains of Scotia we come,
Where the Romans endeavour'd our country to gain,
But our ancestors fought, and they fought not in vain.

Such our love of liberty, our country, and our laws,
That like our ancestors of old, we stand by freedom's
cause ;
We'll bravely fight, like heroes bold, for honour and
applause,
And defy the French, with all their art, to alter our
laws.

No effeminate customs our sinews unbrace,
No luxurious tables enervate our race ;
Our loud-sounding pipe bears the true martial strain,
So do we the old Scottish valour retain.
  Such our love, &c.

We're tall as the oak on the mount of the vale,
Are swift as the roe which the hound doth assail ;
As the full-moon in autumn our shields do appear,
Minerva would dread to encounter our spear.
  Such our love, &c.

As a storm in the ocean when Boreas blows,
So are we enrag'd when we rush on our foes ;
We sons of the mountains, tremendous as rocks,
Dash the force of our foes with our thundering strokes.
  Such our love, &c.

Quebec and Cape-Breton, the pride of old France,
In their troops fondly boasted till we did advance ;
But when our claymores they saw us produce,
Their courage did fail, and they su'd for a truce.
  Such our love, &c.

In our realm may the fury of faction long cease,
May our counsels be wise, and our commerce increase ;
And in Scotia's cold climate may each of us find,
That our friends still prove true, and our beauties
  prove kind.

Then we'll defend our liberty, our country, and our laws,
And teach our late posterity to fight in freedom's cause,
That they like our ancestors bold, for honour and ap-
   plause,
May defy the French and Spaniards to alter our laws.

BANNOCK-BURN.

ROBERT BRUCE'S ADDRESS TO HIS ARMY.

[This beautiful ode was composed by BURNS in the midst of a
  storm, in the moor between Kenmore and Gatehouse, in Galloway.]

Scots, wha hae wi' Wallace bled;
Scots, wham Bruce has aften led;
.Velcome to your gory bed,
  Or to glorious victorie.

Now's the day, and now's the hour;
See the front o' battle lour;
See approach proud Edward's power—
  Edward! chains and slaverie!

Wha will be a traitor knave?
Wha can fill a coward's grave?
Wha sae base as be a slave?
  Traitor! coward! turn and flee!

Wha for Scotland's king and law
Freedom's sword will strongly draw,
Free-man stand, or free-man fa',
  Caledonian! on wi' me!

By oppression's woes and pains!
By your sons in servile chains;
We will drain our dearest veins,
　　But they shall be—shall be free!

Lay the proud usurpers low!
Tyrants fall in every foe;
Liberty's in every blow!
　　Forward! let us do, or die!

THE FLOWERS OF THE FOREST.

[Written by the sister of Sir Gilbert Elliot, about the year 1755.
—BURNS's *Works*, vol. i. p. 282. It laments in elegant and
tender strains the effects of the fatal battle of Flodden, fought
on the 9th September, 1513, in which James IV., most of his
nobility, and the greater part of his army, composed of the
flower of the nation, were slain. The tune is one of the most
beautiful, and considered as the most ancient, of our Scottish
melodies.]

I'VE heard them lilting, at the ewe milking,
　　Lasses a' lilting, before dawn of day;
But now they are moaning, on ilka' green loaning;
　　The flowers of the forest are a' wede awae.

At bughts, in the morning, nae blithe lads are scorning;
　　Lasses are lonely, and dowie, and wae;
Nae daffing, nae gabbing, but sighing and sabbing;
　　Ilk ane lifts her leglin, and hies her awae.

In har'st, at the shearing, nae youths now are jearing;
　　Bandsters are runkled, and lyart or gray;
At fair, or at preaching, nae wooing, nae fleeching;
　　The flowers of the forest are a' wede awae.

At e'en, in the gloaming, nae younkers are roaming
  'Bout stacks, with the lasses at bogle to play;
But ilk maid sits dreary, lamenting her deary—
  The flowers of the forest are weded awae.

Dool and wae for the order, sent our lads to the border!
  The English, for ance, by guile wan the day;
The flowers of the forest, that fought aye the foremost,
  The prime of our land are cauld in the clay.

We'll hear nae mair lilting, at the ewe milking;
  Women and bairns are heartless and wae:
Sighing and moaning, on ilka green loaning—
  The flowers of the forest are a' wede awae.

THE FLOWERS OF THE FOREST.

[" The late Mrs Cockburn, daughter of Rutherford of Fairnalie,
in Selkirkshire, and relict of Mr Cockburn of Ormiston (whose
father was Lord Justice-Clerk of Scotland), was the authoress
[of this song]. Mrs Cockburn has been dead but a few years.
Even at an age, advanced beyond the usual bounds of hu-
manity, she retained a play of imagination, and an activity of
intellect, which must have been attractive and delightful in
youth, but was almost preternatural at her period of life. Her
active benevolence, keeping pace with her genius, rendered her
equally an object of love and admiration.
" The verses were written at an early period of life, and without
peculiar relation to any event, unless it were the depopulation
of Ettrick forest."—*Border Minstrelsy*, vol. i. pp. 279, 280.
edition 1803.]

I've seen the smiling of fortune beguiling,
  I've tasted her favours, and felt her decay;
Sweet is her blessing, and kind her caressing,
  But soon it is fled—it is fled far away.

I've seen the forest adorned of the foremost,
With flowers of the fairest, both pleasant and gay:
Full sweet was their blooming, their scent the air
    perfuming,
But now they are wither'd, and a' wede awae.

I've seen the morning, with gold the hills adorning,
And the red storm roaring, before the parting day;
I've seen Tweed's silver streams, glittering in the
    sunny beams,
Turn drumly and dark, as they rolled on their way.

O fickle fortune! why this cruel sporting?
Why thus perplex us poor sons of a day?
Thy frowns cannot fear me, thy smiles cannot cheer
    me,
Since the flowers of the forest are a' wede.awae.

KILLIECRANKIE.

[In Johnson's *Musical Museum* this song is marked with the
letter Z. as being an old song with corrections or additions.]

Whare hae ye been sae braw, lad?
  Whare hae ye been sae brankie, O?
Whare hae ye been sae braw, lad?
  Cam ye by Killiecrankie, O?
    An ye had been whare I hae been,
    Ye wad na been sae cantie, O;
    An ye had seen what I hae seen,
    I' th' braes o' Killiecrankie, O.

I've faught at land, I've faught at sea,
  At hame I faught my auntie, O;
But I met the devil and Dundee
  On th' braes o' Killiecrankie, O.
    An ye had been, &c.

The bauld Pitcur fell in a fur,
　　An' Clavers gat a clankie, O;
Or I had fed an Athole gled
　　On th' braes o' Killiecrankie, O.
　　An ye had been, &c.

~~~~~~~~~~~~

AWA, WHIGS, AWA!

Awa, Whigs, awa!
　Awa, Whigs, awa!
　Ye're but a pack o' traitor louns,
　Ye'll do nae gude at a'.

Our thrisles flourish'd fresh and fair,
　And bonnie bloom'd our roses,
But Whigs cam like a frost in June,
　And wither'd a' our posies.
　　Awa, Whigs, &c.

Our ancient crown's fa'n in the dust,
　Deil blin' them wi' the stoure o't;
And write his name in his black beuk,
　Wha gae the Whigs the power o't.
　　Awa, Whigs, &c.

Our sad decay in church and state
　Surpasses my descriving;
The Whigs cam o'er us for a curse,
　And we hae done wi' thriving.
　　Awa, Whigs, &c.

Grim vengeance lang has ta'en a nap,
　But we may see him wauken:
Gude help the day, when royal heads
　Are hunted like a maukin!
　　Awa, Whigs, &c,

In the copy of the preceding song in CROMEK'S *Remains of Nithsdale and Galloway Song*, the two last verses are omitted, and the three following inserted, from the recitation of a lady, which were never before printed, probably from their strong and direct severity :—

A foreign Whiggish lown brought seeds
  In Scottish yird to cover,
But we'll pu' a' his dibbled leeks,
  An' pack him to Hanover.
    Awa, Whigs, &c.

The deil he heard the stoure o' tongues,
  An' ramping came amang us ;
But he pitied us sae wi' cursed Whigs,
  He turned an' wadna wrang us.
    Awa, Whigs, &c.

The deil sat grim amang the reek,
  Thrang bundling brunstane matches ;
An' croon'd 'mang the beuk-taking Whigs,
  Scraps of auld Calvin's catches !
    Awa, Whigs, awa,
    Awa, Whigs, awa,
    Ye'll run me out o' wun spunks,
    Awa, Whigs, awa.

The rival claims of the houses of Stuart and Brunswick have long ceased to be matter of dispute, and indeed are no more to the present generation than those of Bruce and Baliol. The question was decided by the sword, and is now set at rest for ever ; yet posterity would be doing injustice to the character of the brave men who devoted their lives and fortunes in a cause which they conceived just, and in defence of a family who had sat upon the throne for so many centuries, not to admire their heroic actions in the field, and undaunted firmness in adversity, which throw a lustre on their names, that time will rather increase than diminish. Although the nation was overawed, the feelings of the people were not subdued ; they saw with grief the unrelenting fury with which those concerned in the Rebellion, and in particular the Highlanders, were persecuted after the battle of Culloden, and sympathised with the unfortunate objects, in many cases proprietors of large estates, men of amiable dispositions, carried away by a mistaken zeal for a family, who, from its tyranny, was unworthy of their assistance :

to see these men pursued to their hiding-places, dragged forth, and ignominiously put to death, must have excited the most poignant grief in every bosom not deadened by party prejudices, which, when the first transports were over, would settle into a hate against the power that sanctioned such proceedings. The poets of the time took the side of the unfortunate, and produced a multitude of songs, several of which are among the finest specimens of lyrical composition : they were necessitated to conceal their names for fear of prosecution, but their lays were eagerly sought after, and treasured up in the memory of the peasantry. It is somewhat remarkable, that all the songs of both periods which have been recovered, breathe the same strain of invective, passion, and hatred against the reigning family, or of pity and tender sympathy for the miseries of their persecuted countrymen.

We have selected a few of the most popular from the Collections of Ritson and Cromek, the latter of whom, by his indefatigable but praiseworthy exertions, has recovered from oblivion many songs composed during the Rebellions of 1715 and 1745.

TO DAUNTON ME.

[There are several variations of this song, all bearing the same
 stamp of desperate resolution. One of the verses is character-
 istic of the noble Lochiel :—

> " Up came the gallant chief Lochiel,
>   An' drew his glaive o' nut-brown steel,
>   Says, ' Charlie, set your fit to me,
>   An' shaw me wha will daunton thee !"]

To daunton me an' me sae young,
An' gude King James's auldest son !
O that's the thing that ne'er can be,
For the man's unborn that will daunton me !

O set me ance on Scottish land,
An' gie me my braid-sword in my hand,
Wi' my blue bonnet aboon my bree,
An' shaw me the man that will daunton me !

It's nae the battle's deadlie stoure,
Nor friends pruived fause that'll gar me cower;
But the reckless hand o' povertie,
O! that alane can daunton me.

High was I born to kingly gear,
But a cuif came in my cap to wear,
But wi' my braid-sword I'll let him see
He's nae the man will daunton me.

THE HIGHLAND LADDIE.

[The Chevalier is probably meant as the hero of this song. It is
printed from the recitation of a young girl in the parish of
Kirk-bean, in Galloway.—CROMEK's *Remains*, p. 150.]

PRINCELY is my luver's weed,
 Bonnie laddie, Highland laddie,
His veins are fu' o' princely blude,
 My bonnie Highland laddie.

The gay bonnet maun circle roun',
 Bonnie laddie, Highland laddie;
The brows wad better fa' a crown,
 My bonnie Highland laddie.

There's a hand the sceptre bruiks,
 Bonnie laddie, Highland laddie;
Better it fa's the shepherd's creuk,
 My bonnie Highland laddie.

There's a hand the braid-sword draws,
 Bonnie laddie, Highland laddie;
The gowd sceptre it seemlier fa's,
 My bonnie Highland laddie.

He's the best piper i' the north,
  Bonnie laddie, Highland laddie;
An' has dang a' ayont the Forth,
  My bonnie Highland laddie.

Soon at the Tweed he mints to blaw,
  Bonnie laddie, Highland laddie;
Here's the lad ance far awa'!
  The bonnie Highland laddie!

There's nae a Southron fiddler's hum,
  Bonnie laddie, Highland laddie;
Can bide the war-pipe's deadlie strum,
  My bonnie Highland laddie.

An' he'll raise sic an eldritch drone,
  Bonnie laddie, Highland laddie;
He'll wake the snorers round the throne,
  My bonnie Highland laddie.

And the targe an' braid-sword's twang,
  Bonnie laddie, Highland laddie;
To hastier march will gar them gang,
  My bonnie Highland laddie.

Till frae his daddie's chair he'll blaw,
  Bonnie laddie, Highland laddie;
Here's the lad ance far awa'!
  My bonnie Highland laddie.

KENMURE'S ON AN' AWA.

[William Gordon, Viscount Kenmure, was commander in chief
of the Chevalier's forces in the south of Scotland. Having
joined General Forster, and marched to Preston in Lancashire,
he there surrendered himself prisoner at discretion, and was
beheaded on Tower-hill, 24th February 1716. He was a de-
vout member of the Protestant church, was much regretted,
and his memory is still revered by the peasantry of Galloway
and Nithsdale.]

Kenmure's on an' awa, Willie,
  Kenmure's on an' awa;—
An' Kenmure's lord's the bonniest lord
  That ever Gallowa' saw.

Success to Kenmure's band, Willie,
  Success to Kenmure's band;
There was never a heart that fear'd a Whig
  E'er rade by Kenmure's land.

There's a rose in Kenmure's cap, Willie,
  There's a rose in Kenmure's cap,
He'll steep it red in ruddie hearts' blede,
  Afore the battle drap.

For Kenmure's lads are men, Willie,
  For Kenmure's lads are men;
Their hearts an' swords are metal true,
  An' that their faes shall ken!

They'll live an' die wi' fame, Willie,
  They'll live an' die wi' fame;
But soon wi' soun' o' victorie
  May Kenmure's lads come hame!

Here's Kenmure's health in wine, Willie,
  Here's Kenmure's health in wine;
There ne'er was a coward o' Kenmure's blude,
  Nor yet o' Gordon's line.

He kissed his ladie's hand, Willie,
  He kissed his ladie's hand;
But gane's his ladie's courtesie,
  Whan he draws his bludie brand.

His ladie's cheek was red, Willie,
  His ladie's cheek was red;
Whan she saw his steely jupes put on,
  Which smelled o' deadlie feud.

Here's him that's far awa, Willie,
  Here's him that's far awa!
And here's the flower that I lo'e best,
  The rose that's like the snaw!

LEWIS GORDON.

[Lord Lewis Gordon, younger brother to the then Duke of Gordon, commanded a detachment for the Chevalier in 1715, and acquitted himself with great gallantry and judgment. He died in 1754.
" The supposed author of this song was a Mr Geddes, priest, at Shenval in the Ainzie."—BURNS.]

Oh! send Lewis Gordon hame,
And the lad I winna name;
Tho' his back be at the wa',
Here's to him that's far awa.

Oh hon! my Highlandman,
Oh! my bonny Highlandman;
Weel wou'd I my true love ken
Amang ten thousand Highlandmen.

Oh! to see his tartan trews,
Bonnet blue, and laigh-heel'd shoes,
Philabeg aboon his knee;
That's the lad that I'll gang wi'.
  Oh hon! &c.

The princely youth that I do mean,
Is fitted for to be a king;
On his breast he wears a star;
You'd take him for the god of war.
  Oh hon! &c.

Oh to see this princely one,
Seated on a royal throne!
Disasters a' wou'd disappear;
Then begins the jub'lee year.
  Oh hon! &c.

~~~~~~~~~~

THERE'LL NEVER BE PEACE TILL JAMIE COMES HAME.

[By Burns; the air is old.]

By yon castle wa', at the close of the day,
I heard a man sing, though his head it was grey;
And as he was singing the tears fast down came,—
There'll never be peace till Jamie comes hame.

The church is in ruins, the state is in jars,
Delusions, oppressions, and murderous wars;
We dare na weel say't, but we ken wha's to blame:
There'll never be peace till Jamie comes hame.

My seven braw sons for Jamie drew sword;
And now I greet round their green beds in the yird;
It brak the sweet heart of my faithfu' auld dame:
There'll never be peace till Jamie comes hame.

Now life is a burden that bows me down,
Sin I tint my bairns, and he tint his crown;
But till my last moment my words are the same,
There'll never be peace till Jamie comes hame.

SUCH A PARCEL OF ROGUES IN A NATION!

Fareweel to a' our Scottish fame,
   Fareweel our ancient glory;
Fareweel even to the Scottish name,
   Sae fam'd in martial story!
Now Sark rins o'er the Solway sands,
   And Tweed rins to the ocean,
To mark where England's province stands:
   Such a parcel of rogues in a nation!

What force or guile could not subdue,
   Thro' many warlike ages,
Is wrought now by a coward few,
   For hireling traitors wages.
The English steel we could disdain,
   Secure in valour's station;
But English gold has been our bane:
   Such a parcel of rogues in a nation!

O would, or I had seen the day
  That treason thus could sell us,
My auld grey head had lien in clay,
  Wi' Bruce and loyal Wallace!
But pith and power, till my last hour
  I'll mak this declaration,
We're bought and sold for English gold:
  Such a parcel of rogues in a nation!

YE JACOBITES BY NAME.

YE Jacobites by name, give an ear, give an ear;
  Ye Jacobites by name, give an ear;
    Ye Jacobites by name,
      Your fautes I will proclaim,
        Your doctrines I maun blame,
          You shall hear.

What is right, and what is wrang, by the law, by the
    law?
  What is right, and what is wrang, by the law?
    What is right, and what is wrang?
      A short syord, and a lang,
        A weak arm, and a strang
          For to draw.

What makes heroic strife, fam'd afar, fam'd afar?
  What makes heroic strife, fam'd afar?
    What makes heroic strife?
      To whet th' assassin's knife,
        Or hunt a parent's life
          Wi' bludie war.

Then let your schemes alone, in the state, in the state;
Then let your schemes alone, in the state;
Then let your schemes alone,
Adore the rising sun,
And leave a man undone
To his fate.

THE CHEVALIER'S LAMENT.

[Composed by BURNS while riding through the muirs between
Galloway and Ayrshire.]

Tune—*Captain O'Kean.*

THE small birds rejoice in the green leaves returning,
The murmuring streamlet runs clear thro' the vale,
The hawthorn trees blow in the dews of the morning,
And wild scatter'd cowslips bedeck the green dale.
But what can give pleasure, or what can seem fair,
While the lingering moments are number'd by care?
No flowers gaily springing, nor birds sweetly sing-
ing,
Can soothe the sad bosom of joyless despair.

The deed that I dar'd cou'd it merit their malice,
A king and a father to place on his throne!
His right are these hills, and his right are these vallies,
Where the wild beasts find shelter, but I can find
none.
But 'tis not my sufferings thus wretched, forlorn,
My brave gallant friends, 'tis your ruin I mourn;
Your deeds prov'd so loyal in hot bloody trial,
Alas! can I make you no better return!

STRATHALLAN'S LAMENT.

[Written by Burns before 1788. The lamentation is supposed
to be uttered by James, Viscount Strathallan, while concealed
in some cave of the Highlands after the battle of Culloden, at
which engagement his father Viscount William was killed.
He escaped to France.]

Thickest night o'erhang my dwelling!
  Howling tempests o'er me rave!
Turbid torrents, wintry swelling,
  Still surround my lonely cave!

Chrystal streamlets gently flowing,
  Busy haunts of base mankind,
Western breezes softly blowing,
  Suit not my distracted mind.

In the cause of right engaged,
  Wrongs injurious to redress,
Honour's war we strongly waged,
  But the Heavens deny'd success:

Ruin's wheel has driven o'er us,
  Not a hope that dare attend,
The wide world is all before us—
  But a world without a friend!

BANNOCKS O' BARLEY.

[A mutilated copy of this song is in JOHNSON's *Musical Museum;* to the research of Mr Cromek the public are indebted for a complete copy of the song.]

BANNOCKS o' bear-meal, bannocks o' barley,
Here's to the Highlandman's bannocks o' barley!
Wha in a brulzie will first cry—A parley!—
Never the lads wi' the bannocks o' barley!
 Bannocks o' bear-meal, bannocks o' barley,
 Here's to the Highlandman's bannock's o' barley!

Wha drew the gude claymore for Charlie?
Wha cow'd the lowns o' England rarely?
An' claw'd their backs at Falkirk fairly?—
Wha but the lads wi' the bannocks o' barley!
 Bannocks o' bear-meal, &c.

Wha, when hope was blasted fairly,
Stood in ruin wi' bonnie Prince Charlie?
An' 'neath the Duke's bluidy paws dreed fu' sairly?—
Wha but the lads wi' the bannocks o' barley! *
 Bannocks o' bear-meal, &c.

---

* " Of all the men who preserved an unshaken fidelity to the Chevalier in his fallen fortunes, the most heroic was Roderick M'Kenzie, who sacrificed his life for him, with a presence of mind, and a self-devotion, unparelleled either in ancient or in modern story.
' About this time, one Roderick M'Kenzie, a merchant of Edinburgh, who had been out with the Prince, was skulking among the hills about Glenmorriston, when some of the soldiers met with him. As he was about the Prince's size and age, and not unlike him in the face, being a genteel man, and well dressed, they took him for the Prince. M'Kenzie tried to escape them, but could not, and

THE STUART'S GREAT LINE.

Tune—*Alloa House.*

Oh! how shall I venture, or dare to reveal,
Too great for expression, too good to conceal,
The graces and virtues that illustriously shine
In the prince that's descended from the Stuart's great
    line!

O! could I extoll, as I love the dear name,
And suit my low strains to my prince's high fame,
In verses immortal his glory should live,
And ages unborn his merit survive.

But O! thou great hero, just heir to the crown,
The world, in amazement, admires thy renown;
Thy princely behaviour sets forth thy just praise,
In trophies more lasting than poets can raise.

being determined not to be taken and hanged (which he knew, if taken, would be his fate), he bravely resolved to die sword in hand; and, in that death, to serve the Prince more than he could do by living. The bravery and steadiness of M'Kenzie confirmed the soldiers in the belief *that he was the Prince*, whereupon one of them shot him; who, as he fell, cried out, ' You have killed your Prince, you have killed your Prince,' and expired immediately. The soldiers, overjoyed with their supposed good-fortune in meeting with so great a prize, immediately cut off the brave young man's head, and made all the haste they could to Fort Augustus, to tell the news of their great heroical feat, and to lay claim to the thirty thousand pounds, producing the head, which several said they knew to be the Prince's head. This great news, with the head, was soon carried to the Duke, who, believing the *great work* was done, set forward to London from Fort Augustus, on the eighteenth of July."

CROMEK'S *Remains*, pp. 193, 194.

Thy valour in war, thy deportment in peace,
Shall be sung and admir'd, when division shall cease ;
Thy foes in confusion shall yield to thy sway,
And those who now rule be compell'd to obey.

THE WEE, WEE GERMAN LAIRDIE.

[There are several variations of this curious old song; the first
verse of one of them runs thus :—

      " Wha the deil hae we got for a king ?
        But a wee bit German lairdie ;
      An' when we gade to bring him hame,
        He was delving in his yardie !
      He threw his dibble owre the dyke,
        An' brint his wee bit spadie ;
      An' swore wi' a' the English he could,
        He'd be nae mair a lairdie !"

There are others which run,—

      " He'll ride nae mair on strac sonks,
        For gawing his German hurdies ;
      But he sits on our gude King's throne,
        Amang the English lairdies.
        *   *   *   *

      Auld Scotland, thou'rt owre cauld a hole,
        For nursing siccan vermin ;
      But the vera dogs o' England's court
        Can bark an' howl in *German !*"]

WHA the deil hae we got for a king,
  But a wee, wee German lairdie !
An' whan we gade to bring him hame,
  He was delving in his kail-yardie.
Sheughing kail an' laying leeks,
But the hose and but the breeks,
Up his beggar duds he cleeks,
  The wee, wee German lairdie.

An' he's clapt down in our gudeman's chair,
   The wee, wee German lairdie ;
An' he's brought fouth o' foreign leeks,
   An' dibblet them in his yardie.
He's pu'd the rose o' English lowns,
An' brak the harp o' Irish clowns,
But our thristle will jag his thumbs,
   The wee, wee German lairdie.

Come up amang the Highland hills,
   Thou wee, wee German lairdie ;
An' see how Charlie's lang-kail thrive,
   He dibblit in his yardie.
An' if a stock·ye daur to pu',
Or haud the yoking of a pleugh,
We'll break yere sceptre o'er yere mou',
   Thou wee bit German lairdie !

Our hills are steep, our glens are deep,
   Nae fitting for a yardie ;
An' our norlan' thristles winna pu',
   Thou wee, wee German lairdie !
An' we've the trenching blades o' weir,
Wad lib ye o' yere German gear ;
An' pass ye 'neath the claymore's sheer,
   Thou feckless German lairdie !

WELCOME, CHARLEY STUART.

You're welcome, Charley Stuart,
You're welcome, Charley Stuart,
You're welcome, Charley Stuart,
   There's none so right as thou art.

Had I the power to my will,
I'd make thee famous by my quill,
Thy foes I'd scatter, take, and kill,
   From Billingsgate to Duart.
     You're welcome, &c.

Thy sympathizing complaisance
Made thee believe intriguing France;
But woe is me for thy mischance,
   Which saddens every heart.
     You're welcome, &c.

Hadst thou Culloden battle won,
Poor Scotland had not been undone,
Nor butcher'd been, with sword and gun,
   By Lockhart and such cowards.
     You're welcome, &c.

Kind Providence, to thee a friend,
A lovely maid did timely send,
To save thee from a fearful end,
   Thou charming Charley Stuart.
     You're welcome, &c.

Great glorious prince, we firmly pray
That she and we may see the day,
When Britons all with joy shall say,
   You're welcome Charley Stuart.
     You're welcome, &c.

Tho' Cumberland, the tyrant proud,
Doth thirst and hunger after blood,
Just Heaven will preserve the good,
   To fight for Charley Stuart.
     You're welcome, &c.

Whene'er I take a glass of wine,
I drink confusion to the Swine, *
But health to him that will combine
    To fight for Charley Stuart.
        You're welcome, &c.

The ministry may Scotland maul,
But our brave hearts they'll ne'er enthrall;
We'll fight, like Britons, one and all,
    For liberty and Stuart.
        You're welcome, &c.

Then haste, ye Britons, and set on
Your lawful king upon the throne;
To Hanover we'll drive each one
    Who will not fight for Stuart.
        You're welcome, &c.

THE LOVELY LASS OF INVERNESS.

[Burns has a beautiful song on this interesting subject, beginning
" The lovely lass o' Inverness," the first half stanza of which
is perhaps all that remains of an older song than this.]

There liv'd a lass in Inverness,
    She was the pride of a' the town,
She was blythe as a lark on the flower-tap,
    Whan frae the nest it's newly flown.
At kirk she wan the auld folks luve,
    At dance she wan the ladses' een;
She was the blythest ay o' the blythe,
    At wooster-trystes or Halloween.

* The Duke of Cumberland.
2 B 3

As I came in by Inverness,
  The summer-sun was sinking down,
O there I saw the weel-faur'd lass,
  And she was greeting through the town.
The gray-hair'd men were a' i' the streets,
  And auld dames crying, (sad to see!)
The flower o' the lads o' Inverness,
  Lie bluidie on Culloden-lee!

She tore her haffet-links of gowd,
  And dighted ay her comely ee;
My father lies at bluidie Carlisle,
  At Preston sleep my brethren three!
I thought my heart could haud nae mair,
  Mae tears could never blin' my ee;
But the fa' o' ane has burst my heart,
  A dearer ane there ne'er could be!

He trysted me o' luve yestreen,
  Of love tokens he gave me three;
But he's faulded i' the arms o' gory weir,
  Oh ne'er again to think o' me!
The forest-flowers shall be my bed,
  My food shall be the wild-berrie,
The fa' o' the leaf shall co'er me cauld,
  And wauken'd again I winna be.

O weep, O weep, ye Scottish dames,
  Weep till ye blin' a mither's ee;
Nae reeking ha' in fifty miles,
  But naked corses sad to see.
O spring is blythesome to the year,
  Trees sprout, flowers spring, and birds sing hie;
But oh! what spring can raise them up,
  Whose bluidie weir has scaled the ee?

The hand o' God hung heavie here,
  And lightly touched foul tyrannie!
It strake the righteous to the ground,
  And lifted the destroyer hie.
But there's a day, quo' my God in prayer,
  Whan righteousness shall bear the gree;
I'll rake the wicked low i' the dust,
  And wauken, in bliss, the gude man's ee.

THE HIGHLAND WIDOW'S LAMENT.

[The fifth, sixth, and seventh verses of this song are by BURNS, the others are old.]

O! I am come to the low countrie,
  Ochon, ochon, ochrie!
Without a penny in my purse
  To buy a meal to me.

It was nae sae in the Highland hills,
  Ochon, ochon, ochrie!
Nae woman in the country wide
  Sae happy was as me.

For then I had a score o' kye,
  Ochon, ochon, ochrie!
Feeding on yon hill sae high,
  And giving milk to me.

And there I had threescore o' yowes,
  Ochon, ochon, ochrie!
Skipping on yon bonnie knowes,
  And casting woo to me.

I was the happiest of a' the clan,
  Sair, sair may I repine;
For Donald was the bravest man,
  And Donald he was mine!

Till Charlie Stewart cam at last
  Sae far to set us free;
My Donald's arm was wanted then,
  For Scotland and for me.

Their waefu' fate what need I tell!
  Right to the wrang did yield;
My Donald and his country fell
  Upon Culloden field!

I hae nocht left me ava,
  Ochon, ochon, ochrie!
But bonnie orphan lad-weans twa,
  To seek their bread wi' me.

I hae yet a tocher band,
  Ochon, ochon, ochrie!
My winsome Donald's durk an' bran',
  Into their hands to gie.—

There's only ae blink o' hope left,
  To lighten my auld ee,
To see my bairns gie bluidie crownes
  To them gar't Donald die! *

* " The determined fierceness of the Highland character urges
to acts of desperate resolution and heroism.   One of a clan, at the
battle of Culloden, being singled out and wounded, set his back
against a park-wall, and with his targe and claymore bore singly the
onset of a party of dragoons. Pushed to desperation he made resistless
strokes at his enemies, who crowded and encumbered themselves to
have each the glory of slaying him. ' Save that brave fellow,' was
the unregarded cry of some officers. *Golice Macbane* was cut to
pieces, and thirteen of his enemies lay dead around him."—
CROMEK's *Remains*, p. 200.

THE YOUNG MAXWELL.

[" This ballad is founded on fact. A young gentleman of the
family of Maxwell, an honourable and potent name in Galloway and Nithsdale, being an adherent of Charles, suffered in
the general calamity of his friends.

" After seeing his paternal house reduced to ashes; his father
killed in its defence; his only sister dying with grief for her
father, and three brothers slain; he assumed the habit of an
old shepherd; and in one of his excursions singled out one of
the individual men who had ruined his family. After upbraid-
ing him for his cruelty, he slew him in single combat."—
CROMEK's *Remains.*]

" Whare gang ye, thou silly auld carle?
  And what do ye carry there?"
" I'm gaun to the hill-side, thou sodger gentleman,
  To shift my sheep their lair."

Ae stride or twa took the silly auld carle,
  An' a gude lang stride took he:
" I trow thou be a feck auld carle,
  Will ye shaw the way to me?"

And he has gane wi' the silly auld carle,
  Adown by the green-wood side;
" Light down, and gang, thou sodger gentleman,
  For here ye canna ride."

He drew the reins o' his bonnie gray steed,
  An' lightly down he sprang:
Of the comeliest scarlet was his weir coat,
  Whare the gowden tassels hang.

He has thrown aff his plaid, the silly auld carle,
    An' his bonnet frae 'boon his bree;
An' wha was it but the young Maxwell!
    An' his gude brown sword drew he!

" Thou killed my father, thou vile South'ron!
    An' ye killed my breth'ren three!
Whilk brake the heart o' my ae sister,
    I lov'd as the light o' my ee!

" Draw out yere sword, thou vile South'ron!
    Red wat wi' blude o' my kin!
That sword it crapped the bonniest flower
    E'er lifted its head to the sun!

" There's ae sad stroke for my dear auld father!
    There's twa for my brethren three!
An' there's ane to thy heart, for my ae sister,
    Wham I lov'd as the light o' my ee!" *

---

* " The noble strength of character in this ballad is only equal-
led by the following affecting story :—

" In the Rebellion of 1745, a party of. Cumberland's dragoons
was hurrying through Nithsdale in search of rebels.—Hungry and
fatigued they called at a lone widow's house, and demanded refresh-
ment. Her son, a lad of sixteen, dressed them up *lang kale and
butter*, and the good woman brought new milk, which she told them
was all her stock. One of the party inquired, with seeming kindness, how she lived—' Indeed,' quoth she, ' the cow and the kale-
yard, wi' God's blessing's a' my *mailen*.' He arose, and with his
sabre killed the cow, and destroyed all the kale.—The poor woman
was thrown upon the world, and died of a broken heart—the dis-
consolate youth, her son, wandered away, beyond the inquiry of
friends, or the search of compassion. In the Continental war, when the
British army had gained a great and signal victory, the soldiery were
making merry with wine, and recounting their exploits—A dragoon
roared out, ' I once starved a Scotch witch in Nithsdale—I killed her

CROOKIE DEN.

Were ye e'er at Crookie Den?
  Bonnie laddie, Highland laddie;
Saw ye Willie and his men?
  My bonnie Highland laddie.

They're our faes, wha brint an' slew,
  Bonnie laddie, Highland laddie;
There at last they gat their due,
  My bonnie Highland laddie.

The hettest place was fill'd wi' twa,
  Bonnie laddie, Highland laddie;
It was Willie and his papa,
  My bonnie Highland laddie.

The deil sat girning i' the neuk,
  Bonnie laddie, Highland laddie;
Breaking sticks to roast the Duke,
  My bonnie Highland laddie.

The bluidy monster gied a yell,
  Bonnie laddie, Highland laddie;
An' loud the laugh gade round a' hell,
  My bonnie Highland laddie.

cow and destroyed her greens; but,' added he, ' she could live for all that, on her God, as she said !' ' And don't you rue it,' cried a young soldier, starting up, ' don't you rue it ?' ' Rue what ?' said he, ' rue aught like that !' ' Then, by my God,' cried the youth, unsheathing his sword, ' that woman was my mother ! draw, you brutal villain, draw.'—They fought; the youth passed his sword twice through the dragoon's body, and, while he turned him over in the throes of death, exclaimed, ' *had you rued it you should have only been punished by your God !*"—Cromek's, *Remains*, p. 187.

CUMBERLAND AND MURRAY'S DESCENT INTO HELL.

[Keenly satirical as is the foregoing song, it sinks into the shade
  compared with this, in which the ludicrous and the horrible
  are combined with a skill not unworthy the genius and humour
  of Dunbar or Burns.]

Ken ye whare cleekie Murray's gane?
He's to dwall in his lang hame;
The beddle clapt him on the doup,
" Hard I've earned my gray groat:
Lie thou there, and sleep thou soun',
God winna waken sic a lown!"

Whare's his gowd, and whare's his gain,
He rakit out 'neath Satan's wame?
He has nae what'll pay his shot,
Nor caulk the keel o' Charon's boat.
Be there gowd whare he's to beek,
He'll rake it out o' brunstane-smeek.

He's in a' Satan's frything pans,
Scouth'ring the blude frae aff his han's;
He's washing them in brunstan lowe,
His kintra's blude it winna thowe!
The hettest soap-suds o' perdition
Canna out thae stains be washin'.

Ae devil roar'd till hearse and roupet,
" He's pyking the gowd frae Satan's poupit!"
Anither roar'd wi' eldritch yell,
" He's howking the key-stane out o' hell,
To damn us mair wi' God's day-light!"—
And he douked i' the caudrons out o' sight.

He stole auld Satan's brunstane leister,
Till his waukit loofs were in a blister;
He stole his Whig-spunks tipt wi' brunstane,
And stole his scalping whittle's set-stane;
And out of its red hot kist he stole
The very charter rights o' hell.

" Satan tent weel the pilfering villain,
He'll scrimp your revenue by stealin':
Th' infernal boots in which you stand in,
With which your worship tramps the damn'd in,
He'll wyle them aff your cloven cloots,
And wade through hell fire i' yere boots."

Auld Satan cleekit him by the spaul',
And stappit him i' the dub o' hell;—
The foulest fiend there doughtna bide him,
The damn'd they wadna fry beside him:
Till the bluidy Duke came trysting hither,
An' the ae fat butcher fry'd the tither!

Ae devil sat splitting brunstane-matches,
Ane roasting the Whigs like bakers' batches;
Ane wi' fat a Whig was basting,
Spent wi' frequent prayer an' fasting;
A' ceas'd whan thae twin butchers roar'd,
And hell's grim hangman stapt an' glowr'd!

" Fye! gar bake a pye in haste,
Knead it of infernal paste,"
Quo' Satan:—and in his mitten'd hand,
He hynt up bluidie Cumberland,
An' whittlet him down like bow-kail castock,
And in his hettest furnace roasted.

Now hell's black table-claith was spread,
The infernal grace was reverend said:
Yap stood the hungry fiends a' o'er it,
Their grim jaws gaping to devour it,
When Satan cried out, fit to scouner,
" Owre rank a judgment's sic a dinner."

*   *   *   *   *

KILLICRANKIE.

[The battle of Killicrankie was fought at the pass so named, on the 27th July 1689, between the Highland clans under Graham Viscount Dundee, and the forces of William III. commanded by General Mackay. The latter were totally routed. Viscount Dundee received a mortal wound under his arm, elevated in the act of encouraging his men to the pursuit.]

CLAVERS, and his Highlandmen,
   Came down upo' the raw, man,
Who, being stout, gave mony a clout;
   The lads began to claw then.
With sword and targe into their hand,
   Wi' which they were nae slaw, man,
Wi' mony a fearful heavy sigh,
   The lads began to claw then.

O'er bush, o'er bank, o'er ditch, o'er stank,
   She flang amang them a', man;
The Butter-box got mony knocks,
   Their riggings paid for a' then.
They got their paiks, wi' sudden straiks,
   Which to their grief they saw, man;
Wi' clinkum-clankum o'er their crowns,
   The lads began to fa' then.

Her skipt about her, her leapt about,
　And flang amang them a', man;
The English blades got broken heads,
　Their crowns were cleav'd in twa then.
The durk and door made their last hour,
　And prov'd their final fa', man;
They thought the devil had been there,
　That play'd them sic a pa then.

The Solemn League and Covenant
　Come whigging up the hills, man;
Thought Highland trews durst not refuse
　For to subscribe their bills then:
In Willie's name they thought nae ane
　Durst stop their course at a', man;
But her nainsell, wi' mony a knock,
　Cry'd, Furich, Whigs awa', man.

Sir Evan Du, and his men true,
　Came linking up the brink, man;
The Hogan Dutch they feared such,
　They bred a horrid stink then.
The true Maclean, and his fierce men,
　Came in amang them a', man;
Nane durst withstand his heavy hand,
　All fled and ran awa then.

Oh' on a ri! Oh' on a ri!
　Why should she lose King Shames, man?
Oh' rig in di! Oh' rig in di!
　She shall break a' her banes then:
With *furichinish,* an' stay a while,
　And speak a word or twa, man,
She's gi' a straike out o'er the neck,
　Before ye win awa then.

O fy for shame, ye're three for ane,
   Her nainsell's won the day, man;
King Shames' red-coats should be hung up,
   Because they ran awa then:
Had bent their brows, like Highland trows,
   And made as lang a stay, man,
They'd sav'd their King, that sacred thing,
   And Willie'd run awa then.

THE BATTLE OF SHERIFF-MUIR.

[Written by BURNS. The battle of Sheriff-muir was fought on
the 13th November 1715, between the Highland army commanded by the Earl of Mar, and the royal troops under the
Duke of Argyle. From the circumstance of the left wing of
either army being routed, both sides claimed the victory.]

Tune—*The Cameronian rant.*

O CAM ye here the fight to shun,
   Or herd the sheep wi' me, man?
Or ware ye at the Sherra-muir,
   And did the battle see, man?
I saw the battle, sair and tough,
And reekin-red ran mony a sheugh,
My heart for fear gae sough for sough,
To hear the thuds, and see the cluds
O' clans frae woods, in tartan duds,
   Wha glaum'd at kingdoms three, man.

The red-coat lads wi' black cockades,
   To meet them were na slaw, man;
They rush'd and push'd, and blude outgush'd,
   And mony a bouk did fa', man:

The great Argyle led on his files,
I wat they glanced twenty miles;
They hough'd the clans like nine-pen kyles,
They hack'd and hash'd, while broad-swords clash'd,
And thro' they dash'd, and hew'd and smash'd,
    Till fey men died awa, man.

But had you seen the philabegs,
    And skyrin tartan trews, man,
When in the teeth they dar'd our Whigs,
    And covenant true blues, man;
In lines extended lang and large,
When bayonets oppos'd the targe,
And thousands hastened to the charge,
Wi' Highland wrath, they frae the sheath
Drew blades o' death, till, out o' breath,
    They fled like frighted doos, man.

O how deil Tam can that be true?
    The chase gaed frae the north, man:
I saw myself, they did pursue
    The horsemen back to Forth, man;
And at Dumblane, in my ain sight,
They took the brig wi' a' their might,
And straught to Stirling wing'd their flight;
But, cursed lot! the gates were shut,
And mony a huntit poor red-coat,
    For fear amaist did swarf, man.

My sister Kate cam up the gate,
    Wi' crowdie unto me, man;
She swore she saw some rebels run
    Frae Perth unto Dundee, man:
Their left-hand general had nae skill,
The Angus lads had nae good will
That day their neebors' blood to spill;
    2 c 3

For fear, by foes, that they should lose
Their cogs o' brose ; all crying woes,
   And so it goes you see, man.

They've lost some gallant gentlemen,
   Amang the Highland clans, man ;
I fear my lord Panmure is slain,
   Or fallen in Whiggish hands, man.
Now wad ye sing this double fight,
Some fell for wrang, and some for right ;
But mony bade the world gude-night ;
Sae ye may tell, how pell and mell,
By red claymores, and muskets knell,
Wi' dying yell, the Tories fell,
   And Whigs to hell did flee, man.

TRANENT MUIR.

[Written by the late Mr Skirvan, a respectable farmer near Haddington. The battle was fought on the 22d September, 1745, in a plain between Prestonpans and Tranent, where the English forces under Sir John Cope were completely routed by the Young Chevalier, Prince Charles Stuart, at the head of his Highland army.]

Tune—*Killicrankie.*

The Chevalier, being void of fear,
   Did march up Birsle brae, man,
And thro' Tranent, ere he did stent,
   As fast as he could gae, man :
While General Cope did taunt and mock,
   Wi' mony a loud huzza, man ;
But ere next morn proclaim'd the cock,
   We heard another craw, man.

The brave Lochiel, as I heard tell,
    Led Camerons on in clouds, man;
The morning fair, and clear the air,
    They loos'd with dev'lish thuds, man:
Down guns they threw, and swords they drew,
    And soon did chase them aff, man;
On Seaton-crafts they buft their chafts,
    And gart them rin like daft, man.

The bluff dragoons swore blood and 'oons,
    They'd make the rebels run, man;
And yet they flee when them they see,
    And winna fire a gun, man:
They turn'd their back, the foot they brake,
    Such terror seiz'd them a', man;
Some wet their cheeks, some fyl'd their breeks,
    And some for fear did fa', man.

The volunteers prick'd up their ears,
    And vow gin they were crouse, man;
But when the bairns saw't, turn to earn'st,
    They were not worth a louse, man:
Maist feck gade hame; O fy for shame!
    They'd better staid awa, man,
Than wi' cockade to make parade,
    And do nae good at a', man.

Monteith * the great, when hersell shit,
    Un'wares did ding him o'er, man;
Yet wad nae stand to bear a hand,
    But aff fou fast did scour man,

* " The minister of Longformacus, a volunteer; who, happening
to come, the night before the battle, upon a Highlander easing nature at Preston, threw him over, and carried his gun as a trophy to
Cope's camp."—RITSON.

O'er Soutra hill, ere he stood still,
 Before he tasted meat, man ;
Troth he may brag of his swift nag,
 That bare him aff sae. fleet, man.

But Simpson * keen, to clear the een
 Of rebels far in wrang, man ;
Did never strive wi' pistols five,
 But gallopp'd with the thrang, man :
He turn'd his back, and in a crack
 Was cleanly out o' sight, man ;
And thought it best ; it was nae jest
 Wi' Highlanders to fight, man.

'Mangst a' the gang nane bade the bang
 But twa, and ane was tane, man ;
For Campbell † rade, but Myrie ‡ staid,
 And sair he paid the kain, man ;
Fell skelps he got, was war than shot,
 Frae the sharp-edg'd claymore, man ;
Frae many a spout came running out,
 His reeking-het red gore, man.

But Gard'ner § brave did still behave
 Like to a hero bright, man ;
His courage true, like him were few
 That still despised flight, man :

* " Another volunteer Presbyterian minister, who said he would convince the rebels of their error by the dint of his pistols ; having, for that purpose, two in his pockets, two in his holsters, and one in his belt."—RITSON.
 † George Campbell, wright in Edinburgh.
 ‡ Mr Myrie, a student of physic, from Jamaica, who was miserably mangled by the broad-swords.
 § Colonel James Gardner, who, when he found himself abandoned by his dragoons, was slain by a Highlander with a Lochaber ax in endeavouring to join the foot.

For king and laws, and country's cause,
    In honour's bed he lay, man;
His life, but not his courage, fled,
    While he had breath to draw, man.

And Major Bowle, that worthy soul,
    Was brought down to the ground, man;
His horse being shot, it was his lot
    For to get many a wound, man:
Lieutenant Smith,* of Irish birth,
    Frae whom he cried for aid, man,
Being full of dread, lap o'er his head,
    And wadna be gainsaid, man.

He made sic haste, sae spurr'd his beast,
    'Twas little there he saw, man;
To Berwick rade, and falsely said,
    The Scots were rebels a', man;
But let that end, for well 'tis kend
    His use and wont to lie, man;
The Teague is naught, he never faught
    When he had room to flee, man.

And Caddell drest, amang the rest,
    With gun and good claymore, man,
On gelding grey he rode that way,
    With pistol set before, man:

---

* "I have heard the anecdote often," says Burns; "that Lieutenant Smith, came to Haddington after the publication of the song, and sent a challenge to Skirvan to meet him at Haddington, and answer for the unworthy manner in which he had noticed him in his song.—'Gang awa back,' said the honest farmer, 'and tell Mr Smith that I hae na leisure to come to Haddington; but tell him to come here; and I'll tak a look o' him, and if I think him fit to fecht him, I'll fecht him; and if no—I'll do as he did—I'll rin awa."—Reliques of Burns, pp. 232, 233.

The cause was good, he'd spend his blood,
  Before that he would yield, man;
But the night before he left the cor,
  And never fac'd the field, man.

But gallant Roger, like a soger,
  Stood and bravely fought, man;
I'm wae to tell, at last he fell,
  But mae down wi' him brought man:
At point of death, wi' his last breath,
  (Some standing round in ring, man,)
On's back lying flat, he wav'd his hat,
  And cried, " God save the King,"—man.

Some Highland rogues, like hungry dogs,
  Neglecting to pursue, man,
About they fac'd, and in great haste
  Upon the booty flew, man;
And they, as gain, for all their pain,
  Are deck'd wi' spoils of war, man;
Fow bald can tell how her nainsell
  Was ne'er sae pra' before, man.

At the thorn-tree, which you may see
  Be-west the meadow-mill, man,
There mony slain lay on the plain;
  The clans pursuing still, man:
Sic unco' hacks, and deadly whacks,
  I never saw the like, man;
Lost hands and heads cost them their deads,
  That fell near Preston-dyke, man.

That afternoon, when a' was done,
  I gaed to see the fray, man;
But had I wist what after past,
  I'd better staid away, man:

On Seaton-sands, wi' nimble hands,
    They pick'd my pockets bare, man;
But I wish ne'er to drie sic fear
    For a' the sum and mair, man.

~~~~~~~~~~~~

JOHNIE COUP.

[This satirical song was composed to commemorate Sir John
Cope's defeat at Preston in 1745.]

Tune—*Will ye go to the coals in the morning.*

COUP sent a challenge frae Dunbar
Charlie, meet me an ye dare,
And I'll learn you the art of war,
If you'll meet wi' me in the morning.
    Hey Johnie Coup are ye waking yet?
    Or are your drums a beating yet?
    If ye were making I would wait
    To gang to the coals i' the morning.

When Charlie look'd the letter upon,
He drew his sword the scabbard from,
Come follow me, my merry merry men,
And we'll meet Johnie Coup i' the morning.
    Hey Johnie Coup, &c.

Now, Johnie, be as good as your word,
Come let us try both fire and sword,
And dinna rin awa like a frighted bird,
That's chas'd frae its nest in the morning.
    Hey Johnie Coup, &c.

When Johnie Coup he heard of this,
He thought it wadna be amiss
To hae a horse in readiness,
To flie awa i' the morning.
   Hey Johnie Coup, &c.

Fy now Johnie get up and rin,
The Highland bagpipes makes a din,
It's best to sleep in a hale skin,
For 'twill be a bluidie morning.
   Hey Johnie Coup, &c.

When Johnie Coup to Dunbar came,
They speir'd at him, Where's a' your men?
The deil confound me gin I ken,
For I left them a' i' the morning.
   Hey Johnie Coup, &c.

Now, Johnie, trouth ye was na blate,
To come wi' the news o' your ain defeat,
And leave your men in sic a strait,
So early in the morning.
   Hey Johnie Coup, &c.

Ah! faith, co' Johnie, I got a fleg,
With their claymores and philabegs,
If I face them again, deil break my legs,
So I wish you a good morning.
   Hey Johnie Coup, &c.

HERE'S TO THE KING, SIR.

Tune—Hey tutti taiti.

Here's to the king, sir,
Ye ken wha I mean, sir,
And to every honest man
    That will do't again.
      Fill up your bumpers high,
      We'll drink a' your barrels dry;
      Out upon them, fy! fy!
      That winna do't again.

Here's to the chieftains
Of the Scots Highland clans;
They hae done it mair than ance,
    And will do't again.
      Fill up, &c.

When you hear the trumpet sounds,
Tutti taiti to the drum;
Up your swords, and down your guns,
    And to the louns again.
      Fill up, &c.

Here's to the King o' Swedes,
Fresh laurels crown his head!
Pox on every sneaking blade
    That winna do't again!
      Fill up, &c.

But to mak a' things right, now,
He that drinks maun fight too,
To shew his heart's upright too,
    And that he'll do't again.
      Fill up, &c.

2 D

FOR A' THAT AND A' THAT.

[By Burns.]

Tune—*For a' that.*

Is there, for honest poverty
  That hangs his head, and a' that;
The coward-slave, we pass him by,
  We dare be poor for a' that!
For a' that, and a' that,
  Our toils obscure, and a' that,
The rank is but the guinea's stamp,
  The man's the gowd for a' that.

What tho' on hamely fare we dine,
  Wear hoddin grey, and a' that;
Gie fools their silks, and knaves their wine,
  A man's a man for a' that;
For a' that, and a' that,
  Their tinsel show, and a' that;
The honest man, though e'er sae poor,
  Is king o' men for a' that.

Ye see yon birkie, ca'd a lord,
  Wha struts, and stares, and a' that;
Tho' hundreds worship at his word,
  He's but a coof for a' that:
For a' that, and a' that,
  His ribband, star, and a' that,
The man of independent mind,
  He looks and laughs at a' that.

A prince can mak a belted knight,
  A marquis, duke, and a' that;
But an honest man's aboon his might,
  Gude faith he mauna fa' that!
For a' that, and a' that,
  Their dignities, and a' that,
The pith o' sense, and pride o' worth,
  Are higher ranks than a' that.

Then let us pray that come it may,
  As come it will for a' that,
That sense and worth, o'er a' the earth,
  May bear the gree, and a' that.
For a' that, and a' that,
  It's coming yet, for a' that,
That man to man, the warld o'er,
  Shall brothers be for a' that.

DONALD MACDONALD.

[By JAMES HOGG, author of *The Queen's Wake*, and other poems:
Written in 1803, at the breaking out of the war with France.]

Tune—*Woo'd and married and a.*

My name it is Donald Macdonald,
  I live in the Highlands sae grand;
I've follow'd our banner, an' will do,
  Wharever my Maker has land.
When rankit amang the blue bonnets,
  Nae danger can fear me awa;
I ken that my brethren around me
  Are either to conquer or fa',
    Brogs an' brochen an' a',
    Brochen an' brogs an' a',
    And is na the laddie weel aff
    Wha has brogs an' brochen an' a'.

Short syne we war wonderfu' canty
  Our friends an' our country to see;
But since the proud Consul's grown vaunty,
  We'll meet him by land or by sea.
Wherever a clan is disloyal,
  Wherever our King has a foe,
He'll quickly see Donald Macdonald
  Wi' his Highlanders all in a row.
    Guns an' pistols an' a',
    Pistols an' guns an' a';
    He'll quickly see Donald Macdonald
    Wi' guns an' pistols an' a'.

What though we befriendit young Charlie!
  To tell it I dinna think shame;
Poor lad! he came to us but barely,
  An' reckon'd our mountains his hame:
'Tis true that our reason forbade us,
  But tenderness carried the day;
Had Geordie come friendless amang us,
  Wi' him we had a' gane away.
    Sword an' buckler an' a',
    Buckler an' sword an' a';
    For George we'll encounter the devil
    Wi' sword an' buckler an' a'.

An' O, I would eagerly press him
  The keys o' the East to retain,
For should he gic up the possession,
  We'll soon hae to force them again:
Than yield up an inch wi' dishonour,
  ·Though it war my finishing blow,
He aye may depend on Macdonald,
  Wi's Highlandmen all in a row.

Knees an' elbows an' a',
Elbows an' knees an' a';
Depend upon Donald Macdonald,
His knees an' elbows an' a'.

If Bonaparte land at Fort-William,
  Auld Europe nae langer shall grane;
I laugh, whan I think how we'll gall him
  Wi' bullet, wi' steel, an' wi' stane:
Wi' rocks o' the Nevis an' Gairy
  We'll rattle him aff frae the shore;
Or lull him asleep in a cairney,
  An' sing him *Lochaber no more!*
    Stanes an' bullets an' a',
    Bullets an' stanes an' a';
    We'll finish the Corsican callan'
    Wi' stanes an' wi' bullets an' a'.

The Gordon is gude in a hurry,
  An' Campbell is steel to the bane;
An' Grant, an' Mackenzie, an' Murray,
  An' Cameron will hurkle to nane;
The Stuart is sturdy an' wannle,
  An' sae is Macleod and Mackay;
An' I, their gude-brither Macdonald,
  Sall never be last i' the fray.
    Brogs an' brochen an' a',
    Brochen an' brogs an' a',
    An' up wi' the bonny blue bonnet,
    The kilt an' the feather an' a'.

BANNOCKS O' BARLEY MEAL.

I AM an auld sodger just come from the camp,
And hame to the Highlands I am on a tramp;
My heart it beats light when I think on the shiel,
Whare I fed on bannocks o' barley meal.
In the cause o' my country (my breast's dearest wish),
For ten years and mair, I've had mony a brush;
Now peace has reliev'd me, and hame I sall reel,
To feast upon bannocks o' barley meal.

A drap o' gude whisky, and Nancy my dear,
An auld vet'ran comrade to taste o' our cheer,
Will be a reward for my toils in the fiel',
Wi' plenty o' bannocks o' barley meal.
Of a' our auld feats at our leisure we'll crack,
Syne cour down and sleep a' the night like a tap
Baith care and its cankers may gae to the deil,
If I hae gude bannocks o' barley meal.

When cauld weather comes and the winds rudely blaw,
And cleeds hill and valley whiles knee-deep wi' snaw,
Wi' ease and content, I'm fu' snug in our shiel,
Thrang feasting on bannocks o' barley meal.
In simmer, when a' the cauld blasts flee away,
I'll beak in the sun on the gowany brae;
Sometimes to the pipe may be shake my auld heel,
Syne feed upon bannocks o' barley meal.

LIZZY LIBERTY.

[By the late Rev. JOHN SKINNER.]

Tune—*Tibbie Fowler i' the glen.*

THERE lives a lassie i' the braes,
  And Lizzy Liberty they ca' her,
When she has on her Sunday's claes,
  Ye never saw a lady brawer ;
So a' the lads are wooing at her,
  Courting her, but canna get her,
Bonny Lizzy Liberty,
  There's ow'r mony wooing at her !

Her mither ware a tabbit mutch,
  Her father was an honest dyker,
She's a black-eyed wanton witch,
  Ye winna shaw me mony like her ;
So a' the lads are wooing at her,
  Courting her, but canna get her,
Bonnie Lizzy Liberty,
  Wow, so mony's wooing at her !

A kindly lass she is, I'm seer,
  Has fowth o' sense and smeddum in her,
And nae a swankie far nor near,
  But tries wi' a' his might to win her :
They're wooing at her, fain would hae her,
  Courting her, but canna get her,
Bonnie Lizzy Liberty,
  There's ow'r mony wooing at her.

For kindly tho' she be nae doubt,
  She manna thole the marriage-tether,
But likes to rove and rink about,
  Like Highland cowt amo' the heather:
Yet a' the lads are wooing at her,
  Courting her, but canna get her,
Bonny Lizzy Liberty,
  Wow, sae mony's wooing at her.

It's seven year, and some guid mair,
  Syn Dutch Mynheer made courtship till her,
A merchant bluff and fu' o' care,
  Wi' chuffy cheeks, and bags o' siller;
So Dutch Mynheer was wooing at her,
  Courting her, but cudna get her,
Bonny Lizzy Liberty
  Has ow'r mony wooing at her.

Neist to him came Baltic John,
  Stept up the brae, and leukit at her,
Syne wear his wa wi' heavy moan,
  And in a month or twa forgat her:
Baltic John was wooing at her,
  Courting her, but cudna get her,
Filthy elf, she's nae herself
  Wi' sae mony wooing at her.

Syne after him cam Yankie Doodle,
  Frae hyne ayont the muckle water;
Tho' Yankie's nae yet worth a boddle,
  Wi' might and main he would be at her:
Yankie Doodle's wooing at her,
  Courting her, but canna get her,
Bonny Lizzy Liberty,
  Wow, sae mony's wooing at her.

Now Monkey French is in a roar,
    And swears that nane but he sall hae her,
Tho' he sud wade thro' bluid and gore,
    It's nae the King sall keep him frae her :
So Monkey French is wooing at her,
    Courting her, but canna get her,
Bonny Lizzy Liberty
    Has ow'r mony wooing at her.

For France, nor yet her Flanders frien',
    Need na think that she'll come to them ;
They've casten aff wi' a' their kin,
    And grace and guid have flown fae them :
They're wooing at her, fain wad hae her,
    Courting her, but canna get her,
Bonny Lizzy Liberty,
    Wow, sae mony's wooing at her.

A stately chiel, they ca' John Bull,
    Is unco thrang and glaikit wi' her ;
And gin he cud get a' his wull,
    There's nane can say what he wad gi'e her :
Johnny Bull is wooing at her,
    Courting her, but canna get her,
Filty ted, she'll never wed
    As lang's sae mony's wooing at her.

Even Irish Teague, ayont Belfast,
    Wadna care to speir about her ;
And swears, till he sall breathe his last,
    He'll never happy be without her :
Irish Teague is wooing at her,
    Courting her, but canna get her,
Bonny Lizzy Liberty
    Has ow'r mony wooing at her.

But Donald Scot's the happy lad,
    Tho' a' the lave sud try to rate him;
Whan he steps up the brae sae glad
    She disna ken maist whare to set him:
Donald Scot is wooing at her,
    Courting her, will may be get her,
Bonny Lizzy Liberty,
    Wow, sae mony's wooing at her.

Now Donald tak a frien's advice,
    I ken fu' weel ye fain wad hae her,
As ye are happy, sae be wise,
    And ha'd ye wi' a smackie frae her:
Ye're wooing at her, fain wad hae her,
    Courting her, will may be get her,
Bonny Lizzy Liberty,
    There's ow'r mony wooing at her.

Ye're weel, and wat'sna, lad, they're sayin',
    Wi' getting leave to dwall aside her;
And gin ye had her a' your ain,
    Ye might na find it mows to guide her.
Ye're wooing at her, fain wad hae her,
    Courting her, will may be get her,
Cunning quean, she's ne'er be mine,
    As lang's sae mony's wooing at her.

AULD LANG SYNE.

[By Burns.]

Should auld acquaintance be forgot,
    And never brought to min'?
Should auld acquaintance be forgot,
    And days o' lang syne?

For auld lang syne, my dear,
For auld lang syne,
We'll tak a cup o' kindness yet,
For auld lang syne.

We twa hae run about the braes,
    And pu'd the gowans fine ;
But we've wander'd mony a weary foot,
    Sin auld lang syne.
        For auld, &c.

We twa hae paidl't i' the burn,
    Frae mornin sun till dine :
But seas between us braid hae roar'd,
    Sin auld lang syne.
        For auld, &c.

And here's a hand, my trusty fiere,
    And gie's a hand o' thine ;
And we'll tak a right guid willie-waught,
    For auld lang syne.
        For auld, &c.

And surely ye'll be your pint-stowp,
    And surely I'll be mine ;
And we'll tak a cup o' kindness yet
    For auld lang syne,
        For auld, &c.

BAGRIE O'T.

Wʜᴇɴ I think on this warld's pelf,
And how little I hae o't to myself ;
I sigh when I look on my thread-bare coat,
And shame fa' the gear and the bagrie o't.

Johnny was the lad that held the plough,
But now he has got gowd and gear enough;
I weel mind the day when he was na worth a groat,
And shame fa' the gear and the bagrie o't.

Jenny was the lass that mucked the byre,
But now she goes in her silken attiré:
And she was a lass who wore a plaiding coat,
And shame fa' the gear and the bagrie o't.

Yet a' this shall never danton me,
Sae lang's I keep my fancy free;
While I've but a penny to pay t'other pot,
May the deil tak the gear and the bagrie o't.

MY LOVE SHE'S BUT A LASSIE YET.

My love she's but a lassie yet,
My love she's but a lassie yet,
We'll let her stand a year or twa,
 She'll no be half sae saucy yet.

I rue the day I sought her, O,
I rue the day I sought her, O.
Wha gets her needs na say he's woo'd,
 But he may say he's bought her, O.

Come draw a drap o' the best o't yet,
Come draw a drap o' the best o't yet:
Gae seek for pleasure whare ye will,
 But here I never misst it yet.

We're a' dry wi' drinking o't,
We're a' dry wi' drinking o't:
The minister kisst the fidler's wife,
  He could na preach for thinkin o't.

THE TOAST.

Tune—Saw ye my Peggy.

COME let's ha'e mair wine in,
Bacchus hates repining,
Venus loves nae dwining,
  Let's be blyth and free.
Away with dull, Here t'ye, Sir;
Ye'r mistress, Robie, gi'es her,
We'll drink her health wi' pleasure,
  Wha's belov'd by thee.

Then let Peggy warm ye,
That's a lass can charm ye,
And to joys alarm ye,
  Sweet is she to me.
Some angel ye wad ca' her,
And never wish ane brawer,
If ye bare-headed saw her
  Kiltet to the knee.

Peggy a dainty lass is,
Come let's join our glasses,
And refresh our hauses
  With a health to thee.
Let coofs their cash be clinking,
Be statesmen tint in thinking,
While we with love and drinking,
  Give our cares the lie.

2 E

JOHN BARLEYCORN.

[By BURNS, on the plan of an old song known by the same name.]

THERE were three kings into the East,
　Three kings both great and high,
An' they hae sworn a solemn oath
　John Barleycorn should die.

They took a plough and plow'd him down,
　Put clods upon his head,
And they hae sworn a solemn oath
　John Barleycorn was dead.

But the cheerful spring came kindly on,
　And show'rs began to fall;
John Barleycorn got up again,
　And sore surpris'd them all.

The sultry suns of summer came,
　And he grew thick and strong,
His head weel arm'd wi' pointed spears,
　That no one should him wrong.

The sober autumn enter'd mild,
　When he grew wan and pale;
His bending joints and drooping head
　Show'd he began to fail.

His colour sicken'd more and more,
　He faded into age;
And then his enemies began
　To show their deadly rage.

They've taen a weapon, long and sharp,
  And cut him by the knee;
Then ty'd him fast upon a cart,
  Like a rogue for forgerie.

They laid him down upon his back,
  And cudgell'd him full sore;
They hung him up before the storm,
  And turn'd him o'er and o'er.

They filled up a darksome pit
  With water to the brim,
They heaved in John Barleycorn,
  There let him sink or swim.

They laid him out upon the floor,
  To work him farther woe,
And still as signs of life appear'd,
  They toss'd him to and fro.

They wasted, o'er a scorching flame,
  The marrow of his bones;
But a miller us'd him worst of all,
  He crush'd him between two stones.

And they hae taen his very heart's blood,
  And drank it round and round;
And still the more and more they drank,
  Their joy did more abound.

John Barleycorn was a hero bold,
  Of noble enterprise,
For if you do but taste his blood,
  'Twill make your courage rise.

'Twill make a man forget his woe;
  'Twill heighten all his joy :
'Twill make the widow's heart to sing,
  Tho' the tear were in her eye.

Then let us toast John Barleycorn,
  Each man a glass in hand ;
And may his great posterity
  Ne'er fail in old Scotland !

AULD GUDEMAN, YE'RE A DRUNKEN CARLE.

Auld gudeman, ye're a drunken carle, drunken carle,
A' the lang day ye wink and drink, and gape and
    gaunt ;
Of sottish loons ye're the pink and pearl, pink and
    pearl,
  Ill-far'd, doited, ne'er-do-weel.
Hech, gudewife ! ye're a flyten body, flyten body ;
Will ye hae, but, gude be prais'd ! the wit ye want ;
The puttin cow should be ay a doddy, ay a doddy,
  Mak na sic an awsome reel.

        Ye're a sow, auld man,
        Ye get fou, auld man ;
        Fye shame ! auld man,
        To your wame, auld man :
      Pinch'd I win, wi' spinin tow,
      A plack to cleed your back and pow.

        It's a lie, gudewife,
        It's your tea, gudewife ;

Na, na, gudewife,
Ye spend a', gudewife;
Dinna fa' on me pell-mell,
Ye like a drap fu' weel yoursell.

Ye'se rue, auld gowk, your jest and frolic, jest and
frolic;
Dare ye say, goose, I ever lik'd to tak a drappy?
An 'twerna just for to cure the cholic, cure the cholic,
Diel a drap wad weet my mou.

Troth, gudewife, ye wadna swither, wadna swither,
Soon to tak a cholic, when it brings a drap o' cappy;
But twa score years we hae fought thegither, fought
thegither,
Time it is to 'gree, I trow.

I'm wrang, auld John,
Owre lang, auld John,
For nought, gude John,
We hae fought, gude John;
Let's help to bear ilk ither's weight,
We're far owre feckless now to fight.

Ye're right, gudewife,
The night, gudewife,
Our cup, gude Kate,
We'll sup, gude Kate;
Thegither frae this hour we'll draw,
And toom the stoup atween us twa!

OUR GUIDWIFE'S AY IN THE RIGHT.

Our guidwife's ay in the right,
   Ay in the right, ay in the right,
Our guidwife's ay in the right,
   And I am ay in the wrang, jo!
Right or wrang she's ay in the right,
   She's ay in the right, she's ay in the right;
Right or wrang she's ay in the right,
   And I am ay in the wrang, jo!

There's gowans grow at our kirk wa',
   At our kirk wa', at our kirk wa',
Owre monie a dinsome carlin law
   Fu' blythe to win aboon, jo!
Wad ance that winsome carle Death,
   But rowe her in his black mort-claith,
I'd make a wadset o' an aith
   To feast the parishen, jo!

~~~~~~~~~

WILLIE BREW'D A PECK O' MAUT.

[" This air is [Mr Allan] Masterton's; the song mine.—The oc-
casion of it was this.—Mr William Nicol of the High School,
Edinburgh, during the autumn vacation being at Moffat, honest
Allan, who was at that time on a visit to Dalswinton, and I
went to pay Nicol a visit. We had such a joyous meeting,
that Mr Masterton and I agreed, each in our own way, that we
should celebrate the business."—Burns.]

O Willie brew'd a peck o' maut,
   And Rob and Allan cam to see:
Three blyther hearts, that lee-lang night,
   Ye wad na find in Christendie.

We are na fou, we're nae that fou,
  But just a drappie in our e'e;
The cock may craw, the day may daw,
  And ay we'll taste the barley brec.

Here are we met, three merry boys,
  Three merry boys I trow are we;
And mony a night we've merry been,
  And mony mae we hope to be!
  We are na fou, &c.

It is the moon, I ken her horn,
  That's blinkin in the lift sae hie;
She shines sae bright to wyle us hame,
  But by my sooth she'll wait a wee!
  We are na fou, &c.

Wha first shall rise to gang awa,
  A cuckold, coward loun is he!
Wha first beside his chair shall fa',
  He is the king among us three!
  We are na fou, &c.

CONTENTED WI' LITTLE.

[By BURNS.]

Tune—*Lumps o' Pudding.*

TENTED wi' little, and cantie wi' mair,
ne'er I forgather wi' sorrow and care,
: them a skelp, as they're creepin alang,
a cog o' gude swats, and an auld Scottish sang.

I whyles claw the elbow o' troublesome thought;
But man is a soger, and life is a faught:
My mirth and gude humour are coin in my pouch,
And my freedom's my lairdship nae monarch dare
    touch.

A towmond o' trouble, should that be my fa',
A night o' gude fellowship sowthers it a':
When at the blythe end o' our journey at last,
Wha the deil ever thinks o' the road he has past?

Blind chance, let her snapper and stoyte on her way;
Be't to me, be't frae me, e'en let the jade gae:
Come ease, or come travail; come pleasure, or pain;
My warst word is—Welcome and welcome again!

THEN GUIDWIFE COUNT THE LAWIN.

[By BURNS, with the exception of the chorus, which is part of
an old song.]

G<small>ANE</small> is the day and mirk's the night,
But we'll ne'er stray for faut o' light,
For ale and brandy's stars and moon,
And bluid red wine's the rysin sun.
Then guidwife count the lawin, the lawin, the lawin,
Then guidwife count the lawin, and bring a coggie mair.

There's wealth and ease for gentlemen,
And semple folk maun fecht and fen';
But here we're a' in ae accord,
For ilka man that's drunk's a lord.
   Then guidwife count, &c.

My coggie is a haly pool,
That heals the wounds o' care and dool;
And pleasure is a wanton trout,
An ye drink it a' ye'll find him out.
Then guidwife count, &c.

˙˙˙˙˙˙˙˙˙˙˙

HEY TUTTI TAITI.

[" I have met the tradition universally over Scotland, and parti-
cularly about Stirling, in the neighbourhood of the scene, that
this air was Robert Bruce's march at the battle of Bannock-
burn."—BURNS.

Mr Ritson attaches no credit to this tradition. " It does not
seem at all probable," he says, " that the Scots had any martial music in the time of this monarch; it being their custom,
at that period, for every man in the host to bear a little horn,
with the blowing of which, as we are told by Froissart, they
would make such a horrible noise as if all the devils of hell had
been among them. It is not, therefore, likely, that these un-
polished warriors would be curious

——— ' to move
In perfect phalanx to the Dorian mood
Of flutes and soft recorders.'

These horns, indeed, are the only music ever mentioned by
Barbour, to whom any particular march would have been too
important a circumstance to be passed over in silence; so that
it must remain a moot point, whether Bruce's army were chear-
ed by the sound of even a solitary bagpipe."—RITSON'S *Scottish Songs,* vol. i. p. xcii.]

LANDLADY count the lawin,
The day is near the dawin;
Ye're a' blind drunk, boys,
And I'm but jolly fou.
  Hey tutti taiti,
  How tutti taiti,
  Hey tutti taiti,
    Wha's fou now?

Cog an ye were ay fou,
Cog an ye were ay fou,
I wad sit and sing to you,
   If ye were ay fou.
     Hey tutti, &c.

Weel may we a' be!
Ill may we never see!
God bless the king
   And the companie!
     Hey tutti, &c.

THE PAWKY LOON, THE MILLER.

Young Peggy's to the mill gane
   To sift her daddie's meller;
A kindlie maid I trow she was;—
   A pawky loon the miller!
An' she coost aff her high-heel'd shoon,
   Laced down wi' thread o' siller;
O maiden, kilt your kirtle high,
   Quo' the young pawky miller.

The new-meal flushed the lassie's cheek,
   Ere the black cock was crawing;
An' luve began to light her ee,
   By the ruddie morn was dawing.
O dight, quo' she, yere mealy mou',
   For my twa lips yere drauking;
But the pawky loon he keppit the words
   Wi' his clapping and his smacking.

Young Peggy has unkilt her coat,
　An' hame she's gane fu' cheerlie;
Aften she dighted her bonnie mealy mou',
　An' lilted awa' fu' clearlie:—
Dustie is the miller's coat,
　An' dustie is the colour;
An' mealie was the sweet, sweet kiss
　Which I gat frae the miller!

O what has keeped ye, Peggy lass,
　At sifting o' the meller?
An' what has tuffled yere gowden locks,
　Kepped up wi' kame o' siller?
An hae ye been licking the mouter, lass,
　Or kissing the dusty miller? *

A pawky cat came frae the mill ee—
　Wi' a bonnie, bowsie tailie,
An' it whiskit cross my lips I trow,
　Which made them a' sae mealie.
An' three gude dams ran down the trows,
　Before was grun' the meller.
An' I'm gaun back for shellen seeds
　To the young pawkie miller!

～～～～～～～～

MEDLEY.

As I cam in by Calder fair,
　And yont the Lappard Lee, man,
There was braw kissing there,
　Come butt an' kiss wi' me, man:
There was Highland folk and Lawland folk,
　Unco folk and kend folk,

* In singing, the two last lines of this verse are repeated.

Folk aboon folk i' the yard;
 There's nae folk like our ain folk.
  Dirum dum, &c.

Hech, hey ! Bessy Bell,
 Kilt your coat, Maggy,
Ye'se get a new gown,
 Down the burn Davie.
The Earl o' Mar's bonie thing,
 And muckle bookit wallet;
Play the same tune o'er again,
 And down the burn, for a' that.
  Dirum dum, &c.

Gin ye had been whare I had been,
 Ye wadna been sae wantin,
I gat the lang girdin o't,
 An' I fell thro' the gantrin;
O'er the hills an' far awa,
 My bonnie winsome Willie;
Whare shall our guidman lye?
 The gleed Earl o' Kelly.
  Dirum dum, &c.

Toddle butt, and toddle ben,
 Hey, Tam Brandy;
Crack a louse on Maggy's wame,
 Littly Cocky Bendy.
Three sheep's skins,
 The barber an' his bason:
The bonnie lass o' Patie's Mill,
 Wi' the free and accepted mason.
  Dirum dum, &c.

JEANY WHERE HAST THOU BEEN?

[Written about 1700 by T. D'URFEY, and altered by RAMSAY.]

O JEANY, Jeany, where hast thou been?
  Father and mother are seeking of thee,
Ye have been ranting, playing the wanton,
  Keeping of Jocky company.
O Betty, I've been to hear the mill clack,
  Getting meal ground for the family,
As fow as it gade I brang hame the sack,
  For the miller has taken nae mowter frae me.

Ha! Jeany, Jeany, there's meal on your back,
  The miller's a wanton billy, and slee,
Though victual's come hame again hale, what reck!
  I fear he has taken his mowter aff thee.
And, Betty, ye spread your linen to bleach,
  When that was done, where could you be?
Ha! lass, I saw you slip down the hedge,
  And wanton Willy was following thee.

Ay, Jeany, Jeany, ye gade to the kirk;
  But when it skail'd, where could thou be?
Ye came na hame till it was mirk,
  They say the kissing clerk came wi' ye.
O silly lassie, what wilt thou do?
  If thou grow great, they'll heeze thee hie.
Look to yoursell, if Jock prove true;
  The clerk frae creepies will keep me free.

2 E

HEY HOW, JOHNY LAD.

Hey how, Johny lad,
  Ye're no sae kind's ye sud hae been,
Hey how, Johny lad,
  Ye're no sae kind's ye sud hae been,
Sae weel's ye might hae touzled me,
  And sweetly pried my mou' bedeen.
    Hey how, Johny lad, &c.

My father he was at the pleugh,
  My mother she was at the mill,
My billy he was at the moss,
  And no ane near our sport to spill;
The feint a body was therein,
  Ye need na fley'd for being seen.
    Hey how, Johny lad, &c.

But I maun hae anither jo,
  Whose love gangs never out o' mind,
And winna let the moment pass,
  When to a lass he can be kind;
Then gang yere wa's to Blinkin' Bess,
  Nae mair for Johny sall she green.
    Hey how, Johny lad, &c.

~~~~~~~~~~

JOHN OCHILTREE.

[In the Tea Table Miscellany this song is marked with the
  Z. as being an old song.]

Honest man, John Ochiltree;
Mine ain auld John Ochiltree,

Wilt thou come o'er the moor to me,
And dance as thou was wont to do!
 Alake, alake! I wont to do!
  Ohon, ohon, I wont to do!
 Now wont to do's away frae me,
  Frae silly auld John Ochiltree.

Honest man, John Ochiltree;
Mine ain auld John Ochiltree;.
Come anes out o'er the moor to me,
And do but what thou dow to do.
 Alake, alake! 1 dow to do!
  Walaways! I dow to do!
 To whost and hirple o'er my tree,
  My bonny moor-powt, is a' I may do.

Walaways! John Ochiltree,
For mony a time I tell'd to thee,
Thou rade sae fast by sea and land;
And wadna keep a bridle-hand;
Thou'd tine the beast, thysell wad die,
My silly auld John Ochiltree.
 Come to my arms, my bonny thing,
  And cheer me up to hear thee sing;
 And tell me o'er a' we hae done,
  For thoughts maun now my life sustain.

Gae thy ways, John Ochiltree:
Hae done! it has nae sa'r wi' me.
I'll set the beast in throw the land,
She'll may be fa' in a better hand;
Even sit down there and drink thy fill,
For I'll do as I wont to do still.
 Wont to do, &c.

OUR GOODMAN CAME HAME AT E'EN.

OUR goodman came hame at e'en,
  And hame came he ;
And then he saw a saddle horse,
  Where nae horse should be.

O how came this horse here?
  How can this be?
How came this horse here,
  Without the leave o' me?

    A horse ! quo' she :
    Ay, a horse, quo' he.
Ye auld blind dotard carle,
  Blind mat ye be,
It's naething but a bonny milk cow,
  My minny sent to me.

    A milk cow ! quo' he :
    'Ay, a milk cow, quo' she.
Far hae I ridden,
  And meikle hae I seen,
But a saddle on a cow's back
  Saw I never nane.

Our goodman came hame at e'en,
  And hame came he ;
He spy'd a pair of jack-boots,
  Where nae boots should be.

What's this now, goodwife?
  What's this I see?
How came these boots here
  Without the leave o' me?

    Boots! quo' she:
      Ay, boots, quo' he.
Shame fa' your cuckold face,
  And ill mat ye see,
It's but a pair of water stoups
  The cooper sent to me.

    Water stoups! quo' he:
      Ay water stoups, quo' she.
Far hae I ridden,
  And farer hae I gane,
But siller spurs on water stoups
  Saw I never nane.

Our goodman came hame at e'en,
  And hame came he;
And then he saw a siller sword,
  Where a sword should nae be:

What's this now, goodwife?
  What's this I see?
O how came this sword here
  Without the leave o' me?

    A sword! quo' she:
      Ay, a sword, quo' he.
Shame fa' your cuckold face,
  And ill mat you see,
It's but a parridge spurtle
  My minnie sent to me.

A parridge spurtle! quo' he:
　　Ay, a parridge spurtle, quo' she.
Well, far hae I ridden,
　　And muckle hae I seen,
But siller-handed parridge spurtles
　　Saw I never nane,

Our goodman came hame at e'en,
　　And hame came he;
There he spy'd a powder'd wig,
　　Where nae wig should be.

What's this now, goodwife?
　　What's this I see?
How came this wig here,
　　Without the leave o' me?

A wig! quo' she:
　　Ay, a wig, quo' he.
Shame fa' your cuckold face,
　　And ill mat you see,
It's naething but a clocken hen
　　My minnie sent to me.

A clocken hen! quo' he:
　　Ay, a clocken hen, quo' she.
Far hae I ridden,
　　And muckle hae I seen,
But powder on a clocken hen,
　　Saw I never nane.

Our goodman came hame at e'en,
　　And hame came he;
And there he saw a muckle coat,
　　Where nae coat should be.

O how came this coat here?
How can this be?
How came this coat here
Without the leave o' me?

A coat! quo' she:
Ay, a coat, quo' he.
Ye auld dotard carl,
Blind mat ye be,
It's but a pair of blankets
My minnie sent to me.

Blankets! quo' he:
Ay, blankets, quo' she.
Far hae I ridden,
And muckle hae I seen,
But buttons upon blankets
Saw I never nane.

Ben went our goodman,
And ben went he;
And there he spy'd a sturdy man,
Where nae man should be.

How came this man here?
How can this be?
How came this man here,
Without the leave o' me?

A man! quo' she:
Ay, a man, quo' he.
Poor blind body,
And blinder mat ye be,
It's a new milking maid,
My minnie sent to me.

A maid! quo' he:
 Ay, a maid, quo' she.
Far hae I ridden,
 And muckle hae I seen,
But lang-bearded maidens
 Saw I never nane..

~~~~~~~~

THE AULD MAN'S BEST ARGUMENT.

Tune—*Widow, are ye wawking?*

O WHA's at my chamber door?
 Fair widow are ye wawking!
Auld carl, your suit give o'er,
 Your love lies a' in tawking.
Gi'e me a lad that's young and tight,
 Sweet like an April meadow ;
'Tis sic as he can bless the sight,
 And bosom of a widow.

O widow, wilt thou let me in?
 I'm pawky, wise, and thrifty,
And come of a right gentle kin ;
 I'm little mair than fifty."
Daft carle, dit your mouth,
 What signifies how pawky,
Or gentle born ye be— bot youth,
 In love you're but a gawky.

Then widow let these guineas speak,
 That powerfully plead clinkan,
And if they fail, my mouth I'll steek,
 And nae mair love will think on.

These court indeed, I maun confess,
I think they make you young, Sir,
And ten times better can express
Affection, than your tongue, Sir.

THE BOATIE ROWS.

O WELL may the boatie row,
  And better may she speed;
And leesome may the boatie row,
  That wins the bairns' bread:
The boatie rows, the boatie rows,
  The boatie rows indeed;
And well may the boatie row,
  That wins the bairns' bread.

I coost my line in Largo Bay,
  And fishes I catch'd nine;
There was three to boil, and three to fry,
  And three to bait the line.
The boatie rows, the boatie rows,
  The boatie rows indeed;
And happy be the lot o' a',
  That wish the boatie speed.

O well may the boatie row,
  That fills a heavy creel,
And cleads us a' frae head to foot,
  And buys our parridge meal:
The boatie rows, the boatie rows,
  The boatie rows indeed;
And happy be the lot o' a',
  That wish the boatie speed.

Whan Jamie vow'd he wad be mine,
  And wan frae me my heart,
O muckle lighter grew my creel;
  He swore we'd never part;
The boatie rows, the boatie rows,
  The boatie rows fu' weel;
And muckle lighter is the load,
  Whan love bears up the creel.'

My curtch I put upo' my head,
  And drest mysel fu' bra',
I true my heart was douf and wae
  Whan Jamie ga'ed awa';
But well may the boatie row,
  And lucky be her part,
And lightsome be the lassie's care;
  That yields an honest heart.

Whan Sandy, Jock, and Janety,
  Are up and gotten lear;
They'll help to gar the boatie row,
  And lighten a' our care.
The boatie rows, the boatie rows,
  The boatie rows fu' weel;
And lightsome be her heart that bears
  The murlain and the creel.

And whan we're worn down wi' age,
  And hirpling round the door,
They'll row to keep us dry and warm,
  As we did them before.
Then well may the boatie row,
  She wins the bairns' bread;
And happy be the lot o' a',
  That wish the boatie speed.

SHE RAISE AND LOOT ME IN.

[Written by D'URFEY, and altered to its present state by RAMSAY, who conceived the original too indelicate for his Miscellany.]

THE night her silent sable wore,
   And gloomy were the skies;
Of glitt'ring stars appear'd no more
   Than those in Nelly's eyes.
When at her father's yate I knock'd,
   Where I had often been,
She, shrouded only with her smock,
   Arose and loot me in.

Fast lock'd within her close embrace,
   She trembling stood asham'd;
Her swelling breast, and glowing face,
   And every touch enflam'd.
My eager passion I obey'd,
   Resolv'd the fort to win;
And her fond heart was soon betray'd
   To yield and let me in.

Then, then, beyond expressing,
   Transporting was the joy;
I knew no greater blessing,
   So blest a man was I.
And she, all ravish'd with delight,
   Bid me oft come again;
And kindly vow'd, that ev'ry night
   She'd rise and let me in.

But ah! at last she prov'd with bairn,
   And sighing sat and dull,
And I that was as much concern'd,
   Look'd just e'en like a fool.

Her lovely eyes with tears ran o'er,
　Repenting her rash sin:
She sigh'd, and curs'd the fatal hour
　That e'er she loot me in.

But who cou'd cruelly deceive,
　Or from such beauty part?
I lov'd her so, I cou'd not leave
　The charmer of my heart,
But wedded and conceal'd our crime:
　Thus all was well again;
And now she thanks the happy time
　That e'er she loot me in.

~~~~~~~~~

THE STEP DAUGHTER'S RELIEF,

[By RAMSAY.]

Tune—*The Kirk wad let me be.*

I WAS anes a well-tocher'd lass,
　My mother left dollars to me;
But now I'm brought to a poor pass,
　My step-dame has gart them flee.
My father he's aften frae hame,
　And she plays the deil with his gear;
She neither has lawtith nor shame,
　And keeps the hale house in a steer.

She's barmy-fac'd, thriftless, and bauld,
　And gars me aft fret and repine;
While hungry, half-naked, and cauld,
　I see her destroy what is mine:

But soon I might hope a revenge,
   ,And soon of my sorrows be free,
My poortith to plenty wad change,
   If she were hung up on a tree.

Quoth Ringan, wha lang time had loo'd
   This bonny lass tenderly,
I'll tak thee, sweet May, in thy snood,
   Gif thou wilt gae hame with me.
'Tis only yoursell that I want,
   Your kindness is better to me
Than a' that your step-mother, scant
   Of grace, now has taken frae thee.

I'm but a young farmer, it's true,
   And ye are the sprout of a laird ;
But I have milk-cattle enow,
   And rowth of good rucks in my yard;
Ye shall hae naething to fash ye,
   Sax servants shall jouk to thee:
Then kilt up thy coats, my lassie,
   And gae thy ways hame with me.

The maiden her reason employed,
   Not thinking the offer amiss,
Consented ;—while Ringan o'erjoyed,
   Receiv'd her with mony a kiss.
And now she sits blythly singan,
   And joking her drunken step-dame,
Delighted with her dear Ringan,
   That maks her good-wife at hame.

THE COUNTRY LASS.

Altho' I be but a country lass,
  Yet a lofty mind I bear—O,
And think mysell as good as those
  That rich apparel wear—O.

Altho' my gown be hame-spun grey,
  My skin it is as saft—O,
As them that satin weeds do wear,
  And carry their heads aloft—O.

What tho' I keep my father's sheep,
  The thing that must be done—O,
With garlands of the finest flowers,
  To shade me frae the sun—O.

When they are feeding pleasantly,
  Where grass and flowers do spring—O,
Then on a flowery bank at noon,
  I set me down and sing—O.

My Paisley piggy cork'd with sage,
  Contains my drink but thin—O,
No wines do e'er my brain enrage,
  Or tempt my mind to sin—O.

My country curds, and wooden spoon,
  I think them unco fine—O,
And on a flowery bank at noon,
  I set me down and dine—O.

Altho' my parents cannot raise
  Great bags of shining gold—O,
Like them whase daughters now-a-days
  Like swine are bought and sold—O;

Yet my fair body it shall keep
    An honest heart within—O ;
And for twice fifty thousand crowns,
    I value not a prin—O.

I use nae gums upon my hair,
    Nor chains about my neck—O,
Nor shining rings upon my hands,
    My fingers straight to deck—O.

But for that lad to me shall fa',
    And I have grace to wed—O,
I'll keep a jewel worth them a',
    I mean my maiden-head—O.

If canny Fortune give to me
    The man I dearly love—O,
Tho' we want gear, I dinna care,
    My hands I can improve—O,

Expecting for a blessing still,
    Descending from above—O ;
Then we'll embrace, and sweetly kiss,
    Repeating tales of love—O.

MY JOCKY BLYTH.

Tune.—*Come kiss with me, come clap with me, &c.*

My Jocky blyth, for what thou'st done,
    There is nae help nor mending ;
For thou hast jogg'd me out of tune,
    For a' thy fair pretending.

My mither sees a change on me,
　For my complexion dashes,
And this, alas! has been with thee
　Sae late amang the rashes.

My Peggy, what I've said I'll do,
　To free thee frae their scouling;
Come then and let us buckle to,
　Nae langer let's be fooling.
For her content I'll instant wed,
　Since thy complexion dashes;
And then we'll try a feather-bed,
　'Tis safter than the rashes.

Then, Jocky, since thy love's so true,
　Let mither scoul, I'm easy:
Sae langs I live I ne'er shall rue
　For what I've done to please thee.
And there's my hand I's ne'er complain:
　Oh! well's me on the rashes;
Whene'er thou likest I'll do't again,
　And a fig for a' their clashes.

* * *

A WAUKRIFE MINNIE.

[Burns picked up this old song and tune from a country-girl in
　Nithsdale.]

Whare are you gaun, my bonny lass?
　Whare are you gaun, my hinnie?
She answer'd me right saucilie,
　An errand for my minnie.

O whare live ye, my bonny lass?
  O whare live ye, my hinnie?
By yon burn-side, gin ye maun ken,
  In a wee house wi' my minnie.

But I foor up the glen at e'en,
  To see my bonny lassie;
And lang before the grey morn cam,
  She was na hauf sae saucey.

O weary fa' the waukrife cock,
  And the foumart lay his crawin!
He wauken'd the auld wife frae her sleep,
  A wee blink or the dawin.

An angry wife I wat she raise,
  And o'er the bed she brought her;
And wi' a meikle hazel rung
  She made her a weel-pay'd dochter.

O fare thee weel, my bonny lass!
  O fare thee weel, my hinnie!
Thou art a gay and a bonny lass,
  But thou hast a waukrife minnie.

JENNY NETTLES.

O saw ye Jenny Nettles,
  Jenny Nettles, Jenny Nettles?
Saw ye Jenny Nettles,
  Coming frae the market;
Wi' bag and baggage on her back,
  Her fee and bountith in her lap;
Wi' bag and baggage on her back,
  And a babie in her oxter?

I met ayont the kairny,
   Jenny Nettles, Jenny Nettles,
Singing till her bairny,
   Robin Rattle's bastard;
To flee the dool upo' the stool,
   And ilka ane that mocks her,
She round about seeks Robin out,
   To stap it in his oxter.

Fy, fy! Robin Rattle,
   Robin Rattle, Robin Rattle;
Fy, fy! Robin Rattle,
   Use Jenny Nettles kindly:
Score out the blame, and shun the shame,
   And without mair debate o't,
Tak hame your wean, mak Jenny fain
   The leel and leesome gate o't.

THE TAYLOR.

[The first and third stanzas are old, the other two are by BURNS.
The air is the March of the Corporation of Tailors.]

THE taylor fell thro' the bed, thimble an' a',
The taylor fell thro' the bed, thimble an' a';
The blankets were thin, and the sheets they were sma',
The taylor fell thro' the bed, thimble an' a'.

The sleepy bit lassie she dreaded nae ill,
The sleepy bit lassie she dreaded nae ill;
The weather was cauld and the lassie lay still,
She thought that a taylor could do her nae ill.

Gie me the groat again, cany young man,
Gie me the groat again, cany young man;
The day it is short, and the night it is lang,
The dearest siller that ever I wan.

There's somebody weary wi' lying her lane,
There's somebody weary wi' lying her lane;
There's some that are dowie, I trow wad be fain
To see the bit taylòr come skippin again.

WHEN SHE CAM BEN SHE BOBBED.

O when she cam ben she bobbed fu' law,
O when she cam ben she bobbed fu' law,
And when she cam ben she kiss'd Cockpen,
And syne deny'd she did it at a'.

And was na Cockpen right saucy witha',
And was na Cockpen right saucy witha',
In leaving the dochter of a lord,
And kissin a collier lassie an' a'.

O never look down, my lassie at a',
O never look down, my lassie at a',
Thy lips are as sweet and thy figure compleat,
As the finest dame in castle or ha'.

Tho' thou has nae silk and Holland sae sma,
Tho' thou has nae silk and Holland sae sma,
Thy coat and thy sark are thy ain handywark,
And Lady Jean was never sae braw.

JOCKY BLYTHE AND GAY.

Blythe Jocky young and gay
 Is all my heart's delight;
He's all my talk by day,
 And all my dreams by night.
  If from the lad I be,
  'Tis winter then with me;
  But when he tarries here,
  'Tis summer all the year.

When I and Jocky met
 First on the flow'ry dale,
Right sweetly he me tret,
 And love was a' his tale.
  You are the lass, said he,
  That staw my heart frae me;
  O ease me of my pain,
  And never shaw disdain.

Well can my Jocky kythe
 His love and courtesy,
He made my heart fu' blythe
 When he first spake to me.
  His suit I ill deny'd,
  He kiss'd, and I comply'd:
  Sae Jocky promis'd me
  That he wad faithful be.

I'm glad when Jocky comes,
 Sad when he gangs away;
'Tis night when Jocky glooms,
 But when he smiles 'tis day.
  When our eyes meet I pant,
  I colour, sigh, and faint;
  What lass that wad be kind
  Can better tell her mind?

AULD ROB MORRIS.

[Marked Q. in Ramsay's Miscellany as an old song with additions.]

AULD Rob Morris that wins in yon glen,
He's the king of gude fallows, and the wale of auld
   men,
Has fourscore of black sheep, and fourscore too;
Auld Rob Morris is the man ye maun lo'e.

Had your tongue, mither, and let that abee,
For his eild and my eild can never agree:
They'll never agree, and that will be seen;
For he is fourscore, and I'm but fifteen.

Had your tongue, doughter, and lay by your pride,
For he's be the bridegroom, and ye's be the bride:
He shall ly by your side, and kiss ye too;
Auld Rob Morris is the man ye maun lo'e.

Auld Rob Morris, I ken him fou weel,
His back it sticks out like ony peet-creel,
He's out-shin'd, in-knee'd, and ringle-ey'd too;
Auld Rob Morris is the man I'll ne'er lo'e.

Though auld Rob Morris be an elderly man,
Yet his auld brass it will buy a new pan;
Then, doughter, ye shouldna be sae ill to shoe,
For auld Rob Morris is the man ye maun lo'e.

But auld Rob Morris I never will hae,
His back is sae stiff, and his beard is grown gray:
I had titter die than live wi' him a year;
Sae mair of Rob Morris I never will hear.

AULD ROB MORRIS.

[By BURNS.]

THERE's auld Rob Morris, that wins in yon glen,
He's the king of gude fellows, and wale of auld men;
He has gowd in his coffers, he has sheep, he has kine,
And ae bonny lassie, his darling and mine.

She's fresh as the morning, the fairest in May,
She's sweet as the ev'ning among the new hay;
As blythe and as artless as the lambs on the lea,
And dear to my heart as the light to my e'e.

But, oh! she's an heiress; auld Robin's a laird,
And my daddie has nought but a cot-house and yard;
A wooer like me mauna hope to come speed:
The wounds I maun hide, which will soon be my dead.

The day comes to me, but delight brings me nane;
The night comes to me, but my rest it is gane;
I wander my lane, like a night-troubled ghaist,
And I sigh as my heart it wad burst in my breast.

Oh! had she but been of a lower degree,
I then might ha'e hop'd she wad smil'd upon me;
Oh! how past describing had then been my bliss!
As now my distraction no words can express!

BUSK YE, BUSK YE.

BUSK ye, busk ye, my bonny bride;
Busk ye, busk ye, my winsome marrow;

Busk ye, busk ye, my bonny bride,
  Busk and go to the braes of Yarrow:
There we will sport and gather dew,
  Dancing while lav'rocks sing in the morning;
There learn frae turtles to prove true;
  O Bell, ne'er vex me with thy scorning.

To westlin breezes Flora yields,
  And when the beams are kindly warming,
Blythness appears o'er all the fields,
  And Nature looks mair fresh and charming.
Learn frae the burns that trace the mead,
  Tho' on their banks the roses blossom,
Yet hastily they flow to Tweed,
  And pour their sweetness in his bosom.

Haste ye, haste ye, my bonny Bell,
  Haste to my arms, and there I'll guard thee,
Wi' free consent my fears repel,
  I'll wi' my love and care reward thee.
Thus sang I saftly to my fair,
  Who rais'd my hopes with kind relenting.
O queen of smiles! I ask nae mair,
  Since now my bonny Bell's consenting.

JOCKY FOU, AND JENNY FAIN.

[Marked Q. in the Tea-Table Miscellany, as being an old song
with additions.]

  JOCKY fou, and Jenny fain,
  Jenny was nae ill to gain,
  She was couthy, he was kind,
  And thus the wooer tell'd his mind.

Jenny, I'll nae mair be nice,
Gi'e me love at ony price;
I'll ne'er prig for red or white,
Love alane can gi'e delyte.

Ithers seek they kenna what,
Features, carriage, and a' that;
Gi'e me love in her I court:
Love to love maks a' the sport.

Let love sparkle in her e'e;
Let her lo'e nae man but me;
That's the tocher gude I prize,
There the lover's treasure lies.

Colours mingl'd unco fine,
Common motives lang sinsyne,
Never can engage my love,
Until my fancy first approve.

It is na meat but appetite
That maks our eating a delyt;
Beauty is at best deceit;
Fancy only kens nae cheat.

TARRY WOO.

[The first half of this song, as well as the tune itself, are conjectured
by Burns to be much older than the rest of the words, which were
probably RAMSAY's.]

TARRY woo, O tarry woo,
Tarry woo is ill to spin,
Card it weel, oh card it weel,
Card it weel ere ye begin.

When 'tis carded, row'd and spun,
Then the work is haflens done;
But when woven, dress'd, and clean,   •
It may be cleading for a queen.

Sing, my bonny harmless sheep,
That feed upon the mountains steep,
Bleating sweetly as ye go
Thro' the winter's frost and snow!
Hart, and hind, and fallow-deer,
No by half so useful are;
Frae kings to him that hauds the plow,
All are oblig'd to tarry woo.

Up, ye shepherds, dance and skip,
O'er the hills and valleys trip,
Sing up the praise of tarry woo,
Sing the flocks that bear it too:
Harmless creatures, without blame!
That clead the back, and cram the wame;
Keep us warm and hearty fou;
Leeze me on the tarry woo.

How happy is the shepherd's life,
Far frae courts and free frae strife,
While the gimmers bleat and bae,
And the lambkins answer mae:
No such music to his ear;
Of thief or fox he has no fear,
Sturdy kent, and colly true,
Will defend the tarry woo.

He lives content, and envies none;
Not even a monarch on his throne,
Tho' he the royal sceptre sways,
Has not sweeter holidays,

2 H

Who'd be a king, can ony tell?
When a shepherd sings so well;
Sings sae well, and pays his due,
With honest heart and tarry woo.

~~~~~~~~~~

O AN YE WERE DEAD, GUDEMAN.

O AN ye were dead, gudeman,
A green turf on your head, gudeman:
I wad bestow my widow-hood
Upon a ranton Highlandman.
There's sax eggs in the pan, gudeman,
There's sax eggs in the pan, gudeman;
There's ane to you, and twa to me,
And three to our John Highlandman.
   O an' ye were dead, &c.

A sheep-head's in the pot, gudeman,
A sheep-head's in the pot, gudeman;
The flesh to him, the broo to me,
An' the horns become your brow, gudeman.
   Sing round about the fire wi' a rung she ran,
   An' round about the fire wi' a rung she ran:
   Your horns shall tie you to the staw,
   And I shall bang your hide, gudeman.

~~~~~~~~~~

JOHN HIGHLANDMAN.

[By BURNS.]

Tune—O an ye were dead, gudeman.

A HIGHLAND lad my love was born,
The Lawland laws he held in scorn;
But he still was faithfu' to his clan,
My gallant braw John Highlandman.

Sing, hey my braw John Highlandman!
Sing, ho my braw John Highlandman!
There's not a lad in a' the lan'
Was match for my John Highlandman.

With his philebeg an' tartan plaid,
And gude claymore down by his side,
The ladies' hearts he did trepan,
My gallant braw John Highlandman.
    Sing, hey, &c.

We ranged a' from Tweed to Spey,
And liv'd like lords and ladies gay;
For a Lawland face he feared nane,
My gallant braw John Highlandman.
    Sing, hey, &c.

They banish'd him beyond the sea,
But ere the bud was on the tree,
Adown my cheeks the pearls ran,
Embracing my John Highlandman.
    Sing, hey, &c.

But, oh! they catch'd him at the last,
An' bound him in a dungeon fast;
My curse upon them every one,
They've hang'd my braw John Highlandman.
    Sing, hey, &c.

And now a widow, I must mourn
The pleasures that will ne'er return;
Nae comfort but a hearty can,
When I think on John Highlandman.
    Sing, hey, &c.

THE HAWS OF CROMDALE.

[It is probable that this song was originally composed on the victory
gained by the gallant Marquis of Montrose, over Sir John Ury at
the village of Aulderne in Nairn; and the descriptive part of the
song, in reference to that battle, is borne out by historical facts.
The Marquis having accomplished a very skilful retreat from
Dundee to the skirts of the Highlands, before the forces of Ge-
nerals Baillie and Ury, was there joined by a considerable reinforcement under Lord Gordon, with which he commenced offensive
operations. Ury marched northwards to prevent Lord Gordon
from levying men for the service of King Charles; but finding he
was too late, continued his march to Inverness, where the Earl of
Seaforth was waiting to join him with a body of men, and while
halting at Elgin, received the unexpected intelligence that Montrose was rapidly approaching, who he imagined to be still on the
south side of the Grampians. The General of the Covenanters
retreated with the utmost precipitation to Inverness, whither he
was closely pursued by Montrose, who encamped at Aulderne.
Montrose's army scarcely exceeded seventeen hundred, while the
reinforcement under Seaforth increased General Ury's to four
thousand men: thinking himself therefore able to oblige Montrose to retreat in his turn, he marched to attack him in his
camp, and suffered a most complete defeat, three thousand of his
men being killed, and five hundred made prisoners, he himself
with the cavalry however effected a retreat, and joined Baillie.
The loss on the part of the victors is scarcely credible, only fifteen
men having been killed.
It was upwards of forty years after the defeat and execution of Montrose, that any action was fought at Cromdale; there would
therefore be the most glaring anachronisms in the song ascribing
to that nobleman the command in the engagement, and styling
the English army, " Cromwell's men," were we not to suppose
it to have been composed on the battle above referred to.]

As I came in by Achindown,
A little wee bit frae the town,
When to the Highlands I was bown,
  To view the haws o' Cromdale.

I met a man in tartan trews,
I speer'd at him what was the news?
Quo' he, the Highland army rues,
 That e'er we came to Cromdale.

We were in bed, sir, every man,
When the English host upon us came;
A bloody battle then began
 Upon the haws of Cromdale.
The English horse they were so rude,
They bath'd their hoofs in Highland blood,
But our brave clans they boldly stood,
 Upon the haws of Cromdale.

But alas we could no longer stay,
For o'er the hills we came away,
And sore we do lament the day
 That e'er we came to Cromdale.
Thus the great Montrose did say,
Can you direct the nearest way,
For I will o'er the hills this day,
 And view the haws of Cromdale?

Alas, my lord, you're not so strong,
You scarcely have two thousand men,
And there's twenty thousand on the plain,
 Stand rank and file on Cromdale.
Thus the great Montrose did say,
I say, direct the nearest way,
For I will o'er the hills this day,
 And see the haws of Cromdale.

They were at dinner every man,
When great Montrose upon them came,
A second battle then began
 Upon the haws of Cromdale.

The Grants, Mackenzies, and Mackays,
Soon as Montrose they did espy,
O then they fought most vehemently
    Upon the haws of Cromdale.

The Macdonalds they return'd again,
The Camerons did their standard join,
Macintosh play'd a bonny game
    Upon the haws of Cromdale.
The Macgregors faught like lyons bold,
Macphersons none could them controul,
Maclauchlins faught like loyal souls
    Upon the haws of Cromdale.

Macleans, Macdougalls, and Macneals,
So boldly as they took the field,
And made their enemies to yield
    Upon the haws of Cromdale.
The Gordons boldly did advance,
The Frazers fought with sword and lance,
The Grahams they made their heads to dance
    Upon the haws of Cromdale.

The loyal Stuarts, with Montrose,
So boldly set upon their foes,
And brought them down with Highland blows
    Upon the haws of Cromdale.
Of twenty thousand Cromwell's men,
Five hundred went to Aberdeen,
The rest of them lyes on the plain
    Upon the haws of Cromdale.

CARL AN THE KING COME.

Carl an the king come,
Carl an the king come ;
Thou shalt dance and I will sing,
Carl an the king come.

An somebodie were come again,
Then somebodie maun cross the main,
And every man shall hae his ain,
Carl an the king come.
 Carl an, &c.

I trow we swapped for the warse,
We gae the boot and better horse ;
And that we'll tell them at the cross,
Carl an the king come.
 Carl an, &c.

Coggie an the king come,
Coggie an the king come,
I'se be fou and thou'se be toom,
Coggie an the king come.
 Coggie an, &c.

~~~~~~~~~

OE'R THE WATER TO CHARLIE.

Come boat me o'er, come row me o'er,
 Come boat me o'er to Charlie ;
I'll gie John Ross another bawbee,
 To boat me o'er to Charlie.

We'll o'er the water, well o'er the sea,
We'll o'er the water to Charlie;
Come weal, come woe, we'll gather and go,
And live or die wi' Charlie.

I lo'e weel my Charlie's name,
  Tho' some there be abhor him:
But O, to see auld Nick gaun hame,
  And Charlie's faes before him!
    We'll o'er, &c.

I swear and vow by moon and stars,
  And sun that shines so early!
If I had twenty thousand lives,
  I'd die as aft for Charlie.
    We'll o'er, &c.

~~~~~~~~~

RISE AND FOLLOW CHARLIE.

I'M inspir'd, inspir'd, and fir'd!
I'm inspir'd, nay, fiercely fir'd!
I'm all on fire with strong desire
  To rise and follow Charlie!

Flush from France, that hot-land, sirs,
Charlie's come to Scotland, sirs;
Push round the quaich and bottle, and, sirs,
  Quaff a health to Charlie!
    Ha teen fo'am, fo'am, fo'am,
    Ha teen fo'am, fo'am, fo'am,
    Ha teen fo'am, fo'am, fo'am,
      To rise and follow Charlie!

Highlandman and Lowlandman,
The princely youth will follow, man!
To beat the red-coats hollow, man,
  Wha wadna rise wi' Charlie?
    Ha teen, &c.

Let burly Wull frae Flanders come,
Wi' brazen trump and kettle-drum!
Bang up the bag-pipe! 'tis our trum'!
  Let's trim the German rarely!
    Ha teen, &c.

We fear nae foes nor foreign loons,
Wi' hairy lips and pantaloons;
Nor Saxons stern, nor bluff dragoons,
  Up! up! and waur them fairly!
    Ha teen, &c.

Ilka loyal heart and leal,
Ye wha love auld Albyn's weal,
Come, drive the rebels to the deil!
  And do't again for Charlie!
    Ha teen, &c.

The tongue is an unruly thing;
Whence imps o' hell in words tak wing!
See, James the Third and Eighth—The King!
  And—not forgettin' Charlie!
    Ha teen, &c.

~~~~~~~~~~~

CHARLIE HE'S MY DARLING.

'Twas on a Monday morning,
  Right early in the year,
That Charlie came to our town,
  The young Chevalier.

An' Charlie he's my darling,
My darling, my darling,
Charlie he's my darling,
The young Chevalier.

As he was walking up the street,
   The city for to view,
O there he spied a bonny lass
   The window looking thro'.
     An' Charlie, &c.

Sae light's he jimped up the stair,
   And tirled at the pin;
And wha sae ready as hersel,
   To let the laddie in.
     An' Charlie, &c.

He set his Jenny on his knee,
   All in his Highland dress;
For brawlie weel he ken'd the way
   To please a bonnie lass.
     An' Charlie, &c.

It's up yon hethery mountain,
   And down yon scroggy glen,
We daurna gang a-milking,
   For Charlie and his men.
     An' Charlie, &c.

HIGHLAND LADDIE.

THE bonniest lad that e'er I saw,
   Bonnie laddie, Highland laddie;
Wore a plaid and was fu' braw,
   Bonnie Highland laddie.

On his head a bonnet blue,
 Bonnie laddie, Highland laddie,
His royal heart was firm and true,
 Bonnie Highland laddie.

Trumpets sound and cannons roar,
 Bonnie lassie, Lawland lassie,
And a' the hills wi' echoes roar,
 Bonnie Lawland lassie.
Glory, honour, now invite,
 Bonnie lassie, Lawland lassie,
For freedom and my king to fight,
 Bonnie Lawland lassie.

The sun a backward course shall take,
 Bonnie laddie, Highland laddie,
Ere ought thy manly courage shake,
 Bonnie Highland laddie.
Go, for yoursel procure renown,
 Bonnie laddie, Highland laddie,
And for your lawful king his crown,
 Bonnie Highland laddie!

BONNY LADDIE.

WHAR' ha'e ye been a' day,
 Bonny laddie, Highland laddie;
Ha'e ye seen him that's far away,
 Bonny laddie, Highland laddie.

On his head a bonnet blue,
 Bonny laddie, Highland laddie,
Tartan plaid, and Highland trew,
 Bonny laddie, Highland laddie.

When he drew his gude braid sword,
  Bonny laddie, Highland laddie,
Then he ga'e his royal word,
  Bonny laddie, Highland laddie—

That frae the field he ne'er wou'd flee,
  Bonny laddie, Highland laddie,
But wi' his friends wad live or die,
  Bonny laddie, Highland laddie.

Geordie sits in Charlie's chair,
  Bonny laddie, Highland laddie;
De'il cock him gin he bide there,
  Bonny laddie, Highland laddie.

I hope to see him mount the throne,
  Bonny laddie, Highland laddie;
Weel ye ken it is his own,
  Bonny laddie, Highland laddie.

Wearie fa' the Lawland lown,
  Bonny laddie, Highland laddie,
Wha took frae him the British crown,
  Bonny laddie, Highland laddie:

But weels me on the kelted clan,
  Bonny laddie, Highland laddie,
Wha fought for him at Prestonpan,
  Bonny laddie, Highland laddie.

Ken ye the news I ha'e to tell,
  Bonny laddie, Highland laddie—
Cumberland's awa' to hell!
  Bonny laddie, Highland laddie:

When he cam' to the Stygian shore,
   Bonny laddie, Highland laddie,
The De'il himsel' wi' fright did roar!
   Bonny laddie, Highland laddie:

Then Charon grim came out to him,
   Bonny laddie, Highland laddie—
You're welcome here, ye devil's limb!
   Bonny laddie, Highland laddie.

He put on him a philabeg,
   Bonny laddie, Highland laddie,
And in his nose they ram'd a peg,
   Bonny laddie, Highland laddie.

How he did skip and he did roar!
   Bonny laddie, Highland laddie;
The de'ils ne'er saw sic fun before,
   Bonny laddie, Highland laddie.

They took him neist to Satan's ha',
   Bonny laddie, Highland laddie,
There to lig wi' his grand-papa,
   Bonny laddie, Highland laddie.

The De'il sat girnin' in the nook,
   Bonny laddie, Highland laddie,
Rivin' sticks to roast the Duke,
   Bonny laddie, Highland laddie.

They pat him neist upon a spit,
   Bonny laddie, Highland laddie,
And roasted him baith head and feet,
   Bonny laddie, Highland laddie.

Wi' scalden brunstane, next wi' fat,
  Bonny laddie, Highland laddie,
They flamm'd his carcase well wi' that,
  Bonnie laddie, Highland laddie.

They eat him up baith stoop and roop,
  Bonnie laddie, Highland laddie;
And that's the gate they guided the Duke,
  Bonny laddie, Highland laddie.

CULLODEN.

[By Mr WILLIAM NICHOLSON of Kirkcudbright, author of a collection of " Poems descriptive of Rural Life and Manners," published at Edinburgh in 1810.]

    Tune—*O! are ye sleepin', Maggie?*

THE heath-cock craw'd o'er muir an' dale,
  Red raise the sun, the sky was cloudy,
While must'ring far, wi' distant yell,
  The north'ren bands march'd stern an' steady.
    O! Duncan, Donald's ready!
    O! Duncan, Donald's ready!
    Wi' sword an' targe he seeks the charge,
    An' frae his shouther flings the plaidy!

Nae mair we chase the fleet-foot roe,
  O'er down an' dale, o'er mountain flyin';
But rush like tempests on the foe,
  Thro' mingled groans the war-note cryin',
    O! Duncan, Donald's ready, &c.

A prince is come to claim his ain,
  A stem o' Stuart, frien'less Charlie ;
What Highlan' han' its blade wou'd hain,
  What Highlan' heart behint would tarry ?
    O ! Duncan, Donald's ready, &c.

I see our hardy clans appear,
  The sun back frae their blades is beamin' ;
The south'ren tramp falls on my ear,
  Their banner'd lions proudly streamin'.
    Now, Donald, Duncan's ready !
    Now, Donald, Duncan's ready !
    Within his hand he grasps his brand ;
    Fierce is the fray, the field is bluidy !

But lang shall Scotlan' rue the day,
  She saw her flag sae fiercely flyin' ;
Culloden's hills were hills o' wae ;
  Her honour lost, her warriors dyin'.
    Duncan now nae mair is ready !
    Duncan now nae mair is ready !
    The brand is fa'en frae out his han',
    His bonnet blue lies stain'd and bluidy !

Fair Flora's gane her love to seek ;
  Lang may she wait for his returnin' ;
The midnight dews fa' on her cheek ;
  What han' shall dry her tears o' mournin' ?
    Duncan now nae mair is ready, &c.

BAULDY FRASER.

[By Mr James Hogg, author of the " Queen's Wake," &c. and published by him in the " Forest Minstrel," a selection of songs printed in 1810.]

Tune—*Whigs o' Fife.*

My name is Bauldy Fraser, man;
I'm puir an' auld, an' pale an' wan,
I brak my shin, an' tint a han'
    Upon Culloden lee, man.
Our Highlan' clans war bauld an' stout,
An' thought to turn their faes about,
But gat that day a desperate rout,
    An' owre the hills did flee, man.

Sic hurly-burly ne'er was seen,
Wi' cuffs, an' buffs, an' blindit een,
While Highlan' swords, o' metal keen,
    War gleamin' grand to see, man.
The cannons rowtit in our face,
An' brak our banes, an' raive our claes;
'Twas then we saw our ticklish case
    Atween the deil an' sea, man.

Sure Charlie an' the brave Lochyell
Had been that time beside theirsell,
To plant us in the open fell
    In the artillery's e'e, man:
For had we met wi' Cumberland
By Athol braes or yonder strand,
The bluid o' a' the savage band
    Had dy'd the German sea, man. *

* Six weeks before the battle of Culloden, some officers proposed
sending up meal to several places in the Highlands, and in particular

But down we drappit dadd for dadd;
I thought it sude hae put me mad,
To see sae mony a Highlan' lad
    Lie bluth'rin on the brae, man.

towards Badenoch, that in the event of the Duke of Cumberland's marching to Inverness, before the army was gathered, they might retreat for a few days, till they could assemble; or, if a misfortune should happen by a defeat, there might be some provisions in those parts; but this was reckoned a timorous advice; and was rejected as such; though I have reason to think it was the opinion of almost all the Highland officers, who were not for precipitating any thing. There is no doubt to be made, but that the Highlanders could have avoided fighting, till they had found their advantage by so doing: They could have made a summer's campaign, without running the risque of any misfortune; they could have marched through the hills to places in Banffshire, Aberdeenshire, the Mearns, Perthshire, Lochaber, and Argyllshire, by ways that regular troops could not have followed; and if they had ventured among the mountains, it must have been attended with great danger and difficulty; their convoys might have been cut off, and opportunities would have offered to attack them with almost a certainty of success: and though the Highlanders had neither money nor magazines, they would not have starved in that season of the year, so long as there were sheep and cattle; they could also have separated themselves in two or three different bodies, got meal for some days provision, met again at a place appointed, and might have fallen upon the enemy where they least expected; they could have marched in three days what would have taken regular troops five; nay, had these taken the high roads (as often they would have been obliged, upon account of their carriages) it would have taken them ten or twelve days; in short, they might have been so harrassed and fatigued, that they must have been in the greatest distress and difficulties, and at length probably been destroyed, at least much might have been expected by gaining of time; perhaps the Highlanders might have been enabled to have made an offensive, instead of a defensive war. This was the opinion of many of the officers who considered the consequences of losing a battle: they knew well, that few Highlanders would join heartily against them so long as they continued entire; but would upon a defeat. But any proposition to postpone fighting was ill received, and was called discouraging the army.—*Lord George Murray's Account of the Battle of Culloden.*

2 I 3

I thought we ance had won the fray;
We smasht ae wing till it gae way;
But the other side had lost the day,
    An' skelpit fast awa, man.

When Charley wi' Macpherson met, *
Like Hay, he thought him back to get;
" We'll turn," quo' he, " an' try them yet;
    We'll conquer or we'll dee, man."
But Donald jumpit owre the burn,
An' sware an aith she wadna turn,
Or sure she wad hae cause to mourn;
    Then fast awa did flee, man.

O! had you seen that hunt o' death! †
We ran until we tint our breath,
Aye looking back for fear o' skaith
    Wi' hopeless shinin' e'e, man.
But Britain ever may deplore
That day upon Drumossie moor,
Whar thousands ta'en war drench'd in gore, ‡
    Or hang'd outowr a tree, man,

---

* The Macphersons were met about five or six miles from the field of battle, on their march to Inverness, and on learning the unfortunate issue of the battle, returned to their own country.

† The cavalry under Lord Ancrum pursued so close, and made such terrible slaughter, that not only the field of battle, but the road to Inverness, for four miles, was covered with mangled or dead bodies; and the slaughter was so undistinguished, that many of the poor inhabitants of Inverness, who had come out of curiosity to see the battle, being clad in the Highland dress, and therefore impossible to be distinguished, were indiscriminately put to the sword among the fugitives.

‡ The glory of the victory was sullied by the barbarity of the soldiers. They had been provoked by their former disgraces to the most savage thirst of revenge; not contented with the blood which

O, Cumberland! what mean'd ye then
To ravage ilka Highlan' glen? *
Our crime was truth an' love to ane;
　　We had nae spite at thee, man.
An' you or yours may yet be glad
To trust the honest Highlan' lad;
The bonnet blue an' belted plaid
　　Will stand the last o' three, man.

was so profusely shed in the heat of action, they traversed the field after the battle, and massacred those miserable wretches who lay maimed and expiring; nay some officers acted a part in this cruel scene of assassination !—*Smollett's History.*

The moor was covered with blood; and our men, what with killing the enemy, dabbling their feet in the blood, and splashing it about one another, looked like so many butchers.—*Letter on the Battle.*

* Wherever the royal troops came they left nothing that belonged to the inhabitants, carrying fire and sword through the country, and driving off the cattle, which were brought in to head-quarters in great numbers, sometimes two thousand in a drove, by which the people were in a most deplorable state, and perished either by sword or famine. Lochiel's house, at Achnacary, was burnt on the 28th of May; Kinlochmoidart's (who had been a prisoner at Edinburgh since November), Keppoch's, Glengary's, and Cluny's were served in the same manner. Vast numbers of the common people's houses or huts were likewise laid in ashes; all the cattle, sheep, goats, &c. were carried off; and several poor people, especially women and children, were found dead in the hills, supposed to be starved. A body of seven hundred troops entered Balquhidder, and proceeded to the braes of Monteith, in search of Glengyle, but not finding him, they burnt his house, and all the houses in Craigroyston possessed by the Macgregors, and carried the cattle to Crieff. Even places of worship were not exempt from the ravages of the soldiery; several mass-houses about Strathbogie were pulled down by them; some Nonjurant Episcopal meeting-houses were likewise burnt and destroyed, and they were generally shut up all over the kingdom.—*History of the Rebellion* 1745.

WAES ME FOR PRINCE CHARLY.

[By Mr WILLIAM GLEN of Glasgow, and first published in a small collection of songs printed at Edinburgh, 1816.]

Tune—*Johnny Faa.*

A WEE bird cam to our ha' door,
   He warbled sweet and clearly,
An' aye the o'ercome o' his sang
   Was, " Waes me for Prince Charly !"
O ! when I heard the bonny soun',
   The tears cam happin rarely ;
I took my bannet off my head,
   For weel I lo'ed Prince Charly.

Quoth I, " My bird, my bonny bonny bird,
   Is that a sang ye borrow ?
Are these some words ye've learnt by heart,
   Or a lilt o' dool an' sorrow ?"
" Oh ! no, no, no," the wee bird sang,
   " I've flown sin' mornin' early ;
But sic a day o' wind an' rain—
   Oh ! waes me for Prince Charly.

" On hills that are by right his ain,
   He roves a lonely stranger ;
On ev'ry side he's prest by want,
   On ev'ry side is danger. *

* About the middle of July, while Prince Charles was in Bora-
dale, he was hemmed in by the troops on all sides. In this situation
he was advised to get if possible to the braes of Glenmoriston, to

Yestreen I met him in a glen,
    My heart maist burstit fairly ;
For sadly chang'd indeed was he—
    Oh ! waes me for Prince Charly.

" Dark night came on, the tempest roar'd
    Loud o'er the hills and vallies ; .
An' whar was't that your Prince lay down,
    Whase hame should'been a palace ?
He row'd him in a Highland plaid,
    Which cover'd him but sparely,
An' slept beneath a bush o' broom— ...
    Oh ! waes me for Prince Charly."

sculk there, and in Lovat's country, till the passes should be opened.
He sent for Donald Cameron of Glenpean to be his guide. That
gentleman came accordingly, and in the night conducted the Prince
safe through the guards who were. in. the pass ;. being obliged to
creep upon all fours, so close to the tents, that they heard the soldiers
talking to one another, and saw them walking between them and the
fires.—The Prince and Macdonald of Glenaladale got safe into
Glenmoriston about the 24th, but were almost famished, having been
forty-eight hours without meat, when Glenaladale found out eight
men, who had been in the Prince's army, and rejoiced to have it in
their power to do him further service, which they accordingly did of
various kinds.—With Glenaladale and these men the Prince continued between the braes of Glenmoriston and Glen-strathferrar, till
the guards were removed, and the passes opened.—About the 14th
of August, he went' with his new retinue into Lochaber, to Achnasual, on the side of Loch-Arkaig, two miles from Achnacarie, the
seat of Lochiel.—They found it burnt, and all the cattle drove
away ! In great distress they remained for some time, when, at last,
one of the Glenmoriston men spied a single hart, which he took aim
at and shot ; and this, without bread or salt, afforded present sub-
sistence to the Prince and his company. The Prince and Lochiel
now sent in quest of each other. Lochiel's messenger found the
Prince in a hut built on purpose, between Achnasual and Loch-
Arkaig. He was bare-footed, had a long beard, a dirty shirt, an old
black kelt coat, durk by his side ; but chearful withal, and in good
health.—*Narrative of the several Passages of the Young Chevalier.*

But now the bird saw some red-coats,
  An' he shook his wings wi' anger—
" Oh ! this is no a land for me,
  I'll tarry here nae langer."
He hover'd on the wing a while,
  Ere he departed fairly ;
But weel I mind the fareweel strain
    Was, " Waes me for Prince Charly !"

GUDE NIGHT AND JOY.

THE night is my departing night,
  The morn's the day I maun awa,
There's no a friend or fae o' mine,
  But wishes that I were awa.
What I hae done for lack o' wit,
  I never never can reca' ;
I trust ye're a' my friends as yet,
  Gude night and joy be wi' you a'.

HERE'S A HEALTH.

HERE's a health to them that's awa,
Here's a health to them that's awa ;
Here's a health to them that were here short syne,
But canna be here the day.
Its gude to be merry and wise,
Its gude to be honest and true,
Its gude to be aff wi' the auld love
Before ye be on wi' the new.

IT WAS A' FOR OUR RIGHTFU' KING.

It was a' for our rightfu' King
  We left fair Scotland's strand;
It was a' for our rightfu' King,
  We e'er saw Irish land, my dear,
    We e'er saw Irish land.

Now a' is done that men can do,
  And a' is done in vain:
My love and native land fareweel,
  For I maun cross the main, my dear,
    For I maun, &c.

He turn'd him right and round about
  Upon the Irish shore,
And gae his bridle reins a shake,
  With, adieu for evermore, my dear,
    With, adieu, &c.

The soger frae the wars returns,
  The sailor frae the main,
But I hae parted frae my love,
  Never to meet again, my dear,
    Never to meet, &c.

When day is gane, and night is come,
  And a' folk bound to sleep;
I think on him that's far awa,
  The lee-lang night and weep, my dear,
    The lee-lang, &c.

LASSIE LIE NEAR ME.

Lang ha'e we parted been,
  Lassie, my dearie;
Now are we met again,
  Lassie, lie near me:
    Near me, near me,
    Lassie, lie near me;
  Lang hast thou lain thy lane,
    Lassie, lie near me.

Frae dread Culloden's field,
  Bluidy and dreary,
Mourning my country's fate,
  Lanely and weary:
    Weary, weary,
    Lanely and weary;
  Become a sad banish'd wight,
    Far frae my dearie.

Loud, loud the wind did roar,
  Stormy and eerie,
Far frae my native shore,
  Far frae my dearie:
    Near me, near me,
    Dangers stood near me;
  Now I've escap'd them a',
    Lassie, lie near me.

A' that I ha'e endur'd,
  Lassie, my dearie,
Here in thine arms is cur'd,
  Lassie lie near me.
    Near me, near me,
    Lassie, lie near me;
  Lang hast thou lain thy lane,
    Lassie, lie near me.

FAREWEEL TO AULD SCOTIA.

[By ANDREW BAIN, and first published in a small collection of songs, printed at Edinburgh in 1816.]

Tune—*Logan Water.*

FAREWEEL to Scotia's hills and dales,
Her heath-clad moors an' flow'ry vales,
Where thistles bloom, an' roses blaw,
    Perfuming Caledonia.
Fareweel the lightsome knowes and braes,
Where blythe I've spent my youthfu' days;
These happy scenes, I leave them a',
    An' sail frae Caledonia.

To India's distant shores I bend,
Wi' fickle fortune to contend;
But whatsoe'er will me befa',
    I'll still love Caledonia.
No worldly wealth, nor storms o' fate,
Can e'er frae me eradicate
That glorious name aboon them a',
    My native Caledonia.

Fareweel the burns that sweetly glide,
Whar brier and breckan fringe ilk side;
Where cooling breezes saftly blaw,
    Refreshing Caledonia.
Fareweel each fountain, glen, an' grove,
Where warblers chaunt their notes o' love.
Fareweel ilk shadow, bower, an' shaw
    That's seen in Caledonia.

2 K

Fareweel ye happy nymphs an' swains,
That dwell in Scotia's blest domains,
May freedom, peace, content an' a',
    Still smile on Caledonia!
Fareweel the lassie neist my heart,
She grieves me sair that we sude part;
She's gude, she's fair without a flaw,
    The flower o' Caledonia.

O Scotia! maun I frae thee gang?
Wi' mournfu' voice I sing the sang.
To say fareweel, the sa't tears fa',
    In love for Caledonia.
Fareweel my cronies, time flies fleet;
We maybe part nae mair to meet;
Fareweel my friends, my faes an' a';
    Fareweel sweet Caledonia.

LOUDEN'S WOODS AND BRAES.

[By TANNAHILL. It is figurative of the parting of Earl Moira and
the Countess of Loudon, shortly after their marriage.]

Tune—*Moira's welcome to Scotland.*

LOUDEN'S bonny woods and braes,
    I maun leave them a', lassie;
Wha can thole whan Britain's faes
    Wad gie Britons law, lassie?
Wha wad shun the field o' danger?
Wha frae fame wad live a stranger?
Now, when Freedom bids avenge her,
    Wha wad shun her ca', lassie?
Louden's bonny banks and braes
Hae seen our happy bridal days,
And gentle Hope shall soothe thy waes,
    When I am far awa, lassie.

Hark ! the swelling bugle sings,
   Yielding joy to thee, laddie,
But the dolefu' bugle brings
   Waefu' thoughts to me, laddie ;
Lanely I'may climb the mountain,
Lanely stray beside the fountain,
Still the weary moments countin',
   Far frae love and thee, laddie :
O'er the gory fields of war,
Where Vengeance drives her crimson car,
Thou'lt may be fa' frae me afar,
   And nane to close thy ee, laddie.

O resume thy wonted smile !
   O suppress thy fear, lassie !
Glorious honour crowns the toil
   That the sodger shares, lassie !
Heaven will shield thy faithfu' lover
Till the vengeful strife be over,
Then we'll meet, nae mair to sever,
   Till the day we die, lassie ;
Midst our bonny woods and braes,
We'll spend our peaceful happy days,
As blythe's yon lightsome lamb that plays
   On Louden's flowery lea, lassie.

CALEDONIA.

[By WILLIAM L———T, Edinburgh.]

SAIR, sair was my heart, when I parted frae my Jean ;
And sair, sair I sigh'd, while the tears stood in my een ;
For my daddy is but poor, and my fortune is sae sma',
It gars me leave my native Caledonia.

When I think on days gane, and sae happy I hae been,
While wand'ring wi' my deary, whare the primrose
blaws unseen,
I'm wae to leave my lassie, and my daddy's cot ava,
Or to leave the healthfu' breeze of Caledonia.

But wherever I wander, still happy be my Jean,
Nae care disturb her bosom, whare peace has ever been;
Then tho' ills on ills befa me, for her I'll bear them a',
Tho' aft I'll heave a sigh for Caledonia.

But should riches e'er be mine, and my Jeanie still be
true,
Then blaw, ye fav'ring breezes, till my native land I
view;
Then I'll kneel on Scotia's shore, while the heartfelt
tear shall fa',
And never leave my Jean nor Caledonia.

HOW LANG AND DREARY.

Tune—*Cauld Kail in Aberdeen.*

How lang and dreary is the night
  When I am frae my dearie!
I restless lie frae e'en to morn,
  Tho' I were ne'er so weary:
    For oh her lonely nights are lang,
    And oh her dreams are eirie;
    And oh her widow'd heart is sair
    That's absent frae her dearie!

When I think on the lightsome days
    I spent wi' thee, my dearie,
And now what seas between us roar,
    How can I be but eirie!
      For oh, &c.

How slow ye move, ye dreary hours;
    The joyless days, how dreary!
It was na sae ye glinted by
    When I was wi' my dearie.
      For oh, &c.

CAPTAIN O'KAINE.

[By RICHARD GALL.—*Vide p.* 211.]

Row saftly, thou stream, thro' the wild-spangl'd valley,
O green be thy banks, ever bonny and fair!
Sing sweetly, ye birds, as ye wanton fu' gaily,
Yet strangers to sorrow, and strangers to care.
    The weary day lang
    I list to your sang,
And waste ilka moment, sad, cheerless, alane:
    Each sweet little treasure
    O' heart cheering pleasure,
Far fled frae my bosom wi' Captain O'Kaine.

Fu' aft on thy banks hae we pu'd the wild gowan,
And twisted a ringlet beneath the hawthorn:
Ah! then each fond moment wi' pleasure was glowin;
Sweet days o' delight, which can never return!
    Now ever, waes me!
    The tear fills mine ee,
And sair is my heart wi' the rigour o' pain;
    Nae prospect returning
    To gladden life's morning,
For green waves the willow o'er Captain O'Kaine.

2 K 3

THE LASS O' BALLOCHMYLE.

[By Burns, who iń one of his wanderings in the woods along the banks of the Ayr, in 1786, met a young lady, a celebrated beauty of the west of Scotland, of whose charms he was instantaneously enraptured. Her station in life prevented him from disclosing at that moment the passion he had conceived, but his mind in these matters disdained restraint, and on his return home he composed and sent the young lady the following song, inclosed in a letter, to which however, as might be expected, she returned no answer. —See Currie's *Life of Burns*.]

'Twas even—the dewy fields were green,
   On every blade the pearls hang ;
The Zephyr wanton'd round the bean,
   And bore its fragrant sweets alang :
In every glen the mavis sang,
   All Nature listening seemed the while,
Except where green-wood echoes rang,
   Amang the braes o' Ballochmyle.

With careless step I onward strayed,
   My heart rejoiced in Nature's joy,
When, musing in a lonely glade,
   A maiden fair I chanc'd to spy ;
Her look was like the morning's eye,
   Her air like Nature's vernal smile,
The lily's hue and rose's dye
   Bespoke the lass o' Ballochmyle.

Fair is the morn in flow'ry May,
   And sweet is night in Autumn mild;
When roving through the garden gay,
   Or wandering in the lonely wild :

But woman, Nature's darling child!
 There all her charms she does compile;
Even there her other works are foil'd
 By the bonny lass o' Ballochmyle.

O had she been a country maid, .
 And I the happy country swain,
Tho' sheltered in the lowest shed
 That ever rose on Scotland's plain,
Thro' weary winter's wind and rain,
 With joy, with rapture, I would toil,
And nightly to my bosom strain
 The bonny lass o' Ballochmyle.

Then pride might climb the slippery steep,
 Where fame and honours lofty shine;
And thirst of gold might tempt the deep,
 Or downward seek the Indian mine;
Give me the cot below the pine,
 To tend the flocks, or till the soil,
And every day have joys divine
 With the bonny lass o' Ballochmyle.

* * * * * * *

THE ABSENT LOVER.

WHAT ails this heart of mine?
 What ails this watry e'e?
What gars me ay turn cauld as death,
 When I tak leave o' thee?
When thou art far awa,
 Thou'lt dearer grow to me;
But change o' fouk, and change o' place,
 May gar thy fancy jee.

Then I'll sit down and moan,
- Just by yon spreading tree,
An' gin a leaf fa' in my lap,
    I'll ca't a word frae thee !
Syne I'll gang to the bower
    Which thou wi' roses tied,
'Twas there by mony a blushing bud
    I strove my love to hide.

I'll doat on ilka spot
    Whar I hae been wi' thee;
I'll ca' to mind some fond love tale,
    By ev'ry burn and tree.
'Tis hope that cheers the mind,
    Tho' lovers absent be;
An' when I think I see thee still,
    I think I'm still wi' thee.

O MARY, TURN AWA.

O MARY, turn awa
    That bonny face o' thine,
And dinna, dinna shaw that breast,
    That never can be mine !
Can ought o' warld's gear,
    E'er cool my bosom's care?
Na, na, for ilka look o' thine,
    It only feeds despair.

Then, Mary, turn awa
    That bonny face o' thine;
O dinna, dinna shaw that breast,
    That never can be mine !

Wi' love's severest pangs
  My heart is laden sair,
An' o'er my breast the grass maun grow,
  Ere I am free frae care.

~~~~~~~~~~

WILLIE'S RARE.

WILLIE's rare, and Willie's fair,
  And Willie's wondrous bonny,
And Willie hecht to marry me,
  Gin e'er he married ony.

Yestreen I made my bed fu' braid,
  This night I'll make it narrow ;
For a' the live-lang winter-night
  I'll ly twin'd o' my marrow.

O came you by yon water side ?
  Pu'd you the rose or lily ?
Or came you by yon meadow green ?
  Or saw ye my sweet Willie ?

She sought him east, she sought him west,
  She sought him braid and narrow ;
Syne in the cleaving of a craig,
  She found him drown'd in Yarrow.

~~~~~~~~~~

SWEET KITTY O' THE CLYDE.

A BOAT danc'd on Clyde's bonny stream,
  When winds were rudely blowing,
There sat what might the goddess seem
  Of the waves beneath her flowing ;

But, no! a mortal fair was she,
  Surpassing a' beside;
And youths a' speer'd her choice to be—
  Sweet Kitty of the Clyde.

I saw the boatman spread a sail,
  And, while his daftness noting,
The boat was upset by the gale,
  I saw sweet Kitty floating;
I plung'd into the silver wave,
  Wi' Cupid for my guide,
And thought my heart weel lost to save
  Sweet Kitty o' the Clyde.

But Kitty is a high-born fair,
  A lowly name I carry,
Nor can wi' lordly thanes compare
  Who woo the maid to marry;
But she not scornfu' looks on me,
  And joy may yet betide,
For hope dares flatter mine may be
  Sweet Kitty o' the Clyde.

~~~~~~~~~~

THOU ART GANE AWA.

Thou art gane awa, thou art gane awa,
  Thou art gane awa frae me, Mary!
Nor friends nor I could make thee stay,
  Thou hast cheated them and me, Mary:
Until this hour I never thought
  That ought could alter thee, Mary;
Thou'rt still the mistress of my heart,
  Think what you will of me, Mary.

Whate'er he said, or might pretend,
 . That staw that heart o' thine, Mary ;
True love, I'm sure, was ne'er his end,
  Or nae sic love as mine, Mary.
I spake sincere, nor flatter'd much,
  Nae selfish thoughts in me, Mary ;
Ambition, wealth, nor naething such ;
  No, I lov'd only thee, Mary.

Tho' you've been false, yet, while I live,
  I'll lo'e nae maid but thee, Mary ;
Let friends forget, as I forgive
  Thy wrangs to them and me, Mary.
So then, fareweel ! of this be sure,
  Since you've been false to me, Mary ;
For a' the world I'd not endure
  Half what I've done for thee, Mary.

THE BARD STRIKES HIS HARP.

[By RICHARD GALL.]

THE bard strikes his harp the wild valleys amang,
  Whare the tall aiken trees spreading leafy appear,
While the murmuring breeze mingles sweet wi' his
      sang,
  And wafts the saft notes till they die on the ear ;
But Mary, whase presence sic transport conveys,
  Whase beauties my moments o' pleasure control,
On the strings o' my heart ever wantonly plays,
  And ilk languishing note is a sigh frae my soul.

Her breath is as sweet as the green-scented brier,
  That blossoms and blaws in the wild lanely glen ;
When I ee her fair shape, which nae mortal can peer,
  A something o'erpow'rs me I dinna weel ken.

Her smiles are as sweet as the mild sunny rays,
   The blink o' her bonny black ee wha can thole?
On the strings o' my heart she bewitchingly plays,
   And ilk languishing note is a sigh frae my soul.

THE HAWTHORN.

[By —— HAMILTON, late teacher of music in Edinburgh.]

ONE midsummer morning, all nature look'd gay,
I met my dear Jamie a-tedding the hay,
Who said, my lovely treasure, come see where I dwell,
Beside the bonny hawthorn that blooms in the vale:
   That blooms in the valley, that blooms in the vale;
   Beside the bonny hawthorn that blooms in the vale.

He prais'd me, and said that his love was sincere,
Not one on the green was so charming and fair;
I listen'd with pleasure to Jamie's tender tale,
Beside the bonny hawthorn that blooms in the vale.
   That blooms, &c.

O hark, bonny Bess, to the birds in yon grove,
How delightfu' they sing, how inviting to love;
The briers, deck'd wi' roses, perfume the fanning gale,
Beside the bonny hawthorn that blooms in the vale.
   That blooms, &c.

His looks were so pleasing, his words soft and kind,
They told me the youth had no guile in his mind;
My heart, too, confess'd him the flower of all the dale,
Beside the bonny hawthorn that blooms in the vale.
   That blooms, &c.

I tried for to go, and oft said I could not stay,
But he would not leave me, nor let me away;
Still pressing his suit, at last he did prevail,
Beside the bonny hawthorn that blooms in the vale.
That blooms, &c.

Now tell me, ye maidens, how I could refuse,
His lips were so sweet, and so binding his vows;
We went and were married, and most cordially we
  dwell,
Beside the bonny hawthorn that blooms in the vale.
That blooms, &c.

THE BIRKS OF INVERMAY.

[By DAVID MALLET, the friend of Thomson, author of the ballad
  of " William and Margaret," and some plays and poems.]

THE smiling morn, the breathing spring,
Invite the tunefu' birds to sing;
And while they warble from each spray,
Love melts the universal lay;
Let us, Amanda, timely wise,
Like them improve the hour that flies,
And in saft raptures waste the day
Amang the birks of Invermay.

For soon the winter of the year,
And age, life's winter, will appear;
At this thy lively bloom will fade,
As that will strip the verdant shade;
Our taste of pleasure then is o'er,
The feather'd songsters please no more;
And when they droop and we decay,
Adieu the birks of Invermay.

2 L

The lav'rocks now and lintwhites sing,
The rocks around wi' echoes ring,
The mavis and the blackbird vye
In tunefu' strains to glad the day;
The woods now wear their summer-suits,
To mirth a' nature now invites;
Let us be blythsome then, and gay
Amang the birks of Invermay.

Behold the hills and vales around
With lowing herds and flocks abound;
The wanton-kids and frisking lambs
Gambol and dance about their dams;
The busy bees with humming noise,
And a' the reptile kind rejoice;
Let us, like them, then sing and play
About the birks of Invermay.

Hark how the waters as they fa',
Loudly my love to gladness ca';
The wanton waves sport in the beams,
And fishes play throughout the streams;
The circling sun does now advance,
And all the planets round him dance;
Let us as jovial be as they
Amang the birks of Invermay.

THE MILLER'S DAUGHTER.

I HAE been courting at a lass,
  These twenty days and mair;
Her father winna gi'e me her,
  She's sic a gleib of gear;

But gin I had her where I wou'd,
 Amang the hether here,
I'd strive to win her kindness
 For a' the miller's care.

For she's a bonny, sonsy lass,
 An armsfu', I swear;
I wou'd marry her without a coat,
 Or e'er a plack o' gear;
For, trust me, when I saw her first,
 She ga'e me sic a wound,
That a' the doctors i' the earth
 Can never mak me sound.

For when she's absent frae my sight,
 I think upon her still,
And when I sleep, or when I wake,
 She does my senses fill;
May Heaven guard the bonny lass,
 That sweetens a' my life;
And shame fa' me gin e'er I seek
 Anither for my wife.

MY SHEEP I NEGLECTED.

[Written in 1743 by Sir GILBERT ELLIOT on the marriage of his mistress, Miss Forbes, with Ronald Crawfurd, Esq.]

Tune—*My Apron, deary.*

My sheep I neglected, I lost my sheep-hook,
And all the gay haunts of my youth I forsook,
Nae mair for Amynta fresh garlands I wove,
For ambition, I said, would soon cure me of love.

O what had my youth with ambition to do?
Why left I Amynta? why broke I my vow?
O gi'e me my sheep, and my sheep-hook restore,
I'll wander frae love and Amynta no more.

Through regions remote in vain do I rove,
And bid the wide ocean secure me from love!
O fool! to imagine that ought can subdue
A love so well founded, a passion so true.
   O what had my youth, &c.

Alas! 'tis o'er late at thy fate to repine;
Poor shepherd! Amynta nae mair can be thine:
Thy tears are a' fruitless, thy wishes are vain,
The moments neglected return not again.
   O what had my youth, &c.

JAMIE O' THE GLEN.

Auld Rob the laird o' muckle land,
  To woo me was nae very blate,
But spite o' a' his gear, he fand
  He came to woo a day o'er late.
    A lad sae blyth, sae full o' glee,
     My heart did never never ken,
    And nane can gie sic joy to me,
     As Jamie o' the glen.

My minny grat like daft and rar'd,
  To gar me wi' her will comply;
But still I wadna hae the laird
  'Wi' a' his ousen, sheep, and kye.
    A lad sae blyth, &c.

Ah what are silks and sattins bra?
  What's a' his warldly gear to me?
They're daft that cast themselves awa
  Where nae content or luve can be.
    A lad sae blyth, &c.

I cou'd na bide the silly clash
  Cam hourly frae the gawky laird;
And sae to stop his gab and fash
  Wi' Jamie to the kirk repair'd.
    A lad sae blyth, &c.

Now ilka simmer's day sae lang,
  And winter's clad wi' frost and snaw,
A tunefu' lilt and bonny sang
  Ay keep dull care and strife awa.
    A lad sae blyth, &c.

THE LASS THAT WINNA SIT DOWN.

What think ye o' the scornfu' quine
  'Ill no sit down by me;
I'll see the day that she'll repine,
  Unless she does agree.
O she did hoot, and toot, and flout,
  'Cause I bade her sit down;
But the next time that e'er I do't,
  I'll be whip't like a loon.
    Wi' a tirry, &c.

And yet she is a charming quine,
  She's just o'er meikle spice;
I'll see the day that she'll be mine,
  For I'm nae very nice.

I loot the lassie tak' her will,
   An' stand upo' her shanks,
The day may come when I will spoil
   Her bonny saucy pranks.
     Wi' my tirry, &c.

I laid my head upo' my loof,
   I did na' care a strae,
I ken'd fow weel that in a joof
   Stand lang she wad nae sae.
At last a blythesome lass did cry,
   Come, Sandy, gi'es a sang;
O now, Meg dorts, I'll fairly try
   Your heart strings for to twang.
     Wi' a tirry, &c.

The lassie's pride it cou'd na' last,
   I sang wi' meikle glee,
Until at last she fairly cast
   Upo' me a sheep's ee.
Aha! thinks I, my bonnie lass,
   Hae ye laid by your pride,
You're bonnier now than e'er you was,
   And ye sall be my bride.
     Wi' your tirry, &c.

I ga'e the lass a-lovin' squint,
   That made her blush sae red,
I saw she fairly took the hint,
   Which made my heart fou glad.
The bonnie lass is a' mine ain,
   For we twa did agree;
Now ilka night she's unco fain,
   For to lie doun wi' me,
     Wi' her tirry, &c.

O GIN MY LOVE WERE YON RED ROSE.

[To this beautiful old fragment, Burns often tried to add a stanza,
and at length succeeded in producing the two following, which
he proposed should be the beginning of the song :—

"O were my love yon lilac fair
  Wi' purple blossoms to the spring ;
And I a bird to shelter there,
  When wearied on my little wing :

"How I wad mourn when it was torn
  By autumn wild and winter rude !
But I wad sing on wanton wing,
  When youthfu' May its bloom renew'd."]

Tune—*Hughie Graham.*

O GIN my love were yon red rose,
  That grows upon the castle wa' !
And I mysell a drap o' dew,
  Into her bonnie breast to fa'.

Oh ! there beyond expression blest,
  I'd feast on beauty a' the night ;
Seal'd on her silk-saft faulds to rest,
  Till fley'd awa by Phœbus' light.

~~~~~~~~~~~

I CARE NAE FOR YOUR EEN SAE BLUE.

I CARE nae for your een sae blue,
Unless your heart to me is true,
Nor yet that dimpled cheek o' thine,
Till every smile ye hae be mine.

D'ye think I'll roose your shape an' air,
Or ca' you bonie, sweet, an' fair,
Unless ye can to me impart
A look which say ye hae my heart.

I care naé for your witching tongue,
Which pleases a' an' pierces some,
Until I hear that tongue declare
Nane but mysell your heart shall share.
An' gin that saft an' melting ee,
Doth beam on me an' only me,
My fate is seal'd, then I am thine,
An' let me die when I repine.

~~~~~~~~~

I'LL AY CA' IN BY YON TOWN.

[By BURNS.]

I'LL ay ca' in by yon town,
  And by yon garden green again;
I'll ay ca' in by yon town,
  And see my bonny Jean again.
There's nane sall ken, there's nane sall guess,
  What brings me back the gate again,
But she my fairest faithfu' lass,
  And stownlins we sall meet again.

She'll wander by the aiken tree,
  When trystin-time draws near again;
And when her lovely form I see,
  O haith, she's doubly dear again!
    I'll ay ca', &c.

GO TO BERWICK JOHNNY.

Go to Berwick Johnny,
Bring her frae the border,
Yon sweet bonnie lassie,
Let her gae nae farder.
English louns will twine ye
O' the lovely treasure,
But we'll let them ken,
A sword wi' them we'll measure.

Go to Berwick Johnny,
An' regain your honour,
Drive them o'er the Tweed,
An' shaw our Scottish banner.
I am Rab the King,
An' ye are Jock my brither,
But before we lose her,
We'll a' there thegither.

~~~~~~~~~

O', ARE YE SLEEPIN', MAGGIE?

[By TANNAHILL.]

O, ARE *ye sleepin', Maggie?*
 O, are ye sleepin', Maggie?
Let me in, for loud the linn
 Is roarin' o'er the warlock craigie!
Mirk and rainy is the night,
 No a starn in a' the carey,
Lightnings gleam athwart the lift,
 And winds drive on wi' winter's fury.

Fearfu' soughs the boor-tree bank,
  The rifted wood roars wild and dreary,
Loud the iron yate does clank,
  And cry o' howlets maks me eerie.
    O, are ye sleepin', &c.

Aboon my breath I daurna speak,
  For fear I rise your waukrife daddy:
Cauld's the blast upon my cheek,
  O rise, rise, my bonny lady.
    O, are ye sleepin', &c.

She op't the door, she let him in,
  He cuist aside his dreepin' pladdie:
Blaw your warst, ye rain and win',
  Since, Maggie, now I'm in aside ye.
    Now since ye're wauken, Maggie,
      Now since ye're wauken, Maggie,
    What care I for howlets' cry,
      For boor-tree bank, or warlock craigie.

HERE'S HIS HEALTH IN WATER.

Altho' my back be at the wa',
And though he be the fautor,
Although my back be at the wa',
Yet here's his health in water.
O wae gae by his wanton sides,
Sae brawly's he could flatter;
Till for his sake I'm slighted sair,
And dree the kintra clatter:
  But though my back be at the wa',
  Yet here's his health in water.

MY LOVE HAS FORSAKEN ME.

My love has forsaken me,
  Know ye for why?
Because he has flocks and herds,
  And none have I.
    Whether I get him, whether I get him,
    Whether I get him or no;
    I care not three fardins
    Whether I get him or no.

But the rot may come amongst them,
  And they may all die;
And then he'll be forsaken,
  Ay, as weel as I.
    Whether I get him, &c.

Meeting is a pleasure,
  And parting's a grief,
And an inconstant lover
  Is worse than a thief.
    Whether I get him, &c.

A thief will but rob me,
  Take all that I have;
But an inconstant lover
  Will bring me to my grave.
    Whether I get him, &c.

The grave it will rot me,
  And bring me to dus ;
An inconstant lover
  No woman should trust.
    Whether I get him, &c.

A' BODY'S LIKE TO BE MARRIED.

[By —— HAMILTON.]

As Jenny sat down wi' her wheel by the fire,
And thought of the time that was fast fleein' by,
She said to hersel', wi' a heavy heigh-hee,
O, a' body's like to be married but me!
    She said to hersel, &c.

My youthfu' companions are a' worn awa',
And tho' I've had wooers mysel' ane or twa,
Yet a lad to my mind I ne'er yet could see;
O, a' body's like to be married but me!
    Yet a lad, &c.

There's Lowrie, the lawyer, wad ha'e me fu' fain,
Who has baith a house and a yard o' his ain;
But before I'd gang to it, I rather wad die;
A wee stumpin' body! he'll never get me!
    But before, &c.

There's Dickie, my cousin, frae Lun'on come down,
Wi' fine yellow buckskins that dazzled the town;
But, poor deevil, he got ne'er a blink o' my ee:
O, a' body's like to be married but me!
    But, poor deevil, &c.

But I saw a lad by yon saughy-burn side,
Wha weel wad deserve ony queen for his bride;
Gin I had my will, soon his ain I wad be:
O, a' body's like to be married but me!
    Gin I had my will, &c.

I gied him a look, as a kind lassie shou'd;
My friends, if they kend it, wad surely rin wud;
For tho' bonny and good, he's no worth a bawbee:
O, a' body's like to be married but me!
> *For tho' bonny, &c.*

'Tis hard to tak shelter behint a laigh dike;
'Tis hard for to tak ane we never can like;
'Tis hard for to leave ane we fain wad be wi';
Yet it's harder that a' should be married but me.
> *'Tis hard for to leave, &c.*

~~~~~~~~

I WONDER WHEN I'LL BE MARRY'D.

My father has forty good shillings, ha! ha! good
    shillings!
And never a daughter but I;
My mother she is right willing, ha! ha! right
    willing!
That I shall have all when they die.
> *And I wonder when I'll be marry'd, ha! ha! be*
> *   marry'd!*
> *My beauty begins to decay;*
> *It's time to catch ha'd o' somebody, ha! ha! some-*
> *   body!*
> *Before it be a' run away.*

My shoes they are at the mending,
    My buckles they are in the chest;
My stockings are ready for sending:
    Then I'll be as braw as the rest.
> *And I wonder, &c.*

My father will buy me a ladle,
    At my wedding we'll hae a good sang;
For my uncle will buy me a cradle,
    To rock my child in when it's young.
> *And I wonder, &c.*

AULD KING COUL.

Oᴜʀ auld King Coul was a jolly auld soul,
  And a jolly auld soul was he ;
Our auld King Coul fill'd a jolly brown bowl,
  And he ca'd for his fiddlers three :
    Every fiddler had a fine fiddle,
      And a very fine fiddle had he—
Fidell-didell, fidell-didell,
  Quo' the fiddlers three ;
There's no a lass in a' Scotland
  Like our sweet Marjorie.

Our auld King Coul was a jolly auld soul,
  And a jolly auld soul was he ;
Our auld King Coul fill'd a jolly brown bowl,
  And he ca'd for his pipers three :
    Every piper had fine pipes,
      And very fine pipes had he—
Ha didell, ho didell, quo' the pipers ;
  Fidell-fadell, fidell-fadell, quo' the fiddlers three ;
There's no a lass in a' Scotland
  Like our sweet Marjorie.

Our auld King Coul was a jolly auld soul,
  And a jolly auld soul was he ;
Our auld King Coul fill'd a jolly brown bowl,
  And he ca'd for his harpers three :
    Ev'ry harper had a fine harp,
      And a very fine harp had he—
Twingle twangle, twingle twangle, quo' the harpers ;
  Ha didell, ho didell, quo' the pipers ;
Fidell-fadell, fidell-fadell, quo' the fiddlers three ;
  There's no a lass in a' Scotland
Like our sweet Marjorie.

Our auld King Coul was a jolly auld soul,
  And a jolly auld soul was he;
Our auld King Coul fill'd a jolly brown bowl,
  And he ca'd for his trumpeters three:
    Ev'ry trumpeter had a fine trumpet,
      And a very fine trumpet had he—
Twara-rang, twara-rang, quo' the trumpeters;
  Twingle twangle, twingle twangle, quo' the harpers;
Ha didell, ho didell, quo' the pipers;
  Fidell-fadell, fidell-fadell, quo' the fiddlers three;
There's no a lass in a' Scotland.
  Like our sweet Marjorie.

Our auld King Coul was a jolly auld soul,
  And a jolly auld soul was he;
Our auld King Coul fill'd a jolly brown bowl,
  And he ca'd for his drummers three:
    Ev'ry drummer had a fine drum,
      And a very fine drum had he—
Rub-a-dub, rub-a-dub, quo' the drummers;
  Twara-rang, twara-rang, quo' the trumpeters;
Twingle twangle, twingle twangle, quo' the harpers;
  Ha didell, ho didell, quo' the pipers;
Fidell-fadell, fidell-fadell, quo' the fiddlers three;
  There's no a lass in a' Scotland
Like our sweet Marjorie.

SCOTIA'S SONS.

Tune—*Andro and his cutty gun.*

Blythe, blythe, aroun' the nappy,
  Let us join in social glee;
While we're here we'll hae a drappy,
  Scotia's sons hae ay been free.

Our auld forbears, when owre their yill,
 And cantie bickers roun'. did ca',
Forsooth, they cried, anither gill,
 For sweer't we are to gang awa.
  Blythe, &c.

Some heartie cock would then hae sang
 An auld Scotch sonnet aff wi' glee,
Syne pledg'd his cog—the chorus rang,
 Auld Scotia and her sons are free.
  Blythe, &c.

Thus cracks, and jokes, and sangs gaed roun',
 Till morn the screens o' light did draw,
Yet driech to rise, the carls roun'
 Cry'd, *Deuch-an-dhorus*, then awa.
  Blythe, &c.

The landlord then the nappy brings,
 An' toasts fu' happy a' may be,
Syne tooms the cog—the chorus rings,
 Auld Scotia's sons shall ay be free.
  Blythe, &c.

Then like our dads o' auld langsyne,
 Let social glee unite us a',
Ay blythe to meet, our mou's to weet,
 But ay as sweer't to gang awa.
  Blythe, &c.

A COGIE OF ALE.

A cogie of ale, and a pickle ait meal,
And a dainty wee drappy of whisky;
Was our forefathers dose to swiel down their brose,
And mak' them blythe, cheery, an' frisky.

Then hey for the cogie, and hey for the ale,
And hey for the whisky, and hey for the meal;
When mix'd a' the gether they do unco weel,
To mak' a chield cheery and brisk ay.

As I view our Scots lads, in their kilts and cockades,
A' blooming and fresh as a rose, man;
I think wi' mysell', O! the meal and the ale,
And the fruits of our Scottish kail-brose, man.
Then hey for the cogie, &c.

When our brave Highland blades, wi' their claymores
and plaids,
In the field, drive like sheep, a' our foes, man;
Their courage and power, spring frae this, to be sure,
They're the noble effects of the brose, man.
Then hey for the cogie, &c.

But your spindle-shanked sparks, wha but ill set their
sarks,
And your pale-visag'd milksops, and beaus, man,
I think when I see them, 'twere kindness to gi'e them,
A cogie of ale and of brose, man.
Then hey for the cogie, &c.

MEDLEY.

Tune—*Calder Fair.*

Was ne'er in Scotland heard or seen
    Sic dancin' and deray,
As at Patie's weddin' on the green
    To bonny Mary Gray.
Busk ye, busk ye bonny bride,
    Quo' the wife ayont the fire,
And lea' the rock and wee pickle tow,
    And the muckin' o' Geordie's byre.

Syne four-and-twenty fiddlers cam,'
  Wi' piper Rob the ranter,
He made them fain to follow him
  Whan he blew up his chaunter.
Fye let us to the bridal a',
  Cried bonny blue-ey'd Nelly,
For I'll dance, whistle o'er the lave o't there,
  Wi' the glee'd Earl o' Kellie.

Then bonny Jean frae Aberdeen
  Cam' thro' the haughs o' Bogie;
And Johnny Fa cam in sae braw,
  Wi dainty Katharine Ogie.
And wanderin' Willie cam' frae 'mang
  The birks of Invermay;
And Jenny Nettles took the road
  Wi' poor auld Robin Gray.

And honest auld John Anderson
  Cam' tottrin' down the hill;
And dainty Davie he brought in
  The lass o' Pattie's mill.
Poor Duncan Gray sigh'd out and in,
  And made an unco bother,
An' spake o' loupin' o'er a linn
  If he gat na Maggie Lauder.

Sweet Marion frae the ewe-bughts cam',
  A gauger cam' frae Fife,
But the rantin' rovin' Highlandman
  Had maistly ta'en his life.
Hersel' was Highland shentleman,
  The breeks she didna like, man;
She didna like the gauger loun,
  Nor yet the turnimspike man.

Frae up amang the cliffy rocks
    Cam' Robin Adair;
And Sandy o'er the lea has left
    The bush aboon Traquair.
The tailor cam' to clout the claise,
    Wi' fleas he fill'd the ha';
But by my saul they gat the rout
    Frae Donald and Maggie Macraw.

At dinner now they dit their mou'
    Wi mony a reekin' cogie;
There was cauld kail frae Aberdeen,
    And bannocks frae Strathbogie;
And there was brose and butter too,
    And meikle store o' lang kail;
Ye might hae crack'd a louse on Maggie's wame,
    She supp'd sae mony pan-kail.

A ewie wi' a crooked horn,
    The haggies in a pat;
The kail brose o' auld Scotland too,
    And herrins laid in sa't.
And Willie brew'd a peck o' ma't
    That set them a' a-roarin';
The fiddlers rubb'd their fiddle-sticks,
    An' ga'e them Tullochgorum.

Syne Highland folk and Lawland folk
    They danc'd wi' meikle pride;
And merrily danc'd the Quaker's wife
    Wi' the lads frae Erroch-side.
Poor Johnny's grey-breeks burst the steeks,
    And rave up to the gavel;
And Jeanie Diver bade them play
    The catie rade the padel.

And Tibbie Fowler o' the glen,
 For lack o' good folk, pu'd at her;
Fint a ane wad she dance wi'
 But the lads frae Galla water.
But Andrew, wi' his cuttie gun,
 He gae her pride a fa';
The lassie tint her silken snood
 Amang the pease straw.

The auld Stewarts bade the fiddlers play
 The sow's tail to Geordie;
And the Border bowmen knock'd them down
 For saying sic a wordic.
Then Lewis Gordon started up,
 Wi' Highland Harry bra man;
And Donald M'Donald fought like fire,
 Wi' knees and elbows an' a' man.

The laddie wi' the white cockade
 He made an unco play;
But Johnny Cope he tint a' hope,
 I trow he got a fley.
He didna like the lang claymore,
 Nor philabegs ava, man;
So aff he ran wi' might and main,
 Sighing, I'm wearin' awa, man.

But Willie was a wanton wag,
 He bore the gree awa';
And Berwick Johnny skirl'd sae loud,
 Up Willie, war them a'.
When wild war's deadly blast was blawn,
 And peace return'd to a',
The pipers a' play'd up, Gude night,
 And joy be wi' ye a'.

FINIS.

Gilchrist & Heriot, Printers, Leith.